THE WAR YEARS

Part II

The Next Generation

James Allan Matte

Published and distributed throughout the World by
J. A. M. PUBLICATIONS
43 Brookside Drive
Williamsville, New York 14221-6915
Tel: (716) 634-6645 – Fax: (716) 634-7204
E-Mail: editor@jampublications.com
Website: URL: http://www.jampublications.com

ISBN- 978-1-7322114-1-4
Library of Congress Control Number:: 2019901447
Matte, James Allan
The War Years, Part II
The Next Generation

Interior and cover design by: TeaBerryCreative.com
Edited by: John Nash

CONTENTS

ACKNOWLEDGEMENT

This author wishes to express his gratitude to Chief Warrant Officer (Ret) Stanley Snopkowski, for providing invaluable information from his experience as a helicopter pilot in the United States Army's 247 Med-Evac Detachment at Nah Trang, Vietnam, which enhanced the portrayal and accuracy of events in Chapters VII, VIII and IX pertaining to the Vietnam Conflict.

PREFACE

The end of The War Years, Part One, reveals the inescapable reunion of James Longbow and Louise Sontag aboard her *Lightfoot* sailboat, after a long separation, due to Longbow's imprisonment in Nazi Germany, and Songtag's short-lived marriage, ending with her husband's accidental death, that nevertheless troubled her conscience. Their 'coming out' on *Lighfoot* was first observed by their best friends, David Siegel and Susan Hershey Siegel, while standing on the veranda of the Lakebeach Yacht Club with binoculars that left no doubt about their reunion and love.

The War Years, Part Two follows their lives, and the lives of their loved ones and close friends, into the next generation. However, the Korean War draws the two senior aviators, James Longbow and David Siegel, into the conflict, when they thought their active service had ended with World War Two. Their siblings witness and experience the trials and tribulations of their parents in times of war, not realizing that they will be subjected to similar trials, brought about by the Vietnam war, that will leave them with emotional scars, some too profound to be shared with their anxiety-ridden family.

CHAPTER I

The Wedding

It was on a cloudless, midsummer afternoon, when David Siegel and his wife Susan Hershey Siegel, saw through binoculars, while standing on the veranda of the Lakebeach Yacht Club in Olcott, New York, their close friends James Longbow and Louise Sontag sailing together aboard *Lightfoot.*

"My God! Dave," exclaimed Susan, "they finally got together."

"Yeah! Looks like it, and they obviously want to keep their reunion a secret," said David.

"I don't blame them. Her husband's tragic death occurred only a little over a month ago," replied Susan.

"I guess they're afraid their reunion, so soon after Mark's death, will raise objections from the community, and bring social rejection," said David.

"I can understand that, but these two people have been in love since before the war, and that marriage to Mark should never have taken place," said Susan. "Furthermore, they've been separated ever since he was imprisoned in Germany, and you know what that was like, since you were with him as a prisoner of war."

"I agree with you, Susan," replied David. "Those two belong together. Having served as a nurse with Louise in England during the war, you know first-hand how she feels

"

about James. Remember our excursions to London, where the four of us, after realizing the death rate of those bombing missions, decided to have a pre-nuptial honeymoon in London, in case Jim and I failed to return on our next bombing raid."

"Don't I ever," replied Susan. "I don't think I'll ever forget that as long as I live, and neither will Jim and Louise, which explains their quick reunion after Mark's death."

"You think we should go to our boat on the island, and wait for Jim and Louise's return from sailing?" asked David.

"No, I don't think it's a good idea, Dave," replied Susan. "Apparently, for now, they want to keep their reunion a secret, so let's wait for them to reveal their rendezvous."

"I guess you're right, Susan. We don't want to invade their privacy. But on the other hand, if we're sitting on our boat, which is only four slips away from theirs, and they happen to come in from the lake, our meeting will be purely accidental," said David.

"Oh! Dave, you really think they'd buy that?" asked Susan. "In any case, let's give them their privacy, and when they're ready, as best friends, we'll be the first to know."

In the meantime, dark clouds were forming over Lake Ontario, as the *Lightfoot* sloop piloted by James Longbow with Louise Sontag standing beside him, her left arm around his waist, sailed freely without destination. They had no knowledge, that their reunion had been discovered by their long-time, newlywed friends, David Siegel and his wife Susan, from the veranda of the Lakebeach Yacht Club overlooking Lake Ontario.

"I think we'd better turn back, Jim," said Louise, "those dark clouds look ominous."

"I guess you're right, sweetheart," replied James, "turn on the engine, while I furl the sails."

"Do we have to furl them now?" asked Louise.

"Yes, because once the storm hits us, we'll have a hard time furling those sails," said James. "Better be safe than sorry."

"I guess you're right, Jim. I'll turn on the engine now," said Louise, who took over the helm, while James got busy furling the jib and the main sail.

Louise remained at the helm while James sat on the port locker against the bulwark facing Louise admiringly, as the wind blew her blond hair partly over her face and seductive blue eyes. It reminded him how much he loved her, and perhaps it was time for him to pop the ultimate question.

"You know, Louise, we can't hide from our family and friends forever," said James. "I know you feel people might think our reunion is too soon after your husband's funeral, but let's face it, those who truly care about you will understand your need to be with the man you always loved, and were meant to marry."

"I don't know, Jim," replied Louise, "I feel so vulnerable to criticism and condemnation in the press by those envious of my family's social status. Maybe we should wait a little longer before revealing our coupling."

"Well, I know one way of breaking the ice about our reunion," said James. "We could announce our engagement to be married."

"Is that a proposal, James?" asked Louise, smiling.

James stood up and walked over to the helm facing Louise. Dropping to one knee, with both hands inviting her blessing, he pleaded. "My Darling Louise, would you do me the honor and make me the happiest man on the face of the earth, by accepting my humble proposal of marriage?"

"Oh! James," exclaimed Louise, reaching over the helm to embrace him. "Yes, I do, my darling," kissing him fervently.

"This was so spontaneous, that I didn't have time to get you an engagement ring," said James. "But we can shop together for one that you would really like. Besides, I didn't know your ring size."

"That doesn't matter, Jim. I think it's a splendid idea for us to shop together for one. That way I'll get one that really suits my personality," replied Louise. "Take the helm, Jim, that way I can stand close to you. You have no idea how your proposal has lifted my spirits."

"Your acceptance lifted mine into the clouds, sweetheart," replied James.

"I can just see my Dad's face when he learns of our engagement. He always thought of you as the son he never had. This will make him a very happy man," said Louise, "and my mom too."

"There's nothing like being readily accepted into the family of the woman you love," replied James. "I'll ask Dave Siegel to be my best man, and I presume you'll want his wife Susan to be your Maid of Honor."

"Yes, of course. She stood up for me at my wedding," replied Louise. "Would you have any objections for us to be married in Saint Michael's Catholic Church?"

"No, why would I?" replied James.

"Well, because that's the church in which Mark Palmer and I were married," replied Louise.

"Makes no difference to me, sweetheart," replied James, "Mark had his day, and now it's history, and the world moves on."

"I do like the way you think, James," said Louise, "your philosophy is so practical."

"Hey! Life's too short to allow the past to interfere with the present, and our reunion is way overdue, sweetheart," replied James.

"I know just the place for my engagement ring, Jim," said Louise.

"Goldsmith's jewelry store in downtown Buffalo."

"You seem to know more about that than I do, so I leave it up to you, sweetheart," said James. "When would you like to visit the place?"

"How about tomorrow afternoon?" asked Louise.

"You don't waste any time, do you," replied James. "It so happens I'm free tomorrow afternoon, so why don't I pick you up at your house, then go from there."

"You, know, Jim, we're so much alike, you and I," said Louise. "That's why we get along so well. We're both decisive and confident about our capabilities. We complement each other."

"Well, I'm glad you feel that way, because having a positive attitude is half the battle in a relationship," said James.

The following day, James and Louise stood in front of a large glassed counter at Goldsmith's jewelry store in Buffalo, looking at various engagement rings.

"You know, Jim, I don't want a ring that has a protruding stone, because it could interfere with my handling of boat lines," said Louise.

"Well, that does make sense," replied James. "Perhaps you would like a ring of American Indian heritage, such as a multi-colored ring of sterling silver mixed with gold."

Louise waived to the clerk for his help. "What do you have in line with a wide multi-colored wedding ring of American Indian heritage?" asked Louise.

"Actually, we have a new selection of American Indian wedding rings, if you'll step over to the next counter," said the clerk.

Louise excitedly looked over the assortment of wedding rings and bands, with James at her side experiencing her enthusiasm.

"Oh! Look at that gorgeous wedding band with the four rows of small, assorted multi-colored stones on a gold and sterling silver ring," said Louise. "The row of small stones would not interfere with the handling of boat lines."

"Yes, it's beautiful and it suits you, Louise," said James. "But what about an engagement ring?"

"Engagement rings all have protruding stones that would require removal of the ring every time I went sailing, and I might then lose it," replied Louise.

"So, you don't want an engagement ring, just that wedding band, then?" asked James.

"That's right, Jim. I will be very happy with that ring. It's absolutely gorgeous, and I will be proud to wear it for the rest of my life," said Louise.

"Then let me buy it for you, and hopefully they'll have your finger size," said James.

Leaving the jewelry store, James, now in possession of the wedding ring, and accompanied by Louise, walked to the parking lot where his 1932 MG Midget, sky blue convertible sports car, was parked, and once inside the car, Louise asked to see the ring again.

"Oh! Jim, I do love this ring. Thank you, darling," said Louise, who then reached over and kissed him, then handed him back the ring. "I know you must keep the ring until our wedding day, when you'll officially place it on my finger."

"What will you tell your parents, and for that matter, to Susan and Dave, about you're being engaged without an engagement ring on your finger?" asked James.

"I'll tell them the truth," replied Louise. "I don't need to apologize for being pragmatic, and on my wedding day, when they see my wedding band, they'll realize the sensibility of my choice."

"You know, Louise, the more I get to know you, the greater my love for you, if that is possible," said James, looking at her with admiration.

"Oh! James, you can take off your rose colored glasses, now," replied Louise, with reciprocal feelings. "When shall we tell our parents?"

"Anytime you say, sweetheart," replied James. "It's up to you."

"Well, there's no time like the present, Jim," said Louise. "Why don't we tell my parents of our engagement when we get to my house."

"OK!" replied James. "The sooner the better, as far as I'm concerned."

Upon arrival at the Sontag mansion overlooking Lake Erie, in Lackawanna, New York, James parked his sports car in the circular driveway in front of the house where they both exited the car. Without ringing the doorbell, Louise entered the house with James behind her. She quickly found her parents sitting on the covered patio in back of the house, overlooking the lake. Upon seeing their daughter, accompanied by James, Michael Sontag stood up to greet them, while Marie Sontag remained seated. Michael was surprised to see James Longbow with his daughter so soon after the funeral of his son-in-law, but said nothing, and Marie remained silent, waiting for her husband to greet them.

"Nice to see you again, Jim," said Michael reaching to shake his hand. "What have you guys been up to?"

"We went sailing, Dad," replied Louise. "James graciously volunteered to crew for me and I accepted."

"Well, you two are grown-ups, so I don't have to tell you what people will think of you getting together so soon after Mark's funeral," said Michael Sontag, directing his disapproval at Louise more than James.

"We've been very careful about being seen together," replied Louise. "I know what you're saying, Dad, but It's not as if James and I just met. We've been in love since before the war, and if it hadn't been for his imprisonment, we'd be married now."

"It's customary for people in mourning to wait at least one year before getting married again," said Marie, now voicing her opinion in support of her husband.

"Mom, you haven't experienced what I've seen in war torn England, where people were dying by the thousands. I've learnt that life is unpredictably short, and time is the most precious asset we've got. I don't intend to waste a minute of it, in order to conform to some pious tradition or societal custom," said Louise, in a firm voice known only too well by her parents, especially her father from whom she obviously inherited that trait.

"I haven't heard from James," said Michael. "What are your intentions, young man?"

"Well, sir, I feel the same way as Louise," replied James. "Life is too short, and our time together is the most precious thing we have to share with each other. I have asked your daughter for her hand in marriage, and she has accepted my proposal. I hope you will not oppose our engagement, sir, because we love each other and intend to be married as soon as possible."

"I guess you two have already made up your mind, and it would be futile for us to oppose your engagement at this time," said Michael.

James looked at Louise for her to respond to her father's comment, when Marie interrupted their silence.

"Why don't you two keep your engagement private for now, and in six months make the announcement of your intent to be married," said Marie. "I think that would be an acceptable compromise."

"I think your mother's suggestion is most appropriate under the circumstances, Louise," said Michael. "You were just recently exonerated by the Board of Inquiry regarding the accidental drowning of your husband Mark, thanks to Ben Siegel, whom I chose instead of his older brother Simon, because he's the law firm's litigator who handles high profile criminal cases, whereas Simon specializes in contract and business law for corporations. But let's face it, some people may not have agreed with the Board's findings, so it's best if we let sufficient time expire before you two announce your engagement."

"I'm willing to live with that, Mister Sontag," said James, respectfully. What do you think, Louise?"

"I guess you're right, Mom, Dad," replied Louise. "Alright, we'll wait six months, but then the church bells will announce our wedding loud and clear."

"Well, I'm glad that's settled, "said Michael, with relief, thinking that although Mark was a nice fellow, he couldn't think of anyone he would rather have as a son-in-law than James Longbow.

"No doubt we'll have to keep a low profile until we're ready to announce our engagement," said James to Louise with her parents agreeing.

"I know. We'll have to avoid the Yacht Club, and other public places, at least locally anyway," said Louise.

"There's always New York City and Toronto," said Michael.

"That's true, but Toronto can be risky," said Louise. "I would prefer Montreal, and I can practice my French."

"Excellent idea," said James. "We must put that on our calendar."

"What about sailing?" asked Louise.

"*Lightfoot* is your sailboat, so you're expected to visit and sail it," said James. "I could come aboard when no one is around and once we're out on the lake, we're home free. But I think we should inform Dave and Susan of our reunion and forthcoming engagement, because their boat is only four slips away from ours, and sooner or later, they're going to see us together. Besides, they're our best friends."

"I agree, Jim," replied Louise. "I'll call Susan and tell her the news over lunch. You see Dave every day at work,

Jim, so you can tell him of our engagement, and I'm sure they'll both support our decision."

"I can always count on you, Louise, to resolve social issues," said James approvingly.

The Curtiss-Wright Corporation. Located in Cheektowaga, New York, a suburb of Buffalo, converted their manufacturing plants from military to commercial aircraft when the war ended a few month earlier. James Longbow and his former co-pilot and best friend David Siegel, were now working as aircraft designers for the Curtiss-Wright Corporation, on a new Super Constellation four-engine airliner.

James was having lunch with David in the corporate cafeteria, and James decided to tell his friend of his reunion with Louise.

"Louise and I are back together again," said James, expecting a surprised look on Dave's face.

"I know, Jim," replied David in a deliberate nonchalant manner.

"How do you know that?" asked James, knowing that Louise would not be meeting Susan until lunch time.

"Because, Susan and I were standing on the yacht club's veranda with binoculars, and that's when we saw you and Louise sailing *Lightfoot,*" replied James.

"Well I'll be damned!" exclaimed James. "When were you going to tell us about your discovery?"

"Susan and I decided to protect your privacy, and wait until you were ready to tell us about it," said David.

"I really appreciate that, Dave," replied James. "We discussed it with Louise's parents, and it was agreed we would wait for six months before we announced our engagement."

"I suppose her parents are concerned about the social stigma it would bring upon you and Louise if you rushed into it now," said David.

"Yeah! That's about it, Dave," replied James. "Louise is having lunch with your wife today, and she'll tell her the news."

"Actually, I'm glad you decided to tell us about your reunion, because now we're a foursome again, and we can get together at each other's house, and in discreet places, until your formal announcement," said David.

"Yeah! Like old times. Those were the days, my friend. Thank God they have not ended. By the way, Dave, you'll never guess who I ran into a couple of days ago while getting gas for my car," said James. "Major Claude Barclay, now Colonel Barclay."

"You're kidding, he's now a full Colonel," replied David.

"Yep! He's the Wing Commander of the 174th Attack Wing stationed at the Mattydale Bomber Base, located in Syracuse, New York," said James.

"Isn't the Mattydale Bomber Base actually the Hancock Field Air National Guard Base, about four and a half miles Northeast of Syracuse?" asked David.

"That's right, and the Colonel asked me if I wanted to join the Army Air Corps Reserves. When I mentioned that you and I were aircraft designers at Curtiss-Wright, he said joining the reserves would be a perfect fit for what we were doing, because we would then have access to all of the new aircraft, including bombers, manufactured by our competitors, and we would get to train and fly them," said James.

"Susan would never let me join the Army Air Corps Reserves, you kidding," replied David.

"Listen, Dave, we would only have to serve one weekend a month and two weeks in the summer, and get paid for it. Furthermore, we would start as Captains and eventually retire drawing Colonels pay with full benefits, including medical coverage for our family for life. That's got to be a most persuasive argument in our favor, don't you think?" said James.

"Did Colonel Barclay say that?" asked David.

"Yes he did, and we could report once a month by way of the Niagara Falls Air Base, where we can catch a flight to the Mattydale Bomber Base in Syracuse to report for duty. We would receive training and fly the B-29 Superfortress. Eventually, in about two years, we'll get to train and fly the B-36 Peacemaker, which has six 28-cylinder engines and four jet engines. It is the biggest bomber ever built. According to Barclay, it can fly at an altitude where no fighter aircraft or missile can reach it, and it has a range of some 12,000 miles. It was just unveiled a week ago on the 20th of August, but problems with the pusher prop engines have caused delays in its production," said James.

"Holy cow! I can see why you're so excited. I'll bet Stephen Waverly, our President, would be very supportive of our joining the reserves in view of the valuable technical information we would gain, flying those new military aircraft. Who built the B-36 Bomber?" asked David.

"I asked the same question of the Colonel, who said it was built by CONVAIR in San Diego, California," said James.

"You know that Bell, Boeing, Douglas and Grumman, all have government contracts to build military aircraft. I wouldn't be surprised if Steve Waverly may be considering joining the competition," said David, "although I can't see anyone wanting to start a war with the United States, now that we have the atomic bomb."

"Yeah! But in order for it to be an effective deterrent, we have to have a bomber that can deliver the atomic bomb anywhere on the globe, and the B-36 Bomber is the plane that can do it," said James. "But in the meantime, don't underestimate the B-29 Superfortress, which delivered the atom bomb to Japan, ending World War Two."

"I guess that's the aircraft we'll be training and flying at Hancock Field," said David.

"Most likely," replied James.

"You know, Jim, when you look at all the benefits, not to mention the pleasure of flying those new bombers, I'm incline to join the Reserves if you do. I won't do it alone, only as the team we used to be," said David.

"That goes without saying, Dave," replied James. "I won't join without my sidekick, you know that."

"Now the trick is to convince Susan and Louise of our plan," said David. "How do you propose we introduce the idea to Susan and Louise?"

"Well, it has to be at a discreet place, of course, so why not have dinner together at your house in North Buffalo," said James. "The reason I didn't suggest Louise's house in Lewiston is because it's really her deceased husband's house, which makes me feel uncomfortable."

"I understand, Jim. I suppose you'll be wanting Louise to sell that house, and possibly build a new house somewhere near the Yacht Club," said David.

"A new house, yes, but not necessarily near the Yacht Club," replied James. "That's a forty-five minute to an hour drive from Lewiston to Curtiss-Wright in Cheektowaga. That's two hours a day wasted. I saw several empty lots, side by side along Ellicott Creek, only a five minute drive from work. Why don't we take a drive right after work and look at it. I'm telling you, Dave, we could build two houses next to each other, overlooking the creek, where we could canoe and fish. It would also offer us a spectacular view from the houses' large bay windows."

"You know Jim, that sounds very promising. The fact that we're just renting the house, while Susan's realtor searches for a house for us to buy, makes it most feasible. I particularly like the idea of it being only five minutes from work, and we would be neighbors," said David.

"I agree, and our kids would grow up together," said James. "Let's look the place over right after work today."

"Yeah! You think we should present the idea of building our two houses off the creek, before we tell them about our desire to join the Reserves, or vice versa?" asked David.

"Hmm! That's a good question," replied James. "I think we should first present our desire to join the Reserves, pointing out all of the benefits and the increase in income it would bring to the table. Then we can tell them about building our two houses on Ellicott Creek and the fact that the additional income from the Reserves would help defray the cost of those houses."

"Excellent idea, Jim," replied David. "I think our gals will salivate at the thought they'll be able to build their homes the way they like it, in such beautiful surroundings, and next to their best friend."

"So let's go see the lots and the area right after work," said James.

"OK! Then I'll make arrangements for us to have dinner at my house this weekend," replied David.

Louise invited Susan to have lunch with her at the *Eagle House* restaurant in Williamsville, New York, a suburb of Buffalo, rather than the Yacht Club, because she was not yet ready to make an appearance there, where everyone knew her.

"I guess by now, Jim has told Dave of my reunion with him, and I'm here to tell you that Jim proposed marriage and I accepted. But we decided to postpone its announcement for six months to satisfy the mourning period," said Louise, expecting an expression of surprise.

"Dave and I saw you sailing together on *Lightfoot* the other day from the club's veranda, but we decided to wait for you to reveal your reunion," said Susan, "but we didn't know of your engagement. Congratulations."

"Holly Moly! You knew all the time and you kept quiet," replied Louise. "That was very thoughtful of you and Dave. You are truly our best friends."

"We're just glad you two are together again. It's as if nothing has changed since before the war, except that now you'll soon be married and we'll have children to enjoy," said Susan.

"That's true, but for me, the children can wait 'till I've seen a bit more of the world," replied Louise.

"Dave and I don't plan on waiting. We want children while were young and healthy. We've seen enough of the world in Europe, and we're glad to be back in the good old USA," said Susan.

"It's funny, me and my logical mind, I thought I knew everything. But you, armed only with your faith, turned out to be right," said Louise.

"Oh! Louise, don't beat yourself up over the past. You had no way of knowing Jim had survived the explosion of his bomber. You're with Jim now, and that's all that matters," said Susan, empathizing with her friend's guilt and remorse.

"It's easier said than done, but I'll get over it, for Jim's sake," replied Louise.

Ellicott Creek ran East and West, separating Cheektowaga from the Village of Williamsville, New York. Creekside Road, as its name implied, ran along Ellicott Creek for about a half a mile, between Wehrle Drive and Cadman Road. Only two houses had been built on its bank, about two hundred yards apart, in a wooded area with several very large trees that would offer much shade to any nearby houses. The other side of the creek was undeveloped, and adorned with very large trees in a pristine natural setting.

"This scenery is absolutely beautiful," said James, standing near the creek's bank, observing a group of ducks slowly paddling their way upstream, while a family of deer was munching on the wild vegetation across the creek.

Turning to David, also admiring the view, James directed their attention to the area where they would have their houses built.

"I think our houses should have two stories, and they should be made of brick and stone," said James. "What do you think, Dave?"

"Well, it would certainly raise the cost, that's for sure," replied David. "But it would also require a lot less maintenance, and I think that building two houses will put us in a better bargaining position with the contractor."

"That's a good thought," replied James. "We'll need to have a large bay window facing the creek. It offers a million dollar view."

"I think the girls will go crazy over this place," said David.

"Yeah! Let's find out who owns these lots and get a price for them," said James. "Then we can find and negotiate with a building contractor for the total cost of this project."

"My Dad's law firm will handle the legal aspects of this project," said David.

"That's reassuring," replied James. "Well, we know what we have to do now, so let's get to it."

The following day, James, while at work, relayed the information he obtained from the Archer Realty Company regarding the lots for sale on Creekside Drive.

"The lots are 130 feet deep by 100 feet wide, and the cost is $950.00 for each lot. However, I think we should buy three lots which will give us each a front width of 150 feet. We'll need that width to give us enough space to build a three rather than a two-car garage, with sufficient space between us and our future neighbors," said James. "I think we should buy those lots right away, before someone else gets the same idea."

"Why do we need a three-car garage?" asked David. "We only have two cars, my 1934 Cadillac V-16 Convertible, which seats four passengers, and the MG TC two-seat Convertible I bought Susan as a wedding present. At first she had trouble with the floor-shift gear box, but once she got used to it, she loved its handling and its rakish and elegant style, with wire wheels, white side walls and cut-away doors."

"Perhaps that's true in your instance, Dave, but Louise and I each have a two-seat sports car which we love and would never think of parting with," said James. "Our immediate problem is that we can't accommodate another couple, whether it is to pick up friends at the airport or simply travel somewhere with another couple. But eventually, we'll have at least two children which will require at least a four-seat vehicle, which means we'll need a three-car garage."

"I see what you mean," replied David. "Do you have any vehicle in mind?"

"Actually, I do. I have a 1941 Town & Country station wagon in mind, which has a steel roof and mahogany paneling that seats six passengers, and it's built by Chrysler," said James. "I think that's just the ticket for us."

"Man. That sounds like the perfect vehicle for you and Louise," replied David. "When do you intend to buy it?"

"Within the next few days, I'll have Louise take a look at it, and if she likes it, I'll buy it for her," said James.

"I guess that back pay we received from the Army after those years of imprisonment in Germany is now coming in handy," said David.

"You bet, and we earned it, Dave," replied James.

"But you will never have to worry about money, Jim, with Louise at your side, my friend," said David.

"If you're implying that Louise's newly found wealth from Mark's estate will be used to fund our house and car, you're sadly mistaken, Dave," replied James. "Louise knows very well, that we'll live on my income, and her wealth will not be used to support me."

"Jesus, Jim, I didn't mean to imply anything other than as your wife, she has the means to protect your shared investments, that's all," replied David.

"That's alright, Dave, I just want to make my position clear," said James. "So what do you think about a three rather than a two-car garage?"

"Well, for us, we only need a two-car garage," said David. But in your case, I agree that a three-car garage is needed. Besides, we don't want the two houses to be exactly the same."

"That's true. But you do agree on our buying three lots, so we have adequate space between the houses and future neighbors, right?" asked James.

"Yeah! for sure. I'll ago along with that," replied David. "I'm all for it, Jim, but shouldn't we pass this by the girls before we do anything. What if they reject the idea," said David.

"Buying the lots is not a big investment, and the timing is important. Besides, we can always sell the lots and get our money back with interest," said James.

"Yeah! I guess you're right. OK then, let me write you a check. The three lots total $2850.00 divided by two equals $1425.00. So I'll write you a check for that amount. Now you can make the purchase," replied David. "You got any ideas about the selection of a building contractor?"

"Not yet, but I'm sure that once our gals approve the project, we can then consult with our parents and friends for testimonials and referrals," said James.

The comfortable weather that Saturday evening at Dave and Susan Siegel's residence in North Buffalo, provided the perfect setting for an outdoor barbeque in their backyard patio. New York strip steaks with baked potatoes and an assorted salad was accompanied by both red and white wine in celebration of their reunion as a foursome, reminiscent of pre-war times.

"You have no idea how good it is to see you two together again," said Susan, with David smiling agreeably.

"Believe me, we're just as happy that bridge has been crossed, and we're finally together at last," replied Louise, squeezing James' hand with a loving look.

David then looked at James to broach the topic of their joining the Army Air Corps Reserves.

"I have some fantastic news that will make our lives richer and safer for us and our future children," said James, with a pause for effect.

"Really! Exclaimed Louise. "Please go on...the suspense is killing us."

"Remember Major Claude Barclay, our Flight Commander at RAF Station Chelveston," said James. "Well, he's now Colonel Barclay, and I ran into him a few days ago while at a gas station, and we reminisced about old times over a cup of coffee. He's now the Wing Commander at the Mattydale Bomber Base, in Syracuse, New York. He said that if Dave and I joined the Army Air Corps Reserves, we would only have to serve one weekend a month and two weeks in the summer, starting at the rank of Captain with future promotions as well as pay and allowances."

"You're not thinking of joining the Reserves, are you?" asked Louise, remembering the time when, as Army Air Corps nurses, Susan and she, with a pit in their stomach, waited alongside the runway at RAF Station Chelveston, England for the return of Jim and Dave's bombing raid over Germany which never came.

"Before you shoot down the idea, please let me finish, Sweetheart," replied James.

"We would only be going to the Hancock Field Air National Guard Base, also known as the Mattydale Bomber base, to serve in the Reserves. We will be getting full pay according to our grade as Captains and that would increase with promotions leading to full Colonel. Then when we complete the equivalent of 20 years of service, which includes the time we already served, we get retirement pay at the highest held grade for life, with full medical benefits for our whole family, even after our death, you and Susan would continue to receive medical benefits for the rest of your lives, and the children until they reach 21 years of age. You would also receive half of our retirement pay. I think that the Reserves offer not only an additional income, but a significant insurance package against any unforeseen event that could destabilize our current situation."

"Looks like Colonel Barclay did an excellent job of promoting his Reserves Unit," said Louise. "But what happens if another war breaks out? Won't the Reserves be the first ones to be called to active duty?"

"That's a fair question, and I asked myself that question too," replied James. "Colonel Barclay told me they just unveiled the biggest bomber ever built, the B-36 Peacemaker, which can fly some 12,000 miles without refueling, at altitudes where no fighter plane or missile can reach it. This means that we can deliver the atomic bomb anywhere in the world and return to the US without stopping for fuel. Knowing this, no country will want to start a war with us or any of our allies. So you really don't have to worry about us being called to active duty."

"I'd like to mention that our boss at work is all for us joining the Reserves, because the training and information we would gain from it, would benefit the company, and the company will pay us in full for the time we serve in the Reserves, which is in addition to the pay we'll receive from the Reserves," said David.

"Did you talk to your Director, Bob Polanski about this?" asked Susan.

"Yes we did, and he totally supports our joining the Reserves, emphasizing its benefit to the company," said David.

"Well, in that case, I'm all for it, Dave," said Susan. "The benefits alone are worth it. Don't you think so, Louise?"

"If what the Colonel told you is all true, then I'm agreeable, but I think you guys should verify what the Colonel has told you before you join the Reserves," said Louise.

"Absolutely. In fact, I'll arrange for you and Susan to meet with Colonel Barclay. Then you can ask him any questions you like. In addition, I think there's a pamphlet setting forth the benefits of joining the Reserves. Keep in mind, that as the Wing Commander, Colonel Barclay, who will undoubtedly be promoted to Brigadier General, will be a valuable ally, come time for promotion," said James.

"I'll say one thing for you, James, you could sell ice in the winter," said Louise, "and right now it tastes like ice cream, so unless the Colonel is lying, which I doubt, I believe that your joining the Reserves is a great idea, and you have my full support. But please bring me that pamphlet."

Everyone laughed at Louise's last remark, but James was not finished with his salesmanship. He now decided to strike the iron while it was still hot.

"On another topic, Dave and I ran across a piece of land in the Village of Williamsville, that would be the perfect place for us to build two houses, side-by-side, overlooking Ellicott Creek. It's surrounded by large trees and wildlife, yet close to everything worthwhile to visit," said James.

"What prompted that idea, James?" asked Louise. "Did you suddenly discover a gold mine?"

"In a way, yes, "replied James. "Let me explain. As veterans, Dave and I are eligible for the G.I. Bill that affords us a 100 percent VA guaranteed loan for housing. Furthermore, the salary we'll be getting from the Reserves will satisfy the monthly payments. That leaves our salaries from Curtiss-Wright Corporation free and clear of that debt."

"I'd like to add, that residing in the Village of Williamsville, will save Jim nearly two hours of driving back and forth to work from Lewiston. It will take us only five minutes to drive from the Village to work at Curtiss-Wright each day. That in itself is worth the investment," said David.

"I guess you guys have really put a lot of thought into this, and it sounds very convincing," said Louise. "What do you think, Susan?"

"I tend to agree with Jim and Dave's explanation of all the benefits this would bring us, as long as they don't get pulled into another war flying bombers," replied Susan.

"Listen, Susan, there's not going to be another war anytime soon, and we'd be too old anyway," replied David.

"Did you guys find out how much a house on that creek would cost?" asked Louise.

"Each lot, which is 130 feet deep by 100 feet wide, is listed as $950.00. However, in order to have sufficient room between the houses and also for us, Louise, to have a three rather than a two-car garage, we're buying three lots and splitting the cost in two. Furthermore, I estimate that to build an all-brick, two-story, four-bedroom house would probably cost about $8000.00, but this is negotiable, of course," said James.

"Why do we need a three-car garage?" asked Louise.

"Because our two sports cars are two-seaters, and we need a car that will seat at least four passengers, for invited guests and especially for the children we'll eventually have," said James.

"I must admit, James, that a four-seater is needed. What did you have in mind?" asked Louise.

"Actually, a Chrysler, 1941 Town & Country station wagon, which has a steel roof and mahogany paneling, and it seats six passengers," said James.

"I saw one of those station wagons last week, and that wood paneling gives it a country flavor. It really looks very utilitarian," said Susan. "If we didn't have Dave's Cadillac, I would have Dave buy one of them.

"Is it available at a local dealership?" asked Louise.

"Yes, at the Chrysler dealership in Buffalo," replied James. "Would you like to go there this Saturday? You could test-drive it."

"Yes, I would," replied Louise. "It's a date. But coming back to the house, you said that this could all be financed through the Veterans Administration. Is that correct?"

"Yes, that's correct," replied James.

"That looks promising," replied Louise. "You believe that your Reserve pay will take care of the house payments, then."

"Yes I do, but if not, we can certainly supplement it with what we make at Curtiss-Wright," replied James, becoming a bit annoyed at Louise's inquisition, which Louise sensed.

"I'm not questioning your judgment, Jim, or yours, Dave," said Louise. "But as your lifetime partners, I'm sure you'd want and respect Susan's and my opinion regarding matters of importance, such as where and in what type of house we'll be living in."

"Of course we do," replied James. "That's why we're having this conversation. We'd never take action without your approval. You know that."

"Well, I hope so," replied Susan, who so far had remained relatively quiet. "I'm sure you guys have covered all the bases, and we girls respect your judgment, so unless Louise has something to add, I'm for moving forward with this project."

"I agree with Susan," replied Louise. "Let's get some solid figures concerning the cost of the houses. By the way, what would be the dimensions of the two lots when the three lots are divided?

"Each lot will be 130 feet deep with a frontage of 150 feet, costing $1425.00" said James.

"That's a good size lot," said Louise. "I'll talk to my father about the selection of a contractor."

"And I'll consult with my father whose law firm deals with contractors for his recommendation," said David. "The fact that we'll be negotiating for two houses should bring the price down a bit."

"Well, it looks like we've got our work cut out for us, Dave," said James. "We'll keep you gals in the loop as we move on this project."

The following day, James called Colonel Barclay, who provided him with the necessary instructions for joining the Reserves. The following Monday afternoon, James and

David visited the Wing Commander's office at Hancock Field Air National Guard Base in Syracuse, where they were sworn in by Colonel Barclay as Captains in the Reserves, with assignment at the 174th Attack Wing located on that base.

Wearing their military uniform with Captain's bars on their shoulders, James and David returned by air to Niagara Falls Air Force Station where they had left their vehicles.

"See you tomorrow at work, Jim," said David, getting into his car. "Are you heading to Lewiston, or your father's house?"

"I'm not moving into Louise's house in Lewiston, not now nor when we're married, Dave, and Louise understands and agrees with my decision. That's why having our house built in the village is the best solution," said James.

"That's a wise decision, Jim. Take care, buddy," replied David.

The two lots along Ellicott Creek were purchased, after much negotiation, for the total price of $2500.00. The contractor, Joel Frankel, well-known to Simon Siegel's law firm, was awarded the contract to build the two houses on Creekside Road. Louise and Susan didn't waste any time working with the contractor, pouring over blueprints, and making numerous suggestions that invariably increased the cost of the houses. However, it was decided, that due to the creeks substantial rise in elevation during the Fall and Spring seasons which saturated the ground, it was best to forego a basement in favor of a thick concrete slab over a terrain of bedrock. It was explained by the contractor, that one of the benefits of having the house built on bedrock was that its flooring extended to the floor of the creek, whose water had a cooling effect during the summer, reducing the temperature inside the house by about ten degrees Fahrenheit.

However, an unforeseen additional expense became apparent when they looked at the creek's shoreline. The end of the backyard that abutted the creek fell approximately six feet. It became obvious that a stone wall supported with cement would have to be erected to prevent erosion of the backyard from the elevated and fast moving current of the creek during flood season, especially at their location which was at the creek's narrowest point, offering no comfort to mosquitos, and the least likely section to freeze during winter.

The final blueprints for the two houses, laid out on the dining room table at Dave and Susan's rented house in North Buffalo, were now being studied by James and David with Louise and Susan standing over them.

"I guess you girls don't have a problem with both houses being nearly the same," said David.

Susan looked at Louise. "No, not at all, Dave. We both agreed that four bedrooms were ideal for our future plans, and the rest of the layout of the house was perfectly coordinated to meet all of our needs," said Susan.

"The construction of the houses may be the same, except for the garages, but the interior decorations will be different, I'm sure," said Louise.

"Well, I'll be glad to leave that part to you girls," said James.

"That goes for me too," said Dave. "The house needs a woman's touch to make it a home."

"You'll notice that there's a utility room next to the kitchen, and it leads to the garage," said James. "The utility room is where the washing machine and dryer will be located, along with the furnace and hot water tank."

"Why there?" asked Susan.

"Because we don't have a basement, and it's the only place for those items to be located," replied David. "Actually, It's most convenient. You don't have to go down to a basement to do your laundry."

"What about storage space," asked Louise. "We always accumulate stuff that has value which we want to keep, and the garage must be free to house the three cars."

"Actually, Dave and I thought of that and so we'll have the contractor build a large walk-in floored area in the attic for storage. In addition, we're having a shed built in the back yard opposite the garage to house the lawn mower and other horticulture items. Ours will be painted red and white, while Dave wants his shed to be painted blue and white so we don't look altogether like twins."

"That's a great idea, Jim," said Louise. "Looking at these blueprints, all the bedrooms will be upstairs, each with a full bath and shower. Am I reading this right?"

"Yes, you are, Louise," replied James. "Dave and I discussed this at length, and realized that if each family is blessed with a son and a daughter, they'll need separate bathrooms. The guest room also needs a full bath, and of course the master bedroom, which you'll notice is much larger than the other three bedrooms, will have a full bath."

"But what happens if we accidently conceive a third child. Where will the child sleep?" asked Susan.

"He or she will occupy the guest room, and we'll just pitch a tent in the back yard for our guests," said James, smiling at the thought.

"Well, Susan, I don't plan on having such an accident," said Louise. All I want is a son and a daughter, God willing."

"The downstairs apparently has bay windows on both the street side and the back yard overlooking the creek. But as I see it, they're different sizes according to their location," said Louise. Am I seeing things or does the master bedroom have six side-by-side tall windows overlooking the creek?"

"That's right. It gives us a panoramic view of the creek and its surrounding foliage," replied James. "I might add that the dining room has a large bay window overlooking the creek. The view of the creek has a therapeutic quality that soothes the soul as well as the eyes."

"I think we're all in agreement about the creek's esthetics," said Louise. "I see you have two half-baths downstairs. One between the dining room and the utility room, and one between the home office and the library. I can see having your home office, Jim, but a library?"

"I thought we discussed that," replied James, quickly looking to Dave for support.

"Not that I remember," replied Louise, looking at Susan for confirmation.

"We do a lot of reading and research, Dave and I, and we'd like to have our own library of books, and I'm sure you'd also like to maintain a library of your favorite books and a quiet place to read them," said James.

"I suppose you're right. Our own private library would be a nice place to seek solace and peace," said Susan. "I think that when our houses are completely built, we'll be so content that we won't even want to go on vacations."

"I wouldn't go that far, Susan," said Louise. "Sometimes, getting away makes us appreciate what we have at home."

"Well, while you gals contemplate the future, we guys have to deal with the present, and the contractor wants our approval as soon as possible, so he can lay the foundation and exterior structure of the houses before winter sets in," said James.

"Is everyone in agreement with the plans for building the two houses?" asked James.

They all looked at each other, then Dave spoke first.

"I'm in agreement with the plans," said David. "What about you, Susan?"

"Yes, of course. I'm looking forward to choosing the wallpaper and other interior decorations," replied Susan.

"What about you, Louise," asked James. "Are you satisfied with the plans, or do you have some changes in mind?"

"No, Jim, I think we've covered everything. If I'm hesitant, it's because I'm trying to think if we've forgotten anything," said Louise. "No, I think we've got everything, Jim, go ahead and approve the plans."

Louise joined Susan in the kitchen, where she was preparing a pot of coffee to go along with apple pie for dessert.

"You, know, Susan, I am so proud of Jim and Dave. Those two guys are such close friends, and to have you and Dave as neighbors is a true blessing," said Louise.

"Dave and I feel the same way, Louise, and you are more than a mere friend. You are the sister I never had."

"Cut it out, Susan. You'll have me blushing," replied Louise with a hearty laugh.

"There's something I must tell you," said Susan.

"What's that?" asked Louise with a frown.

"I'm pregnant," said Susan.

"Oh! My God. When did you find out?" asked Louise.

"This morning when I saw Doctor Goodchild," replied Susan.

"Does Dave know yet?" asked Louise.

"No, I plan on telling him tonight, after you guys have left," said Susan.

"When is the baby expected?" asked Louise.

"In about seven and a half months," replied Susan, "I hope it's a boy because Dave wants a boy first, then a girl."

"How do you feel, Susan?" asked Louise.

"Wonderful. It's hard to explain the miracle that's happening inside me. When I think that Dave and I are creating a new human being with a soul; it makes me feel close to God, and fulfilled as a woman," said Susan. "There is nothing comparable on this earth."

"I've never seen you look so radiant, Susan," said Louise. "I never envied anyone before, but I envy you now, my dearest friend, and I do hope it's a boy."

"Thank you, Louise. Once you're married, don't wait too long before you conceive your first child. It's a gift from heaven."

With their guests gone for the evening, Susan approached David who was pouring himself a scotch.

"Would you like a drink before we retire?" asked David.

"No, thank you, Dave," replied Susan. "I have an important announcement to make."

"Oh! Really. If it's that important, I'd better sit down," said David humorously.

"I saw Doctor Goodchild this morning and I'm six weeks pregnant," said Susan now seating herself next to him on the couch.

"Oh! God. I'm going to be a father," exclaimed David who took her hands in his, not sure if he should hug her due to her delicate condition. But then he hugged her in a soft embrace.

"I love you so much, Susan. This is so unexpected. You'll have to be careful and take it easy, now. We want a healthy boy," said David.

"But what if it's a girl, Dave," said Susan.

"I'll love her just as much, honey. We'll just have a boy next time, that's all," replied David.

"Well, I hope so, David. "God decides those things, and we're just lucky he chose us to bear his children, because many parents can't."

"You are the heart of this family, Susan, and I adore you," said David, gently embracing her with a soft kiss on her lips.

The two houses were taking shape fast, their foundations already in place and their structure erected with roofs installed. The contractor had two crews working on both houses simultaneously to beat the forthcoming winter weather. In the meantime, James and David were getting ready to attend their first monthly weekend at Hancock Field Air National Guard Base in Syracuse, New York.

Colonel Barclay welcomed James and David, introducing them to his Deputy, Lieutenant Colonel Tom Levin, and Group Commander, Major Paul Thompson.

"You're both assigned to Major Thompson's group," said Colonel Barclay. "He'll familiarize you with the area and our mission. You'll also receive qualification training to fly the B-29 Superfortress, a four-engine, propeller-driven heavy bomber. It's the first bomber to house its crew in pressurized compartments. It's capable of flying at altitudes of up to 32,000 feet and speeds of up to 375 miles per hour. It has a General Electric Central Fire Control System that directs four remotely controlled turrets, each armed with .50 caliber machine guns. In addition, there are five sighting stations, all interconnected, located in the nose and tail positions. There are also three Plexiglas blisters in the central fuselage. Each sighting station has an analog computer that compensates for airspeed, gravity, humidity and temperature, increasing the machine guns' accuracy. The best part of it all, is that the computers permit one gunner to operate two or more turrets simultaneously. You'll also notice that the B-29 has the same number of crew members as the B-17. That would be the pilot, co-pilot, bombardier, navigator, flight engineer, radio operator, gun commander, left gunner, right gunner, and tail gunner. In case you're wondering, the B-29 is the bomber that delivered the first atomic bomb over Japan, resulting in its unconditional surrender."

"We're looking forward to flying that Superfortress, sir," said James, speaking for Dave as well.

"I'm sure you are. I also happen to know of your fine record flying B-17's over Germany, and I'm elated to have you back under my command," said Colonel Barclay. "These two fine officers, Paul, were shot down over Germany, and survived German imprisonment, while many perished under horrible conditions. Take good care of them, Paul."

"It will be my pleasure, sir," replied Paul Thompson, who then escorted James and David to Group Headquarters for further orientation.

Upon their return to Buffalo, David and Susan joined James and Louise for dinner at the Sontag Mansion in Lackawanna overlooking Lake Erie, while Louise's parents,

Michael and Marie Sontag, were on vacation in their beach house at West Palm Beach, Florida.

"So how did it go on your first assignment in the Reserves?" asked Louise.

"We were given the usual cook's tour of the base by our Group Commander, after meeting briefly with Colonel Claude Barclay," said James. "Then we were given a chance to see and climb aboard the B-29 Superfortress, which is the type of aircraft that dropped the atomic bomb on Japan. That is one impressive bomber."

"Did you get to fly it?" asked Susan.

"No, we first have to get checked out on it before we can fly one of them," replied David.

"What do you mean 'checked out'?" asked Susan.

"Well, we have to receive some training on this new aircraft, and get qualified before they'll let us fly it," said David.

"It's just routine for any new aircraft, Susan," said James. "It's no big deal."

"Whatever happened to that B-36 Peacemaker you told us about that could fly higher than any fighter aircraft or missile?" asked Louise.

"You've got a good memory, Louise. That was the unveiling of a prototype B-36. It has to go into production, and won't be delivered to the Army Air Corps until sometime in 1952, according to Major Thompson, our Group Commander," replied James, withholding the fact that its production was delayed due to engine problems.

"So, until then, you'll be flying the B-29 Superfortress, huh!" said Louise.

"Yeah! And possibly other aircraft," said David. "If I get a chance, I'd like to fly one of the latest fighter aircraft, but don't worry, Susan, they're only local flights, not combat missions."

"Yeah! But how safe is it?" asked Susan.

"Safer then driving a car on the highway amongst a lot of incompetent drivers," said David.

"Oh! Susan, let the boys play with their big, expensive toys," said Louise, chuckling.

"So how's the construction of our houses coming along?" asked James. "We haven't had a chance to go by there since we got back from Hancock Field."

"All the windows are in. The plumbing is done, but the electrical work is not yet finished. The contractor for the stone wall on the creeks' embankment had to wait for the Corps of Engineers to give the OK, before he could get started. It seems that any work on the creek is the domain of the Corps of Engineers, and the Village permit is contingent on their approval," said Louise with Susan nodding in agreement.

"So, everything is going on schedule, then," said James.

"Yes, so far so good," replied Louise.

"When do you think the houses will be ready for us to move in?" asked David.

"In about forty-five days, maybe a week or so later, but you never know with contractors," said Louise. "Susan and I visit them almost every day to motivate them."

"To motivate them, I like that," said David.

"Hey! Don't underestimate the power of a woman's charm, mister," said Louise.

"Oh! We don't, believe me, look what happened to us," replied James, with a loud laughter.

"Oh! Yeah! Just for that, you're having beans for dinner, smart ass," replied Louise, eliciting laughter from everyone.

"I think it's a good idea for you two gals to pay the contractor a daily visit," said James. "It keeps him on his toes, if you know what I mean."

"And listen, while you're there, make sure they insulate the water pipes before they close up the walls," said David. "These contractors like to save money by cutting corners, and that's one of the ways they can do that. It's too bad we can only pay them a visit on weekends, and they don't work on Sundays."

"So, I'm glad you girls are staying on top of this construction," said James. "If you do see some irregularities that need our attention, keep in mind we're only a five minute drive from the construction, and hopefully one of us is able to leave work."

It was the last week in November 1946, when the two houses were finally completed, and all that was needed was for them to pass final inspection by the Building Department of the Village of Williamsville. Louise and Susan were now busy shopping for furniture and other household items, but they soon learned that their individual tastes were significantly different. Hence, while very close friends, they decided to do much of their shopping with their husbands, who, among other things, footed the bills.

With only two weeks left before the Christmas Holidays were upon them, they realized that the furnishing for their houses, which had yet to be ordered, would not arrive until sometime in mid-January 1947.

"Since we can't move into our new homes until sometime in January, why don't the four of us get away from this winter weather, and spend Christmas at my folks' beach house in West Palm Beach, Florida," said Louise to Dave and Susan with whom she and Jim were having dinner. "Besides, Jim and I can't be seen together during the holidays."

"I hadn't thought of that," said David. "Florida would be a safe bet, and it would explain our absence with our folks during the Christmas holidays."

"How big a house is it? I mean, can it accommodate the four of us?" asked Susan.

"Yes, quite easily. It's a three-story house with an octagonal shape tower atop the roof. It has five bedrooms, and the house is located right on the beach. I can't wait to sink my toes in that warm sand, away from this cold weather," said Louise.

"What's the tower used for?" asked Susan.

"It's a large room on top of the third floor, with a huge bay window overlooking the ocean, and side windows for a view of the beach. It's similar to the tower we have over our house in Lackawanna," replied Louise, glancing at

James with whom she had shared a romantic evening in that tower. 'In fact, my father used the Lackawanna plans for the beach house on a smaller scale, with minor alterations. It's our home away from home."

"Well, that sounds very inviting. I'm all for it," said Susan. "How about it, guys, Christmas and New Year, or just Christmas?"

"If we're going to spend the holidays in West Palm Beach, then we might as well stay there for the duration of the holidays, which would include Christmas and New Year," said James, looking at Dave for confirmation.

"I agree with Jim," replied David. "If we're going to spend the holidays in West Palm Beach, we might as well stay 'till after the New Year. How do you propose we get there?"

"That's a good question, and I have an idea," said James. "Why don't we use the company's Travel Air 6000-B, which is a 6-seat single engine aircraft used by company executives, and I doubt it will be used during the holidays."

"Is that a safe aircraft?" asked Susan.

"Well, it's used regularly by Curtiss-Wright executives on business trips. It has a range of about 550 statute miles, so we'd have to make two to three stops for refueling," said James.

"Probably in West Virginia and South Carolina," said David.

"You said it seats six people, is that right?" asked Louise.

"Yes, that's right," replied James.

"Have you flown that aircraft before?" asked Louise.

"Actually, I have, twice, and Dave was with me. It's an easy plane to fly, we're both licensed pilots, and after flying B-17's, this is child's play," said James.

"But you still have to find out if the plane is available for us to use during the holidays," said Louise.

"I'll find out tomorrow," replied James.

The following day, James and David, together visited the president of the company, Stephen Waverly, who admired these two young veteran pilots since their first encounter, and were now on a first name basis.

"What can I do for you two young men?" asked Waverly.

"We'd like your permission, sir, to use your Travel Air 6000-B aircraft to fly with our wives to West Palm Beach for the Christmas and New Year holidays," said James.

"I wasn't aware you were married, Jim," said Waverly.

"Actually, I'm engaged to Louise Sontag, but we're keeping it quiet for the time being," replied James.

"Oh! OK! I understand, Jim," replied Waverly. "Did you renew your private aircraft license since your return to civilian life?"

"Yes, we both did, and with instrument flying included, as a result of our military training," said James.

"Well, in that case, that aircraft is available for your use, and I'll make sure Jeff in maintenance is aware of it. So tell me, Jim, if I'm not invading your privacy. Have you set a date for the wedding?" asked Waverly.

"We decided to wait for six months, so that leaves four months before the wedding, which will take place in the Saint Michaels' Church in Buffalo."

"Well, I hope you'll invite me to your wedding, Jim," said Waverly. "My wife loves weddings and their receptions which she finds so uplifting."

"I'll definitely make it a point for a formal invitation to be sent to you and your wife," said James.

"I'm looking forward to your wedding, Jim, and I wish you a good flight and safe passage to Florida," said Waverly, ending their conversation.

Back in their design department, James conferred with David.

"I think we'd better get reacquainted with the Travel Air before we fly to Florida," said James.

"Not a bad idea," replied David. "I estimate that it's about 1300 miles from Buffalo to West Palm Beach, and with only a 550-mile range, we'll need to find out what airports are available for refueling on the way there."

"When do you think we should leave Buffalo?" asked David.

"Maybe three days before Christmas Eve, to give us a chance to get settled into the beach house," replied James. "By the way, Louise has been at the beach house many times since she was just a kid. She said the house has a four-car garage occupied by two cars for our use."

"What airport is available at West Palm Beach?" asked David.

"Lantana Airport, located about six miles south of West Palm Beach. It's a small airport, and the only one not taken over by the Army Air Corps during the war," said James.

"Probably a puddle jumper," replied David. "But that's alright, because there won't be any sizable air traffic to contend with."

"That's right and the cost of landing and parking will be a lot less," replied James. "Can you take care of the flight plan, Dave?"

"Sure, I'll get right on it," said David.

The morning sun was bright and shiny on that 22d of December, when James and David, accompanied by Louise and Susan, boarded the Air Travel 6000-B, with two large suitcases and two satchels that barely fitted into the six-seat aircraft.

"This is going to be an exciting trip," said Louise to Susan, "with our guys flying this light aircraft."

"Luckily, we're not facing any snowy weather, and it gets better as we fly south," said James to Louise and Susan.

"That's good to hear," replied Louise.

"OK! Girls, buckle up, 'cause we're getting ready to take off," said James, with David sitting to his right as his navigator.

They had to make only two stops for refueling, due most likely to the favorable weather and wind, landing at Lantana Airport in time for a mid-afternoon lunch.

At the Lantana Airport's minor terminal, Louise called the Gable Security Company which provided year-around security for the Sontag beach house. As prearranged, she requested a pick up from the airport for their transportation to the beach house.

"How long do we have to wait for transportation?" asked James.

"About half an hour. We might as well get a cup of coffee while we wait," said Louise, as she eyed the small counter in the corner offering beverages and donuts.

As predicted by Louise, a Plymouth 1940 Woodie, 4-door station wagon arrived and parked in front of the entrance to the small, one-story terminal. The driver beeped his horn announcing his arrival, prompting Louise and her companions to exit the terminal. While Louise greeted the driver, her companions loaded their baggage in the back of the station wagon, and then seated themselves in the vehicle.

"I'm Louise Sontag. I presume you're here to drive us to the Sontag beach house in West Palm Beach."

"That's right, Miss Sontag. My name is Ted, and I have the directions to your beach house."

"Good, you get us there safely, Ted, and I'll give you a good tip," said Louise, who then seated herself next to James in the first row of seats.

Upon arrival at the beach house, Ted parked his vehicle in the wide driveway facing the four garage doors. He then unloaded the two suitcases and satchels to improve his gratuity, and was not disappointed when Louise gave him five dollars.

They first stared at the large beach house with wonderment, and then turned towards the long beach and the ocean's crashing waves.

"Wow! What a spectacular view. Can't wait to get my bathing suit on for a dip in that inviting ocean," said Susan.

"I think you'd better cool it, Susan, remember your pregnancy," said David.

"I'm not made of chocolate, Dave, I won't melt," replied Susan with a chuckle.

"I think I'll join you, Susan," said Louise. "But let's get settled in first."

"I hope you've got a key to the front door, Louise," said James jokingly.

They all walked up to the front door, and Louise unlocked it, allowing everyone to enter the spacious house, which they found especially clean, due to the cleaning service used by Louise's parents.

"You strong men can take the suitcases upstairs, and I'll show you which bedrooms you'll occupy," said Louise, marching up the stairs ahead of James and David, while Susan followed behind them.

"Alright, James, you can put the suitcase and satchel in this bedroom, which is the one I've been using ever since I can remember.

You can put your baggage in the bedroom at the end of the hall, Dave," said Louise.

"Why that one at the end of the hall?" asked Susan.

"Because it's soundproofed by the rooms in-between," replied Louise, which brought laughter from everyone.

"I suppose you mean my snoring, huh!" remarked David.

"Yeah! That's it, Dave, your snoring," replied Louise. "You believe that, and my lips will be sealed forever."

"Boy, these are large rooms, and with a full bath," said David.

"I could get used to this real easy."

"Well, you've got the entire Christmas and New Year holiday to enjoy it," said Louise. "When you guys are settled in, come on downstairs and acquaint yourselves with the rest of the house, while we gals look into the kitchen to see what food if any is in the fridge and freezer."

"Looks like my parents got rid of any excess food, except for the freezer which has a dozen frozen steaks and vegetables," said Louise to Susan standing next to her.

"Where do you shop for food around here?" asked Susan.

"There are stores in West Palm Beach, which is only about five miles from here. We'll drive over there tomorrow and stock up for the holidays,"

James and David appeared in the large kitchen, wondering what food was available.

"We do have frozen steaks and vegetables, but I don't think you want to wait for the steaks to thaw out, so I suggest we drive to West Palm Beach for dinner. Tomorrow, Susan and I are going shopping for food," said Louise.

"Actually, I did some research before coming here, and found out that Morrison Field, which is home to the Air

Transport Command, is located near West Palm Beach. It has an Officers Club, and since Dave and I are now Reserve Officers, we can frequent the 'O' Club with you as our guests, and have dinner there," said James.

"I forgot to mention that to you Susan," said David. "We both belong to the Officers Club at Hancock Field, which has reciprocal privileges with other Officers Club."

"Is Morrison Field a big base?" asked Louise.

"The Air Transport Command involves not only transport services, but from what I learned, more than 40,000 pilots trained there, and the Women's Army Corps also served there during the war," said James. "I think they referred to those women as WACS."

"That's a derogatory term used only by you chauvinists," said Susan.

"They only used that term to describe enlisted women, not the female officers," said James, "and I don't think they took offense to the use of that term."

"Did you ever ask them, Jim?" asked Louise.

"Well, no, but enlisted men were often referred to as G.I.'s, which stands for Government Issue, and I know they didn't mind being called that. In fact, they were kind of proud of it," said James. "So why should enlisted women find the term WACS offensive?"

"I guess women are more sensitive to labels," said Susan.

"Well, in the military you usually become desensitized to those labels," replied James.

"I don't know why we're so concerned about this," said David. "I vote for having dinner at the Officers Club in Morrison Field. All those in favor say Aye."

Everyone yelled Aye, and David posed the question of time for dinner to Susan and Louise.

"It's now 1645," said James. "It will take us maybe a half hour to get to Morrison Field, and we do have to check out those two cars in the garage. So, hopefully, if we have an operational vehicle, we could leave at 1800 hours in time for dinner at 1830, a most reasonable time."

"There should be only two cars in the garage," said Louise. "One is a Lincoln Model K series with a V-12 engine and a bronze metallic colored body. It seats four passengers. The other is a Lincoln Le Baron Roadster convertible two-seater, with a yellow body and red fenders. My Dad loved Lincolns."

"Those are expensive cars," said James. "Let's go look at them. Obviously, we'll have to use the Lincoln with four seats."

In the garage, as Louise had predicted, the two vehicles stood next to each other in mint condition, and admired by all present.

James immediately lifted the hood of the Lincoln Model K and inspected the motor and its accessories, with David standing on the other side of the motor commenting on its engineering.

" I love the way they put this engine together," said James. "Why don't you get in the driver's seat and start it up. Hopefully, the battery won't be dead."

David got behind the wheel and pumped the gas pedal a few times, then turned on the ignition with the key given to him by Louise, standing by with Susan.

The engine cranked up but didn't start. David, being an engineer, didn't need any advice from James, also an engineer, nor was any given. David waited a few minutes, then turned the ignition on, and this time the engine started, at first with a tremor, then it smoothed itself into a purr, like a satisfied kitten.

"How much gas is in the tank, Dave?" asked James.

"Near a full tank," replied David. "Looks like she's ready to go."

"Not yet. Turn on the lights and the signals to see if they work," said James.

David followed James' instructions, and satisfied that everything worked, turned off the engine.

"Let's take a look at the Roadster while we're at it," said James.

"Man, she's a beauty. I'm going to drive this roadster before we leave," said Dave. "I'm sure the girls will want to as well."

"Louise, you got the key to this car?" asked David.

"Yes," she replied, handing him the car key.

"I'm going to start the engine, Jim, while you check under the hood," said Dave.

This time the roadster's engine responded immediately without any prompting. "Let it run for a few minutes, Dave," said James, still looking at the engine. "OK, turn on the lights and signals."

"I can see those two guys running around town in that roadster while we sweat in the kitchen," said Louise. "But I've got the key."

"Well, let's give them some time with their new toy," said Susan. "We'll keep them busy barbequing our dinners, when we're not eating out."

"You're getting to think like me, Susan," said Louise. "You're supposed to be the softie for these guys, which is an admirable trait."

"I'm getting my pointers from you, Louise, but you're right, our differences are what make us a great team," said Susan.

"Let's go inside," said Louise. "I'm going to fix us some cold lemonade."

The two couples, with James at the wheel, drove their Lincoln K automobile the approximate six miles to Morrison Field, and after James presented his military identification card and received a salute from the guard-on-duty, they proceeded to the Officers Club.

The parking lot was surprisingly full of cars, necessitating they park their car four rows back from the front facing the Club.

The four of them, wearing casual dress, but the men wearing jackets, inasmuch as they were not in uniform, entered the Club. James and David, each presented their Hancock Field Officers Club membership card.

"Welcome to the Morrison Officers Club, Captains," said the Receiving Desk Manager. "Are you and your guests here for dinner, or the bar?"

"We're here for dinner," replied James.

The Manager turned to his assistant, also wearing a civilian suit.

"Have them seated at table number seven."

As the two couples were being led to their table, James mentioned to Louise that being seated at table number seven was a good luck sign.

"I didn't know you were superstitious, Jim," said Louise.

"I'm not, but there must be something to number seven; so many people believe it's a lucky number," said James. "Where there's smoke there must be fire."

"You know, Jim, as long as I've known you, you've never been without a plausible answer to anything I've ever questioned," said Louise.

"Well, you'll never be able to accuse me of being boring," replied James. "Besides, sweetheart, I don't think you'd want me any other way."

"I do love you, Jim, and that's what matters," said Louise, smiling profusely, as they sat down at the four-sided dinner table.

"I would have thought we'd have to wait a while before being seated, with all those cars in the parking lot," said

David. "But, it's the bar area that attracted most of them, luckily for us."

"This is a nice Club," said Louise. "I see some women in uniform having dinner and also at the bar."

"Like I said earlier, there's a unit of the Women's Army Corps stationed here at Morrison Field," said James.

Looking at the menu, David turned to Susan. "They've got some great choices of meat and fish, Susan. Anything that tempts your palate?"

"Yes, that filet mignon with lobster," replied Susan.

"I think I'll have the same," said Louise, also looking at the menu. "What about you, Jim."

"The sixteen ounce prime rib with backed potato is just what the doctor ordered," replied James, now looking at Dave for his choice.

"You know, Jim, I'm tempted to order that too, but I think I'm going to order the porterhouse steak," said David.

"Chacun a son gout," said James. "Each to his own taste."

"Even though there's a dance floor and a band stand, I don't think we're going to have any live music this evening, because it's a week day," said David.

"Yeah! But I'm sure they'll have live music Saturday night," replied James.

"You guys want to come back, Saturday?" asked Louise.

"Let's see how good the food is first, then we can decide," replied David.

"When you look at those low prices, you can't help wanting to return," said Susan.

"Frankly, we're on vacation for the Christmas Holidays, so I don't really care about the prices," said David. "But otherwise, you're right, without seeing what's available in West Palm Beach, I doubt if any restaurant or club can match what's offered here."

"Amen to that, Dave," said James. "What kind of wine shall we order?"

"White wine for me, James," said Louise.

"I'm going to order a bottle of Beaujolais, a red wine," said James. "Anybody else want the same?"

"Yes, I'll go for that," replied David. "What about you, Susan?"

"I'll have the same as you, Dave," she replied.

Their sumptuous dinner having been pleasurably consumed, and now waiting for their desert with coffee, they were approached by a man in Army Air Corps uniform wearing Captains bars on his shoulders.

"Dave Siegel," said the Captain with hesitation. "Is that you?"

Dave stood up, "Bill Kaufman. Well, I'll be damned," shaking his hand vigorously. "Where the hell did you come from?"

Kaufman then saw Jim stand to greet him. "Jim Longbow, my God, I never thought I'd see you guys again," said Kaufman shaking his hand.

David waived the waiter over and asked him to bring them a chair for Kaufman.

Sitting between Jim and Dave, facing Louise and Susan, Kaufman ached to learn about his two officer companions at the Nazi concentration camp.

"Let me introduce you, Bill, to my wife Susan and Jim's fiancée Louise," said David.

"It's my great pleasure to meet you ladies," said Kaufman. "Dave, Jim and I were confined in the same prison barracks in Germany, and we manage to survive the ordeal while many others didn't."

"I see you're still in uniform, Bill. Are you stationed here?" asked David.

"Yes, I'm an aviation instructor here," replied Kaufman. "I decided to make the Army Air Corps a career. So what are you guys doing here?"

"We're on vacation for the Christmas Holidays. Jim and I are in the Army Air Corps Reserves, stationed at Hancock Field Air National Guard, located in Syracuse, New York," said David.

"Really, so what rank did they give you?" asked Kaufman.

"We're both Captains, like yourself, Bill, so you can't pull rank on us," said David, laughing.

"If I remember correctly, you guys hail from Buffalo, New York," said Kaufman.

"Yeah! That's right," replied Dave. "The Hancock Field was the closest Air National Guard installation where we could serve our reserve commitment, and you'll never guess who is our Wing Commander."

"I haven't a clue," replied Kaufman.

"Major Claude Barclay, now Colonel Barclay," said James.

"You're kidding, Colonel Barclay. Things are looking up for you guys. Having him as your Wing Commander is a big plus, come promotion time."

"The nice thing about it, is that we don't have to prove ourselves all over again. He knows and respects our track record," said James.

"So what do you guys do when you're not serving in the Reserves?" asked Kaufman.

"Jim and I are employed as aircraft designers for the Curtiss-Wright Corporation in Cheektowaga, New York," replied David.

"Really, that sounds like a great job. Congratulations to you both," said Kaufman, who then hesitated, looking at Louise and Susan.

"There's something I'd like to discuss with you, Dave, but I don't know if it's appropriate with your wife and Jim's fiancée present," said Kaufman.

"If it's about our time in prison, Bill, they know all about it, so ask your question," said David.

Looking in the girls direction, Kaufman explained, "Dave and I were the only Jews in our prison barracks, and Jim was the only one that knew that. If it had been known to the Germans, and an SS Captain in particular, we would have been summarily executed. As Dave and Jim can attest to, that SS Captain, Hans Gunther, whose name I will never forget, shot and killed at least five of our officers one day while standing in formation, and several more during our imprisonment. When we were liberated by the US Army, I noticed that Captain Gunther had disappeared a couple of days before. I reported Captain Gunther's activities to the C.I.D. at the Provost Marshall General's Office, and when I didn't hear from them, after I was returned to the United States, I followed up with a letter. About a month later, I received a reply that their C.I.D. investigation failed to locate SS Captain Hans Gunther, and he was either deceased or else had acquired a new identify, and immersed himself into the German population. I even followed up with a letter to the F.B.I. and got the same response. I was wondering if you or Jim had heard anything about the whereabouts of Captain Gunther?

"I haven't heard anything," replied David, "Have you, Jim?"

"No, and frankly, Bill, I doubt if anyone will ever find him. Many German soldiers who returned to civilian life, immigrated to Canada, and some with high profiles went to Brazil and Argentina. If he changed his identity, he could easily assimilate into Canadian society without the risk of being discovered by one of his former American Prisoners of War," said James.

"Why don't you just forget about this guy, Bill," said David. "We survived, and that's our revenge."

"He's right, Bill. Forget him and move on with your life," said James, who felt that Kaufman was carrying too much of a grudge which would have an adverse impact on his life.

"So, I don't see a wedding ring on your finger, Bill," said David. "You're not a confirmed bachelor, are you?"

"No, I've just been too busy, but eventually I'll meet that special woman, who'll sweep me off my feet and make me her king," said Bill, with a big grin on his face.

"Isn't that line for the man to sweep the girl off her feet and make her his queen," said James.

"So I improvised a bit," said Kaufman. "No harm done if it works."

"Well, Bill, we all wish you luck, because you certainly deserve nothing but the best, my friend," said David. "Here's my card with my address and phone number. If you should come into the Buffalo area, please don't hesitate to give us a call for a get-together."

"I don't have a card, but here's my phone number, Dave," said Kaufman. I'll send you a note with my full address."

"Well, I don't want to overstay my welcome, folks," said Kaufman, standing up. "It was certainly a wonderful surprise seeing you guys, and a pleasure meeting you Susan and Louise."

"The pleasure is all ours, Bill," said David, now standing with Jim to shake hands with Kaufman.

"By the way guys, stay away from those B-24's, they're flying coffins. If you don't believe me, just ask Colonel Barclay, he should know. In the bombing raid over the German-held Romanian oil complex at Ploiesti, of the 177 B-24s, 54 were lost," said Kaufman, who then turned and walked back to the bar to join his friends.

"Bill Kaufman," said James to David, both looking at their comrade's departure. "He's one of a kind."

"I heard about the B-24 bomber's poor performance from one of the pilots incarcerated with us," said David. "They called it the Constipated Lumberer."

"I hope you guys take Bill's advice," said Susan.

"Never fear, my dear. Those B-24s have since been retired to the heap pile," said David.

"Why is Bill so obsessed with finding this Captain Gunther?" asked Louise.

"That's because one of the officers shot by Gunther was his co-pilot, standing next to him....he was also his cousin," replied Longbow.

"Good God! How awful. I can't say I blame him," replied Louise, with Susan nodding her head in agreement.

"I don't think Bill will ever give up looking for that SS Captain," said Susan.

Upon return to the beach house, Dave and Susan announced they were bushed and were calling it a night.

"We're sleeping in, so don't expect us for breakfast In the morning," said Dave standing at the foot of the stairs with Susan.

"I don't think we're going to be up early in the morning, either, so goodnight," replied James.

"Good night Susan," said Louise.

After David and Susan had climbed the stairs to their bedroom, Louise turned to James.

"Would you like to stay up for a while or are you ready to retire?" asked Louise.

"I'm ready to retire, sweetheart, if you are," replied James.

"Yeah! It's been a long day, let's call it a night," she replied with humor.

Inside their bedroom, Louise took off her shoes, blouse and skirt, then dressed only in her panties and bra, went to the bathroom. James stripped to his jockey shorts and lay on the bed propped up with two pillows, waiting for the bathroom to be free. Finally, Louise exited the bathroom and walked up to the edge of the bed.

"Jim, I misplaced my diaphragm, it's not amongst my toilet articles. I must have left it at home," said Louise, "do you by any chance have a condom?"

"No, I never use them. It's like taking a shower with a raincoat on," replied James. "Any suggestions?"

"Well, I'm in the 24th day of my menstrual cycle, which is a safe period to engage in sex without protection," said Louise.

"In that case, sweetheart, let's do what comes naturally," replied James with a laugh. He then got off the bed and went into the bathroom to brush his teeth and wash his face. Leaving the bathroom, he found only the side lamp was lit, and Louise was lying on the bed stark naked with her head propped up against the two pillows, waiting for him.

Upon seeing James, she opened her stretched arms and invited him to embrace her. He quickly removed his shorts exposing his erected penis, and climbed onto the bed, joining her in an embrace that began with a soul kiss while fondling her voluptuous breasts, and then sucking one of her large nipples. Now equally aroused with passion, Louise grabbed his penis with her right hand, guiding it towards her vagina, which he eagerly pushed inside her with a rhythmic movement that brought them together into a climactic state of euphoria that transcended all pleasures with unequal contentment.

"Oh! Jim, I love you so much, that sometimes it scares me," said Louise in a soft voice, now resting beside him.

"And I love you, too, sweetheart. But why does it scare you?" asked James.

"Well, because I'm afraid that something might happen to you, which I couldn't bear," replied Louise.

"Oh! Sweetheart, nothing's going to happen to me," replied James. "You can't live life, fearful of everything. It'll drive you crazy."

"Yes, I know, darling. It's just that I've never been in love before, and I've found out that my love for you runs so very deep and absolute, that life without you would be intolerable," said Louise, leaning towards him, placing her left arm across his chest.

"You can be sure of one thing, sweetheart," said James. "I will always love you and be totally faithful to you, for the rest of your life. That should ease any insecurity."

Louise moved closer to James and kissed him passionately on the lips, arousing them both into another round of lovemaking that ended with them falling asleep in each other's arms.

For the next several days, they spent their time on the beach, swimming, playing volleyball and barbequing in the evening, followed by drinking beer sitting around a stone fire pit, exchanging stories. They then went shopping for a Christmas tree but being in a tropical climate, they only found a tall, fake, decorated Christmas tree, whose only redeeming quality was that it was green. They bought it and brought it back to the beach house, and stood it up in the living room facing the large bay window.

"Well, we're the only ones who are going to see it, so it doesn't matter if it isn't a real tree," said Louise, examining its stance.

"Yeah! At least it gives us the feeling of Christmas," replied Susan.

"Louise, is there a Catholic Church around here that's holding midnight Mass this Christmas eve?" asked James.

"I don't think so, Jim," replied Louise. "I've never been here during the Christmas holidays, so I don't really know, but I don't think so."

"I would doubt it, too," said David. "Although being Jewish, I wouldn't be a reliable source."

"We'll just make up for it when we get back to Buffalo," said James to Louise, knowing that David and Susan, being of the Jewish faith, wouldn't be interested in attending Mass.

"I think we should spend New Year's Eve at the Officers Club," said Louise. "What do you think?"

"I think it's an excellent idea," replied David with Susan nodding her head in agreement.

"Then that's settled," said James. "Let's make reservations for dinner and then we'll stay for the festivities."

Fortunately, the Officers Club was quite large, because the place was packed with officers, most of them wearing their dress uniforms, and accompanied by their wives or girlfriends. There were several female officers that came in pairs or trios not accompanied by a male escort, but a few were with a man also in uniform. The mix gave a cheerful atmosphere.

"It's a good thing we made reservations," said Louise, after being seated at a table for four in the dining room. "This place is crammed. I hope the service can handle this crowd."

"I'm sure they got ready for it," said James. "It's not as if they were novices at this. They've been running Officers Clubs for decades."

"I see that the band has arrived," said David. "This place will be jumping soon."

"This is exciting. I'm glad we decided to spend New Year's Eve here," said Susan.

"I'd better get the attention of a waiter, so we can at least order some drinks to start the evening," said James.

"Yeah! And let's also order champagne," said David.

Finally a waiter came over, when James waived a five dollar bill at him.

"First, I would like to order two bottles of champagne on ice. In addition, we'll need two bottles of red wine, one bottle of white wine, a whiskey sour, a gin and tonic, and two scotch and sodas. I presume you have California wines, right?" asked James.

"Yes sir, we do," replied the waiter. "What type of red and white wines would you like?"

"Christian Brothers or Paul Masson wines will do. Surprise us with a semi-sweet red wine and a dry white wine," said James.

"Are you ready to order your dinner?" asked the waiter.

James looked around at his companions for an answer.

"Do you need more time?" asked the waiter.

"No, we'll order now," replied James, fearful of not getting another chance at service for a long time.

Everyone ordered steaks to their liking, and soon thereafter, the alcoholic beverages arrived, followed several minutes later with the champagne in a bucket of ice.

The conversation during dinner practically required a megaphone, due to the loud music and the chatter from several hundred party goers. But it did make everyone feel jovial as the New Year approached, inviting James, Louise, David and Susan to take their place on the dance floor, while there was still room. Although the dance floor was large, it had quickly filled to capacity.

Finally, the countdown by the band leader started, and when the clock struck midnight, the traditional folk song of *Auld Lang Syne* bidding farewell to the old year, came through the speakers, joined by the crowd of revelers who were now busy kissing their mate and wishing them a Happy New Year for 1947.

The flight back home to Buffalo aboard the Air Travel 6000-B was uneventful, due to unusual mild winter weather conditions in Western New York.

While James and David got busy at work in the design department of the Curtiss-Wright Corporation, Louise and Susan wasted no time in shopping for furniture and other accessories, so they could soon move into their new homes.

It wasn't until the end of January, when the two houses on Creekside Road were ready to be occupied, and the two couples celebrated its opening with the customary glass of champagne.

However, two weeks later, another event occurred that also presented an unanticipated celebration.

James arrived at his new home on Creekside Road at about 5:30 p.m. to find Louise busy in the kitchen preparing a sumptuous dinner with lit candles on the dining room table where dinner was to be served rather than in the kitchen.

"Hmm! Smells good," said James. "What's the occasion?"

"That's a surprise, darling. It'll wait until after dinner," replied Louise.

Throughout dinner, James wondered what the imminent surprise could possibly be. After having coffee with their dessert, Louise invited James to sit with her on the couch in the living room.

"OK! Sweetheart," said James. "What's the surprise."

"I went to see the doctor, this morning, and as I suspected, I'm pregnant," said Louise, looking into James' eyes for his reaction.

"Are you sure? I mean, I thought we had sex during your safe menstrual cycle," said James.

"I'm sure, Jim. The doctor examined me and said I'm six weeks pregnant," said Louise. "But after seeing how happy and contented Susan is with her pregnancy, I've changed my mind about waiting 'till I'm thirty. So I'm not upset about being pregnant, Jim, and I hope you're happy about it too."

"Of course, I'm happy, sweetheart. I just hope it's a boy, so I can take him fishing and boating with me," said James.

"Oh! Jim, I'm glad you feel that way, because I was so worried you'd be upset over it," said Louise.

"No, I just thought you'd be upset over an unexpected pregnancy," said James.

"I was talking to Susan the other day, and the way she talked about how it felt to have a living human being growing inside your body, and the miracle of it all, just overwhelmed her with the purpose of her life on this earth," said Louise. "Haven't you noticed the glow in her face since her pregnancy?"

"Actually, I think Dave has fallen in love with her all over again since her pregnancy," said James. "It is indeed a miracle."

"I do hope it's a boy, Jim," said Louise. "But I hope you'll love our baby just as much if she's a girl."

"Sweetheart, any child we create will receive all the love I have. You know that," said James. "If it's a girl, then we'll try again, and this time we'll hope for a boy, that's all."

"If it's a boy, you name him, and if it's a girl, I'll name her," said Louise. "Does that sound fair to you?"

"Frankly, I would never name any of our children without your input and approval, sweetheart," said James.

"That's very kind of you, Jim. But I do have a preference for the name of our daughter, when she does arrive," said Louise. "You want to hear it?"

"Sure, what is it?" asked James.

"*Jacqueline,*" said Louise. "I just love that name, and her friends can call her *'Jackie'* for short. What do you think?"

"I like it very much. I think it's perfect," replied James.

"Oh! Jim, no wonder I love you so much," said Louise. "You're such an easy and understanding man."

"Sweetheart, our tastes are so much alike. That's why we get along so well," said James. "You know, opposites attract, but they don't stay together. On the other hand, couples whose tastes are similar and compatible, are less likely to have serious differences that invite confrontations."

"I agree, but I also think that empathy plays a significant role in relationships," said Louise. "We're very sensitive to each other's needs and emotional state."

"We keep up this analysis and we're going to have to hang out a sign," said James, with a laugh.

"So, if it's a boy, Jim, what would you like to name him?" asked Louise.

"I hadn't thought about it, but the first thing that comes to mind is the name of *Garreth* which means *Brave Spear.* His friends could also call him Gary for short," said James.

"I like that name. *Brave Spear* has an American Indian flair to it," said Louise.

"It's funny that I should have thought of that name so quickly, almost as if it was destined to be his name," said James. "Do you really like it?"

"Yes, I do, Jim," replied Louise. "Are you not sure?"

"Yes, I'm sure, and if you like it, then so be it. His name will be *Garreth,*" said James, with finality.

"Listen, sweetheart. Now that you are pregnant, you must be careful of your activities, not lift anything, and watch your diet," said James. "We want a healthy child, but then I'm preaching to the choir. Please forgive me. I am acting like a new father, which I am."

"Oh! James. I know that if it's a girl, you'll spoil her rotten, and she'll wrap you around her little finger, because you'll simply adore her," said Louise with a knowing smile.

"Yeah! I know, you're right," replied James in total agreement. "But, your pregnancy brings up another matter, sweetheart.

I don't think we should wait for another four months to get married," said James. "I think we should talk to your parents about this, and I think that under the circumstances, they'll agree that our marriage in church should be scheduled as soon as possible."

"I hadn't thought that far ahead," replied Louise. "You're right. I don't want to walk up the aisle advertising my pregnancy."

"The sooner the better, so let's visit your parents tomorrow evening. My father trusts my judgement and will agree to whatever we decide," said James.

"We'll go right after dinner, so why don't I call them now, while my father is home, and tell them we'll be there at about 7:00 p.m." said Louise.

"Afterwards, with your parents' blessings, we can tell Dave and Susan, since he'll be my best man and Susan will be your Maid of Honor," said James.

James and Louise enjoyed dinner at the Sontag mansion in Lackawanna, then Louise sprung the news of her pregnancy to her parents.

"How far along is your pregnancy?" asked her mother, Marie.

"Seven weeks now," replied Louise. "It's not something we planned."

"Well, what are your plans now?" said her father, Michael, looking at James for an answer.

"We want to get married as soon as possible, before her pregnancy shows," said James.

"Under the circumstances, I guess you have no choice," replied Michael.

"We want to get married at Saint Michael's Church, but with no fanfare, and a reception only for our immediate family and closest friends," said Louise.

"That's going to be a difficult task to keep the press from knowing and advertising the event," said Michael. "I'll talk to Father Timmons at Saint Michael's and arrange for the marriage to be kept private and unannounced."

"Well, my dear, now that you're going to be a wife and a mother, you're gonna learn what it is to be selfless and without free time for escapades," said Marie. "But don't worry, I'll be there to help you in any way I can, Louise."

"And that goes for me too, Louise, and you too Jim," said Michael. "You're the parents of our forthcoming grandchild, and whatever you need, we'll provide with our love."

"Thank you, Dad," said Louise, "and I'll need your help and advice more than ever, Mom."

"You're our daughter and only child, Louise, and I'm glad you chose Jim as your husband and father of our grandchild," said Michael, looking at James as the son he never had, but whose traits he admired.

"You can be sure I'll do my best to make your daughter happy, and hopefully meet all of your expectations," replied James.

"I'm sure you will, Jim," said Michael. "Just consider this your second home."

"How soon do you think our marriage can take place, Dad?" asked Louise.

"I don't really know. It depends on the church's schedule. But I'll contact Father Timmons tomorrow, and hopefully he'll be able to give us a date," said Michael.

"Have you decided on where you'll spend your honeymoon," asked Marie, addressing Louise and James.

"We talked about that, Mom. By the time we get married, I'll be almost three months pregnant. I don't want to be away from home and my doctor, in the event that some medical issue arises that could endanger my baby. So we agreed that we'll forego a trip and spend our honeymoon in our new home and its wonderful surroundings, while close to you and my doctor," said Louise.

"You know, Louise, you've suddenly grown into a very mature woman, and I'm so proud of you," said Marie. "I think you two have made a very wise decision, and we'll be here, whenever you need us."

The following evening, Louise received a telephone call from her father.

"Louise, I spoke with Father Timmons and the wedding is set for the 20th of February which is ten days from now," said Michael. "It'll be a small wedding like you wanted, and then the reception will be held at our house, if that's alright with you."

"Thanks Dad. Of course I expected the reception to be held at your house which is ideal for such an occasion," said Louise. "I'd better get things going, like a wedding dress and other arrangements."

"Whose going to be Jim's best man, and your Maid of Honor?" asked Michael.

"Dave Siegel will be Jim's best man, and his wife Susan will be my Maid of Honor," replied Louise.

"I think you've got things under control, Louise," said Michael. "I've already made arrangements with Father Timmons for the church wedding, so that's one thing you and Jim don't have to concern yourself with."

"You're the best father a girl could ever have. I love you, Dad," said Louise, concluding their conversation.

Now being next door neighbors, Louise gave a quick telephone call to Susan, and arranged for her and David to come over after dinner the following day.

It was 7:15 p.m. when David and Susan walked over to their neighbor's house, where they were enthusiastically received by James and Louise into their new home.

"Oh! I like your new furniture, Louise," said Susan. "It finally came in."

"Yes. Of course you've seen the rest of the house. Why don't we sit in the living room where it's more comfortable." said Louise, noticing that Susan's pregnancy was now showing. "How many months now?"

"Four and a half months," replied Susan. "Thank God I'm over the morning sickness. But now I can feel the baby moving inside me, and it feels so strange.

"Well, the reason we invited you over, is to tell you that I am two months pregnant," said Louise.

"Oh! My God! Really?" exclaimed Susan. "How did that happen?"

"I think the baby was conceived on that first night we stayed at the beach house in Florida."

"Well, I'll be damned, so you're going to be a father, Jim," said David. "When is the wedding going to take place?"

"That's the other reason we invited you over," said James. "The wedding is going to take place at Saint Michael's Church on the 20th of February, and I would like you to be my Best Man."

"And for you Susan to be my Maid of Honor," said Louise.

"Good God! So soon?" said David.

"It's obvious, Dave, they want to get married before her pregnancy shows," said Susan. "I presume your parents already know?"

"Yes, Jim and I had dinner with my folks yesterday, and my father arranged for the wedding to take place at Saint Michael's on the 20th," said Louise.

"And I told my father about it, and he thought it was a good idea to have the wedding as soon as possible," said James.

"Well, in that case, we're at your complete disposal my friends," said David with Susan nodding in agreement.

"Just think, Louise, we're going to each have a baby only a few months apart. We're hoping it's a boy," said Susan.

"We do too," replied Louise. "But if it's a girl, that's OK too. We'll just try for a boy next time."

"That's the way we look at it too," said David.

"Have you been suffering from morning sickness?" asked Susan.

"Yes, but not as bad and frequent as what you had, Susan. Nevertheless, it does curtail my activities," said Louise.

"I didn't know you were suffering from morning sickness," said James.

"Well, I didn't want to bother you with our female problems, Jim," replied Louise. "But I think that phase is over now."

"That's good to hear," replied James.

"I'm glad you agreed not to travel far during your pregnancy, sweetheart," said James, then turning to David and Susan. "We decided to forego a honeymoon, so Louise could be near her doctor and parents, in the event of medical complications. We just don't want to take any chances," said James.

"I think that's very smart," said Susan. "It's just not worth the risks. Besides, I can't think of a more wonderful place to spend your honeymoon, than here in your beautiful home, surrounded by nature's wonderful foliage."

"Not to mention next to our best friends," said Louise.

"Since we're not planning on putting up a fence between our houses, our kids will be able to play together along the creek. I think that building our houses next to each other is the best decision we've ever made," said David.

"And the best years are ahead of us," said James.

At 10:00 a.m. on Wednesday, the 20th of February 1947, James Longbow and Louise Sontag were married in Saint Michael's Roman Catholic Church, with only a small number of worshippers in attendance. The bride wore a long, cream colored wedding gown with a conservative neckline. She did not want to wear the same wedding gown she wore when she married Mark Palmer, now deceased. Her hair was pulled up into a beehive held by a slender diamond studded silver crown, from which a three-foot veil hung over her shoulders and back. She looked like the Queen of Sheba, and upon first seeing her walk up the aisle to the alter, James swallowed hard with awe at her beauty and majesty, undoubtedly shared by many of the spectators in attendance. James silently thanked God for the privilege of marrying and being loved by the woman of his dreams.

On the 10th of July of that year, a son was born to Susan Hershey Siegel, whom she named Alexander, whose astrological sign was Cancer.

On the 18th of September of that same year, the temperature in Buffalo reached a record 89 degrees Fahrenheit, greeting the newborn son of Louise Sontag Longbow, whom she named Garreth, with the astrological sign of Virgo.

There was much rejoicing in the Siegel and Longbow households, watching their two sons steadily growing from infants to babies, when fate conspired with nature to provide Susan with another baby, only twelve months after the birth of her son Alexander. This time, to their delight, it was a girl whom they named Rachel, whose astrological sign was Cancer, like her brother, but as fate would have it, also compatible with Capricorn.

Not to be outdone, fate nudged nature to have Louise conceive and give birth on the 7th of July 1948, to a girl whom they named Jacqueline, with the astrological sign of Capricorn, coincidentally compatible with Cancer.

The compatibility of those astrological signs did not escape Louise and Susan, who thought that God was perhaps playing Cupid with their children, which enlivened the predictability of their children's future.

As the years went by, with the four children sharing the same playground in their backyard overlooking Ellicott Creek, a special bond developed between them that promised to last a lifetime. They were now becoming of age for entry into their first school, with the two boys first, followed the next year by the two girls who were a year younger. Preparations were made for Garreth and Alexander to be matriculated into Catholic and Jewish schools respectively Then Jacqueline and Rachel would follow the same path for girls' schools, Catholic and Jewish. But, when eligible for entry into high school, it was decided by the Longbow and Siegel couples, that their children could then be enrolled into private non-denomination schools that would enable the four children to share those school years together.

CHAPTER II

The Korean War

As the Longbow and Siegel families were planning their children's education, the world and local newspapers announced on 24 June 1950, the invasion of the pro-Western Republic of South Korea, by the Soviet-backed Democratic People's Republic of North Korea. More than 75,000 soldiers from the North Korean People's Army crossed the 38th parallel of latitude, which formed the boundary between North and South Korea. President Harry S. Truman of the United States, ordered U. S. troops to the aid of South Korea, and convinced the United Nations to also send military assistance to South Korea. It was described by the Administration as a Police Action. Nevertheless, conscription was quickly instituted, and all American men between the ages of 18 and 26 were required to register for the Draft, with a 24-month commitment, which swelled the ranks of the United Nations to a mostly American military force.

"Thank God, you're over 26, Jim," said Louise, "otherwise you'd be drafted. You think your Reserve Unit will be activated?"

"I haven't heard anything yet," replied James. "It's really too soon to tell. We're not technically at war with North Korea. The President referred to it as a Police Action."

"Yeah! But he's still drafting our young men to join our troops in South Korea," said Louise. "I have a very uneasy feeling about this, Jim."

The door-bell at the Longbow residence rang, and Dave, accompanied by Susan, were invited inside.

"My mother is staying over watching the kids, so we decided to come over to talk about this Korean War," said Susan.

"It looks like General MacArthur pulled a whole Army Division from Japan to fight the North Koreans, and he's been pushed back to the southern peninsula of South Korea," said David. "It's no wonder President Truman called on the draft to augment his forces."

"As I told Jim, it's a lucky break that you and Jim, are beyond the draft age," said Louise. "But what about your Reserve Unit being called to active duty?"

"It's a possibility, but this police action appears to involve the Army, not the Air Force, which, since 1947, is now a separate branch of the service, and no longer part of the US Army," said David.

"That's something I didn't know, being so busy raising my two children," said Louise. "Maybe you'll escape being recalled to active duty."

"I certainly hope so," said Susan. "I thought the last war had put an end to all of this madness."

"As long as there are people on this planet, there will be conflict," said James.

"Well, I hope our children never see another war," said Susan.

Several weeks transpired, then the news media applauded General MacArthur's brilliant amphibious landing at the Port of Inchon, behind enemy lines, encircling North Korean troops, then driving them back deep into North Korea.

There was rejoicing by the Longbow and Siegel families at the news of MacArthur's bold victory, which appeared to have brought the war to an end. However, the Chinese Army came to the aid of the North Korean Army with 330,000 troops, pushing the United Nations troops back into South Korea.

The dreadful news finally arrived, as James Longbow and David Siegel sat in Longbow's kitchen with their wives, looking sadly at the official orders their husbands had received from the Commander of the 174th Attack Wing.

"You're both being assigned to the 19th Bombardment Group at Kadena Air Base on Okinawa," said Louise. "Why do they need you there?"

"Because, several B-29 Superfortresses have been transferred from Andersen Air Force Base on Guam to Okinawa. I presume those B-29's will be used to bomb North Korea, and they need qualified pilots to fly those bombers," said Longbow.

"I thought you guys were free from further participation in bombing raids, and your reserve status required only one weekend a month and two weeks of active duty in the States," said Susan.

"Normally that's true, Susan, but we're now on a war footing, although it's officially a police action," said David.

"We really don't know what our actual assignment in Okinawa will be," said Longbow. "Besides, flying those B-29 Superfortresses is a lot safer than the B-17s we flew over Germany."

"How long will you guys be gone?" asked Louise.

"Can't be too long. It's just a police action, and North Korea doesn't have the defense capability the Germans had," said David.

"But the news said the Chinese Army was now supporting the North Koreans, and had driven our troops back to South Korea," said Louise. "We're no longer dealing with just North Korea, and China is no small adversary."

"You forgot one thing, Louise," replied Longbow. "We've got atomic bombs which no one else has, and I'm sure that General MacArthur will use them if he has to."

"Good God, Jim," exclaimed Susan. "Do you realize what that means, World War Three."

"C'mon, Susan," replied Longbow. "I don't think it's going to come to that. Cooler heads will prevail, I'm sure."

"I sure hope so, Jim, because I don't want our children to grow up without a father," said Susan.

"We have to report to Hancock Field, and from there I presume to an air base on the west coast, and then to Okinawa," said David.

"Please don't worry, Louise," said Longbow, reassuringly. "I'll write to you as often as time permits, I promise."

"And ditto for me, too, Susan," said David.

Upon arrival at Hancock Field in Syracuse, New York, Longbow and Siegel, now Captains, reported to the Wing Commander, Colonel Claude Barclay for duty and further orders.

"Welcome back, gentlemen," said Colonel Barclay, coming around his large imposing desk to greet and shake hands with Longbow and Siegel, who had served under him in England before they became prisoners of war in Nazi Germany.

"Being under your command, sir, makes this active duty assignment a lot more agreeable," said Longbow. "I just hope this *police action* doesn't turn into another world war."

"You can relax, Jim," replied Colonel Barclay, "this Korean incident will be over by the end of the year. General MacArthur has ordered the stockpiling of fifty atomic bombs in Okinawa. Most of them are being delivered by ship, but in the event of immediate need, we're delivering twelve of them by air, using B-29 SuperFortresses."

Longbow looked at Siegel with a concerned look. "Is that why we're here, sir, to deliver an atomic bomb to Okinawa?" asked Longbow.

"The answer to that question, Jim, is yes, and it is classified information," answered Colonel Barclay.

"I presume that the bomb we'll be carrying will not be armed," said Siegel.

"That's correct, Dave," replied Colonel Barclay. "Nevertheless, all precautionary measures must be taken to insure there won't be any chance of that bomb falling into the hands of the enemy."

"You can be sure, sir, that we will deliver the bomb to Okinawa in pristine condition," replied Longbow.

"I'm sure you will," replied Colonel Barclay. "You're both experienced and war tested pilots, which is why you were chosen for this mission, along with other similarly experienced pilots."

"Where do we pick-up the nuclear device?" asked Siegel.

"That's in your special orders, which I'm about to give you," said Colonel Barclay. "You made such a good team, in England, that I decided to keep you together on this mission to fly a B-29 to March Air Force Base, where you will have a nuclear bomb loaded onto your aircraft for transportation to Kadena Air Base, Okinawa."

"What happens after we deliver the nuclear bomb, sir?" asked Siegel.

"Your orders reassign you to the 19th Bombardment Group whose mission includes the use of B-29s to conduct bombing raids over North Korea, and possibly over the Yalu power plants on the Chinese border," said Colonel Barclay.

"Does that mean we'll remain on Okinawa for the purpose of conducting bombing raids over North Korea, sir?" asked Longbow.

"Yes, that's correct, Jim," replied Colonel Barclay, handing him and Dave their special orders. "The exigencies of the service must come first, you know that."

"Yes, sir, I understand," replied Longbow, quickly reading his orders. "According to these orders, sir, we're leaving the day after tomorrow. That gives us only one day to inspect the aircraft and remedy any malfunctions, sir."

"Yes, so you'll have to report to Major Paul Thompson, who'll direct you to your billets, where the rest of your skeleton crew is housed. You'll then be assigned your B-29 bomber, and provided with whatever equipment is required for your mission. So I guess I'd better let you guys go, so you can get your aircraft ready for departure on time. Good luck to you both, and I hope to see you safe and sound upon your return," said Colonel Barclay, returning their salute.

Walking out of the Wing Headquarters building, Siegel turned to Longbow. "Man, I don't like this arrangement, Jim. We may be dropping atomic bombs over China. I don't think I'm going to mention this to Susan. She'll have a fit."

"First of all, Dave, that's classified information, which you must not mention in any of your letters," said Longbow. "I just think that the shipment of atomic bombs to Okinawa is merely a strategic warning for China to convince North Korea to negotiate a settlement."

"I sure hope you're right, Jim," replied Siegel.

"Let's just concentrate on doing our job, and getting that nuclear device to Okinawa, then let the chips fall where they may," said Longbow, in a fatalistic mood.

The wooden barracks at Hancock Field were of World War Two vintage, and the skeleton crew assigned to the B-29 Bomber with tail number 528, were already settled into barracks number 719, with their flight equipment, awaiting the arrival of their pilot and co-pilot. It was 1410 hours when James Longbow and David Siegel entered barracks 719, where they received a warm reception from their crew.

"I'm Jim Longbow, your skipper, and this is Dave Siegel, my co-pilot. It looks like you're all here, so let's get acquainted before we get to work."

"I'm Lieutenant Steven Brody, your Navigator, sir," shaking Longbow's and Siegel's hands.

"I'm Lieutenant William Marcus, your Bombardier, sir," also shaking hands with Longbow and Siegel.

"I'm Tech Sergeant Tom Walton, your Flight Engineer, sir," he said, starting to salute the officers, when Longbow extended his hand which Walton shook with a smile of appreciation for not pulling rank and accepting him as an equal.

"I'm Tech Sergeant Bruce McCarthy, your Radio Operator, sir," now feeling comfortable with shaking hands with his informal skipper and co-pilot.

"Well, it appears that you form the nucleus of our crew, and I expect that the Gun Commander, and his three gunners, will be assigned to us when we arrive at Kadena Air Base in Okinawa," said Longbow. "Have all of you been checked out on the B-29?"

"Yes sir, we have," replied Lieutenant Brody, speaking for all of them.

"Well, tomorrow, after breakfast, we'll all meet at our bomber, and familiarize ourselves with its equipment. Then we'll take her for a short flight to make sure everything is in working order," said Longbow.

On the morning of their departure aboard B-29 Superfortress number 528, Longbow and Siegel, with their skeleton crew of airmen, took off at exactly 0800 hours, with destination March Air Force Base, Riverside County, California.

Longbow and Siegel sat side-by-side in the cockpit while the bombardier sat in front of them in the nose of the aircraft. In fact, the seating arrangement of the crew on the B-29 was remarkably different from that of the B-17 bomber they had flown in World War Two. This was due to the General Electric Central Fire Control System, its analog electrical instrumentation, and the computerized gun turrets.

"Man, this is one hell of an aircraft, and a far cry from the old B-17," said Siegel to Longbow.

"Yeah! She handles like a cutter-rigged sailboat," said Longbow. "steady as she goes, and built to weather any storm."

"Speaking like a true sailor, Jim," replied Siegel. "I can see why she was chosen to deliver the atomic bomb over Japan. Her carry-on capacity is 16,000 pounds, and the Mark-4 Plutonium bomb we'll be carrying, thankfully without its plutonium core, weighs 10,800 pounds with room to spare."

"I just wonder if they'll have us conducting daylight or nighttime bombing raids," said Longbow.

"Well, at least now we'll have P-51 fighters escorting us to target and back....I hope," said Siegel.

"I don't see why not," replied Longbow. "But let's not worry about that 'till we get there."

Longbow and his crew landed safely at March Air Force Base, and remained there for five days, while a Mark-4 Plutonium bomb was carefully loaded onto their B-29 Superfortress. However, at Siegel's insistence, Longbow made sure the Plutonium bomb was not armed with its essential nuclear core. Longbow understood his best friend's concern, having witnessed serious screw-ups by armament and maintenance personnel in the past.

"How's the Plutonium core being shipped?" asked Siegel.

"They don't weigh much, so they're being shipped separately by air to Okinawa," said Longbow. "They may already be there for all I know. It's a safety measure."

"A smart one too," replied Siegel. "We've got a long flight ahead of us, Jim. I think we should stock up on coffee, and I brought my own thermos for the occasion."

"You mean you're dissatisfied with the Air Force standard issue," said Longbow.

"Hey! This one is double the capacity and it's nearly shock proof," replied Siegel.

"If that's all it takes to keep you happy, my friend, I'm all for it," said Longbow, with a big grin.

"You know, Jim. I think I'm going to use this long flight to write Susan a letter which I can mail from Kadena Air Base," said Siegel.

"That's not a bad idea, Dave. I think I'll do the same and surprise Louise," said Longbow. "But make sure you don't mention our cargo."

"Don't worry, I know the drill," replied Siegel.

Upon arrival at Kadena Air Force Base, Longbow and his crew were met by Lieutenant Colonel Dean Crawford who identified himself as the Base Operations Officer.

"Welcome to Kadena Air Base, Captain," said Crawford. "Any problems with the cargo?"

"No sir, everything went well," replied Longbow. "This is Captain David Siegel, my co-pilot. I was directed by the control tower to park the aircraft in this location. Due to its cargo, sir, do you want the aircraft to remain here?"

"Yes, we'll attend to it from here, Captain. Extra security is being implemented to safeguard the aircraft and its cargo," said Crawford.

Longbow and his crew were billeted in Quonset hut number 28 located only a hundred yards from the Mess Hall, and one street over from Wing Headquarters. Nevertheless, Longbow was provided with a jeep for him and his three officers to navigate through the air base. His remaining crew was also provided a jeep for quick transit to their aircraft.

Longbow and Siegel were ordered to report to Colonel Frank Madison, Commander of the 19th Bombardment Wing.

After being officially greeted by Colonel Madison, with his Deputy Commander, Lieutenant Colonel Peter Savage in attendance, Longbow and Siegel were invited to be seated.

"You're now assigned to the 19th Bomb Wing, and here are your official orders," said Madison, sliding the one-page orders across his desk for Longbow and Siegel to retrieve and examine.

"You're one of twelve aircrews to bring us a Plutonium nuclear bomb. They will be unloaded and stored in a secure area. Your aircraft will be loaded with 260-pound fragmentation bombs and photoflash bombs, which have proven effective on suspected North Korean troops," said Colonel Madison.

"Are those the only bombs we'll be carrying, sir?" asked Longbow, a bit puzzled by its restrictiveness.

"If you're thinking of incendiary bombs, Captain, such as those used on Japanese cities at the end of the Second World War, their use has been denied for political reasons," said Lieutenant Colonel Savage.

"May I ask, sir, what type of fighter aircraft will escort us during our bombing raids?" asked Longbow.

"P-51s and P-80 jet fighters," replied Savage. "They've gained control of the air space over North Korea against North Korea's prop-driven Yaks and Sturmoviks."

"That's very reassuring, sir. I just wished our B-17s had been provided such escort during our bombing raids over Germany," said Longbow, with Siegel yielding the floor to his able skipper.

"Yes, I know. You and Captain Siegel come highly recommended by Colonel Barclay, with whom I served as aviation cadets," said Colonel Madison, with an approving smile.

"Well, sir, we'll do our best," replied Longbow.

"That's all we can expect. Lieutenant Crawford will be in touch with you tomorrow, to get you acquainted with the rest of the staff and our mission," said Colonel Madison, who then stood up, signaling the interview was over.

Longbow and Siegel stood at attention and saluted Colonel Madison who returned their salute. The two captains then did an about face and exited the Wing Commander's office.

"What did you learn from that interview, Jim?" asked Siegel.

"That we won't be dropping atomic bombs anytime soon," replied Longbow.

"I got that impression too...for political reasons, of course," said Siegel with a chuckle.

"And no incendiary bombs, either," said Longbow. "This is indeed a *police action*, certainly no way to fight a war."

"You think we should have our Indian emblem painted on the nose of our B-29?" asked Siegel.

"Naw! I don't think we'll be here that long, I hope," replied Longbow.

"I didn't think so," said Siegel. "Let's go meet our gunners."

At Quonset hut number 28, Longbow and Siegel were surprised to find all eight remaining crew members assembled in the hut. They were quickly introduced by Lieutenant Steven Brody, the navigator, to Tech Sergeant Charlie Olson, Gun Commander, Staff Sergeant Zachary Nielsen, gunner, Staff Sergeant Sam Wehrle, gunner, and Staff Sergeant Peter O'Reilly, gunner.

"Have any of you gunners seen action?" asked Longbow.

"Both Zach and I have flown three missions over North Korea aboard a B-29, sir," replied Charlie Olson.

"Well, you all made it back, so you must have had great fighter escort," said Longbow.

"Yes sir, we sure did," said Olson. "Those P-51 Mustangs and the F-80 Shooting Stars did a bang up job of clearing the skies for us."

"That's good to hear," said Siegel. "We could have used that kind of cover in our B-17's over Germany."

"Wow! You flew missions over Germany, sir!" said Zachary Nielsen, unabashedly impressed.

"Yes, Captain Siegel and I flew several missions over Germany without any fighter escort, so we are delighted to learn we'll have fighter escort to target and back," said Longbow.

"You'll love the B-29 Superfortress sir," said Olson. "It's the Cadillac of bomber aircrafts, sir."

" Glad to hear that, Sergeant Olson," replied Longbow. "I'm sure we won't be disappointed. Tomorrow, you'll have your leisurely breakfast, but be at the aircraft at 0930 with full gear for a trial run."

During the trial flight, Longbow with Siegel at his side as co-pilot, took the B-29 to 30,000 feet and found the pressurized cabins withstood the compression, and the gunners didn't have to suffer the extreme cold temperatures experienced on the B-17 bombers. Longbow and Siegel agreed that the B-29 Superfortress was indeed the Cadillac of bombers, and they were ready for action.

The following afternoon, Longbow and Siegel, accompanied by their navigator and bombardier, reported to the briefing room adjacent to Wing Headquarters. Present at the briefing were the officers from eighteen B-29 bombers, awaiting the arrival of Deputy Commander Lieutenant Colonel Peter Savage, Lieutenant Colonel Dean Crawford from Base Operations, and Major Robert Duval from Mission Control.

The crews immediately stood at attention as Lieutenant Colonel Savage entered the briefing room with his two colleagues.

"At ease men," said Lieutenant Colonel Savage as he stood on the small, elevated platform facing the aircrews.

"Many of you are going on your first air raid over North Korea, and while some of you have much experience conducting bombing raids in Europe or the Far East during World War Two, this experience promises to be quite different, inasmuch as our targets are restricted to North Korea, and China is off limits, even though they supply North Korea with arms, equipment and fighter aircraft, not to mention their movement of some 300,000 Chinese troops into North Korea in support of their invasion of South Korea," said Savage.

"Does this mean that our fighter escort can't follow hostile aircraft in hot pursuit over the Chinese border, sir?" asked one of the pilots.

"That's exactly right, Lieutenant," replied Savage. "Those are our orders from headquarters. "That also means we cannot conduct bombing raids on legitimate targets located on Chinese soil."

There was much murmur among several of the crew members, obviously unhappy about those restrictions, which Lieutenant Savage decided to address.

"I know what you're thinking," said Savage. "That this is no way to fight a war, and General MacArthur has already voiced his discontent to Washington. He believes as I do, that we should pull all the stops and bomb the hell out of Manchuria, which borders on North Korea, to send the Chinese a message they understand. In the meantime, we must follow our current orders and restrict our bombing raids to North Korean targets."

"Excuse me, sir," said another pilot. "Why are we stock piling atomic bombs on this air base if we're not permitted to bomb China?"

"General MacArthur can be very persuasive, and I wouldn't be surprised if those restrictions were soon lifted," replied Savage, not wanting to elaborate on this sensitive matter, as yet not decided.

Savage turned the podium over to Lieutenant Colonel Crawford.

"We are continuing our daylight bombing using our SHORAN Navigation Bombing System, which enables us to accurately place bombs on the target area. Our target for this mission is the Cho-Sen Nitrogen Explosives Plant at Konan. You'll be dropping the usual 2000 pound bombs. This mission, code named Blockbuster, consisting of thirty-five B-29's, will be escorted by P-51 Mustangs and F-80 Shooting Stars. Your mission departure time is tomorrow morning at 0800 hours," said Crawford. "Any questions?"

"Woudn't incendiary bombs be more effective, sir?" asked one of the crew members.

"Probably, but we have been ordered not to use them, in view of the negative press we received after using them on Tokyo, Japan in the last war," said Crawford.

"So the politicians are directing this war, then!" said another crew member.

"You do the math, Mister, and draw your own conclusions," replied Crawford to a Chief Warrant Officer, normally addressed as either Mister or Chief, and highly respected due to their many years of service, rendering them as experts in their field of endeavor.

After the briefing, Longbow and Siegel were joined by Lieutenants Steve Brody and Bill Marcus as they walked towards the Officers Club for the usual free hors-d'oeuvres before dinner.

"I think that if General MacArthur gets his way, we're gonna be dropping those atomic bombs over Manchuria," said Brody.

"The big question is whether General MacArthur has enough juice to override the President of the United States, who I hear is against the use of atomic weapons against China for fear of starting a third world war," said Siegel.

"General MacArthur is the highest ranking general of the armed forces. He's also politically connected and very popular with the media, while President Truman is viewed simply as a haberdasher of men's clothing, from his previous employment," said Marcus.

"All that is true, but President Truman is the Commander-in-Chief of all US Armed Forces, therefore General MacArthur must obey orders from the President, or else get relieved of duty," said Longbow.

"Yeah! But President Truman may be afraid of the political ramifications, if he gets into a fight with General MacArthur and relieves him of duty," said Siegel.

"In the meantime, we're sitting here in Okinawa with some fifty atomic bombs, ready for deployment and the start of a world war," said Siegel.

"And we thought this was just a police action," said Brody.

"The thought of dropping some 50 atomic bombs over the Manchurian border separating China from North Korea, is most bothersome if they are used primarily against the civilian population, which could amount to the death of some fifteen to twenty million Chinese civilians, not to mention the after effects of radiation," said Siegel.

"Actually, General MacArthur made it known that he would only use the atomic weapons against military and industrial targets such as railroad marshalling yards, bridges, factories, hydroelectric plants, airfields, and supply centers," said Lieutenant Marcus.

"That sounds great for the media, but how do you limit the devastation of an atomic bomb," said Siegel, "especially when you're dropping fifty of them, spreading a belt of radioactive cobalt from the Sea of Japan to the Yellow River for at least 70 years. Granted it would effectively prevent any invasion of Korea from the North, but at what cost. What do you think, Jim?" asked Siegel turning his attention to Longbow.

"I think you present a very strong argument against the use of atomic bombs, especially in this limited police action. The consequences of adopting General MacArthur's action plan could very well precipitate World War III," replied Longbow.

"I sure hope that cool heads prevail in Washington," said Brody.

"Amen, brother," replied Siegel, with the others nodding in agreement.

"Listen, men, let's keep this discussion regarding the use of atomic bombs to ourselves, and not disturb the rest of the crew with what may never happen," said Longbow.

"Our lips are sealed, Skipper," replied Brody, with a grin.

"Smart advice, Jim," said Siegel as the four officers entered the Officers Club for their anticipated free hors-d'oeuvres before dinner.

With clear skies, the group of thirty-nine B-29 Superfortresses took off at 0800 sharp for Konan, North Korea. Escorted by two squadrons of P-51 Mustangs and F-80 Shooting Stars, the B-29's climbed to 29,000 feet upon entry into North Korean skies where they were immediately met with North Korean prop-driven Yaks and Sturmoviks. While the gunners aboard the B-29's were busy defending their aircraft, the Mustangs and Shooting Stars took over the challenge and quickly downed several enemy fighters, sending the rest into retreat.

"Man, this is a far cry from what we experienced over Germany," said Siegel to Longbow at the helm. "There's nothing like having a fighter escort. I just love those guys."

"Yeah! They do make a huge difference," replied Longbow. "Marcus, we're near the target area. Get ready."

"Got it, skipper. OK! I'll take over from here," said Marcus.

After releasing their bomb load, all of the bombers returned home to Kadena Air Base, without the loss of a single bomber. However, one P-51 Mustang was shot down by a North Korean Yak- fighter aircraft, but six enemy aircraft were also shot down by American fighters, causing a retreat of remaining hostile aircraft.

On Creekside Drive in Williamsville, New York, sat Susan Siegel and Louise Sontag in their backyard, overlooking the activities of their children, to make sure they didn't venture too close to the retaining stone wall abutting Ellicott Creek, which at this time of the year, was nearly at its lowest depth of a couple of feet. Nevertheless, the stone wall was nearly six feet high with a stone platform below to sit or stand on, that ran the width of both properties. A portable aluminum staircase hung over the wall, allowing people to descend to the platform below, giving access to the creek.

"I just got a letter from Dave," said Susan. "They flew their first mission over North Korea and didn't lose a single bomber."

"That's a relief," replied Louise. "Jim never mentioned it. But then he doesn't like to talk about his bombing missions."

"Well, in any case, so far it looks like they may come out of this without a scratch, and hopefully they'll be home soon," said Susan.

"Look at those kids, don't they remind you of our child-hood days," said Louise.

"The four of them get along so well," said Susan, "I hope they always remain close friends like the four of us."

"Yes, and I don't see any reason why they can't have the same close relationship that we've had all these years, with our husbands being brothers-in-arms," said Louise.

"Our children have us to emulate and hopefully, they'll overlook our imperfections," said Susan.

"Said like a true Girl Scout," said Louise. "I think it's time to feed our kids. Let's gather them around the picnic table."

And so went the afternoon and evening for the Longbow and Siegel families, secure and relieved that their husbands' service in the Far East did not imperil their safety.

Two months and several bombing missions later, Longbow and his crew were again scheduled for a bombing raid over North Korea.

Thirty B-29 Superfortresses were scheduled to conduct a bombing raid against bridges in Sunchon, North Korea. To the B-29 crews, it was considered just another routine bombing mission.

The Superfortresses took off in early morning, including Longbow, Siegel and their crew, comforted by the sight of their Mustang and Shooting Star fighter escort. Because of their previous success, they had reduced their bombing altitude from 30,000 feet to 20,000 feet for better accuracy of their bombs to target. As the group of B-29s approached

Sunchon, they suddenly found themselves under heavy attack by ten Soviet MiG-15 jet fighters with astonishing speed that overwhelmed the prop-driven Mustangs and even the Shooting Star jet fighters.

"Longbow and Siegel could hear their gunners cursing that the MiG-15's speed prevented them from getting a bead on them. Unable to protect the bombers, due to the loss of several Mustangs and Shooting Stars, eight B-29's were shot down. Luckily, Longbow and his crew returned to Kadena Air Base unarmed, but stunned by the loss of so many aircraft, both bombers and fighters.

Immediately upon arrival at Kadena Air Base, the crews of the remaining twenty-two B-29 bombers assembled in the Briefing Room for a thorough debriefing by Lieutenant Colonel Dean Crawford of Base Operations, with Colonel Frank Madison and his Deputy Lieutenant Colonel Peter Savage, Major Robert Duval of Mission Control and Captain Louis Sturm, Base Operations, in attendance, due to the seriousness of the aircraft losses and the sudden appearance of Soviet MiG-15 jet aircraft.

"The sudden advent of Soviet MiG-15 fighters is largely responsible for the unacceptable losses of bomber and fighter aircraft suffered on this latest mission over Sunchon. I would like to hear from any of you who have heard pilot chatter from those MiG-15's, such as the language they used, etc.," said Crawford.

"I'm Lieutenant Foreman, sir, co-pilot with Captain Cid Porter. I heard one of the MiG-15's talking briefly to another MiG-15 pilot in Chinese,"

"How do you know it was Chinese, Lieutenant?" asked Crawford. "Because my mother is Professor of Chinese Literature at the University of California, and I was raised bilingual, sir," replied Lieutenant Foreman.

"What was the pilot saying to the other Chinese pilot?" asked Foreman.

"It was quick chatter, mostly about the selection of aircraft targets, sir," replied Foreman.

"Are you convinced these MiG-15 pilots were Chinese?" asked Crawford.

"Yes sir," said Foreman.

"Anyone else who has information to offer about this mission?" asked Crawford.

"Those MiG's were the fastest and most maneuverable jet fighters I've ever seen, Sir. One unique feature about those MiG's was their swept-wings. We need faster fighter aircraft to escort us to targets in North Korea, or else we're gonna have a lot more losses of B-29's," said Longbow who didn't identify himself.

Colonel Madison took over the podium from Lieutenant Colonel Crawford.

"I'm suspending daylight bombing until we are provided with the F-86 Sabre which is also a swept-wing fighter aircraft that is now available, and should arrive at Kadena Air base shortly. In the meantime, we will commence nighttime bombing raids over North Korea using SHORAN navigation radar to accurately pinpoint targets.

The enemy is now using radar guided anti-aircraft searchlights capable of illuminating our bombers for several minutes, giving their MiGs a bright target. You now will have at your disposal shaft, strips of foil to be dropped over the source of the searchlights as a countermeasure, in an effort to knock out the radar guidance system and evade their searchlights. The flak from anti-aircraft artillery can be just as devastating as those MiGs, so use those countermeasures the moment you see the searchlights. Any questions?" asked Colonel Madison.

"How do we know those F-86 Sabres can handle the MiGs?" asked one the B-29 Commanders.

"A North Korean pilot defected and landed his MiG-15 at Kimpo Airport outside Seoul. The MiG-15 was sent to Wright Field, Dayton, Ohio, where it was studied and used in simulated combat against F-86 Sabres, and the Sabres won hands down," said Colonel Madison. "This is not for dissemination, fellows."

"I'm sure I speak for all of us, sir, when I say that those F-86 Sabres can't get here soon enough," said another B-29 Commander.

"Their arrival will not be quiet. Just be patient," concluded Colonel Madison, ending the briefing.

Within two days, the crews from twenty-five B-29 Superfortresses were gathered in the Briefing Room for their first nighttime bombing raid over North Korea.

"Gentlemen, tonight's operation is code named *Fastball* and your target is the chemical plant at Namsan-Ri. Those radar guided searchlights and anti-aircraft guns are going to be actively searching for you, with MiGs waiting to pounce on you, so be alert and use the shaft countermeasure as soon as your aircraft is lit up," said Lieutenant Colonel Dean Crawford, who then turned over the briefing to Captain Louis Sturm, Base Operations.

As the crews dispersed from the briefing, Longbow and Siegel, accompanied by Lieutenants Brody and Marcus, walked over to the snack bar for coffee and donuts.

"How many bundles of those strips of aluminum foil do we have, Bill?" asked Longbow.

"Three bundles, I believe," replied Bill Marcus, the bombardier.

"Listen, Bill, we still have time, get us three more bundles from supply," said Longbow. "It's our only defense against those radar guided searchlights."

"I agree with you, Skipper, and I'll get right on it," replied Marcus.

David Siegel felt more concerned about this nighttime bombing raid than any previous raids since his B-17 was shot down over Germany, but he didn't want to express his concern to his best friend Jim Longbow, who had admonished him regarding his negative thinking. Positive thinking, he told him, is the only path to success.

The group of twenty-five B-29 Superfortresses took off the runway at Kadena Air Base in the semi-darkness of the evening with the expectation of total darkness over North Korea, until the artillery searchlights began their search for them.

"How long before we reach our target, Bill?" asked Sergeant Olsen, the Gun Commander.

"About fifteen minutes," replied Bill Marcus, the bombardier.

Suddenly several wide beams of light from radar guided searchlights appeared against the underside of some of the bombers around the Longbow bomber, with flak following their flight paths, hitting some of the bombers, setting them on fire.

"Bandits at twelve o'clock high," yelled Olsen, gun commander.

"The MiGs have downed two of our bombers at eight o'clock," yelled Pete O'Reilly, the tail gunner, over the noise of the machine guns.

"Bill, drop a couple of bundles of shaft," ordered Longbow, "and get ready to drop more when we get lit up."

The deafening noise of the .50 caliber machine guns was actually reassuring to the officer crew, whose survival depended on the skill of their sergeants manning the guns. This was a true team effort that bonded them as brothers-in-arms.

"Bill, we're three minutes to target," said Longbow. "Are you ready to take control?"

"I've got it, skipper, the SHORAN is on the target.... bombs away," said Bill Marcus.

"OK! Now drop another bundle of shaft, Bill," ordered Longbow, but before Bill had time to execute the order, a sea of light engulfed their aircraft from a radar guided searchlight.

Bill Marcus immediately dropped two bundles of aluminum shaft while Longbow, having dropped his bomb load, was now able to take evasive action. This double maneuver successfully evaded the focus of the searchlight.

"Phew! That was close," said Siegel to Longbow.

"Bill, do we have any more bundles of shaft?" asked Longbow over the intercom.

"No, we don't, skipper. We used all of them," replied Marcus.

"This is your skipper. We're heading home, so far unscathed, but we're out of shaft, so you gunners stay alert for those MiGs," said Longbow.

Having joined the remaining bombers who had escaped the onslaught of the MiGs, and the radar directed flak, and were now heading home to Kadena Air Base in Okinawa, the crew wondered about their loses.

"Good grief, Jim," said Siegel, "how many bombers did we lose?"

"I really don't know, Dave," replied Longbow. "I know three definite loses, but there may be more. We'll find out at the debriefing."

"Man, Bill dropped that last bundle of shaft just in time," said Siegel. "We were lit up like a Christmas tree."

"Yeah! I know. We made it out of there by the skin of our teeth," said Longbow.

"Next time we may not be so lucky," replied Siegel. "This is getting to be just as dangerous as those missions over Germany."

"It does seem that way, but hopefully we'll get those F-86 Sabres to escort us, which will change the odds in our favor, but those radar guided searchlights and artillery are still a serious threat," said Longbow.

"Well, the shaft was effective," replied Siegel.

"That may be because in addition to the dropping of the shaft, I was able to take evasive action, which would not have been permitted, if we had not dropped our bombs over the target," replied Longbow.

"You do have a valid point, Jim. I sure hope our tech guys come up with something else to neutralize those radar guided searchlights," said Siegel.

"Yeah! But in the meantime, the bombing raids continue on schedule," said Longbow.

"We'd better not mention any of this in our letters to the girls, otherwise I wouldn't put it past them to somehow make their way over here like they did in England," said Siegel.

"Oh! C'mon Dave," said Longbow, laughing at Dave's remark. "They've got four young kids to take care of. There's no way they would ever contemplate coming over here, even if their parents offered to take care of the kids."

"Yeah! I guess you're right, Jim," replied Siegel. "Nevertheless, no sense worrying them over something that may never happen."

"That's the only way to look at it, Dave," replied Longbow.

"This is your skipper. We're not out of reach of enemy flak and fighters yet, but Job well done. We'll be home shortly," said Longbow, who liked to keep his crew informed.

The Briefing Room was crowded with the crews from the returning B-29s, who had just learned they had lost eleven bombers, primarily from attacks by Soviet Migs, assisted by the radar guided searchlights.

"Skipper, ...Sergeant Clift Harrison, our new gunner, who replaced Sam Wehrle, wants to ship back to the States for medical reasons. He looked kind of shook up when we landed," said Steve Brody, the navigator. "When I asked him if anything was wrong, he said he'd rather talk to you."

"Hmm! This was his first combat mission, wasn't it," said Longbow.

"That's right, skipper," replied Brody.

"That may have had something to do with his behavior," said Longbow. "I'll take care of it as soon as this debriefing is over."

Colonel Frank Madison, accompanied by his Deputy Lieutenant Colonel Peter Savage, Lieutenant Dean Crawford from Base Operations and Captain Louis Sturm, also from Base Operations, took to the stage with Colonel Madison stepping behind the lectern with microphone.

"As you well know, we lost eleven B-29s, four P-51 Mustangs and three F-80 Shooting Stars on this mission, and much of it was the work of those Soviet MiGs, with the help of their ground radar guided searchlights," said Madison. "Now, I know how you must feel frustrated by the lack of adequate fighter escort, but I have good news for you. Tomorrow we're getting eighteen F-86 Sabres, followed by another thirty-four by the end of the week. That should make you smile."

"We're retiring the P-51 Mustangs and also the F-80 Shooting Stars. They're being shipped back to the States," said Savage, relieving Madison and taking over the lectern. "From now on, you'll be escorted by F-86 Sabres which will make a world of difference. We're also adding another defense against those infernal searchlights; the painting of black glass lacker on the bellies and underside of the wings of all B-29s, which our tech people tell us, will make the bombers significantly less visible in the darkness of the night. Any questions?"

"Yes, sir. Has the painting of the underside of B-29s or similar aircraft been tested?" asked Longbow.

"Not in Korea, but during the Second World War, the British tested the theory with their bombers in raids over Germany and it appeared to be effective," said Savage.

"What will be the ratio of Sabres per B-29s on our bombing raids, sir?" asked another flight commander.

"Initially it will be one Sabres to two B-29s, which will be quickly increased to one to one, and possibly more escorts, depending on the results we get," said Savage. "MacArthur intends to dominate the sky over North Korea."

"Those are very encouraging words, sir," replied the flight commander. "I hope those Sabres meet the challenge."

"You tell us after the next debriefing, commander," replied Savage, with a confidence that resonated with the crew members in attendance.

After the debriefing, Longbow told Siegel he was going to have a private meeting with Sergeant Clift Harrison.

"He probably just needs a pep talk, Jim," said Siegel. "It was his first combat mission."

"You're probably right, Dave. Anyway, I'll talk to him and find out what's troubling him. Where do you think he might be right now?" asked Longbow.

"Probably in the snack bar with the other gunners," said Siegel.

"Alright. I'll see you later, back at the hut," said Longbow.

Inevitably, Longbow found Sergeant Harrison sitting at a table alone with a cup of coffee and a donut.

"Hiya! Clift, mind if I join you?" asked Longbow.

"No sir, please do," replied Harrison, who had stood up in the presence of an officer also his flight commander.

"At ease, Clift, I just would like to talk to you about this last mission, which I understand was your first one," said Longbow.

"I guess you talked to Lieutenant Brody," said Harrison.

"Well, he thought that being your first bombing raid, you were perhaps a little unnerved by this first experience, which is normal. We all go through that during our first few missions, until we realize that the odds are with us most of the time, and in fact, probably better than when you drive your vehicle on the road full of problematic people," said Longbow. "So tell me, Clift, are you able to handle this experience or do you need help?"

"I always wanted to be a gunner on a bomber, and never thought I would react this way. But when a MiG came at me with guns blazing, I just froze up. Luckily he missed us, and my failure to shoot back didn't cost us the loss of our aircraft, but I now wonder if I'm capable of functioning as a gunner, sir," said Harrison.

"You know, Clift, any normal person will experience fear at some time in their life, and especially in a combat situation. The difference between courage and cowardice is whether you can control that fear or succumb to it, and you don't strike me as a coward, Clift," said Longbow. "You just instinctively reacted before you had a chance to evaluate the situation, which is perfectly normal. When we face a threat to our well-being, Clift, our autonomic nervous system activates a self-preservation system called the sympathetic system, which causes us to fight, flee or freeze, and our training and experience guides us into a fight mode because it provides us with the best odds of survival."

"I guess it does make a lot of sense, the way you put it, sir," said Harrison.

"You're part of my crew, Clift, so you can drop the sir. Skipper will do just fine," said Longbow. "You ever been in a fist fight or a boxing match, Clift?"

"I did some amateur boxing, but it never amounted to much," replied Harrison.

"Well, you do know that as long as you're throwing punches at your opponent, he has to go onto the defensive, and can't return punches. It's the old saying that the best defense is an offense," said Longbow. "So as long as you're firing that machine gun at your opponent, you're putting him in a defensive position, and that's your best defense. You keep that in mind, Clift, and you'll do just fine as a dependable and effective gunner."

"You know, skipper, I can see why they made you the flight commander. I'll be alright, sir, you can depend on me from now on," said Harrison.

"I'm sure of it, Clift, I have complete faith in you. You are an important member of our flight crew. So take care, and see you on our next mission," said Longbow.

The following morning, Longbow and Siegel went to the orderly room to collect their mail, and they both received letters from their wives. They went back to their jeep, which gave them privacy, and opened their letters.

"Louise included a picture of her and the kids," said Longbow.

"They sure have grown the short time I've been away."

"Susan also sent me a picture of her with Alex and Rachel," said Siegel, handing the picture to Longbow who reciprocated with his picture.

"You know, Alex looks a lot like you, Dave, while Rachel has Susan's features," said Longbow. "They're good looking kids."

"Thanks, Jim. I think Gary has some of Louise's facial features, but overall, he's much like you, while Jacqueline, with her blue eyes and blond hair is the spitting image of Louise," said Siegel. "I can't wait for us to get back home, so we can enjoy our families."

"Amen, brother," replied Longbow. "Louise says that the kids are fully engaged in their school classes and homework, which gives her time to shop with Susan, and do things they didn't have time for before."

"Yeah! Susan wrote the same thing in her letter, enjoying the limited freedom for a well-deserved rest from those ultra-energetic kids. That's one thing I'll be able to do when I get back, is to take some of that burden from her. She's such a darling. I sure miss her," said Siegel.

"I know just how you feel, Dave. I miss Louise more than I ever thought possible," replied Longbow.

"Well, this police action can't last forever," said Siegel.

"Yes, but I'm afraid we're going to be spending the Christmas holidays here at Kadena Air Base," said Longbow.

"Yeah! I think you're right, Jim. Hopefully it'll be our last Christmas in Okinawa," replied Siegel.

"In the meantime, I'm learning to play my ukulele, which is really a simple instrument, with four nylon strings, and only 24 inches long, making it easy to carry," said Longbow.

"So that's where you've been hiding, huh!" said Siegel.

"I've just been taking lessons at the on-base education office, mostly evenings, when we're not on a mission," said Longbow.

"Can you play anything yet?" asked Siegel.

"Sure, I can play chords, that's simple, and with practice I'll be able to accompany myself, singing songs that I've converted from some of the poems I wrote," said Longbow.

"I've known you for how many years, Jim, yet you never told me you wrote poetry," said Siegel. "Does Louise know you write poems?"

"Yes, she does. I wrote a few poems with her in mind," replied Longbow.

"Do you have some with you, I can read?" asked Siegel.

"No, they're at home in Williamsville," replied Longbow. "But I can recite some of them from memory, but I don't want to bore you, Dave."

"Haw! C'mon, Jim, give me a taste of what you've written," said Siegel.

"Naw! Some other time, Dave," replied Longbow. "I've got to go to the education office for another lesson."

"You sure are a man of mystery, James," said Siegel. "When I think I know all about you, I discover how little

I do know. But what I do know I like, and that's what matters, my friend."

"Thank you for your vote of confidence, Dave," replied Longbow with a big grin on his face.

"So when will you reveal to Louise that you play the ukulele and converted some of your poems to songs?" asked Siegel.

"I'm thinking of making a tape recording of one song with the ukulele, which I will mail to Louise as a surprise," said Longbow.

"Man, what a surprise that will be," said Siegel.

"Yeah! I wish I was there to see the expression on her face," said Longbow.

"Jesus! There's never a dull moment with you, is there?" said Siegel.

"Hey! Life is what you make it, Dave," said Longbow. "But I must admit, that I can't take all the credit for my poetry. Louise is my inspiration, without her, I doubt I would have written anything of substance."

"Man, and I thought my love for Susan was unmatched, but I think you have me beat, my friend, and more power to you," said Siegel, with renewed admiration for his best friend.

The following evening after dinner, Longbow pulled out his ukulele from his wall locker in the Quonset Hut, and sitting on his footlocker, started playing 'Mister Sandman' with only Siegel and Steve Brody present. The rest of the crew was not expected until near bedtime. Siegel and Brody joined in with the lyrics to this most popular song, which Longbow had obviously mastered with much practice before allowing himself to be heard by his fellow officers and crew.

"Hey! That was great," exclaimed Siegel, "You sure got the hang of it with the ukulele. Know any other tunes?"

"Yeah! Singing the Blues, and Que Sera Sera," said Longbow.

"I don't know the words to Singing the Blues, but I do know the lyrics to Que Sera Sera. How about you , Steve?" asked Siegel.

"Hell! Everybody knows that song," replied Brody. "It's on the radio all the time."

"OK! Let's do it, maestro," said Siegel to Longbow.

Afterwards, Siegel looked at Longbow. "You know, Jim. When we get back home, you're going to be a popular guy with that ukulele on the beach at the Lakeshore Yacht Club, and on the *Lightfoot* and *Viking* sailboats, with a case of beer and vocal chords."

The next day, Longbow and his three officers were summoned to Base Operations for an emergency briefing. They were joined by officers from 24 other B-29 crews. Also in attendance were all 18 pilots of the recently arrived F-86 Sabrejet fighters, assigned to escort the B-29 Superfortresses.

Colonel Madison, accompanied by his Deputy Lieutenant Colonel Savage, Lieutenant Colonel Crawford and his assistant Captain Sturm from Base Operations entered the Briefing Room, and Madison yielded to his Deputy Savage to address the attending aircrews. As Savage stood behind the lectern, Captain Sturm pulled the black curtain open, revealing a map of North and South Korea, and the Chinese border including Manchuria.

"Gentlemen, the code name for this mission is *Operation Rainfall*. Our target is the Chinese airbase at Uiju Airfield in North Korea. We hope that this will lure MiG-15s into battle where our F-86 Sabrejets can destroy them," said Savage. "That notwithstanding, the mission is to destroy Uiju Airfield, and that's the job of the B-29 Bombers. Take off time is 0900 hours tomorrow morning, and yes, it's a daylight raid. Any questions?"

"Why are we switching from nighttime to a daylight raid, sir?" asked Siegel.

"Because you now have a Sabrejet escort and they need to see the MiGs in order to shoot them down. This promises to be one hell of a dog fight," said Savage.

"How many MiG-15s can we expect from that airfield" asked one of the Sabrejet pilots.

"Probably fifteen to twenty. Think you can handle it?" replied Savage sarcastically.

"Yes, sir, no problem," replied the fighter pilot in a loud voice.

"Good. Any other questions?" asked Savage, who ended the briefing when no one raised his hand.

At the Quonset Hut, Longbow, in the presence of his entire crew, explained in detail *Operation Rainfall*, and what to expect, including bailout procedure if necessary. Everyone was momentarily quiet after his briefing, pondering what could happen during this raid, considering this would be a daylight raid, with memories of the significant losses in the last one, and whether the F-86 Sabrejets could handle the Soviet MiGs.

The next morning, the Superfortresses took off from Kadena Air Base, and were joined by their Sabrejet escort flying high in overhead formation. It wasn't until the North Korean radar units detected their presence that the Soviet MiGs were scrambled to intercept the group of B-29 bombers, not suspecting and detecting the Sabrejets flying at high altitude above the bombers who offered radar interference.

It didn't take long for the MiGs to appear, and the call of bandits by the gunners in the B-29s and the clatter of their machine guns, spelled 'Hell Fire' with Sabrejets and MiGs in mortal combat at speeds that defied eyesight and measured life and death in seconds.

Longbow called out to his bombardier for his readiness to accept control of the aircraft and drop their bomb load on the target airfield.

"Bill, we're only three minutes to target," said Longbow.

"OK, Skipper, I got it," replied Bill Marcus, focusing on his bombsight, then calling out: "Bombs away, let's go home."

"Dave, take over, I'm going back there to check on the crew," said Longbow, who learned that no damage to crew or aircraft had occurred.

"It looks like we didn't lose a single bomber, Jim," said Dave.

"Yeah! It does look that way, but we may have lost one or more of our Sabrejets," said Longbow.

"Man, they did a terrific job. I saw at least two MiGs go up in flames," said Dave.

As they were heading home with the bomber group, the radio operator, Bruce McCarthy came up to the cockpit to relay information.

"It's been reported, sir, that we lost two Sabrejets, but they destroyed eleven MiGs forcing the rest to retreat," said McCarthy.

"Did we lose any bombers?" asked Siegel.

"No, sir, not one, thank God!" replied McCarthy.

"You can also thank those Sabrejet pilots," said Longbow.

Back at Kadena Air Base, Longbow and his crew were given a week without a call for another bombing raid. Longbow spent a lot of time at the education office learning to play his ukulele, at first to simple tunes and progressing to popular songs. Sometimes Siegel would join him, just to see his progress, amused that his best friend, a superb athlete, would be interested in a musical instrument, especially an ordinary ukulele. He also knew of Longbow's talent in writing quixotic poetry, easily converted to song writing, and he then realized the possibility that his friend might just apply his ukulele to his poetry, and upon his return to the States, woo his wife with a personal ballad. The thought amused him almost into laughter.

"What are you grinning about, Dave?" asked Longbow, interrupting his ukulele practice.

"Oh! The thought occurred to me that you could turn one of your poems into a song for your ukulele," said Siegel.

"Actually, I thought of writing a rhyming poem that I could recite as a monologue in a melodious fashion using my ukulele to give it a musical flair," said Longbow. "You don't have to be a singer for that."

"Actually, I think it's a great idea, Jim," replied Siegel. "Wait a minute, I met this Lieutenant Joe Yansa while having a drink at the Officers Club, and he told me he was the Officer-in-Charge of Broadcasting the Voice of America relayed from the States, which takes place in the control room of the Communications Center. It uses an AMPEX Model 600 tape recording machine which weighs only 28 pounds, versus the old one which weighed 500 pounds. He said it's now available commercially in the States for about $900.00. With Christmas approaching, what a terrific holiday present that would make."

"Man, you're full of crazy ideas, Dave," replied Longbow. "However, that would make one terrific Christmas present to the whole family, if we could make it work. But would Lieutenant Yansa permit us to use his AMPEX recorder to make a personal recording?"

"Maybe. We'll have to talk to him. But if he does, then we'd have to contact your father and mine, and have them locate the store that sells them, and buy two of them, one for Louise and one for Susan. They would then hold them until they get our tape recordings, then your father could bring the recorder and tape to Louise, and my father could bring the second recorder and tape to Susan, at Christmas time, for them and the kids to listen to our desire to be with them on this holiday season and wishes for the future," said Siegel.

"You know, Dave, that's probably the best idea you've come up with that I can remember. That tape recording will be the closest means of being with them, and they'll be able to replay it over and over again," said Longbow.

"Not to mention the private part of the tape dedicated solely to our wives, which I'm sure, they'll cherish many years from now, as a reminder of when we were young," said Siegel. "The question is, how do we get Lieutenant Yansa's cooperation?"

"First of all, Dave, I think that Lieutenant Yansa is an American Indian, probably a Cherokee. He'll realize from my family name, that I'm an Iroquois Indian, which should encourage a friendly relationship," said Longbow. "But that may not be enough to get his cooperation, so we'll have to offer him something that he would value more than money, which is out of the question of course."

"Yeah! That would amount to a bribe. But what could he want that only we can give him, is the sixty-four dollar question?" said Siegel.

"I've got, It. Let's offer him a ride aboard our B-29, and he can take a picture of himself on a B-29 Superfortress, which he can send to his family. Now that's something he would value more than anything available here in Okinawa," said Longbow.

"By God, Jim, you've nailed it right on the head," said Siegel.

"Christmas is not that far away, and the mail from Okinawa to the States is slow, so we'd better get this show on the road right away," said Longbow. "Let's go see him first thing in the morning."

"While we're there, let's find out his size so we can get him a flight suit," said Siegel.

"Not a bad idea. Besides, it'll make him feel part of the crew," said Longbow.

The following morning, Longbow and Siegel met with Lieutenant Joe Yansa at the Communications Center, and as expected, Yansa was quite enthusiastic about the opportunity to fly on a B-29 Superfortress, and have his picture taken in a flight suit on a bomber. In return, he agreed to use his AMPEX recording equipment to record Longbow's ukulele monologue and Christmas greeting to his family, and do the same for Siegel. He even agreed to provide the two reels required for the recordings. Needless to say, everyone was gratified with the arrangement.

The Longbow crew was not apprised of the arrangement until the morning of the training flight, when Lieutenant Yansa appeared on the flight line, dressed in his flight suit. He was introduced to the crew by Longbow as a representative of the Voice of America for a familiarization flight, which was readily accepted by the crew.

Yansa gave Siegel a small camera, which he in turn gave to one of the gunners for him to take a photograph of Yansa standing in front of the B-29 Bomber with Longbow and Siegel on either side of him.

They then all boarded the bomber, and after climbing to 10,000 feet, Longbow allowed one of the gunners to seat Yansa behind one of the machine guns and fire a few rounds, which undoubtedly would remain etched in his mind for the rest of his life.

Yansa's experience aboard the B-29 solidified a very close friendship with Longbow and Siegel, assuring them continued reasonable access to the AMPEX recorder.

With both recordings completed to their satisfaction, Longbow and Siegel, each wrote a letter to their fathers, enclosed in the package containing the reel of their recording, explaining their unusual Christmas gift, with the request to purchase an AMPEX Model 600 recorder. Then on Christmas Eve, for them to bring the AMPEX recorder with the recording to Louise and Susan, as their Christmas present from their husbands.

"Well, Jim, it's two months before Christmas, I sure hope the girls get their present by Christmas Eve," said Siegel.

"Well, if they don't, it won't be because we didn't try. Besides, they'll get it sooner or later, and realize the delay wasn't our fault," replied Longbow.

"That's true. But we don't know how long we're going to be here on this godforsaken island, so why not send our girls periodic tape recordings from both of us. It doesn't have to be all songs and music," said Siegel. "And think of the morale booster this would be for our wives, and the kids too, whom we haven't seen for quite a while."

"I agree, but we don't want to abuse Lieutenant Yansa's hospitality, so we have to place reasonable limits on our use of his recording studio," said Longbow. "It's Friday, let's go the Officers' Club for those hors-d'oeuvres. I especially love those chicken livers wrapped in bacon, I could make a meal of them."

"I forgot about that. Good idea," replied Siegel.

The Club was packed with officers feasting on the hors-d'oeuvres and drinks, mostly beer. Siegel got into a conversation with the officer next to him, also indulging in the various hors-d'oeuvres.

"Hi! I'm Bob Crowley of the 19th Bomb Wing," said the officer wearing Captain's bars on his shoulders.

"I'm Dave Siegel, also of the 19th Bomb Wing," replied Siegel, "and this is Jim Longbow, my flight Commander."

"Please to meet you Bob," replied Longbow, shaking his hand.

"I presume from your rank, you're the Flight Commander of a B-29," said Siegel.

"That's correct. My co-pilot Pete Tolson doesn't care for these hors-d'oeuves, and is imbibing at the bar," replied Crowley.

"Where did you serve before coming here?" asked Siegel.

"In the Pacific Theatre, flying B-29's, and after the war, I joined the reserves at Hancock Field Air National Guard in Syracuse, New York. I never thought I'd end up here in Okinawa," said Crowley.

"So you're from Western New York," said Siegel. "I'll be damned. Jim and I are from Buffalo and we also joined the reserves and were stationed at Hancock Field when the Korean War broke out. Like you, we ended up on this island. Funny we didn't meet at Hancock Field, but it's a big place."

"Yeah! So where did you guys serve before coming here?" asked Crowley.

"We flew B-17's from RAF Station Chelveston, England over Germany," replied Siegel, standing between Longbow and Crowley, holding the conversation in a very noisy club.

"Well, I'm from Rochester, only an hour and a half from Buffalo, so we're neighbors, aren't we?" said Crowley.

"I guess we are at that. When we get back to the States, whenever that will be, we must get together," said Siegel.

"Yeah! My wife is getting weary of my absence, and I'm missing the growth of my two kids who are now 5 and 6 years old. I really don't want to miss any more of their birthdays," said Crowley, pulling out his wallet to retrieve a photo of his wife with their son and daughter.

"You have a very handsome family, Bob," said Siegel, turning to Longbow for him to see the photograph.

"Yes, you have a very attractive family, Bob," said Longbow.

"It just so happens, Bob, that Jim and I both have a son and a daughter of about the same age as your children," said

Siegel, showing him a picture of his wife and two children, while Longbow, now engaged in a conversation with an officer on his left, was not privy to the picture show.

"I just hope that this police action is over soon, 'cause I've got to get home before my kids are grown up and my wife thinks I'm the mailman," said Crowley.

"Yeah! I know what you mean, Bob, but this police action can't last much longer. I hear that MacArthur is threatening to use a series of atomic bombs along the Manchurian border, which should get their undivided attention and their ass at the negotiating table," said Siegel.

"Let's hope you're right, Dave, so we can go home where we belong," replied Crowley.

Two days later, a meeting in the Briefing Room was scheduled for the next bombing mission over North Korea. This time, there were forty-five F-86 Sabrejet pilots in attendance, along with the officer crew of forty B-29 Bombers, which gave the bomber crews a most reassuring feeling of safety for this mission, waiting to be announced.

As usual, the Wing Commander Colonel Madison and his Deputy Lieutenant Colonel Savage, accompanied by Lieutenant Colonel Crawford of Base Operations, and his assistant Captain Sturm, entered the Briefing Room, causing the entire assembly to stand at attention.

"At ease, men," said Colonel Madison standing before the lectern. "I want to welcome the Sabrejet crews of the 51st Fighter Interceptor Wing, which now brings the total number of F-86 Sabrejets to fifty aircraft. However, five of them will not participate in this mission due to required maintenance. Nevertheless, you bomber crews will be escorted by forty-five Sabrejets to your target which is the hydroelectric complex at Sui-ho dam in North Korea, under Operation *Sledgehammer*. Captain Sturm will now give you the details of this operation.

The briefing over, Longbow and Siegel, along with Lieutenants Brody and Marcus walked back to their Quonset Hut where they met the remaining crew.

"Our week's vacation is over, fellows," said Longbow to his enlisted crew. "We're leaving tomorrow morning at 0900 hours on a bombing raid over the hydroelectric complex at Sui-ho Dam in North Korea. The good news is that we're going to be escorted by forty-five F-86 Sabrejets to the target and back," said Longbow.

"Hey! Things are finally looking up," exclaimed the flight engineer, Sergeant Walton.

"How many B-29's are going on this raid, Skipper?" asked Gun Commander Sergeant Olson."

"Forty B-29's," replied Longbow. "Just remember, that although our Sabrejets will take care of those MiG's, we're still going to get a lot of flak from their anti-aircraft artillery. So always be prepared for the worst, and ready to bail out when given the order."

"Man, I don't want to even think about that," said Sergeant McCarthy, the radio operator.

"Alright, guys, let's keep a positive attitude, and do what we were trained to do, and leave the rest to providence," said Siegel.

The silvery Sabrejets could be seen by Longbow and his crew from their B-29 Bomber, lined up on an adjacent runway, ready for takeoff.

"Man, those Sabrejets are the most beautiful thing I've ever seen," said Siegel to Longbow, sitting side-by-side in the cockpit of their bomber.

"Yeah! They look fast just sitting still," remarked Longbow, admiring their configuration.

"OK! It's our turn to take off, everybody take your position," said Longbow over the intercom.

Once in formation with the other B-29's, cruising at 10,000 feet, Longbow turned the helm over to Siegel, then gave the order for the gunners to test fire their six Browning fifty-caliber machine guns, whose excessively loud noise was nevertheless most reassuring to the crew.

"Isn't that Crowley's bomber ahead of us?" asked Siegel. "He said he had his wife's name 'Shirley' painted on the fuselage and his tail number is 333, which I remember because it's a good poker hand. But the numbers are kind of blurry from here."

"I can't see the side of his fuselage, Dave," replied Longbow. "Wait, I'll get the binoculars."

"Yeah! It's Crowley's bomber, alright. I can see his tail number, 333," said Longbow.

"Fancy meeting someone from Rochester over here in this war zone," said Siegel.

"It's a small world, Dave, and getting smaller by the minute," replied Longbow, inferring it could end anytime.

"Alright, we're climbing to 29,000 feet, and approaching enemy territory, so be on the alert," said Longbow to his crew.

The group of forty-five Sabrejets were flying high above the B-29 formation, ready to pounce on any MiG's approaching the bomber formation.

"How long before we reach our target?" asked Siegel on the intercom to navigator Brody.

"Fifteen minutes, give or take a minute," replied Brody, when all of a sudden, puffs of smoke surrounded the aircrafts from ground artillery flak. As if that wasn't enough, Gun Commander Olsen alerted the Skipper and crew of oncoming MiG fighters, quickly engaged by Sabrejets in dog fights taking place over and under the bomber formation, with some of them coming so close to the bombers who could not take evasive action, that it was a miracle there were no collisions, unless the fighter pilot lost control in such close quarters.

The bomber gunners were busy firing their machine guns at MiGs within their view, careful not to hit pursuing Sabrejets, when one MiG flying above the Longbow bomber was hit with machinegun fire from a Sabrejet fighter, causing the MiG to burst into flames. The MiG went into a spin downward in front of the Longbow bomber and into the right wing of Crowley's B-29 aircraft, severing its entire wing from its fuselage. The flaming bomber flew into oncoming flak, as it descended precipitately towards a crash, before the incredulous eyes of Longbow and Siegel, who witnessed the entire dramatic episode.

"My God! I can't believe what I just saw," said Siegel. "This could have been us."

"Yeah! I know, Dave. But keep your cool. We're approaching our target," said Longbow.

"Bill, how close are we to target," asked Longbow to his bombardier Bill Marcus.

"Four minutes and counting, Skipper," replied Marcus.

"OK! Let me know when you're ready," said Longbow.

Two minutes passed, when Marcus, called out to Longbow he was ready to take over control of the aircraft with his SHORAN bombsight system.

Longbow turned over control of the bomber to Marcus, when the bomber to his left suddenly burst into flames, apparently a direct hit from Artillery flak, sending the flaming bomber into a dive to its grave.

"Jesus, this is getting heavy," said Siegel to Longbow.

"Can you see the target, Bill?" asked Longbow.

"Yeah! I got it now, bombs away," replied Bill Marcus.

"OK! Guys, we're going home, but be alert, we're still in enemy territory," said Longbow, slowly turning the aircraft around with the bomber formation, when another bomber got hit with flak losing one of its engines, which they successfully feathered, leaving three other engines to bring them home.

"I wonder if Crowley is the only bomber we lost besides the other one we saw go down," asked Siegel.

"I think so, but we won't know until we get back to base," answered Longbow.

"Man, when I think of Bob Crowley's wife and kids when they get the news, I think, this could be one of us," said Siegel.

"Don't think about it, Dave, otherwise It will drive you crazy," said Longbow. "Just thank God you survived this one, and hope for the best on the next one."

"I think I'm going to visit the Base Chapel, Jim," said Siegel. "They may not have a rabbi, but the chaplain, whether Catholic or Protestant is a man of God, and I could use some spiritual guidance."

"Well, we can all use spiritual guidance, Dave," said Longbow. "If you don't mind, I'll go with you."

"I guess this last mission has made us realize we're not immortal, and were it not for the grace of God, what happened to Bob Crowley could easily have happened to us," said Siegel.

"Well, there's nothing like the present, so let's go to the chapel now," replied Longbow.

The chapel at Kadena Air base was small, accommodating about one hundred people in pews, and another fifty standing. But then, military personnel were not breaking down the door to the chapel to get in. Nonetheless, the chaplain, a Catholic priest, was dedicated to his calling, holding mass every Sunday morning, and attending to the daily needs of military personnel.

It was Friday afternoon, when Longbow and Siegel entered the chapel and found Father O'Reilly exiting the confession kiosk.

"Are you gentlemen seeking to have your confession heard?" asked Father O'Reilly.

"No, Father," replied Longbow. "We're here to confer with you for spiritual guidance about the precarious missions we're conducting as bomber pilots."

"I see, I'm Father O'Reilly, and you are?"

"I'm Captain James Longbow and this is Captain David Siegel, my co-pilot on a B-29 Superfortress."

"Why don't we have a seat in that pew over there, where we can talk in private," said Father O'Reilly.

"You see, Father, on our last mission, we saw with our own eyes, a bomber in front of us, piloted by someone we just met, who had shown us a photograph of his wife and two children, get blown up with no survivors, in a collision with a damaged enemy aircraft. It could just as easily have been our own bomber. Is the loss of lives part of a scheduled plan by God, or is it a crap shoot of random selection?" asked Longbow.

"You must be from New York," said Chaplain O'Reilly. "I haven't heard that term 'crap shoot' since I left New York City to join the clergy."

"Yes, Father, we're both from Buffalo," replied Siegel.

"Well, to answer your question, it is a crap shoot with some exceptions of course," said Father O'Reilly. "We've been given *free will,* and it is up to us to choose right from wrong. Furthermore, the actions we take in life, dictate its outcome and our destiny. God didn't cause that damaged enemy aircraft to collide with your friend's bomber. It was a stroke of bad luck, that's all."

"So what you're saying then, is that no matter how hard we pray, it's not going to change the odds, for or against us, when we go on those bombing raids," said Longbow.

"Normally no, but there are exceptions, as I said, when God feels the circumstances warrant his intervention," said Father O'Reilly.

"Then, there is good reason to pray for his intervention, in the hope that our situation will get his attention and perhaps his help," said Siegel.

"Yes, that is correct. Never give up hope. But as the old saying goes, God helps those who help themselves." said Father O'Reilly.

"Well, then, Father, I seem to remember, that when Colonel Tibbetts was getting ready to fly his B-29 named Enola Gay, carrying an atomic bomb for release over Japan in World War Two, that a chaplain delivered a prayer at the pre-flight briefing blessing the crew," said Longbow.

"Yes, I do remember that event," said Father O'Reilly. "He was a Protestant chaplain named William Downey, and I have a published copy of his blessing, which is appropriate for all religious denominations."

"Could we see and read Chaplain Downey's prayer, Father," asked Longbow. "Our crew is made up of various religious faiths, so as the Flight Commander, I do need to review it before it can be used with our crew. I'm sure you understand."

"Yes, of course. Let's go into the rectory and I'll give you a copy," said Father O'Reilly.

After Longbow and Siegel read the lengthy prayer, Longbow suggested a minor change to the prayer to Father O'Reilly.

"The prayer assumes we fly our missions at night, however, since the arrival of F-86 Sabrejet fighters, we've switched to daylight bombing, therefore that sentence in the prayer which states 'May the men who fly this night be kept safe, etc.' should be changed to 'May the men who fly this day be kept safe, etc.' would be most appropriate in our situation," said Longbow.

"That's no problem, I'll make the change," replied Father O'Reilly.

"I do have one final question, Father. Would you give us the honor and privilege of blessing our crew, using Downey's prayer, on our next mission?" asked Longbow.

"It would be my privilege, Captain Longbow. You just let me know when and where to report, and I'll be there with Downey's prayer to wish your crew safe passage with God's blessing," said Father O'Reilly.

"On behalf of my crew, I thank you with much gratitude, Father. I will notify my crew of your forthcoming blessing, which I'm sure will be received with much relief and hope in these stressful times," said Longbow.

Within forty-eight hours, Longbow and his officer crew found themselves in the Briefing Room with thirty-nine bomber crews and all fifty Sabrejet pilots.

"This is Operation Thunderball, and your target is the hydroelectric complex at Kyosen, North Korea. The raid on the hydroelectric complex at Sui-ho was most successful. Let's knock this one out and put their lights out." said Colonel Madison.

"Your take-off time tomorrow is 0900 hours. Any questions?" asked Lieutenant Colonel Crawford.

"We bomber pilots certainly appreciate the terrific protection the Sabrejet pilots are giving us against the MiGs, but what can be done to silence the anti-aircraft artillery, which is responsible for much of our losses?" asked a flight commander.

"May I answer his question, sir," asked Colonel Mark Stanford, Commander of the 51st Fighter Interceptor Wing.

"Go ahead, Mark," replied Colonel Madison.

"With fifty Sabrejets in the air, it shouldn't take more than half of them to quickly dispose of any attacking MiGs, while the other half will go down and strafe the artillery sites to oblivion," said Colonel Stanford.

"Thank you. That will be most encouraging to our crews," replied the flight commander.

The briefing over, Longbow and Siegel, decided to visit Father O'Reilly.

"The information I'm about to reveal to you, Father, is classified, so I expect you will not divulge this information to anyone," said Longbow.

"I understand. I also wear the uniform and took the oath," replied Father O'Reilly.

"I meant no disrespect, Father. I just had to formalize this understanding," said Longbow. "We're going on a bombing mission tomorrow morning, leaving at 0900 hours. I would be most grateful, Father, if you could deliver your prayer to our crew not later than 0815, but not earlier than 0730 hours. Our aircraft, tail number 528, is parked in front of hangar 4, with no name on its fuselage. See you in the morning, Father," said Longbow, shaking Father O'Reilly's hand, with Siegel nodding approvingly.

Father O'Reilly, wearing his Air Force uniform with Captain's bars on his shoulders, and a cross on his lapel indicating his position as Chaplain, arrived in his assigned jeep at 0745.

As he climbed out of his jeep, he was greeted by Siegel, who invited him to meet the crew.

"Jim Longbow is inside the aircraft, but he'll be out in a moment when he sees you've arrived," said Siegel.

"That's a big bomber, so many guns," said Father O'Reilly, amazed at the size of the aircraft and its formidable armament.

"That's why we have ten crew members," said Siegel.

"How many of those bombers are going on this mission?' asked Father O'Reilly.

"Quite a few, Father," replied Siegel, not wanting to divulge the exact number, even to Father O'Reilly, as it was on a need-to-know basis.

Father O'Reilly realized from Siegel's vague response that he was overstepping his bounds, and decided to restrict his actions to the delivery of his prayer.

Longbow exited the aircraft and greeted Father O'Reilly with an enthusiastic handshake.

"Well, Father, you're just in time to give us your blessing," said Longbow. "I'll have my crew stand in line in front of the aircraft, and you can stand in front of the crew to deliver your prayer. I'm having one of the aircraft mechanics take a photograph of you blessing our crew."

Father O'Reilly pulled out a folded sheet of paper containing the prayer. "I'm ready when you are," said Father O'Reilly.

Longbow walked up to the port side of the aircraft facing him, and ordered the crew to assemble in a single line facing Father O'Reilly. He motioned to the aircraft mechanic holding a camera, to stand on the side, so he could include both the crew and Father O'Reilly in the photograph. He then asked Siegel to stand with him in the middle of the line, with the other two officers standing on each side of Longbow and Siegel, followed by the enlisted crew members.

"OK! Father, we're ready anytime you are," said Longbow.

Father O'Reilly unfolded the paper, and then addressed the crew.

"I'm Father O'Reilly, your Chaplain. I've been invited by your flight commander to deliver this prayer to you, with my blessings, on your hazardous mission."

"Almighty Father, who will hear the prayer of them that love thee, we pray thee to be with those who brave the heights of thy heaven and who carry the battle to our enemies. Guard and protect them, we pray thee, as they fly their appointed rounds. May they, as well as we, know thy strength and power, and armed with thy might may they bring this war to a rapid end. We pray thee that the end of the war may come soon, and that once more we may know peace on earth. May the men who fly this day be kept safe in thy care, and may they be returned safely to us. We shall go forward trusting in thee, knowing that we are in thy care now and forever. Amen."

Father O'Reilly, then made the sign of the cross, blessing the crew and its aircraft, then folded the prayer, inserting it inside his breast pocket.

While the crew dispersed, Longbow and Siegel walked up to Father O'Reilly and thanked him for his blessing.

"I'm sure the crew feels a lot safer, now that you've given your blessing," said Longbow. "Can we expect future blessings, Father?"

"Yes, of course. Just let me know when, and I'll be there," replied Father O'Reilly.

"When we get the developed picture, I'll personally deliver a copy to you, Father," said Longbow.

"Thank you. I will frame it, and hang it on the wall of my rectory," replied Father O'Reilly.

Longbow and Siegel then boarded their bomber, while Father O'Reilly stood back to watch their aircraft start its engines and then taxi to the awaiting runway, getting in line with the other bombers, starting to take off towards North Korea. What Father O'Reilly failed to see, were the fifty F-86 Sabrejet fighters taking off on an adjacent runway, flown by young and eager air cowboys, anxious to engage the enemy and test their flight skill and courage in mortal combat.

Operation Thunderball went without a hitch, and as predicted by Colonel Stanford, the Sabrejet fighters quickly shot down 9 MiGs, routing the rest, while the other half of the Sabrejet Wing silenced the anti-aircraft artillery sites before they could damage the bombers with flak. For the first time in the history of bombing raids over North Korea, there were no loses of B-29 bombers or F-86 fighters, signaling complete control of airspace over North Korea.

It was three weeks before Christmas when Longbow received a letter from his father assuring him that he and David's father, Simon Siegel, each had acquired an AMPEX Model 600 reel-to-reel recorder, and packaged them with the recording provided by Jim and Dave in Christmas wrapping for delivery on Christmas Eve.

Longbow passed the information from his father to Dave Siegel, who hadn't yet received a letter from his father, but did so two days later. Satisfied with their Christmas gift to their families, Longbow and Siegel, went to the Officers Club for a leisurely dinner with red wine to celebrate their creative deed with great expectations of its results.

Eric Longbow and Simon Siegel had agreed to each deliver their sons' Christmas gift at 2:00 p.m. on Christmas Eve, in order to maintain harmony. As planned, the Christmas gifts were delivered with instructions to open the gifts in the presence of the children, as it was intended for the whole family, but not until Christmas day.

After Eric Longbow left the house, Louise immediately called Susan Siegel, residing next door, to inform her of the Christmas gift from her husband.

"Is it a big, heavy box?" asked Susan.

"Yes, it is, why?" asked Louise.

"Because, Dave's father just delivered a Christmas gift from Dave, and it's in a big, heavy box in Christmas wrapping and a card, wishing me and my kids a Merry Christmas," said Susan.

"I got a similar package, and I'll bet it's the same thing." said Louise. "I can't wait to open it, but Eric said I can't open it until Christmas day. I don't know if I can wait until then."

"Well, Simon said we had to open it in the presence of the kids, because it was a present for the whole family. Like you, Louise, I'd like to take a peak, but I dare not 'cause it would spoil the surprise," said Susan.

"I guess you're right. We'll just have to wait until tomorrow," replied Louise.

"Gosh! I wonder what Jim and Dave cooked up this time?" asked Susan.

"They're in Okinawa, so they don't have many items to choose from," said Louise. "But maybe they had their father select the gifts for them."

"Who knows? If we keep this up, we'll end up opening those gifts before we're supposed to. So let's just wait until it's past midnight," said Susan.

"Yeah! But the kids will be asleep by then, and we're to open the gifts in their presence," replied Louise. "So let's wait until the kids are up, then we can open it."

The big gift, along with small ones given by relatives, lay under the Christmas tree until early morning, when Garreth and Jacqueline, now six and five years old, respectively, ran into their mother's bedroom to awaken Louise for their Christmas presents. Susan's children, Alexander and Rachel, about the same age as Louise's children, slept in late, until their mother Susan got up, making breakfast before they were allowed to open their presents.

The excitement in the Longbow residence was felt by all, as Louise pulled the heavy box from under the Christmas tree, and with a pair of scissors, cut the ribbon that encircled the package, then unwrapped the Christmas paper, exposing a heavy cardboard box that had to be cut open, revealing a large cabinet with two closed side-by-side doors.

"Gee, Mom, what is it?" asked Garreth.

"I don't know, Gary, but we'll find out," said Louise, opening the two doors from which an envelope dropped out. It was addressed to Louise. The note inside the envelope informed her that this was a reel-to-reel recorder, and the reel in place was a recording of him, her husband, talking to her and the kids, and a monologue of him playing a ukulele while reciting a poem he composed for her, hoping she would like it.

"This is a note from your father, telling us that this machine has a recording of your father talking to us from Okinawa and wishing us a Merry Christmas. He also composed a song for me which he recorded while playing a ukulele. I guess he learned to play a ukulele while in Okinawa," said Louise.

"Oh! Let's hear it, Mom," said Jacqueline, eagerly.

"First we have to plug it in, then I guess I just press Play, and turn the volume up," said Louise, following the steps she had called out.

"Merry Christmas, Louise, and Merry Christmas to you Gary and Jackie. I'm making this recording in the Control Room of the Communications Center at Kadena Air Force Base in Okinawa. Dave and I have been busy flying a B-29 Superfortress on bombing raids over North Korea, and while it was risky at first, now we've got F-86 Sabrejet fighter escorts, which has made our bombing missions much safer. So there's no need to worry about us, our tour of duty will be over in six months, then we'll be home for good. I see that you kids have grown quite a bit since I was assigned overseas. I promise that I will spend a lot more time with you when I get back. In the pictures Louise sent me, I see a very handsome boy named Gary, standing with a gorgeous girl named Jackie. My crew members can't believe I have such attractive children and believe they must take from their mother, and I kind of agree. Now I'm going to recite a poem I composed for your mother while playing my ukulele. I named it

WHEN WE WERE YOUNG

Remember when we first met
on the raft at Lakebeach
your blond hair and blue eyes
that had me mesmerized
that first kiss under the raft
which left me paralyzed
while you swam away
without saying goodbye
but then we met again
at the Yachtclub ball
where we danced so close
intoxicated by your fragrance
I fell in love forever.

we were ever so young
two dreamy sailors
you rich and me poor
without a care in the world
except being together
those sunny days and starry nights
when we were ever so young
full of hope and dreams
those were the days and nights
we thought would end with the war
when Europe was so far away
but our love never died
because we remembered so well
those days when we were young
we knew they'd never end.
MERRY CHRISTMAS

The recording went silent signaling its end. Louise wiped the tears from her eyes, then withdrew a tissue from a nearby box and dabbed her cheeks.

"Why are you crying, Mom?" asked Jackie.

"Oh! I just miss your father, that's all, Jackie," replied Louise.

"We do too, Mom, and we can't wait for him to come home," said Gary.

"I know. Did you like the recording?" asked Louise.

"Yes, we did, Mom. I hope Dad sends us more of them," said Jackie.

"I hope he tells us more about those bombing raids and the jet fighters," said Gary. "That must be exciting."

"Your father is limited as to what he can tell us about those bombing missions, because the information is mostly classified," said Louise.

"What do you mean 'classified' Mom?" asked Gary.

"Well, it means that he can't reveal certain information. That if it fell into the wrong hands, it could be useful to the enemy, and hurtful to our airmen," said Louise. "So he can only tell us general information that won't help or hurt anyone."

"Gee, Mom, I want to be an airplane pilot like Dad," said Gary, who had been given a toy airplane on his birthday.

"You've got plenty of time to decide what you want to do with your life, Gary," said Louise.

"Hey! It's time for you to open your other presents," said Louise, thankful she had these two wonderful children to keep her company while she waited and endured her husband's absence.

In the meantime, in the Siegel household, where Hanukah, the Festival of Lights is celebrated in conjunction with Christmas, Susan sits on the floor with her son Alex and her daughter Rachel in front of the AMPEX Model 600 recorder.

"OK! Kids, here goes," said Susan, pushing the Play button, whereupon the voice of David comes on with his Christmas greetings, wishing he was there to enjoy the Christmas holidays with them. He tells them of his comings and goings at the Air Base, but omits his flying experiences and bomber raids over North Korea. Susan, at times, detected a sadness in her husband's voice when reminiscing about their times together, but then he put on a happy face for the children whom he adored. All in all, Susan would treasure this recording for replay many years later.

At Kadena Air Force Base, Longbow and Siegel were enjoying the Spring weather, as they leisurely walked from the Mess Hall to Base Operations, that morning of the 11th of April 1951, when upon arrival, they heard the news on the radio, that the President of the United States, Harry S. Truman, as Commander-in-Chief, had fired General Douglas MacArthur for insubordination, and relieved him of his command the previous day. Furthermore, President Truman replaced General MacArthur with General Matthew Ridgeway.

"For those of you who just got in," said Colonel Madison, Wing Commander, "I had a conversation with General Ridgeway's Adjutant earlier this morning who explained to me that General MacArthur's plan to expand the Korean war into Manchuria had been rejected by President Truman, to avoid a third world war. Instead, he was adopting the policy of a limited war that would result in a temporary truce with North Korea to reach an agreement that would reinstate the 38th parallel as the official border between North and South Korea. Apparently, General MacArthur held fast on his plan to invade Manchuria, ignoring President Truman's orders to abandon any plan of a China invasion, resulting in MacArthur's relief of his command and dismissal from the US Army."

"Does that mean that those atomic bombs stored here in Okinawa will not be used in this Korean conflict, and possibly returned to the United States for storage," said one of the flight commanders.

"Yes, that's correct. President Truman wants this *police action* to remain a limited conflict that will not invite China and possibly Russia into the fray that could easily expand into a world war," replied Madison. "Any other questions?"

"Won't MacArthur's dismissal place North Korea in a better negotiating position?" asked Siegel.

"Perhaps, and then maybe not. It depends on who's doing the negotiating and what leverage we have, which we're not privy to at this time," replied Madison. "Let's hope that this latest action will result in an early truce so we can all go home."

"Amen!" Murmured Longbow to Siegel.

Sometime later, Longbow and Siegel learned through the news media, that General Douglas MacArthur, upon his return to the United States, was given a ticker-tape parade on Broadway in New York City. He was further invited to speak before the United States Congress, where he ended his speech with those famous words, "Old soldiers never die, they just fade away."

It was a grand day on that 1st of June, when Longbow and Siegel received their Special Orders reassigning them to the 174th Attack Wing at Hancock Field Air National Guard in Syracuse, New York, where they were to be discharged from active duty, and returned to reserve status, as Majors.

"Hey! Jim, did you notice that we've been promoted to Major," said Siegel.

"Yes, I did," replied Longbow. "I think it's to encourage us to remain in the reserves in case of another *police action*."

"Well, it may just work, because by the time another war starts, we'll be too old to fly combat missions. Besides, we planned on staying for the retirement benefits, remember," said Siegel.

"I agree with you, Dave. I think we should remain in the active reserves, but it'll take some convincing to get Louise and Susan to agree," said Longbow.

"Well, we'll just have to work on them, that's all," replied Siegel.

"The Special Orders say we're to leave Okinawa aboard a MATS aircraft on the 7th of this month, with stopover at Travis Air Force Base, Fairfield, California, then onto Hancock Field where we'll be discharged from active duty," said Siegel to Longbow.

"I don't know if writing a letter to Louise and Susan to let them know of our transfer to Hancock Field will get to them before we arrive," said Longbow.

"I don't think so, Jim. Hey! Let's surprise them," said Siegel with a big grin on his face.

"Huh! Huh! I don't know if Louise will kiss me or punch me for not warning her of our arrival," said Longbow, grinning.

"She'll probably give you a sleepless night to remember," replied Siegel, with a knowing smile, reminiscing about that unforgettable night at London's Regent Hotel during the Second World War, when Siegel and Longbow experienced their first and most memorable love making with their fiancées, Susan and Louise.

"After this long abstinence, I hope I can remember how," replied Longbow.

"Don't worry, Jim, she'll jog your memory," said Siegel, laughing.

"I'm looking forward to seeing the kids," said Longbow. "They're growing so fast."

"Yeah! Me too. That Rachel is just a living doll. I hope she doesn't break too many hearts," said Siegel.

"When you think of it, Dave, we've been pretty lucky, surviving the war, marrying the girl of our dreams, and having children of both genders," said Longbow.

"Yeah! But with every positive there's also a negative. I'm just fearful of that forthcoming negative," replied David Siegel.

"There you go again, Dave, thinking negatively," said James Longbow. "There doesn't have to be a negative, that's all in your negative mind. Think positive so that if a negative thing occurs, it will be a surprise that you did not agonize over, and then cross that bridge when you get there."

"You make things appear so simple. I guess I'm just a worry wart, huh!" replied Siegel.

"That you are, my friend, but you do show signs of improvement," said Longbow with a laugh.

"That's what Susan says," replied Siegel.

"What, that you show signs of improvement?" asked Longbow.

"No, that I'm a worry wart," replied Siegel with a grin.

"Hey! No one is perfect, Dave, so take what I say with a grain of salt," replied Longbow.

After their return to the United States and settling down with their families, Longbow and Siegel wasted no time in visiting their employer at the Curtiss-Wright Corporation. Upon entering the Curtiss-Wright Corporation building, they were immediately greeted by a security officer who asked the reason for their visit.

"My name is James Longbow and this is David Siegel. We're employees of the Curtiss Wright Corporation, who've just been released from active duty as Korean War veterans. We're now returning to our old jobs as Aircraft Designers, and expected to be greeted by Robert Polanski or Alfred Pinetti, upon arrival, inasmuch as we notified the company of our return," said Longbow.

"Just a moment, sir. I'll see if either gentleman is available," said the security officer, who got on the telephone, and after a quick conversation, turned his attention to Longbow.

"Mister Pinetti will be here shortly, sir," said the security guard.

More than five minutes transpired before Alfred Pinetti, the Chief Designer arrived.

"Well, welcome back, Jim, Dave," said Pinetti, shaking their hands. "It's alright, Alvin, they work in my department,"

"Bob Polanski wants to greet you, so we'll go to his office," said Pinetti.

Upon arrival at Polanski's office, the secretary immediately allowed them to enter his office.

"Welcome back," said Polanski, greeting Longbow and Siegel with a smile and handshake. "Please have a seat, gentlemen."

"So, I presume you want to return to your old job of aircraft designer," said Polanski.

"That's what we were promised when we agreed with your blessing to join the active Air Force Reserves, sir," said Longbow.

"Well, that's correct, and in compliance with the Federal Statute governing returning veterans, your previous job is available to you," said Polanski. You'll continue to work under Mister Pinetti, our Chief Designer, and in recognition of your honorable service as Korean veterans, you will get a five percent pay raise."

"Thank you, sir," replied Longbow, while Siegel remained silent.

"You're welcome. So what type of aircrafts did you fly while in the active reserves?" asked Polanski.

"A B-29 Superfortress, sir," replied Longbow.

"Any other aircraft?" asked Pinetti.

"No, sir, the B-29 was the only bomber available to conduct bombing raids over North Korea," replied Longbow.

"Soon the B-29 will be superseded by the B-36, isn't that correct?" asked Pinetti.

"Yes, that's correct, but it won't be available until sometime next year," replied Longbow, who surmised from their questions, that he and David had nothing to offer the company in terms of new aircraft technology.

"Are you planning on remaining in the Active Reserves?" asked Polanski.

"Yes, but we haven't yet discussed the matter with our wives, sir," replied Siegel.

"Well, I hope you do remain in the Active Reserves, and your salary will not be interrupted during your time in the Reserves. In the meantime, welcome back, and I presume you'll be ready to start work this coming Monday," said Polanski.

"Yes sir, and thank you for the raise in pay," said Longbow.

Upon exiting the Curtiss-Wright Corporation building, Siegel expressed his dissatisfaction with the pay raise and the cold reception.

"Did you get the feeling that they were only interested in what new aircraft experience we could bring to the company, and their disappointment when you told them we only flew a B-29 Bomber," said Siegel.

"Yes, I definitely got that impression, Dave, but they're businessmen, and as such, they're only interested in the bottom line," said Longbow.

"Jesus, Jim, are you really satisfied with a five percent pay raise after all we've been through?' asked Siegel.

"Well, of course I would have liked a bigger pay raise, but you must remember that they didn't have to pay us while we were in the active reserves, and they'll continue payment when we join the active reserves again, which they're not obligated to do, so I have no complaints," replied Longbow.

"You do have a valid point, Jim, but as I see it, Pinetti is a long way from retirement, and he stands in the way of advancement. On top of that, he's been taking the credit for most of the innovations we've developed in aircraft design. I think it's time for us to move on to greener pastures, Jim," said Siegel.

"What are you suggesting, Dave?" asked Longbow.

"Why can't we start our own aircraft company? We could get financing from my father, and as you well know, Louise's father is one of the wealthiest men in America, who would surely want to help his daughter and her husband succeed in this promising venture," said Siegel.

"Look Dave, even if we got all of the required financing, there's still the fact that we would no longer be just aircraft designers, but owners with the responsibility of managing a large aircraft company that builds as well as designs aircrafts. We'd be spending twenty hours a day, six to seven days a week at work, while our families would hardly see us, except to sleep. That's not my idea of a family life, Dave. I'm satisfied with a nine-to-five job, five days a week, with a reasonable income, that will allow me to spend ample time with my wife and children, in an unhurried atmosphere of love and devotion," said Longbow.

"Well, that's easy for you to say, Jim. Your wife inherited three and a half million dollars from the estate of her deceased husband, so you have financial security. I, on the other hand, have only my salary, and the measly income from the active reserves to support my family. I certainly don't want to ever go to my father for financial support, so I have to look at other means of income, and starting our own company seems like a good bet," said Siegel.

"First of all, Dave, I made it very clear to Louise from the beginning, that I intend to provide for my family without her financial support or that of her father," said Longbow. "Furthermore, our salaries are significantly more than that of the average person, and our Reservist income is most respectable and useful. I do not intend to sacrifice my precious time with my family for money I don't need.

"You're thinking small, Jim. Open your horizon and think of the possibilities," said Siegel.

"You know, Dave, it's not the greatness of your means, so much as the smallness of your wants that determines your wealth. So I don't think about size, Dave, I think about quality. Sorry to disappoint you, Dave, but I'm a family man, and I'm going home to enjoy a tasty leg of lamb. Say hi to Susan for me, she's your wealth," said Longbow, opening the door to his sports car for Dave to exit, and without another word, sped off.

By the week's end, both Louise and Susan agreed for their husbands to rejoin the active reserves, inasmuch as there was no likelihood of another war in the near future, and after that, they'd be too old for combat duty.

Things went back to normal at the Curtiss-Wright Corporation for Longbow and Siegel, who fell into the routine as if they had never left. Then, early one Monday morning in late August of that year, Longbow was summoned to President Stephen Waverly's office.

"I wonder what's going on?" said Siegel, inquisitively.

"Don't know, but I'm about to find out," replied Longbow, who left the aircraft designer room, wondering what was the apparent urgency of this summons from the President of the corporation.

President Waverly's middle-aged secretary immediately opened the door to Waverly's office with a welcoming smile that eased Longbow's concern.

Waverly instantly walked around from his desk and greeted Longbow with a smile and a handshake.

"I apologize for not greeting you until now since your return from Korea, but I've been so busy with work that my wife complains the only time she sees me is on holidays," said Waverly. "But that's not a valid excuse, I know. Have a seat, Jim."

Waverly returned to his comfortable chair behind his large wooden desk and sat down. "I have some bad news, not for you, but for the company. Yesterday afternoon, Al Pinetti, piloting our Air Travel company aircraft from Chicago with our Chief Salesman Cid Costello, crashed soon after takeoff with no survivors," said Waverly.

"Good God! I'm so sorry to hear that, sir," said Longbow. "Do they know what caused the crash?"

"There was a terrible lightning storm over that area, with a weather warning for all flights scheduled for departure from Chicago International Airport. I guess Al wanted to get back in time for work this morning, and disregarded the weather warning, which cost his and Cid's life," said Waverly.

"I flew that same airplane with Dave this past December, when we went to Florida for the Christmas holidays. As a six-seat single engine aircraft, it provided a stable flight, but a lightning storm does present a significant hazard," said Longbow.

"Well, the reason I asked you into my office, Jim, is to let you know that as of today, you're now the Chief Designer with the same authority, privileges and salary afforded Al Pinetti," said Waverly.

"Thank you, sir, but Dave Siegel is equally qualified, and we've been working extremely well as a team. I believe that he should be promoted as my assistant, and I'm willing to share my increase in pay with Dave so he won't feel unappreciated," said Longbow, which raised Waverly's eyebrows at Longbow's willingness to share his pay raise with his friend.

"Frankly, Jim, is such devotion and loyalty to Dave really warranted. I've appointed you as the Chief Designer, and as such, you are entitled to the salary associated with that position. I'm willing to appoint Dave Siegel as your assistant, and I'll give him a raise appropriate for that position. That way, you won't have to share your raise, and Dave will be adequately compensated for his promotion. I have also instructed Bob Parnell, our Personnel Director, to hire two aircraft designers to work under your supervision," said Waverly.

"You asked me if my devotion and loyalty to Dave is really warranted. My answer is definitely yes. We have shared many life and death experiences, both in the Second World War and the Korean conflict, which makes us brothers-in-arms. However, your suggested alternative does make sense and is acceptable to me, and I'm sure will be to Dave as well. I presume you'll be calling him in to inform him of his promotion, then?" asked Longbow.

"Yes, I will, right after you leave, Jim. I want you to know, that I truly admire your unconditional loyalty to your friend Dave Siegel, and I hope he appreciates such rare and uncommon friendship. I consider you to be an exceptional asset to this corporation, and should you ever need any assistance, Jim, please don't hesitate to call or visit me," said Waverly, who then stood up and walked from behind his desk to shake Longbow's hand, and wish him well in his new job.

CHAPTER III

Discovery of a Former Nazi Camp Officer

Life on Creekside Road in Williamsville with the Longbow and Siegel families couldn't have been better, with the kids now all in school, providing free time for Louise and Susan to visit various stores, and plan for the forthcoming Christmas holidays in about three weeks.

"You changed your hairstyle, Louise. It's shorter but very becoming," said Susan.

"Easier to maintain too," replied Louise. "Betty, that's my hairdresser's name, told me about this fabulous Hungarian restaurant in Toronto which she visited with her husband last Saturday. She said it serves genuine Hungarian food, but what really impressed her and her husband was the gypsy music, played by three violinists that come around each table. It was so romantic, with the gypsy music capturing the essence of Hungarian passion that swelled your heart into teary eyes."

"What's the name of the restaurant?" asked Susan.

"The Budapest-Gypsy Restaurant, a fitting name for it," replied Louise. "I think we should talk Jim and Dave into taking us there for dinner. What do you think?"

"Sounds exciting, and I could use a change of scenery," replied Susan.

"OK! I'll suggest it to Jim at dinner time, and then he can talk to Dave about it," said Louise.

"Why don't I tell Dave about it too, at dinner time. Then they'll both know their wives are anxious to have dinner at the Budapest-Gypsy Restaurant in Toronto," said Susan.

"Good idea, let's suggest this Saturday," said Louise. "We can use my babysitter for all four kids at my house. What do you think?"

"This Saturday, then, and I know your babysitter, so sure, Alex and Rachel will love spending the evening with Gary and Jackie at your house, so consider it done, Louise," replied Susan with a mischievous grin.

The two couples decided to use Dave's new 1951 Cadillac, eight-cylinder, four-door, Silverpine Green Metallic sedan, for which he used his 1934 Cadillac convertible as a trade-in. All agreed Dave's new Cadillac provided a more comfortable ride to Toronto, than James' station wagon.

They arrived at the Budapest-Gypsy Restaurant, which had a prominent dark red marquee over its brightly lit entrance, with the restaurant's name in a neon sign above the marquee. A sign directed customers to park at the rear of the restaurant, which Dave did, with a few parking spaces still available, probably due to their early arrival.

James and Dave, dressed in dark suits with white shirt and contrasting tie, escorted Louise and Susan, both dressed in cocktail dresses, from the parking lot, inasmuch as there was no street doorman to greet the ladies, and the walk was short.

Upon entering the restaurant, they were immediately greeted by the Maitre-D, a dark-haired, middle-age man, dressed in a tuxedo, who asked for their reservation name, which James Longbow provided.

"We have reserved a wonderfully situated table with an unobstructed view of the stage and dance floor for you, Monsieur Longbow," said the Maitre-D, giving the restaurant a flair of French Haute-Cuisine.

"Merci beaucoup, Monsieur," replied longbow, letting him know that even Americans can speak French.

Looking over the Hungarian menu, they all agreed to order the traditional Goulash and Schnitzel, inasmuch as they were not familiar with Hungarian food. Louise had been told by her hairdresser to try the Goulash which she said was exquisitely delicious.

Halfway through the dinner, three men dressed in tuxedos, appeared from back stage, and started playing their violins, whose coordinated musical sound pulled at one's heart strings, conveying the desperation of lost love. As the three violinists came close to their table, the sensitivity of the sound of the bow flowing across the strings of the violin penetrated the hearts of its listeners with wondrous appreciation for this romantic music.

The violinists played several gypsy melodies, and then disappeared for a break.

"My God! What a wonderful performance," said Susan.

"They made those violins sing with excitement and cry the blues like no one I ever heard," said Louise."

"Well, your hairdresser was right about them and this restaurant," said Susan.

"James, what did you think of them?" asked Louise, who then noticed that her husband was staring at someone across the dance floor at a table occupied by two couples.

"James, what are you staring at?" asked Louise.

"Please, Louise, be quiet for a minute," said Longbow.

"Dave, don't look now, but directly across the dance floor, at that table with two couples. The man dressed in a dark suit, white shirt and light blue tie, sitting next to the blond haired woman, is SS Captain Hans Gunther," said Longbow. "Please don't look in his direction, 'cause I don't want him to know he's been spotted."

Unable to contain his curiosity, Siegel quickly looked in the direction cited by Longbow. "It does look like him, but I can only see his profile, and it's kind of dark in here," said Siegel.

"I'd know him anywhere," said Longbow. "Let's go to the Men's restroom and on the way back, we'll walk by his table, and without staring at him, we'll get a good look at him."

"You mean that's the Nazi Captain who shot all those prisoners you told us about?" asked Louise.

"Yeah! That's the one. But we don't want to spook him," said Longbow.

"OK! Let's go to the rest room, I need to get a better look at him," said Siegel.

"God! This dinner is turning out to be a real who-dun-nit mystery," said Louise.

Inside the Men's restroom, Longbow waited for the only customer to leave before he spoke to Siegel.

"How can you be sure, Jim? It's been seven-to-eight years since we've seen this guy," asked Siegel.

"I first saw him on the dance floor with his wife, that blond woman sitting next to him, before the violinists came on. He danced close enough to our table for me to see his eyes, and I'll never forget those cold blue eyes, they never change. I stared into those eyes when he was about to shoot me, remember," said Longbow.

"Jesus, how can I ever forget," replied Siegel. "OK! Let's go check him out."

Longbow led the way with Siegel following close behind him, as they navigated their way up a narrow hallway separating a row of booths from the assortment of tables dispersed around the dance floor, until they faced the one table occupied by Gunther, his wife and another couple.

Captain Gunther, still had a full head of dark hair, but now he also had a dark, slim mustache. He was apparently preoccupied in a heated discussion with the man sitting across from him, which worked to Longbow and Siegel's advantage, inasmuch as he was too busy to take notice of the two men taking mental note of his appearance and voice.

Back at their table, Siegel looked at Longbow with distress in his face.

"Jesus, Jim, it's Captain Gunther, alright. Even his voice sent me shivers," said Siegel, now looking at Susan.

"There is absolutely no doubt in my mind, that he's SS Captain Hans Gunther," said Longbow.

"What are you going to do now?" asked Louise.

"Well, he obviously changed his name before immigrating to Canada, so we must find out what his name is and possibly where he resides," said Longbow.

"When he leaves, he'll either take a taxi or else drive his own car," said Siegel. "If he takes a taxi, we're lost. But If he drove here, then we can get his license plate number which can be traced to his home address."

"If he takes a taxi, I'm going to get into another taxi and follow him to his destination," said Longbow. "In that case, just wait for me. I'll be back. Otherwise, I can casually and discreetly follow him and his wife to their car in the parking lot and get their license plate number, hopefully without getting seen."

"In the meantime, Dave, once Gunther and his wife leave the restaurant, could you approach the person at the reservation desk, and find out under what name he and his entourage registered. You may have to offer a bribe, but whatever it cost, it'll be worth it," said Longbow.

"Excellent idea. No problem, Jim," replied Siegel.

"God! You guys sound like detectives in a movie," said Susan.

"If that man, as you said, is a murderer, he may be armed and not squeamish about shooting you, Jim," said Louise.

"So be careful when you follow him in the parking lot, which is quite dark and isolated."

"Don't worry, sweetheart, I'll be careful," replied Longbow.

"The waiter has just brought them their bill," said Siegel.

"I see he's paying in cash," said Longbow, who took one of the sharp knives from the table and stuck it inside his belt, hidden by his jacket, which made Siegel smile with approval, but a frown from Louise.

"OK! I'm going into the lobby, and hopefully, he won't take a taxi," said Longbow. "You girls remain at the table so my departure won't look suspicious."

Longbow stood in the far corner of the lobby looking through a bunch of magazines for waiting customers, when he observed Gunther, his wife and the other couple retrieve the women's light coats, and when asked by the Maitre D if they wanted him to flag a taxi, Gunther answered in the affirmative, which raised Longbow's anxiety about getting another taxi in time to follow Gunther.

A Taxi arrived in front of the restaurant, and the Gunther group made their exit, but only the unknown couple entered the taxi, with Gunther and his wife wishing them goodnight. Gunther, accompanied by his wife, then walked around the corner and along the wide cement walkway to the rear parking lot, but Longbow, now elated over this turn of events, waited a while before venturing into the parking lot, to give time for Gunther to get into his car with his wife, and drive out into the street. Longbow reasoned that the safest and most productive place for him to be, was at the parking lot exit, where it was lighted, and Gunther would have to stop before entering the street. As predicted by Longbow, Gunther, driving a black, late model Mercedes, stopped at the street entrance to view the traffic, at which time Longbow memorized the rear license plate number, and then walked back into the restaurant where he wrote the number down. Siegel, who had been talking to the reservation clerk, immediately came up to Longbow.

"Did you get the plate number?" asked Siegel.

"Yes, I did, and wrote it down. Here, you write it down as well, in case I lose it," said Longbow.

"By the way, Gunther made the reservations under the name Franz Muller with his telephone number which I wrote down. Apparently the restaurant requires the customer's phone number in case there's a need to change the reservation," said Siegel, with a pleased smile. "Now who do we give this information to, that will get the best results?"

"I think we should call Bill Kaufman, who has a vested interest in the arrest and conviction of Captain Gunther, who shot and killed his co-pilot, who happened to be his cousin," said Longbow. "Bill has already reported Gunther to the Army CID, the Air Force OSI, the FBI and the Immigration Service. I think that we should give him all of the information we have, so he can provide it to the investigative agencies he's already in touch with. That's the only way for this information to be useful for Gunther's identification and apprehension."

"I totally agree with you, Jim. We'd better get back to the table where Louise and Susan have been patiently waiting for our return," said Siegel.

"What did you guys find out?" asked Louise.

"We found out his current name is Franz Muller, and we got his license plate number and car make," said Longbow.

"Now what are you going to do with that information?" asked Susan.

"We think that Bill Kaufman, whom you girls met at the Officers Club at Morrison Field in West Palm Beach, should receive all of that information," said Siegel.

"Why him?" asked Louise.

"If you remember, he told us all of his personal experiences with SS Captain Hans Gunther, while a prisoner of war in Germany, with Jim and me," said Siegel. "Gunther shot and killed Bill's cousin and co-pilot standing next to him in the same line we also were in."

"Bill also reported the incident to several military and federal agencies with an unyielding determination to find Gunther for prosecution," said Longbow. "So we think Bill is in the best position and motivation to make the best use of this information."

"Wow! Is he going to be surprised," said Louise.

"That's an understatement," said Longbow.

"When are you going to call Bill Kaufman?" asked Susan.

"As soon as we get back to Williamsville," replied Longbow.

Kaufman had given Longbow his telephone number for his office at the Aviation Training Center in Morrison Field. However, he would have to wait until the next morning to call him.

"Captain Kaufman," answered the person being called by Longbow.

"Bill, this is Jim Longbow in Williamsville, New York. How are you?"

"Great, how about you, Jim," replied Kaufman.

"I've got some news that's going to make your day, Bill," said Longbow.

"Oh! Yeah, what's that?" asked Kaufman.

"Yesterday, Dave Siegel and our wives had dinner at the Budapest Gypsy Restaurant in Toronto, and while there we encountered none other than Captain Hans Gunther with his wife, also having dinner there. Dave and I discreetly walked by his table for a second and closer look to verify his identity and we're positive he's the SS Captain Hans Gunther we had the misfortune to meet while imprisoned in Germany. We learned that he made his dinner reservations under the name of Franz Muller. I also observed him driving a late model Mercedes and wrote down his license plate number. Are you ready to copy all this?"

"Yes, go ahead, Jim," replied Kaufman with excitement in his voice.

"You got it all?" asked Longbow.

"Yeah! and you just made my day, Jim," said Kaufman. "I never thought I'd see the day when I would ever find this bastard. I'm going to relay this information to the FBI and the Bureau of Immigration as soon as I hang up. I'm sure they'll contact the Canadian authorities and ask for his extradition, either to the United States or Germany for trial. I'll keep you and Dave posted on the progress made. In the meantime, Jim, if there is anything I can go for you or Dave, just holler, and I'll be at your service, my friend."

"I'm just glad this opportunity occurred, Bill. Dave and I also want to see this man prosecuted....we were there, remember," said Longbow.

"I know, and I just hope the Canadian government cooperates with us on his extradition," said Kaufman."

"Well, just remember, Bill, that Dave and I, are willing to give testimony about Captain Hans Gunther's activities at the concentration camp," said Longbow.

"I appreciate that, Jim, and should you guys be needed, I'll let you know in plenty of time. In the meantime, take care and let's keep in touch," said Kaufman.

"Will do, Bill. You got my telephone number, right?" asked Longbow.

"Yeah! I sure do and Dave's also," replied Kaufman.

The conversation with Kaufman over, Longbow looked at Louise who had been standing next to him, with the expected question:

"Was he pleased with the information you gave him?" asked Louise.

"Ecstatically happy. He's now going to contact the FBI and the Bureau of Immigration for them to contact the

Canadian authorities for possible extradition to the US or Germany for trial," said Longbow.

"This could become world news, Jim," said Louise.

"Yes, but I hope our names don't get published, we don't need the publicity," said Longbow. "I'd better call Dave and give him an update."

A fortnight transpired, then the newspapers released an article regarding the United States Attorney General's request to the Canadian government for the extradition of Captain Hans Gunther, also known as Franz Muller, residing in Toronto, Canada, to the United States, for war crimes, while Deputy Commandant of Nazi Concentration Camp Stalag IX-B, located southeast of Bad Orb in Hessen, Germany, during the period 1942-1945.

"I wonder, Jim, if the Canadian government will agree to Gunther's extradition?" asked Louise.

"The article doesn't mention any decision by the Canadians. I guess they're gonna want evidence of Gunther's crimes, not to mention his identification as SS Captain Hans Gunther. I'm sure Franz Muller will claim a mistake in identity," said Longbow.

"Well, three of you surviving prisoners can identify him, so I don't see a problem there," replied Louise.

"That's correct, but will it be enough for the Canadian government?" said Longbow. "I hope the FBI and other security agencies can come up with a set of Gunther's fingerprints from the files of the German government that can be matched to Franz Muller. However, the files of many of those concentration camps were destroyed before the allies got there to rescue their inmates."

"What about the real Franz Muller, you think he's dead?" asked Louise.

"Most likely, Captain Gunther probably selected him for his similar physical appearance and age, then killed him, taking his identification papers, which I doubt contained a fingerprint, but were signed and authenticated by German authorities. That probably got him into Canada, which at the time, was overwhelmed with applications for immigration," said Longbow.

"My God! What a mess," said Louise. "Well, I'm glad it's Bill Kaufman's problem and not yours, Jim."

"I'm sure Bill is enjoying every minute of this challenging situation, because he now has definitive leads to work with, and has the assistance of the FBI, and now the Attorney General," said Longbow.

It was on a Friday in mid-afternoon, four weeks after his last telephone call with Bill Kaufman, when Longbow received a phone call from Bill, whose tone of voice lacked enthusiasm.

"Hi! Jim, this is Bill Kaufman. I called Dave Siegel, but he isn't answering his phone, but the information I'm about to give you pertains to both of you."

"Gee! That sounds ominous, Bill. What is it?" asked Longbow.

"Well, to begin with, it seems that when Franz Muller applied for immigration to Canada shortly after the war, he produced his Dog Tag, an oval disk made of aluminum or tin, containing his name, soldier's number and blood type. He also produced a Soldbuch identification card which did not contain a fingerprint, nor a photograph of Muller, the latter not required until 1943, after he had already been inducted into the German Army. Therefore, all Muller had to do was find an enlisted soldier with his blood type and the rest was a gift," said Kaufman.

"Good Grief, it was that easy, huh! But what about governmental records...aren't there any detailed records of either Franz Muller or Hans Gunther?" asked Longbow.

"The FBI found nothing pertaining to either man, which posed a problem that became significant when the Canadian government asked for evidentiary proof that Franz Muller was in fact Hans Gunther, and that the mere personal identification by former prisoners' of war dating back some eight or nine years, was insufficient evidence for the extradition of a Canadian citizen, which Hans Gunther became shortly after his immigration," said Kaufman.

"So I guess, you need a photograph or a fingerprint of either man to establish Gunther's real identity, which is not available," said Longbow.

"That's correct, and I've been told that as far as the FBI and the Attorney General's Office is concerned, this case is closed, unless new evidence is uncovered," said Kaufman.

"Man, that's got to be very frustrating. So what are you going to do now?" asked Longbow.

"I hate to see that son-of-a-bitch get away with all those murders of American servicemen, and my cousin in particular. There's got to be a way to make him pay for his crimes," said Kaufman.

"Listen, Bill, I hope you're not thinking of taking matters into your own hands. No one gets away with anything, believe me. So he may live unpunished for several years until his death. But eventually, he's gonna have to answer to God for his crimes, and his punishment will far exceed anything he might endure on this earth. So let it be, Bill, and let providence take care of him. He's not worth jeopardizing your soul," said Longbow.

"I know what you're saying is true, Jim, but this is a hard pill to swallow, my friend. Anyway, I thought you and Dave would like to know the outcome of the investigation," said Kaufman.

"Thanks, Bill. Find yourself a good woman that will make you forget that hateful past. Believe me, life will never be better," said Longbow.

Later, that evening, Longbow related his conversation with Bill Kaufman to Dave Siegel.

"Well, that takes care of any extradition of Captain Gunther. But as you said to Bill, Gunther will get what's coming to him sooner or later when he meets his maker. In the meantime, we've got better things to do than worry about that scoundrel," said Siegel.

About a week later, Siegel and Longbow left work together and arrived at their houses located next to each other, and Siegel noticed the newspaper lying at the front door to his house and picked it up for him to read inside his house, while Susan prepared dinner for him and their two children. Longbow's paper had already been picked up by his wife Louise, which he put off reading until after dinner.

It wasn't more than ten minutes, when Longbow's telephone rang.

"This is Dave, did you read today's newspaper?" asked Siegel.

"No, not yet, why?" asked Longbow.

"Check out an article on the second page. It's about the murder of Franz Muller, shot to death next to his car in the Toronto Municipal Parking Ramp, yesterday evening at approximately 1730 hours. They have no suspects so far," said Siegel.

"Good God! I see what you mean. I've got the article in front of me now, and they've developed no suspects. I doubt they ever will," said Longbow.

"I immediately thought of Bill Kaufman," said Siegel.

"I can see why you would think that. He's got plenty of motive, but with the publication of Muller's past life as a possible Nazi, there's no telling how many other former prisoners of war might seek revenge. So let's not go there, Dave. Whoever did it, just expedited Gunther's meeting with God. That all," said Longbow.

On 20 May 1953, President Dwight Eisenhower and the United States National Security Council approved the use of nuclear bombs if North Korea and China did not agree to an Armistice. The threat of using nuclear bombs apparently had its desired effect, because on 27 July 1953, North Korea agreed to the Armistice, and the 38th parallel became a demilitarized zone, with both sides patrolling its border. The armistice ended the conflict, but it did not officially end the Korean War. Hence, in October of that year, The United States and South Korea signed a mutual defense treaty, permitting the United States to establish military bases in South Korea to defend the country against any invasion. The news of this armistice was most appreciated by Louise and Susan, who feared their husbands would be recalled to active duty if the Korean War expanded into a world conflict.

CHAPTER IV

Reconnaissance Flight Over Moscow

It was in the summer season of 1955, when James Longbow and David Siegel, having been promoted to Major, got a chance to train and fly the B-36D Peacemaker, the largest bomber ever built, which could fit a B-29 Superfortress under one of its wings. But Siegel had reservations about spending his annual two weeks of required active duty at Loring Air Force Base in Limestone, Maine. It was the largest airbase of the US Air Force Strategic Air Command, and home of the 42nd Bombardment Wing, and the B-36D Peacemaker.

"Listen, Jim, if we get qualified to fly the B-36D Peacemaker, and there is another was or even a conflict like Korea, we could end up flying combat missions all over again, and I think at that point, Susan would insist I resign my commission and the reserves," said Siegel.

"C'mon, Dave, there's no chance of another war anytime soon.

The B-36 with the letter D, showing it's the fourth prototype with many improvements, was named the Peacemaker, because it deters any enemy from even considering starting a war with the United States. It has six propeller driven engines and four General Electric J-47 jet engines that doubles its power, especially when taking off, climbing to extreme altitudes, and speeding over hostile territory. It has a top speed of 435 miles per hour, and can reach an altitude of over 50,000 feet, which means that enemy fighter aircraft, and even missiles can't reach it. Furthermore, it has a non-stop range of over 12,000 miles, enabling it to drop its bombs over any enemy territory in the world, and return to its airbase in the United States without refueling. Now wouldn't you want to at least learn to fly and experience its performance?" asked Longbow.

"Man, you should be a salesman for Convair, its manufacturer." said Siegel. "Where did you get all of this info?"

"I was talking to Bill Thompson, who's been promoted to Lieutenant Colonel, a couple of days ago, and he said he was going to Loring Air Force Base to receive his training on the B-36D. He said that if you and I were interested, he would arrange for us to spend our next annual two-weeks active duty on TDY at Loring, where we would receive training on the B-36D. Being qualified on the B-36D would certainly improve our position for promotion to Lieutenant Colonel," said Longbow.

"Jesus, Jim, we just got promoted to Major. What are you bucking for, General?" asked Siegel.

"Of course not, Dave. I was just promoting the benefits associated with your training for the B-36, so you would join me as my co-pilot on this exciting adventure, which I wouldn't want to do without my brother-in-arms as my co-pilot," said Longbow.

"Well, when you put it that way, Jim, I guess I can hardly refuse.

I just hope I can persuade Susan that there's no danger involved, and no war in sight," said Siegel.

"Hey! Just mention the benefits of promotion to a supervisory position that will exempt you from combat duty," said Longbow. "That's what I'm going to tell Louise."

"Louise is a sharp gal, Jim. I think she accepts your sales pitch about the security of your job because she loves you, and she knows that's what makes you happy. So she goes along with your adventurous desires, even if it's worrisome," said Siegel.

"Well, maybe you're right. But I haven't disappointed her yet, and I think this is a safe bet," replied Longbow.

"You once called me a 'worry wart' remember. I guess I haven't changed. But you're right, your reasoning that the benefits far outweigh the risks is sound, so you've got yourself a co-pilot on that B-36 Peacemaker," said Siegel.

At home, Longbow and Siegel played down the importance of their forthcoming two-week temporary duty at Loring Air Force base as routine flight training required pursuant to their promotion to Major. Louise and Susan accepted their explanation without a second thought, knowing they'd be home in a fortnight to resume their work at the Curtiss-Wright Corporation as aircraft designers.

Upon their return home to Williamsville, Longbow and Siegel could not contain their enthusiasm about the B-36D Peacemaker, to Louise and Susan, gathered in their backyard with their four children for a mid-afternoon barbeque using Longbow's grill and picnic table.

The children, Gary and Alex, now 9 years old, with Jackie and Rachel, a little over a year younger than their brothers, were all busy fishing from the four-foot wide cement ledge below the stone wall abutting Ellicott Creek, which in the summer season is quite shallow. Louise and Susan were sitting at the picnic table listening to their husbands describing their experience with the fabulous B-36D Peacemaker.

"That bomber has ten engines, can you believe it?" said Longbow as a statement rather than a question, to Louise and Susan.

"Why does it need so many engines?" asked Susan.

"Because of the weight of the bombs it's carrying and the size of the aircraft," replied Siegel.

"The atomic bomb that was dropped on Hiroshima weighed 9700 pounds, whereas the Hydrogen bomb that the B-36D carries, weighs 41,600 pounds and is 700 times more powerful than the atomic bomb. That gives you an idea of the destructive power that the B-36D carries in its belly for delivery anywhere in the world," said Longbow.

"My God! I didn't know the H-Bomb mentioned in the news was that powerful," said Susan. "It could wipe out all of New York City."

"That's right, and that's why we don't anticipate any country wanting to start a war with us," said Siegel.

"That's the plane you guys were trained to fly while at Loring Air Force Base in Maine," said Susan inquiringly.

"Yes, Jim and I flew one of them for certification, and we climbed to 52,000 feet. That's 12,000 feet more than the B-29's altitude ceiling, and the Peacemaker's featherweight model can go even higher," said Seigel.

"Strategic Air Command, which everyone refers to as SAC, has 20 percent of its bombers carrying nuclear weapons in the air at all times, so that in the event of a nuclear attack by another country, those SAC bombers already in the air, can deliver their nuclear bombs on enemy targets in sufficient numbers to destroy the enemy's ability to make war. That's SAC's mission which is well known by our enemies, and a real deterrent against another Pearl Harbor," said Longbow.

"Wow! I hate to pay their fuel bill," said Louise.

"You know, Dave, the B-36D could be used to conduct high altitude surveillance and photography, outside the range of enemy artillery and fighter aircraft," said Longbow.

"I'm sure SAC Headquarters is already thinking of using the Peacemaker for reconnaissance missions," added Siegel.

"You guys sound as if you're planning on flying some of those missions. Are you?" asked Susan.

"Naw! We only have two continuous weeks of active duty per year, plus that one weekend a month, so those missions are flown by active duty personnel, not reservists like us," said Longbow, in a reassuring tone of voice.

"Yeah! But I can detect wishful thinking you were on active duty to fly those Peacemakers," said Louise.

"Well, we can always dream, that's normal, but our interest is in the development of new aircraft design, and flying the B-36D generated much creative thinking that can be applied to commercial aviation in our work at Curtiss-Wright," said Longbow.

"Really, that sounds interesting. I'm sure your Director, Bob Polanski will be happy to hear that," said Louise.

"He's the one who encouraged us to join the Air Force Reserves, for that reason, I'm sure," said Siegel.

A cry of joy and excitement could be heard from Rachel, who had just caught a fish, and now was attempting to reel it in.

"Reel him in slowly, Rachel," said Gary, now standing next to her, "otherwise you'll lose him. That's it, pull him in slowly. I'll get the landing net."

"Oh! He's a beauty," said Rachel, as she pulled the fish close enough for Gary to scoop up into his landing net.

"Oh! Boy, it's my first catch. Is he big enough to keep?" asked Rachel, as she watched Gary remove the hook from the fish.

"I think so, Rachel. I think it's a northern pike. Your Mom will know and she can cook it on the grill," said Gary. "Let's put it in the bag."

"Hey! What did you catch, Rachel?" yelled Jackie, standing with her fishing pole about 20 feet from her.

"I think it's a northern pike, so they're there, Jackie," yelled back Rachel.

About an hour-and-a-half later, the four young fishermen ended their angling, and carrying a bag containing three northern pikes, walked up to their parents sitting at the picnic table.

"We each caught a northern pike, except for Jackie," said Alex, opening the bag for the parents to see.

"Haw! That's too bad, Jackie," said James Longbow. "There'll be other times, sweetheart, so don't fret over it."

"I won't Dad. I'm just glad someone caught some fish," replied Jackie.

"Well, I'll prepare the fish for the three of you to cook on the grill," said Louise, "and you, Jackie, can have a steak, with the rest of us."

"Actually, Missus Longbow, Jackie can have my fish. I much prefer a steak," said Alex Siegel, who fancied Jackie.

"That's very thoughtful and generous of you, Alex, but you caught the fish, therefore you deserve it and must eat it," said Louise.

"Well, it was just a thought, Ma'am," replied Alex.

Louise looked at Susan with a knowing smile of appreciation for their children's discovery of adolescent love, a fact that was also evident from the behavior of Gary towards Rachel.

"You know, Susan, when I see the close relationship between our kids, it's almost a déjà vu of our own lives," said Louise.

"Yes, I noticed. I wouldn't be surprised if it developed into an intense and enduring love story equaling our own," said Susan.

"God! Wouldn't that be something," replied Louise, thoughtfully.

Two weeks before James Longbow and David Siegel were scheduled to report to Hancock Field for their 1956 annual, two-week active duty reserve service, they each received an official letter with Special Orders from the Commanding Officer, 174th Attack Wing, ordering them to report to the 42nd Bombardment Wing, Loring Air Force Base, for duty in fulfillment of their commitment.

Dave Siegel immediately went next door to visit Jim Longbow.

"Did you get these special orders?" asked Siegel.

"Yes, I did, and I wonder what SAC is up to?" said James Longbow.

"I think Bill Thompson talked us into getting qualified for the B-36D Peacemaker so we could then be assigned to fly one of them when SAC needed additional flight crews for its missions," said Longbow.

"Maybe so, Jim, but we're only required to serve two-weeks on active duty each year, so it wouldn't be worth it to use us reservists for a SAC mission," said Siegel.

"That depends on the mission, doesn't it," replied Longbow.

"Good grief, now you've got me thinking of the worst scenarios," said Siegel.

"There you go again, Dave, worrying yourself into a frenzy, before we've even arrived at Loring. You know SAC. They like to play war games all over the globe, and that's probably what they have in mind for us. So relax, buddy. We'll find out soon enough," said Longbow with a reassuring tone that always consoled Siegel, a courageous and patriotic aviator, but mindful of his wife's reaction to any dangerous mission that would threaten his life, which she was repeatedly assured was non-existent for reservists.

Upon arrival at Loring Air Force Base in Limestone, Maine, Longbow and Siegel reported to the commanding officer of the 42nd Bomb Wing for duty as ordered.

"I'm Colonel Gordon Baxter. Welcome aboard, gentlemen."

"Thank you, sir," said Longbow for Siegel and himself.

"You've been chosen for a special mission that does not involve bombing a target. You will be flying the new RB-36D Reconnaissance aircraft equipped with fourteen cameras and eighty T-86 photo flash bombs. This was made possible by replacing the forward bomb bay with a pressurized manned compartment, which includes a small darkroom so the photo technician can develop the film. This required that we add seven more crew members, bringing the total crew to twenty-two. However, the upside to all this is that it allowed an extra 3000 gallon droppable fuel tank, increasing its range and endurance as much as 50 hours, and it also enabled an increase in its altitude ceiling to 58,000 feet," said Baxter.

"What defensive armament did it retain, sir?" asked Longbow.

"The 20 millimeter cannons and the tail turret were retained. Furthermore, it also has electronic counter measures."

"Do we have to decrease our altitude when taking photographs, sir?" asked Siegel.

"Not at all. In fact, it's been shown that at 50,000 feet, the camera can show the identification markings on a golf ball," replied Baxter, with a proud smile.

"The last and obvious question, sir, is the location of the photoshoot target?" asked Longbow.

"The Strategic Air Defense System known as BERKUT, which is designed to defend Moscow against bomber attacks. It has B-200 Radar guided missiles, and possibly V-300 missiles. That's one of the reasons we need this photo-recon mission," said Baxter.

"When are we scheduled to leave, sir?" asked Longbow.

"You will have three days to acquaint yourselves with the RB-36 and its crew, then when you Jim, as the Flight Commander, deem the aircraft and your crew ready, you will alert Combat Operations and be given authorization to proceed on this mission, code named *Operation Pingpong*," said Colonel Baxter, and with no further questions, ended the briefing.

"Well, Dave, let's go meet our crew," said Longbow.

The RB-36 Reconnaissance aircraft, too large with its lengthy wingspan to fit in any hangar, stood on the tarmac in front of hangar number 7. The entire crew was already in place in and around the aircraft when Longbow and Siegel arrived.

"I'm Captain Steve Matlock, your navigator, this is Captain Tom Flattery, our bombardier, and First Lieutenant Bob McCain, your third pilot," he said, shaking his aircraft commander's hand.

"I'm glad to finally meet you and Major Siegel, sir," said Captain Bruce Palmeri. "I'm your senior radar operator, and this is Tech Sergeant Peter Polanski, our radar observer, sir. Lieutenant Tom Brokavich is our flight engineer and Master Sergeant Clive Montblanc is our second flight engineer. Also, Tech Sergeants Adam Pulver and Zachary Scott are our radio operators."

"I'm Lieutenant Robert Calvin, chief gunner, and this is my 20- mm cannon gunnery crew: Tech Sergeants Bill Thornby, George McCabe, Don Messenger, and Sergeant Alvin Sigorski is my turret tail gunner. As you probably know, sir, the sixteen 20-mm cannons were reduced to only five, to make room for the photo-recon equipment."

"Yes, I'm aware of that, Lieutenant. At the altitude we'll be flying, the powers-that-be don't feel we need all that defensive armament," said Longbow.

Captain Charles Copland stepped forward and introduced himself and his five photo-reconnaissance crew members, consisting of Tech Sergeants, Ralph Bottom, Carl Plummer, Sam Fieldman, Vince Sorentino, and Frank Festini.

"We're the reason you're flying this behemoth to Moscow," said Copland. "It's the only aircraft that can carry all of this photographic equipment to its destination and back, hopefully in one piece."

"We'll do our best, if not, you can blame our Intel, which told us that no fighter aircraft or missile can reach us at the altitude we'll be flying," said Longbow.

"What altitude is that?" asked Copland.

"We'll fly past 50,000 feet, more likely at about 56,000 feet," replied Longbow.

"I hope your Intel is right," replied Copland.

"Let me have you attention, men," said Longbow, addressing the entire crew that had assembled on the port side of the aircraft.

"We're going to go right now on a test flight, where you will be able to operate your equipment to insure it's in perfect working order, because we'll only get one shot at the target, flying 435 miles an hour at an altitude of about fifty-six thousand feet. So make sure everything is working properly, and if not, let me or Major Siegel know immediately of the problem."

"When are we scheduled for take-off?" asked Captain Matlock, the navigator.

"As soon as I am satisfied that the aircraft, its equipment and the crew is ready," said Longbow. "Any other questions?"

"Alright, then, let's get the show on the road," concluded Longbow, when no other questions were posed.

Finally, two days later, Operation *Pingpong* was declared a GO, and at 0600 hours the RB-36D Recon Peacemaker took off from the main runway at Loring Air Force Base, Limestone, Maine, destination: Berkut Strategic Air Defense System, Moscow.

The navigator, Captain Matlock, planned the mission's route over the North Pole, descending the globe to Russia towards Moscow.

"This is your skipper," said Longbow, over the intercom. "We're only fifteen minutes to target, so let's be alert and ready to execute Operation *Pingpong*, then we can go home."

Large puffs of smoke suddenly began to appear in front but some distance below the aircraft. However, they soon found the aircraft's altitude.

"Jesus, can we climb any higher?" asked Siegel.

"We're already at 55,000 feet. Their flak has reached our current altitude. Let's see how high this crate will go," said Longbow, slowly climbing to 58,000 feet, when suddenly several missiles hit three of the prop-driven engines on the starboard side and one prop-driven engine caught on fire on the port side, requiring they be shut down and their propellers feathered.

"We're starting to lose altitude, Jim," said Siegel, when suddenly the aircraft took a jolt as a projectile hit the midsection of the fuselage destroying some of the photographic equipment but, luckily not injuring any of the crew.

"We're losing a lot of fuel, Skipper," said Lieutenant Tom Brokavich, the flight engineer. "Some of the damage is too extensive for the self-sealing fuel bladders to handle, sir."

"We're not going to make it home," said Longbow. "Another engine has just failed. We're flying on only two turning and now two burning engines. The fuel loss is too great to sustain, and the chance for explosion is very real."

"I totally agree with you, Jim," said Siegel.

"I agree with you, sir. Will you give the crew the order to bail out?" said Tom Brokavich.

"This is your skipper," said Longbow over the intercom. "Our aircraft is in immediate danger of explosion; therefore I am ordering all crew members to bail out immediately. Captain Matlock, please make sure all crew members bail out immediately, then notify me when it's done. Major Siegel and I will be the last to bail out."

"Lieutenant McCain, we don't need a third pilot, so bail out with the rest of the crew," said Longbow.

"What about me, sir?" asked Brokavich. "Do you need me, or should I bail out with the rest of the crew?"

"No, Tom, you did your job and now it's time for you to bail out. You can use the exit hatch in the forward compartment. See you on terra firma," said Longbow.

Several minutes transpired when one of the two jet engines on the port side started producing white smoke. At that moment, Captain Matlock's voice came on the intercom notifying Longbow that all crew members, except for him, had bailed out from the aft compartment.

"OK Steve, bail out, right now, 'cause Dave and I are going to follow you, and I'm going to pull the demolition handle, giving us only 90 seconds before the aircraft explodes," said Longbow, who then put the aircraft on auto-pilot.

"OK! Dave, let's do it, and remember to wait ten seconds before pulling your rip cord. That will make sure you clear the engines and their 19 foot propellers, and put some distance between you and the aircraft when it explodes," said Longbow.

Siegel bailed out head first from the exit hatch of the forward compartment, followed by Longbow, after he had pulled the demolition handle, both successfully clearing the aircraft with functioning parachutes. As expected, the 90 seconds passed quickly with the explosion of the RB-36 Recon-Peacemaker, disintegrating before their very eyes.

Unknown to Longbow and Siegel who had parachuted several minutes and miles from the crew, Tech Sergeant Peter Polanski, the radar observer, upon bailing out from the rear compartment hatch, got killed when the tip of one of the working propellers severed his head. Furthermore, all of the anti-aircraft artillery from the Berkut Strategic Air Defense System was focused on the RB-36, its only target, filling the sky with a shower of deadly projectiles into which the RB-36 crew members parachuted, with little or no chance for survival.

Longbow and Siegel fortunately bailed out when the aircraft had traveled outside the range of the anti-aircraft artillery. They both landed in proximity to each other in a park next to a school in a town about thirty miles from Moscow. They were quickly surrounded by armed police-men whose numbers convinced Longbow and Siegel to surrender peacefully. They were handcuffed and brought to the local police station where they were searched and confined until the military police arrived and took custody of the prisoners.

While awaiting their transfer to the Soviet military authorities, Longbow and Siegel quietly discussed their perilous situation.

"Well, so much for the credibility of our intelligence service," said Siegel. "I'd like to confront that ass-hole that figured we couldn't be reached by any armament when flying at 50,000 feet."

"Listen, Dave. Right now we must concentrate on what's before us. I expect we'll be individually interrogated by the KGB about our mission, and in particular, the photo-recon equipment we were carrying, which is classified, and the primary reason for the demolition explosives that disinte-grated our aircraft. So, remember, you're only the co-pilot and know nothing about the photo-recon equipment we were carrying. In fact, unless they provide evidence we were carrying that kind of equipment, you should not admit anything and reveal only your name, rank and serial num-ber, in accordance with the Geneva Convention."

"Yeah! Sure, Jim. They'll honor the Geneva Convention.

Let's get real. They'll treat us as combat enemies and we'll be lucky if we ever see our families again," said Siegel.

"C'mon, Dave. Worrying never solved anything. Let's just take one day at a time. Our State Department will surely want to negotiate our release and that of our crew, in exchange for something they want. So don't give up, buddy," said Longbow.

"I'm not giving up, Jim, I'm just stating the facts before us, that's all," replied Dave.

"OK! In the meantime, I wish I could speak Russian. Maybe one of the guards speaks English. I sure could use the bathroom," said Longbow.

Finally, after much verbal manipulation, one of the policemen, who understood some English, escorted Longbow, and then Siegel to the restroom within the station, to their relief. A couple of hours later, four military officers appeared at the police station and took custody of prisoners Longbow and Siegel. They were transported in a weapons-carrier type vehicle to KGB Headquarters in Central Moscow, where they were delivered to two Special Agents of the KGB for interrogation.

Longbow and Siegel were immediately separated and placed in adjoining rooms for debriefing and interrogation. The rooms were windowless. There was a small table with three chairs; one behind the desk, one in front of it and one chair on the side next to the wall.

What was not obvious but expected by Longbow and Siegel, was that the interrogation would be video or at least audio recorded.

Two men dressed in dark suits, white shirts and maroon ties, entered the room. The taller man introduced himself and his colleague.

"I'm Special Agent Mikhail Robokov and this is Special Agent Ivan Rustonovich of the KGB, the Committee for State Security," said Robokov in fluent English.

"I don't understand why we're being interviewed by the KGB. We're officers of the United States Air Force, and as such fall under the purview of military authorities," said Longbow.

"Before I address your question, Major James Longbow, I need to confirm your identity. I have here documents taken from you by the police, consisting of your military identification card, but no other identification. Did they miss anything that would corroborate your identification?" asked Robokov.

"Yes, my dog tags," replied Longbow, removing his metal dog tags from his neck, which he surrendered to Robokov.

"Very good, Major Longbow. Now let me explain the reason for your detention here at KGB Headquarters. Our aviation and forensic experts have reported from the scene of the wreckage of your B-36 bomber, that your aircraft contained no bombs and little armament, but evidence of photographic equipment, which means that your mission was to invade our airspace and conduct external espionage by illegally photographing our Strategic Air Defense System. For your information, Major Longbow, the KGB is responsible for external as well as internal espionage," said Robokov.

"I do appreciate your position, but I don't agree with your conclusions, sir. I wish at this time to exercise my right under the Geneva Convention, limiting further responses to my name, rank and serial number," replied Longbow.

"Major Longbow...you must know that we have the means and the power to extricate all of the information your mind possesses. Therefore, why go through all this unnecessary unpleasantness, when you know we'll eventually get all the information we need and desire," said Robokov.

"You'd only find out that I don't have any of the information you're seeking, because I'm only the pilot who knows nothing about the equipment we might have been carrying. I'm just an airbus driver, and depend on the expertise of my crew for the fulfillment of the mission. That's all I have to say," said Longbow.

"That's a most interesting statement, you just made, Major Longbow, because I have been informed that the bodies of twenty American airmen were found in the vicinity of the crash, many of them identifiable only by their dog tags. How many crew members did you have onboard, Major?" asked Robokov.

"That's all of them," replied Longbow, visibly distressed. "I find it hard to believe they were all killed by anti-aircraft guns or the failure of their chutes."

"Are you suggesting that any of your airmen were deliberately killed by our soldiers while in their parachutes or on the ground?" asked Robokov.

"At this point, without a thorough investigation by an impartial inspector, I have to question the cause of death of my crew," replied Longbow.

"You're entitled to your opinion, Major. Ours is based on the facts found at the scene of the wreckage. This interview is over for now, but we'll meet again, soon," said Robokov, leaving the room with his colleague.

In the adjoining room, a similar interview was conducted with Major David Siegel, who simply exercised his rights under the Geneva Convention, providing only his name, rank and serial number, adamantly refusing to answer any questions. His interview was also terminated, without Siegel learning of the death of his entire crew.

At Loring Air Force Base Headquarters, the mood of the 42nd Bombardment Wing Commander, Brigadier General Howard Taft, and his staff of officers, was somber, as they discussed the loss of the RB-36 Recon Peacemaker and all its crew, except for its pilot and co-pilot.

"The last radio signal we received from the RB-36 indicated they'd been hit by several missiles and anti-aircraft artillery, shutting down several of their engines, at an altitude of 56,000 feet, and were ordered by the Aircraft Commander to bail out. That's the last transmission, sir. However, we did receive a classified message from Intel at the American Embassy in Moscow, that Majors Longbow and Siegel were the only survivors," said Colonel John Islington, Chief of Combat Operations.

"Yes, I know. I thought missiles and ground artillery couldn't reach the RB-36 at altitudes of 50,000 feet," said General Taft. "They were flying at 56,000 feet. What the hell happened to our intelligence?"

"Well, sir, the Soviets must have just recently developed more sophisticated armament that escaped our intelligence gathering," said Lieutenant Colonel Steve Warren, chief, air controller.

"My God! How are we going to explain that to the families of those twenty airmen, and no doubt their congressmen as well as the news media?" said General Taft.

"Right now, sir, I think we need to find out the condition of the two survivors, Major James Longbow and Major David Siegel, currently in their custody," said Colonel Mark Taylor, Deputy Wing Commander. "I also find it hard to believe that all twenty of these airmen died from incoming artillery fire and shrapnel. You would think that at least half of them would have parachuted to safety, perhaps with a broken arm or ankle, but alive as prisoners."

"I agree with you, Mark. We must demand access to the bodies of these airmen, and have them shipped back to the United States for inquest and an autopsy to determine their cause of death," said General Taft.

"We'll have to get the State Department involved, sir," said Lieutenant Colonel Dean Smithers, the Wing Adjutant.

"No doubt, especially since the Soviets have Majors Longbow and Siegel in custody, who they will surely charge with a capital crime against the State, with much international publicity," said General Taft. "What kind of sentence do you think they're facing, Bob?"

"Possibly the death penalty, sir, but I think they'll probably sentence them to life imprisonment at hard labor, to be served somewhere in Siberia, because that punishment is so much more severe, and an effective deterrent," said Lieutenant Colonel Robert Kolenski, the Provost Marshal.

"Well, let's hope the State Department, together with the Central Intelligence Agency, and the Department of Defense can come up with an exchange of prisoners, so we can get these brave men back home," said General Taft.

It was mid-afternoon when Louise Longbow heard the doorbell ring several times. Standing at the entrance door to her two-story house on Creekside Road in Williamsville, New York was a uniformed officer of the United States Air Force.

"I'm Colonel Claude Barclay, Commander of the 174th Attack Wing at Hancock Field Air National Guard Base in Syracuse, New York. Are you Missus Louise Longbow?"

"Yes I am. Would you come in, please," said Louise, opening the door, then leading the Colonel into the dining room overlooking Ellicott Creek, where she invited him to have a seat at the glass covered table.

"I presume your visit has something to do with my husband," said Louise with apprehension.

"Actually, my visit concerns both your husband and Major Siegel, whom I believe from his address, resides next door," replied Colonel Barclay.

"Then maybe I should call his wife Susan to come over," said Louise.

"I believe that would be a good idea, if she is available," replied Colonel Barclay.

Louise left the dining room and called Susan who, upon learning that Colonel Barclay was at Louise's house concerning their husbands, immediately came over.

Colonel Barclay sat at the end of the dining table flanked by Louise and Susan, sitting worriedly about the reason for a visit by a high-ranking Air Force officer.

"As you may know, your husbands were assigned to the 174th Attack Wing at Hancock Field in Syracuse for active reserve duty. When they reported for duty a week ago, they were sent on temporary duty to Loring Air Force Base where they were assigned to fly an RB-36 Reconnaissance aircraft at high altitude to take photographs of a Soviet air defense system near Moscow. Our intelligence assured us that at an altitude of 50,000 feet, no Soviet fighters, missiles and anti-aircraft artillery could reach our RB-36 aircraft. Unfortunately, the Soviets apparently developed a missile capable of reaching invading high altitude aircraft, even at 56,000 feet, which is the altitude our RB-36 aircraft was flying at the time it got hit.

"Oh! My God!" Exclaimed Susan, placing both hands to her face.

"Your husbands are alright, they're safe," said Colonel Barclay, responding quickly to Susan's look and exclamation of despair.

"There were twenty-two airmen aboard the aircraft, and they all were able to bail out of the aircraft, but only your husbands, Major Longbow and Major Siegel, survived the onslaught, according to the Soviet's communique to our State Department. Your husbands are currently being held by the Soviet Security Service, pending negotiations by our governments," said Colonel Barclay.

"So, our husbands are alive and well then," said Susan.

"Yes, according to the Soviet communique," replied Colonel Barclay.

"Could the communique be wrong?" asked Louise.

"I seriously doubt it, because they would have a hard time explaining their death, after they've officially acknowledged their survival and detention," said Colonel Barclay.

"Well, that's good to hear. But I feel so sorry for the families of those twenty airmen that lost their lives," said Louise.

"Yes. At this very moment, we have officers paying official visits to each and every family of the deceased airmen," said Colonel Barclay.

"What do you think our chances are of having our husbands returned to us?" asked Susan.

"That's hard to say, Ma'am. I wouldn't venture a guess at this time, until we've had further communications with the Soviets to learn of their intentions regarding the return of our two aviators. But please rest assured, that I will keep you posted of any progress made, regarding the return of your husbands," said Colonel Barclay, ending his official notification, and accepting a cup of coffee before heading back to Syracuse.

Lieutenant-General Boris Smirnov, the ranking KGB Officer, was having his own meeting at KGB Headquarters located at Lubyanka Square in Moscow with members of the general staff. Included at the meeting were Major-General Grigory Mikhailov, Colonel Feodor Vasiliev, Colonel Aleks Ivanov, Major Igor Lebeden, and Captain Mikhail Robokov the lead investigator who initially interviewed Major Longbow, and privy to Major Siegel's interview by his assistant.

"We've been approached by the United States Department of State to negotiate the return of Major James Longbow and Major David Siegel, in exchange for two of our own agents currently convicted of espionage and incarcerated in a federal prison in the United States," said Lieutenant-General Boris Smirnov. "This is the reason for this meeting, to determine the feasibility of such an exchange, with its advantages and disadvantages."

"Well, I can think of one of our imprisoned agents, namely Colonel Adrian Kolzak, serving a life sentence at Leavenworth Federal Prison, who should be returned to us. I'm sure Oleg Morozov, General of the Army, would be most pleased to see his nephew, Adrian, returned to his family," said Major-General Grigory Mikhailov.

"I must agree with Grigory, that the return of Colonel Kolzak would be a very popular exchange," said Colonel Vasiliev.

"However, who would be a most acceptable candidate for the exchange of the second American pilot?" asked Lieutenant-General Boris Smirnov.

"Actually, sir, I don't think we should exchange the American Aircraft Commander, James Longbow. We should hold him responsible for the actions of his entire crew, and put him on trial for espionage, in full view of the media, as a deterrent to future violations of our airspace. Then we can agree to exchange his co-pilot, Major David Siegel for the return of Colonel Kolzak. I believe this would be our most advantageous course of action," said Colonel Feodor Vasiliev.

"Before we discuss this exchange of prisoners, in what physical condition are the two American pilots? I believe Captain Robokov and his assistant conducted the interrogation of the two pilots, so he can provide us with first-hand information regarding their physical and mental status, and whether they are presentable to the media, which will be present at the trial and also at the exchange of prisoners," said Major Igor Lebeden.

"Actually, sir, my associate, Lieutenant Ivan Rustonovich and I only conducted a preliminary interview of the two American airmen, who would only provide us with their name, rank and military service number. Our intelligence provided us with much information about these two officers. They were merely reserve officers perform-ing their required two-weeks active duty. Apparently, they were selected on this reconnaissance mission because of their prior experience as B-17 and B-29 bomber pilots in the Second World War and the Korean conflict. They were recently trained in the B-36 Bomber, and our agents in the United States have easily acquired all of the particulars regarding that aircraft. So these two reserve pilots have nothing to offer us that we do not already know. Therefore, sir, they are in good physical and mental health and ready for exposure to the media," said Captain Robokov.

"This will also attest to our civilized and humane treatment of hostile invaders, and minimize the fact that twenty of their airmen lost their lives. It will further justify Feodor's recommended course of action. I therefore believe Feodor has made a very good argument for putting the aircraft commander on trial, and exchanging his co-pilot for the return of Colonel Adrian Kolzak," said Lieutenant-General Boris Smirnov. "Anyone disagree with this course of action?"

The six KGB officers looked at each other briefly, then Major-General Grigory Mikhailov, turned to the ranking officer, Boris Smirnov to voice his reply for the group.

"Sir, I'm sure I speak for everyone here, when I submit our approval of Colonel Vasiliev's suggestion, and your endorsement for putting the American aircraft commander on trial, and exchanging his co-pilot for Colonel Adrian Kolzak," said Major-General Grigory Mikhailov.

"Then so be it. I'll pass our decision to the Military Collegium of the Supreme Court of the Soviet Union, for their legal review and approval, prior to notifying the United States Department of State of our decision," said Lieutenant-General Boris Smirnov.

It didn't take more than three days, for the Military Collegium to approve the KGB's decision and plan of action.

The United States Department of State was notified of the decision by the Soviet CPSU Politburo, which generated another meeting. In attendance was the Secretary of State, Marjorie Stanford, Commander of Strategic Air Command, Lieutenant General Clark Beauregard, the Secretary of Defense, Stephen Castleberry, the Director of the Central Intelligence Agency, George Bernard, and the Attorney General Mark Dressler.

"Looks like we're only going to get back Major David Siegel, the co-pilot. They plan on putting the aircraft commander on trial for espionage," said Marjorie Stanford. "There's no mention of the return of the bodies of the twenty airmen who perished."

"I see no problem with the exchange of Colonel Adrian Kolzak, currently imprisoned at Leavenworth for the return of Major David Siegel. However, I believe we should insist on the return of the bodies of the twenty airmen as part of the agreement. I don't think we'd be successful in challenging their authority to put Major James Longbow on trial for espionage," said General Clark Beauregard.

"What's your legal opinion, Mark, on the Soviet's plan to put Commander Longbow on trial for espionage?" asked Marjorie Stanford.

"Well, they've got sufficient evidence from the wreckage of the RB-36 Peacemaker to make a case for external espionage, from a high altitude reconnaissance aircraft. The Soviets want to show the world their military capability and our aggressive behavior towards them. I seriously doubt they would reconsider that decision," replied Mark Dressler, the Attorney General.

"General Beauregard, do you believe that the death of those twenty crewmembers was caused solely by anti-aircraft artillery?" asked Marjorie Stanford.

"No, I do not. I believe many of those airmen were deliberately shot by Soviet Army soldiers with a 'take no prisoners' mentality, as they parachuted or landed. I don't think they'll want us to conduct an autopsy that would reveal the true cause of death of those airmen," said General Clark Beauregard.

"Then our insistence on the return of those twenty deceased crewmen could be a deal breaker in the exchange of prisoners," said Marjorie Stanford.

"It's a real possibility, but we won't know until we make that request. I might add that our request for the return of those dead crewmen should be very strong, because they may want the return of Colonel Kolzak so much more than we know, that they'll yield to our demand for the return of our crewmen," said General Beauregard.

"Alright, then, I believe that the correct course of action is for us to agree to the exchange of Colonel Kolzak for the return of Major Siegel, and the bodies of the twenty deceased crewmen," said Marjorie Stanford. "Is everyone on board?"

"I do have one caveat, Ma'am," said George Bernard, the Director of the CIA. "This exchange should take place at Checkpoint Charlie on the East-West border of Berlin, where we've held previous successful exchanges."

"I agree with George," said General Beauregard. "Checkpoint Charlie is an ideal location for this exchange, and the Soviets have never objected to that location in past exchanges."

"Any other suggestions or recommendations before we adjourn this meeting?" asked Marjorie Stanford.

"I think we've covered all the bases," replied Mark Dressler, the Attorney General, which ended the meeting.

The Soviet CPSU Politburo forwarded the United States Department of State's reply and agreement to the exchange of Colonel Adrian Kolzak for Major Siegel, and the return of the bodies of the twenty crewmen, to the Head of the KGB in Moscow.

Lieutenant-General Boris Smirnov, the ranking KGB Officer, convened a meeting at KGB Headquarters in Moscow. In attendance were Major General Grigory Mikhailov, Colonel Feodor Vasiliev, Colonel Alek Ivanov, and Major Igor Lebeden.

"The Americans agreed to the exchange of Colonel Adrian Kolzak for the return of Major Siegel, and also the return of the twenty dead airmen. There is no mention or objections to the trial of Major Longbow, which surprises me," said General Smirnov.

"I think they realize the futility of objecting to our prosecution of Major Longbow for espionage, so they're concentrating on the return of Major Siegel, and of course, the return of the dead airmen," said General Mickhailov.

"I see a definite problem with the return of those dead airmen.

We all know that many of them were killed by some of our overzealous soldiers, which is bound to be discovered in an autopsy," said Colonel Vasiliev.

"I wouldn't worry about that, Feodor, our coroner's office has assured me that they'll take care of that problem. The Americans want the exchange to take place at Checkpoint Charlie, which we have used in the past, so I don't see any problem with that location. Do any of you?" asked General Smirnov.

"No, actually that location will facilitate the exchange," replied Colonel Ivanov.

"Good, then I'll notify the US State Department of our intention to ratify the agreement and set a date for the exchange," said General Smirnov.

The date and time for the exchange was set for the eleventh of September 1956, at 1300 hours.

The weather was mild but cloudy with threatening rain on that fateful day, as several US Army vehicles consisting of trucks, weapons carriers and covered jeeps, were assembled behind and on the sides of the prefabricated wooden shack bearing a sign 'US Army Checkpoint' above it. The shack, situated in the center of the road dividing the entrance and exit lanes, was fronted by a pile of sandbags five feet high, as a protective measure for the Military Police guarding the checkpoint.

A hundred yards east of Checkpoint Charlie, stood the East German checkpoint with guard towers, cement barriers and a shed used to search departing vehicles with heat scanners for hidden fugitives. The area was busy with personnel and vehicles, and some high ranking Soviet officials were in attendance to execute the pre-arranged exchange of prisoners and dead crewmen. Two Soviet Army officers were using binoculars to observe the activities taking place at Checkpoint Charlie, with fifteen minutes to spare before the official exchange was to take place at 1300 hours.

Colonel Adrian Kolzak, handcuffed and sitting in back of a jeep next to an armed Military Policeman, with several military policemen standing around the jeep, waited for Colonel Ralph Bellamy, the Provost Marshal, to take command of the exchange.

Colonel Bellamy, a tall man with an athletic build that commanded authority and respect, got into the passenger side of the jeep and ordered his driver to proceed to the white line halfway between Checkpoint Charlie and the

East German Checkpoint where the official exchange was to take place. The jeep was followed by two Army trucks for the transport of the dead airmen. As they stood at the while line, Colonel Bellamy observed a black sedan with a truck behind it, slowly approach them and stop. The front passenger of the sedan got out and opened the rear door of the sedan. Major David Siegel, dressed in his flight suit, climbed out of the sedan, still wearing handcuffs. The KGB agent that had been sitting next to him in the sedan, got out and stood by Siegel while the other agent held Siegel by the arm, waiting for the Americans to show themselves with Colonel Kolzak.

"Alright, Lieutenant, bring Colonel Kolzak out of the jeep where the Soviets can see him," said Colonel Bellamy, also exiting the jeep.

The three men standing behind the white line on the American side stood vis-à-vis the three men standing on the other side of the white line on the East German side, measuring each other in silence.

"I'm Colonel Bellamy, the Provost Marshal, and I'm ready to exchange Colonel Kolzak standing next to me for Major David Siegel, who see is standing next to you, sir."

"I'm Colonel Alek Ivanov. If you will remove Colonel Kolzak's handcuffs, we'll remove Major Siegel's handcuffs, and then make the exchange."

"Excuse me, Colonel Ivanov, but I don't see the coffins of the twenty dead airmen you're supposed to return as part of this exchange," said Colonel Bellamy.

"They are in the vehicle behind me, Colonel, and ready for transfer to your vehicle," replied Colonel Ivanov.

"May I see them, Colonel, before we make the exchange," asked Colonel Bellamy.

"Yes, you may Colonel. If you'll step behind this truck you will see two wooden crates containing the remains of the twenty airmen," replied Colonel Ivanov.

Colonel Bellamy looked at the two crates and wondered how the bodies of twenty airmen could fit into two wooden crates, then realized the possibility they may have been individually or mass cremated.

"Exactly how have you reduced the remains of our twenty airmen, Colonel?" asked Colonel Bellamy.

"We have cremated each airman, and placed their ashes in individual bronze vase-shaped urns, with their dog tags attached to the neck of the urns, to identify them. The bodies of most of these airmen were so badly damaged that it became necessary to use cremation, which is widely used in the United States, as the best and most manageable way to return their remains. I hope you will accept their remains with our deepest condolences," said Colonel Ivanov.

"Yes, of course. Can my men open the crates to verify their contents, Colonel?" asked Colonel Bellamy.

"I can have one of my men do that for you, Colonel," said Ivanov, who ordered two of the soldiers who had driven the truck to unload the two crates and open the top of each one.

Colonel Bellamy, counted the top of each bronze urns, and satisfied with the count, told Colonel Ivanov he could close the crates.

"Alright, Colonel Ivanov. Can we make the exchange now, by removing the handcuffs of each man," said Colonel Bellamy.

The cuffs removed, each man was released and walked across the white line into his country. The two crates of bronze vase-shaped urns were loaded onto one of the US Army trucks, and an American flag was secured over each one of the crates, in a show of respect and honor for their service.

Major Siegel, sat in back of the jeep next to the Lieutenant, with Colonel Bellamy sitting in the front passenger seat.

"How do you feel, Major?" asked Bellamy.

"A lot better, now that I'm out of Soviet hands and with Americans," replied Siegel.

"I know you must be tired, and you'll be asked a lot of questions at Headquarters, where they're waiting for your arrival. So, I won't pester you with questions, although I'm sure you have a lot to tell," said Colonel Bellamy.

At Army Headquarters, Major David Siegel, was escorted to a briefing room, where he was greeted by several high ranking military officers, from the Army and Air Force, plus a Special Agent of the Office of Special Investigations (OSI) and also an agent of the Central Intelligence Agency (CIA).

"Welcome back, Major Siegel. You have our deepest sympathy for the loss of your crew, and we intend to do everything possible to gain your aircraft commander's freedom," said Major General Thomas McGuire, Deputy Commander, Strategic Air Command (SAC). "We urgently need to know what happened during your flight over Moscow and the resulting loss of twenty crewmembers.

"We were flying at an altitude of 56,000 feet over our reconnaissance target, the Berkut Strategic Air Defense System, when we were hit by several missiles that crippled four of our prop engines, causing a loss of altitude that put us in range of their anti-aircraft artillery. We suffered no crew casualties on board the aircraft, not until they bailed out. Frankly, I was surprised to learn so many of our crewmembers had lost their lives. The KGB interrogated me and I'm sure Jim Longbow, but I only gave them my name, rank and serial number, and they seemed satisfied with that information, because they terminated the interview and that was the only interview I was subjected to," said Siegel.

"Can you explain why you and Major Longbow escaped injury?" asked one of the officers.

"We were the last ones to bail out, and Jim Longbow wanted to put some distance between the crew that had parachuted and the aircraft he was about to blow up. He had only 90 seconds from the time he pulled the demolition ring and the explosion of the aircraft, so we both got out of the aircraft real fast after he pulled the ring. We landed in a field close to a police station where we were incarcerated, then turned over to the KGB. Having been initially captured and incarcerated by the civilian police, made it impossible for the KGB to later claim our demise," said Siegel.

"Why do you think the Soviets released you, but decided to prosecute Major Longbow?" asked General McGuire.

"I don't know, sir. I can only guess, that as the aircraft commander, they would have a better chance to convict him, than his crew who took orders from him," replied Siegel.

"Very well, Major Siegel. I know you must be tired and looking forward to some rest and recuperation, before flying home to Buffalo. Thank you for your service, Major. Have a safe flight home," said General McGuire, dismissing Major Siegel, but not the committee.

"Is there anyone here who believes all of these crewmembers lost their lives from anti-aircraft fire?" asked General McGuire. "I didn't think so," said McGuire, not receiving any reply.

"The soviets were very clever in hiding the cremation of those crew members until the final hour when the exchange took place at Checkpoint Charlie. There's no way an autopsy can now be performed on the ashes of those airmen. They got away with murder," said General McGuire, and everyone agreed.

Louise Longbow and Susan Siegel received telephone calls minutes from each other, from Colonel Barclay and his deputy, Lieutenant Colonel Tom Levin.

"Missus Longbow. I've just been notified by the Department of State that the Soviets have decided to prosecute your husband for espionage. They have, however, agreed to return Major David Siegel in exchange for a convicted Soviet spy currently incarcerated at Leavenworth Penitentiary, and also to return the bodies of the twenty deceased crewmembers," said Colonel Barclay.

"Is there any chance my husband will be exonerated?" asked Louise, feeling a pit in her stomach.

"To be very frank with you, Missus Longbow, your husband's chances of being exonerated are very slim," replied Colonel Barclay.

"If my husband is found guilty, what could be the sentence?" asked Louise.

"That's hard to say. Please remember that politics always enter into these trials, and the Department of State will be very active in getting the Soviets to ameliorate and reduce the severity of any sentence. But before you form any opinions regarding the fate of your husband, Missus Longbow, I strongly suggest you wait until all the facts are known and the information is verified," said Colonel Barclay.

"I never thought something like this could ever happen to my husband, now that we're not involved in any war. My God, why is this happening?" asked Louise rhetorically.

"I am deeply sorry, Missus Longbow. You have my solemn promise that I will notify you immediately of any news concerning your husband," said Colonel Barclay, who wished a miracle would happen to free Jim Longbow, whom he admired and respected.

Susan Siegel was elated over the news from Lieutenant Colonel Tom Levin, that her husband was in the process of being exchanged for a convicted Soviet spy. However, the fact that her husband would be returned to her was somewhat dampened by the news that her neighbor and best friend's husband, Jim Longbow, would be prosecuted and possibly never return. She called Louise, and during the exchange of information, Susan sensed that her friend was feeling depressed over the thought that her husband might never be returned to her, and expressed her sincere sympathy.

"Listen, Louise, remember what happened when the B-17 Bomber, Jim and Dave were flying over Germany, was shot down, and everyone thought they'd died in the explosion of the aircraft. I remained faithfully hopeful of their return, but you gave up and married Mark Palmer, now deceased, God bless his soul, only to regret it, when both Jim and Dave returned from being prisoners of war. Well, don't make that same mistake again, Louise. Don't ever give up hope. Jim is a most resourceful man, and I'm sure he'll find a way to return home, especially now that he has a wonderful family," said Susan.

"God, I can't believe our role reversal. You're now preaching to me about hope and having a positive attitude," said Louise. "But you're right, and when you're right,

I don't mind admitting it. Thanks for being such a loyal and dependable friend, Susan."

The Niagara Falls Air Base was not crowded that Monday morning, as Susan Siegel, accompanied by David Siegel's parents, Simon and Rebecca, were sitting in the reception room whose large window overlooked the vast runway. They were awaiting the arrival of Major David Siegel, scheduled to land at 1045 hours from McGuire Air Force Base, New Jersey, where he had arrived the evening before from Berlin, Germany.

"What time is it, Dad?" asked Susan.

"It's now 10:30 Susan. Don't worry, he'll be here, maybe a bit late, but he'll be here," replied her father.

"I'm just so anxious to see him, Dad. I didn't want Alex and Rachel to miss school, so I told them about his homecoming, and they'd see him when they got back from school, and they were so excited," said Susan.

"I'm sure they were not worried about his return. Kids are natural optimists, so you did right in not interrupting their school attendance," said her father.

"Besides, kids are impatient. They'd be a handful waiting for his arrival," said her mother.

"I think his plane is landing," said Simon Siegel. "He'll be arriving through the passenger exit over there."

Apparently the aircraft was not carrying many passengers, because there were only a few people waiting near the passenger exit beside the Siegel family.

Several minutes passed, then a few airmen in uniform appeared at the exit, and were greeted by relatives and friends, then finally, Major Siegel appeared, still dressed in his flight suit, and upon seeing Susan, dropped his AWOL bag and hugged and kissed her, oblivious to the presence of his parents, until they got close to him, and his mother got his attention. David then embraced his mother, and then his father welcoming him home. They all left the terminal, and David got into Susan's car, while his parents got into their car to follow Susan and David to their residence in Williamsville, where they could all enjoy their reunion with David together.

As soon as they arrived at David and Susan's residence, Louise Longbow, residing next door, came over to greet David, and join the family to learn first-hand from David about the flight and her husband James' condition.

Louise was greeted by David like a long-lost sister, with whom he had known and shared many exciting experiences.

"Well, I must say, Dave, you don't look any of the worst for wear, considering what you've been through," said Louise looking at him admiringly. "It's so nice to have you back. I just wish James had accompanied you."

"I know, Louise. Jim couldn't make it, due to unforeseen circumstances, but I'm sure he'll find a way to make it back. So don't worry, the Department of State and the Department of Defense are doing everything they can to obtain his release," said David apologetically.

"God, I hope so, Dave," replied Louise with a worried look on her face, which elicited sincere sympathy from everyone present.

"Why don't you all make yourselves comfortable, while I make some coffee and serve some apple strudel," said Susan.

"Please excuse me, while I go upstairs and get out of this flight suit and into some civies. I won't be long," said David.

They all gathered around the rectangular, mahogany dining table overlooking the back yard and Ellicott Creek, affording them a beautiful and tranquil view of nature.

"This view of your backyard is worth the price of this house, Susan," said her mother.

"Yes, I agree, and that's why Jim and I chose this area to build our houses, next door to each other, and we've never regretted it," said David.

"And the kids just love it. They go fishing, and now that we got them a tandem kayak, we can't keep them in the house to do their chores," said Susan.

"Tell me about it. I've got the same problem with Gary and Jackie, but it's not really a problem. At least I know where they are, and they just love this area, not to mention that Jackie has a crush on Alex," said Louise with a smile of approval.

"Funny you should say that, Louise, 'cause I noticed the same affliction between my daughter Rachel and your son Gary," said Susan, with a reciprocal grin.

"Tell us, Dave, what happened on that flight over the Soviet Union?" asked Simon, knowing Louise was dying to ask that question, but was afraid to initiate the conversation.

"Well, without revealing classified information, I'll be glad to tell you that no one got injured while onboard the aircraft. It was only after the crew, there were twenty of them, parachuted from the aircraft that they ran into anti-aircraft artillery and other projectiles that ended their lives. Jim and I waited until they had all bailed out, then Jim pulled a demolition ring which gave us only 90 seconds to bail out before the plane exploded, and we bailed out far from the crew and the anti-aircraft artillery where we landed in a field in back of a Soviet police station. Of course we were arrested and then turned over to the Soviet Secret Police. We later learned that none of the crew survived the jump from the aircraft," said David, whose solemn tone of voice reflected his grief.

"Why did you have to explode the aircraft?" asked his mother.

"Because some of the equipment on board is classified and we didn't want the Soviets to have access to its technology," replied David.

"I guess that makes sense," said Simon.

"So what happened after you were turned over to the Secret Police?" asked Susan.

"The Soviet Secret Police is known as the KGB, and they interrogated me and Jim separately, but I gave them only my name, rank and serial number, in accordance with the

Geneva Convention, and they accepted it without the use or threat of harsh interrogation methods, and ended the interview," said David.

"Did you get a chance to see or talk to Jim after you were interrogated?" asked Louise.

"No, I never saw Jim, again. Not since they separated us, just before the interrogation," said David.

"So how do you know if he's alright?" asked Louise.

"I know he's OK, because they're obviously holding him for a public trial, with the news media in attendance, to show the world the aggressive invasion of their country's air space by the United States. So they'll make sure he's well fed and well dressed for his trial," said David.

"What are his chances for acquittal?" asked Simon.

"It's hard to say, Dad, because of the politics involved. You never know with the Russians. This trial could be just a maneuver for better terms in negotiating another deal between the Soviet Union and the United States," said David, not wanting to give Louise, attentively listening, the impression her husband's fate was doomed, which he secretly suspected.

"I would highly recommend, Louise, that you give Gary and Jackie, hopeful news that Jim will eventually return home, safe and sound, but it may take a while because of the politics involved between our two countries," said David.

"In the meantime, let us hope our prayers will be answered," said Susan, with everyone agreeing.

CHAPTER V

Escape from KGB Headquarters, Moscow

At the KGB Headquarters in Lubyanka Square, Moscow, where Major James Longbow was being held in a solitary cell on the seventh floor of the building, he was suddenly moved to a cell occupied by another detainee to make room for a high-profile prisoner.

James Longbow, still dressed in his flight suit bearing his rank of Major on his shoulders, wings over his breast pocket, and the American flag sewed on the right shoulder of his flight suit, entered the cell containing an upper and lower bunk on each side of the cell. Standing in between them, was a dark-haired man with an athletic build, perhaps in his late twenties or thirty, wearing the full-dress uniform of an officer of the Soviet Air Force, with the rank of Major, bearing two rows of colorful ribbons attesting to his courage and exploits as an aviator.

"Welcome to our humble abode, Major," said the Soviet Officer.

"Thank you. I'm Major James Longbow. I'm glad you speak English, because I do not speak Russian."

"In these times of communication technology, learning English has become a necessity. I am Major Fedor Popov, 9th Fighter Aviation Division, Kubinka Air Base, located five kilometers from Moscow."

"Why are you, a Major in the Soviet Air Force, sharing a cell with me, an officer of the United States Air Force awaiting trial?" asked Longbow, curious as to the reason for revealing so much information about himself. Longbow had heard of Nazi agents placed in cells with American prisoners to gain intelligence information, and Popov could be a KGB agent with the same intentions.

"I heard about your failed reconnaissance flight over our Strategic Air Defense System. The news travels fast within the Soviet military. I understand you lost all but one of your crew members, and I'm sorry for that, Major, but your intelligence should have known about our V-300 and V400 missiles' capability. Now you're going to stand trial for espionage, and I predict that you will be sentenced to life imprisonment in Siberia where you will surely die," said Major Popov.

"What do you mean, I lost all but one of my crew members?" asked Longbow.

"Except for your co-pilot, you lost all of your crew members. Haven't they told you that?" asked Popov.

"I see, you included my co-pilot as one of my crew members," said Longbow.

"However, I feel that you were destined to cross paths with me, Major Longbow," said Popov.

"Really, why's that?" asked Longbow.

"Please allow me to tell you why I am being detained here in this cell, and then you will know why fate has brought you into this cell," said Popov.

Longbow moved to the bunk that was unoccupied, and sat down facing Popov sitting in the bunk on the opposite side of the aisle.

"I was engaged to a beautiful woman named Nastasia Bolshov. We grew up together and were planning on getting married, when my superior officer, Colonel Dimitri Volkow, saw her with me at the annual Officers Ball. He became seriously interested in her, even though he was married. He had me transferred to Yakusk Air Base, 280 miles south of the Arctic Circle, and 5000 miles from Moscow, preventing me from seeing Nastasia for several months, while he pursued her, until one day, when he managed to get her alone, he raped her. She was afraid to tell anyone except her mother, for fear of reprisals, and as a damaged woman, I would desert her. The stress became too much and she committed suicide. When I returned to Kubinka Air Base and learned of her suicide, I spoke with her mother and she revealed to me that her daughter had been raped by Colonel Volkov, and the shame brought her to suicide. At that moment, I became so enraged, that I drove to Division Headquarters, where I found Colonel Volkov in his office, and attacked him with all the strength and rage within me, until he collapsed to the floor, and I was subdued by fellow officers. I was arrested and charged with the attempted murder of a superior officer, and scheduled for General Court Martial, where I expect to end up in the same place as you in Siberia."

"That's quite a story, Major. I can understand your fury, and I empathize with your actions, because I probably would have done the same, under the circumstances," said Longbow.

"So now do you see the dynamics of our meeting at this time in this cell. I believe in fate, and I now have a proposition for you that you cannot refuse, if you want your freedom," said Popov.

"I suppose you have an escape plan," said Longbow with aroused curiosity.

"Yes I do, and in order for it to be successful, I need your assistance and cooperation," replied Popov.

"You've got my attention, let's hear it," said Longbow.

"First of all, my lawyer is also my cousin Maxim. My best friend and co-pilot Vigor Sokolov, and several close friends in the 9th Fighter Aviation Division, are willing to help me in the event I wish to escape. The only logical way to flee Russia is to steal an aircraft, a Yakolev Yak-25, radar equipped, two-seater fighter aircraft, with external fuel tanks to give us the range we need to fly to England. This would give us a range of 1677 miles. The flight distance from Moscow to London, England is 1558 miles, giving us a fuel safety net of 119 miles. Now, it's a well-known fact that the United States Air Force has taken over several RAF Stations in England since the Second World War, and they're still there fully operational, with an estimated 40,000 Air Force personnel on active duty on those air bases. With you on board as a United States field grade officer and aviator, we should have no problem entering English air space, and landing on one of the United States air bases in England," said Popov.

"I see you've done your homework, but you could have made your escape without me, and radioed ahead to the nearest air field in England that you were seeking asylum as a defector," said Longbow.

"That may be true, but not a sure thing. They may not trust me and deny me entry, or worse, shoot me down. But the real reason you're needed in this escape plan, is because I need your sponsorship into the United States as an American citizen with a new identity that will prevent the KGB from finding me after I've escaped," said Popov.

"Now things are a lot clearer, thank you. I hope you realize that the CIA and the Department of Defense are going to take a good look at you, and possibly have you submit to a polygraph test to confirm your motive for seeking asylum," said Longbow.

"Yes, I realize that. They'll want to make sure I'm not a KGB operative or a spy. I'll submit to any test they wish to give me. I have no problem with that. So do I have a partner, Major Longbow, and will you sponsor me for citizenship in the United States?" asked Popov.

"My answer is yes, and I would appreciate it, if we would address each other by our first names, if you don't mind," said Longbow.

"OK, Jim, and my first name is Fedor," replied Popov.

"So how do you plan on getting us out of here, and into that Yak-25 aircraft?" asked Longbow.

"Money talks, especially in the Soviet Union. We've talked this over several times, me and my cousin Maxim, about my escape, and as an incentive to help me, I gave him my house, and everything in my bank account, which is substantial, because I can't take it with me where I'm going. With my conviction a certainty, that was my only option. Also, I won't need it, once in the United States. Let's face it, once my escape is discovered, all of my property and holdings will be seized by the government. So Maxim now has the resources to help us escape, and I'm sure he'll use some of it to bribe those who guard us, and also some of the ground crew at Kubinka Air Base, where several Yak-25 fighter aircraft are kept in a ready configuration for instant takeoff in case of alert of hostile entry. Vigor will make sure the auxiliary fuel tanks are installed on the aircraft he'll have ready for us to use," said Popov.

"What about all those radar guided missile stations situated throughout the Soviet Union, and particularly within our flight path? What's the altitude ceiling of the Yak-25?" asked Longbow.

"The altitude ceiling of the Yak-25 is 39, 370 feet, and accessible to the new V-300 and V-400 missiles. But, I happen to know their location and will avoid them, that's all," replied Popov.

"That's reassuring. I might as well tell you, that during the Second World War, I flew B-17 bombers from RAF

Station Chelveston, located in the Midlands of England, and know the station, its runway and landing strips quite well. Although It's been several years since I've been at Chelveston Air Base, I'm still familiar with their general procedures for landing aircraft and the control tower's lexicon. So once in proximity to the coast of England, I should begin to transmit our request for entry into their airspace and landing at RAF Station Chelveston. I will cite my identity and status as a US Air Force pilot, having escaped from a Soviet prison in Moscow. I'm sure they'll ask me certain personal questions to establish my identity, and then we'll receive clearance to land at one of their airstrips. By the way, I have flown jet fighter aircraft in the Reserves for training to satisfy my curiosity, but never in action," said Longbow.

"That's almost too good to be true. Everything seems to fit so perfectly. Now I know fate sent you here. There can be no other explanation. I will be forever indebted to you, my friend. I am due for a visit from Maxim tomorrow morning. I must get him to start things immediately. We have no time to lose, before we go to trial. Luckily the judicial system here is very slow moving, sometimes several months before we are even formally charged," said Popov.

"let's hope the Soviet judicial system remains slow, 'cause I can't wait to get out of here," said Longbow.

The following day, after Popov met with his cousin, he was returned to his cell where he apprised Longbow of the results of his meeting with Maxim.

"The plan is this, Jim," said Popov. "First of all, the Yak-25 with the extra fuel tanks will be parked some distance from the other aircraft, and ready for us to board and takeoff. But it must be done at night when the visibility is limited. In the Control Tower, the controller on duty will be someone whom Maxim took care of. When clearing for takeoff, He will be advised that I'm on a routine night training flight, so he will later be covered when queried about the flight. Maxim is sure he can get the aircraft ready for us in three days' time. He will then have to coordinate our escape from here with the time of our flight departure, so we can go directly from here to the Air Base where our aircraft will be waiting for us to takeoff. The KGB guard is relieved each day at 2000 hours by his night replacement. We'll have someone, dressed as a guard, be that replacement, while the real guard will be temporarily delayed, long enough for us to takeoff and be gone for at least three hours. The flight time from here to England is about three and a half hours. Unless there's a change in plans, we'll be leaving this place shortly after 2000 hours this coming Saturday," said Popov.

"Man, you don't waste any time, do you," said Longbow.

"Hey! Not when my life depends on it. Anyway, you've never flown on a Yak-25, so basically, you'll be in the rear seat, while I'll be seated in the tandem seat in front of you. Your position is usually manned by the radar intercept operator, who also can assist the pilot in guiding the aircraft. We'll also have dual access to the radio and communications system. Therefore, should anything happen to disable me, you'll be able to bring the aircraft to its destination. The Yak-25 is not much different in operation from other jet fighter aircraft. I'll familiarize you with the instrument panel and controls, once we're in the air," said Popov.

"Partner, when we land in England, this time I'm going to kiss the ground," said Longbow, with a grin that elicited a similar joyful grin from Popov.

Saturday evening arrived when Maxim and the imposter guard, who unlocked the cell, escorted Popov and Longbow downstairs to a waiting car, the imposter guard remaining there for appearances, while Maxim and his driver brought Popov and Longbow to the Kubinka Air Base. They entered the main gate showing false identification, then drove to the east end of the terminal where they parked.

"You know this installation better than I do, Fedor," said Maxim. "Your aircraft is parked in front of hangar number A-4 which is just around the corner. You'll recognize it because it's the only one with auxiliary fuel tanks. It's ready to go, cousin, so good luck." Then turning to Longbow, "Sir, your arrival was a Godsend. Take good care of my cousin, he's my favorite relative," shaking his hand with vigor.

"That I will, Maxim, and don't worry, we'll make a yank out of him yet," replied Longbow, with his disarming smile.

Popov gave Maxim a warm hug and a handshake with a heavy heart, knowing they'd never see each other again.

Popov was the first to climb into the front seat, followed by Longbow in the rear seat. While Popov was checking everything from the instrument panel, Longbow was familiarizing himself with the controls and the instrument panel, written in Russian. He fastened his seat belt, and put on the headphones, waiting for Popov to test its transmission. Suddenly, Longbow heard the roar of the two jet engines warming up, then the voice of Popov.

"Jim, can you hear me?" asked Popov.

"Yes, loud and clear," replied Longbow.

"OK! Now get off the radio, until we get into the air, and at least a half hour has gone by, so you don't mistakenly say something in English for the Control Tower to hear. When we get out of range, I'll go to a limited frequency so we can talk. So hang on, here we go," said Popov.

Popov, got clearance from the Control Tower, as expected, and climbed rapidly to a high altitude where he acted as both pilot and navigator, following a previously mapped route that avoided radar-guided missile sites, at full speed ahead. After forty-five minutes had transpired, Popov finally broke his silence and called Longbow.

"We're on our way, and so far, I hear no alert regarding our flight, which is good, and I hope it stays that way until we have crossed the English Channel," said Popov.

"That's very reassuring, Fedor. Can you now clue me in on some of the instrument gauges," said Longbow.

"Sure, be glad to," replied Popov, who then familiarized Longbow with all of the instruments and controls, including the lever for the ejection seat, which hopefully, they would not have to use.

After three hours in flight without interference, Popov called Longbow.

"We're approaching Amsterdam, Holland and facing the English Channel and the East Coast of England, so start sending your radio message to RAF Station Chelveston, requesting clearance to land. You know the drill," said Popov.

"Yeah! I guess we're not going to see the Cliffs of Dover," replied Longbow, who then started calling the Control Tower at RAF Station Chelveston.

"Please repeat your identification, you're transmission is weak and garbled," said the Controller from Chelveston.

"This is Major James Longbow of the United States Air Force, flying a Yak-25 jet fighter aircraft with Major Fedor Popov. We've escaped from KGB Headquarters, Moscow and request permission to land. I was flying a RB-36 Recon Peacemaker over Moscow with Major David Siegel and 20 crewmembers, and we were shot down with only two survivors. Myself and Major Siegel. Contact SAC Headquarters for verification, but be advised that we are very low on fuel and need to land as soon as possible. Please advise," said Longbow.

"We have you on our radar over the Channel. Please wait for verification," replied the Controller.

A few minutes passed which seemed like an eternity.

"Our fuel is running low, Jim. You'd better call them again and tell them we can't wait much longer," said Popov.

At that moment, the radio came on again from RAF Chelveston.

"This is the Controller at RAF Chelveston. Major Longbow, we've received confirmation and you're cleared to land on runway A-5, sir. Then proceed to Area B where you will be met by security,"

"Roger. Thank you," replied Longbow.

"You want to land this aircraft, Jim, since you're familiar with their runways, or shall I?" asked Popov.

"I'm familiar with the runways, Fedor, but not landing this aircraft, so you be my guest, and land this baby on freedom alley," said Longbow.

The landing was perfect, and Popov taxied the aircraft to Area B where several vehicles were parked, some with flashing red lights on their rooftops, apparently military security.

Upon exiting from the Yak-25 Jet Aircraft, Popov and Longbow were met by several field grade Air Force officers, backed up with security guards armed with assault rifles. In order to avoid confusion as to which of the two airmen was the United States aviator, Longbow moved forward and introduced himself to the Colonel leading the group.

"I'm Major James Longbow, United Air Force, and this is Major Fedor Popov, of the Soviet Air Force who assisted me in my escape from KGB Headquarters in Moscow. He is officially defecting, and I am personally sponsoring him for immigration to the United States."

"Welcome back, Major Longbow. I'm Colonel John Savarin, the Base Commander, and welcome to the United States, Major Popov. Your assistance in Major Longbow's escape is most sincerely appreciated by Strategic Air Command and the United States Air Force."

"It is my sincere pleasure to be here, sir," said Popov.

"We've arranged for a short briefing inside the terminal, then your lodgings for the night. Tomorrow will provide more time to go into details surrounding your escape and other related information," said Colonel Savarin.

"Colonel Savarin....may I have a moment with you, sir?" asked Longbow, with Popov standing next to him.

"Yes, what is it, Major?" said Colonel Savarin.

"I don't think anyone should be allowed to take photographs of Major Popov, which could end up in the news media, jeopardizing the anonymity of Major Popov's new identity," said Longbow.

"That's a good point. I'll make sure he's not photographed and his identity remains anonymous," replied Colonel Savarin.

"I also think it's important to remove those two auxiliary fuel tanks from the Yak-25, and either destroy or store them, so that in the event the aircraft is returned to the Soviets, they won't know Popov got help from the ground crew at Kubinka Air Base," said Longbow.

"Yes, I totally agree. You never know when we may need their assistance again," replied Colonel Savarin.

Longbow turned his attention to Popov. "You should wear your sunglasses, Fedor, and maybe get a hat to hide your identity," said Longbow with a smile that Popov returned with gratitude for Longbow's obvious effort to protect him.

The following day being a Sunday, was not a convenient day for holding a detailed briefing, but the high level interest in Major Longbow's escape, and the role played by Major Popov, required immediate attention, and a swift report to Lieutenant General Clark Beauregard, Commander of Strategic Air Command, Stephen Castleberry, the Secretary of Defense, and Marjorie Stanford, the Secretary of State. At the conclusion of the meeting, it was agreed by Colonel John Savarin and his colleagues that Major Fedor Popov appeared to be a genuine defector, and the fact that Major Longbow supported that opinion and intended to sponsor him for immigration with a new identity as a United States citizen, effectively sealed that judgement.

Longbow wished Fedor Popov farewell with a warm handshake, then parted with a few words that both would remember for the rest of their lives.

"We'll never see each other again, Fedor, but the memory of you will remain emblazoned in my mind forever, my friend. God Bless you," said Longbow, who then turned and walked towards the exit with Popov's eyes focused on this man who had changed his life.

It was just after dinner that Sunday, when the telephone in the Longbow household in Williamsville, New York rang at least five times before Gary answered it.

"Mom, It's for you. It's Colonel Barclay," yelled Gary.

Louise ran down the stairs and picked up the telephone.

"This is Missus Longbow."

"Louise Longbow...this is Colonel Barclay. We met a few weeks ago. I have some terrific news for you, Missus Longbow. Your husband James managed to escape in a fighter aircraft with a defecting Russian pilot, and they landed yesterday at RAF Station Chelveston, England. He will be leaving Chelveston tomorrow and will land at McGuire Air Force Base, New Jersey later tomorrow evening, and hopefully will get a connecting flight to Niagara Falls Air Force Base, either tomorrow evening or else the next day. I will let you know when he is expected to arrive at Niagara Falls Air Base."

"Oh! My God. I can't believe it. My prayers have been answered. Thank you Colonel Barclay. Thank you so much for everything you've done for us. You have no idea of the happiness this news is bringing to this family," said Louise, fighting back tears of joy.

"Well, believe me, Missus Longbow, this news is making a lot of aviators who know your husband at Hancock Field, very happy. I expect this news will hit the newspapers within the next day or two with international interest," said Colonel Barclay.

Louise immediately ran next door to announce the news to her best friend, Susan Siegel, and her husband David, who stood stunned as Louise related the news of her husband's escape with a defecting Russian aviator.

"This is an incredible story," said David. "I can't wait to hear the details of his escape. When did you say he'll arrive at Niagara Falls Air Force Base?" asked David.

"Possibly tomorrow night, but most likely the day after. Colonel Barclay said he'll call me when he learns the exact time and date," said Louise.

"You must be ecstatically happy at this news, Louise. Let's have a drink to celebrate his homecoming," said Susan.

"I'll second that," said David, and they all went into the dining room for their favorite mixed drink.

"I'll bet Jim will be bombarded with request to appear on television Talk Shows, because this story is so fantastic that only a screen writer could come up with an event like this. I tell you, Louise, I can't wait to talk to Jim. Because as brothers-in-arms, he'll confide in me, things he won't tell anyone else," said David.

"Wow! You see, Louise, I told you not to give up hope, even when it seems hopeless, and now I can tell you that I thought it was hopeless, but here we are, celebrating his return," said Susan.

The expected phone call from Colonel Barclay finally arrived, and Louise learned that her husband James would be arriving at Niagara Falls Air Force Base the following day at approximately 1430 hours.

The whole Longbow, Siegel, Sontag gang was there, without the children, to greet their returning air warrior with an enthusiasm that rivaled the intensity if not the largesse of Lindbergh's 1927 return from Paris.

As the C-47 military air transport aircraft landed, the small crowd of relatives gathered at the gate to meet their hero. Dressed in a new flight suit provided to him at RAF Station Chelveston, James Longbow was the first person to descend the metal staircase from the aircraft. Carrying an AWOL bag, he nonchalantly walked towards the terminal until he saw Louise standing at the front of the crowd of relatives. When their eyes met, Louise opened the gate and ran towards him, leaping into his arms as he dropped his AWOL bag to hold her with a kiss that seemed to last an eternity, as his father and friends stood behind the gate, waiting for them to break for air, and a respite for later resumption at home. As they walked, arm-in-arm, towards their relatives and friends, with big smiles on their faces, James was greeted with hugs, handshakes and a kiss from Susan, expressing their love and admiration for his bravery and safe return to his family and friends.

"Well, Jim, how does it feel being back to the States after being a prisoner in Moscow?" asked Michael Sontag.

"Like taking a hot shower after being pulled out of a Korean benjo ditch," replied Longbow.

"What's a benjo ditch, Dave?" asked Susan.

"It's a shallow ditch containing human waste, used as a fertilizer of rice paddies in Korea," replied David Siegel, eliciting laughter from nearby listeners.

"Golly, I'm sorry I asked," said Susan, embarrassed.

Upon arrival home in Williamsville, James Longbow was greeted by his son Gary and his daughter Jackie with overwhelming enthusiasm and love.

"Dad, your escape from Moscow was in all the newspapers," said Gary. "They didn't give much detail, only that you managed to steal one of their fighter planes and land in England."

"Gosh, Dad, how'd you manage to steal one of their airplanes?" asked Jackie, in wonderment.

"It's really a long story, some of it is classified information," replied James Longbow.

"Really, why's that, Dad?" asked Gary.

"Because we, the US Government, don't want them to know our methods of escape," said James, evading the question.

"Well, we're sure glad you made it back, Dad. I hope you don't go on any more of those dangerous missions. Mom was really upset and cried a lot, when she learned your plane got shot down," said Jackie.

James looked at Louise, standing nearby, listening to her children's questions, a bit embarrassed at Jackie's revelations.

"OK! Kids, your father is tired from his long flight, so no more questions tonight, alright," said Louise, ending her children's inquisition.

That night, in the bedroom, Louise released all of her pent-up emotions of love nearly lost, on her James, whose only remedy was to make love to her in a most tender and romantic way.

"You know, Jim, I never knew love could be so deep and profound, that one could die from the loss of it. That's how I felt when I initially learned of the loss of your plane. But Susan reminded me of the grave error I made when your B-17 bomber exploded and you survived. I wasn't about to make that mistake again, and believed, against all odds, even after you were charged with espionage and held back for trial, that somehow, you'd find a way to return to us, safe and sound, and by God, you did, my darling, and I hope you never leave us again," said Louise in tears.

"I won't leave on any missions again, sweetheart. I promise," replied James, hoping he would never again be asked to serve his country on a perilous mission.

The following day, it didn't take long for the telephone at the Longbow residence to ring several times from various news media, wanting to speak to James Longbow.

"What do they want?" asked Louise.

"They want me to appear on television for an interview regarding my escape from Moscow. A newspaper wants to interview me regarding the same thing. I refused them all," said James.

"Why don't you want to be interviewed, Jim, especially on television?" asked Louise, rather surprised at his refusal.

"Because they'll expect me to reveal all the details regarding the escape, which would jeopardize the safety of those who helped in my escape," replied James.

"Oh! I didn't realize that. Well, you know best, Jim, so you do what your heart and conscience tells you, and you have my full support, darling," replied Louise.

The telephone rang one more time, but it was not from a solicitor.

"Jim, this is Colonel Barclay, how're you doing, buddy?"

"OK!, Just taking it easy before going back to work at Curtiss-Wright Corporation," replied James Longbow.

"I just got a call from the Commander of SAC, Lieutenant General Beauregard. He saw the news on TV, as I did, where the commentators are making your refusal to appear on their show as unpatriotic, in that the public has a right to know the details of your escape. I hope you haven't agreed to any of their requests. I hear that one of the stations offered you fifty thousand dollars for your appearance, is that right?" asked Barclay.

"Yes, that's right and you can tell General Beauregard that I refused all offers," said Longbow.

"I thought you would, to protect your teammate, and I'll be glad to pass that on to the General," said Barclay.

"To protect not only my teammate, but all others involved," said Longbow.

"That's right, I forgot. You know, Jim, I'm going to recommend to General Beauregard that you be promoted to Lieutenant Colonel, immediately. I believe you deserve it. Give my best to your wife, Jim. Take care buddy," said Barclay.

"Who was that, Jim?" asked Louise.

"Oh! Just Colonel Barclay, supporting my decision not to appear on any television shows or newspaper interviews," said Longbow, who had never mentioned to Louise, he'd been offered fifty thousand dollars to appear on a television program.

Sitting in beach chairs on the cement platform at the bottom of the stone wall bordering Ellicott Creek, Jim Longbow and Dave Siegel quietly watched the ducks paddling upstream while a family of deer across the creek, munched along the grassy shore.

"If you feel up to it, Jim, I'd like to hear the details about your escape from the KGB Headquarters in Moscow," said Siegel.

"As long as you promise not to divulge any of this information to anyone, Dave, because this information was classified as Top Secret by the Air Force," said James Longbow.

"I understand and I promise, Jim, so what happened?" replied Siegel.

"Well, while at KGB Headquarters, I was imprisoned in a cell with a Major Fedor Popov, a fighter pilot who had been charged with aggravated assault on a superior officer. He was just as anxious to escape and exit the Soviet Union as I was, and devised a plan of escape, but for it to work, he needed my assistance," said James Longbow, who related all the details that followed, to his landing with Popov at RAF Station Chelveston.

"That is quite a story, Jim. Somebody up there really likes you, my friend," said Siegel.

"I guess I was just lucky, that's all," replied James Longbow.

"That's more than just luck, Jim. There are too many convenient coincidences. I think God had a lot to do with it, and he wouldn't go through all that, unless he had something else of importance for you to do, before you leave this earth," said Siegel.

"Jesus, Dave. I can't put Louise through this stressful ordeal again. From now on, I'm just a desk jockey," replied James Longbow.

CHAPTER VI

Enrolment at University—Dodging the Draft

Soon after James Longbow's spectacular escape from Moscow and return to the United States Air Force Active Reserves, he was promoted to full Colonel, and his buddy David Siegel became a Lieutenant Colonel, also in the Reserves.

As the years went by, Jim Longbow got promoted again, this time to Brigadier General, and Dave to full Colonel in the Active Air Force Reserves. General Longbow played down his promotion with his family, wearing his uniform only when serving his one-weekend per month and two weeks in the summer on active duty at Hancock Field in Syracuse, New York. Indeed, Longbow didn't even use his military rank on his personal correspondence, to avoid the appearance of self-importance and arrogance. His Reserve status and that of Dave Siegel, to the delight of their wives, did not require any active participation in an armed conflict.

However, 1964 changed all that when the U.S. destroyers USS Maddox, and USS Turner Joy, were attacked by the North Vietnamese in the Gulf of Tonkin. The United States Congress passed the 'Gulf of Tonkin' Resolution authorizing President Lyndon Johnson to wage all-out war against North Vietnam. Men between the ages of 18 and 25 were required to register for the draft and serve a minimum of two years on active duty in the United States Army. Excluded from the draft were men attending a college or university. It didn't take long for the Longbow and Siegel families to review their sons' options.

Gathered together in the Longbow household, were the two families to discuss their sons' standing with the draft.

"You two boys have just graduated from high school and were planning on entering the University of New York at Buffalo next January. However, you, Alex will be 18 this 25th of July and you Gary will turn 18 on the 7th of September, making you both eligible for the draft. That is, unless you get admitted to the University of New York this fall, which will then exclude you from the draft until you graduate," said Jim Longbow, with Dave Siegel agreeing.

"I think they should apply for admission right away, because Alex will turn 18 this July, before the fall registration," said Dave Siegel.

"Maybe we should just get drafted and get it over with," said Gary.

"Don't be a fool, Gary," said Louise. "Listen to you father who has a lot of experience with the military and knows what's best for you."

"You should get your education first, then, if so inclined or required, join the military. With a college education, you get more opportunities for advancement and decision-making positions which will prepare you for civilian life," said James Longbow.

"And that goes for you too, Alex. Get your education first, then perhaps the Vietnam war will be over by the time you graduate, and if not, you'll be better prepared and more mature for the military service," said David Siegel.

"I have to agree with you, Dad," said Alex. "I'm not anxious to visit Vietnam, in any capacity. I want to join the UB baseball team with Gary next year."

"Alright, then. We want you two boys to immediately apply for admission to UB," said Louise, speaking for Susan as well.

Both boys were admitted for entry into the University of New York at Buffalo for the Fall semester, to the relief of their parents. The first thing they did was to join the UB Baseball team; Gary as a pitcher and Alex as a first baseman, the same position they held in their high school baseball team.

After being interviewed by their education counselor regarding their selection of major and minor studies, Gary and Alex met in the UB Cafeteria for lunch.

"What major studies did you select, Gary?" asked Alex.

"Aeronautical engineer, like my Dad," replied Gary. "I didn't tell you before, Alex, because I didn't want to influence your decision. That way, you'd select the major study you personally want to work at the rest of your life."

"Well, I selected aeronautical engineering, like my Dad, who got me interested in that field since I was old enough to understand it, and I can't wait to start getting flying lessons. So let's both go to Falcon Aviation and sign up for lessons. I'm sure my Dad will be more than willing to defray my cost," said Alex.

"That's just great. We're following in our fathers' footsteps, and I think my father will also support my flying lessons. I'm not sure my Mom will be too happy with my decision, because of its potential dangers, but she won't object when my father approves," said Gary.

"OK, then! The best way to approach our parents is to first mention the selection of our major in aeronautical engineering. That will justify our desire to take flight lessons at Falcon Aviation, where our fathers also attended and got their FAA certification," said Alex.

"The only thing left will be for them to offer their financial support for those lessons," said Gary.

"I don't think we'll have a problem with financial support. Shall we announce our plan for flight lessons simultaneously, or do you want to test the waters first?" asked Alex.

"Let's do it simultaneously. How about this evening after dinner?" asked Gary.

"You got it. I'll call you right after I've had a talk with my Mom and Dad," replied Alex.

It was 7:35 p.m. when Gary received a telephone call from Alex.

"Hi Gary. I got my Dad's support and go ahead for the flight training, but not without a lot of explaining to my Mom, who wanted me to become a lawyer and join my grandfather's law firm, as a safer and more lucrative profession. But I won her over with my charming disposition," said Alex, laughing at his last remark.

"Your Mom gave in because she knows you'll be happiest in the profession you, yourself chose and love, not your charm, buddy," said Gary, laughing.

"Yeah! Alright, so what about you? How did it go?" asked Alex.

"They were glad I elected to major in aeronautical engineering, and didn't object to my taking flying lessons. In fact, my Dad immediately offered to defray the cost of those lessons," said Gary.

"Great. When do you want to go to Falcon Aviation to sign up for flight lessons?" asked Alex.

"How about tomorrow morning, after breakfast at about 9:30 a.m." said Gary.

"OK! See you after breakfast," replied Alex.

Gary and Alex subscribed to Falcon Aviation's accelerated flight training program, in order to be free for their entry at the University of New York in September.

With only two months left in the baseball season at the State University of New York at Buffalo (SUNYAB), Gary and Alex were given a chance to try out during practice, given their previous experience in high school.

"OK! Young man, let's see what you've got," said the Coach, Neil Watson to Gary facing a catcher.

"I'm going to throw him a slider," said Gary, knowing he must tell the catcher what he will be throwing so there won't be any surprises or injuries.

Gary went through his windup, and leaping forward with the snap of his wrist, aimed the ball at the shoulder of an imaginary batter, causing the ball to break some 18 inches over the home plate into the catcher's mitt.

"That's some slider you've got there. Let me see you throw another one," said Coach Watson.

Gary threw another slider, equally effective and accurate.

"You've got a very impressive slider, young man. What other pitches have you got?" asked Coach Watson.

"I've got a fast ball," replied Gary.

"OK! Gary...it is Gary?" asked Coach Watson. "Let's see your fast ball.

Gary leaned back, his right hand almost touching the ground, then catapulted forward releasing the baseball with lightning speed that split the center of home plate into a resounding sound in the catcher's mitt.

The coach was visibly impressed with the speed and accuracy of Gary's fast ball, and asked him to repeat it, which Gary obliged with equal accuracy, an important element of any pitch, especially with a fast ball.

"Skip, get the radar gun and stand behind the catcher," said Coach Watson. "This radar gun was mass produced two years ago by an electronics company for use by the police to measure the speed of vehicles. We got a hold of one for our use to measure the speed of a baseball. So we're gonna find out the speed of your fast ball, 'cause I think you've got something special, young man."

"OK! Skip, are you ready?" asked Coach Watson.

"Yes, sir," replied Skip.

"Alright, Gary, throw Jake the best fastball you've got, straight over home plate," said Coach Watson.

Gary did his windup and threw his fast ball. It seemed like only a second before it found its mark in the catcher's mitt.

"Holy cow!" Said Skip, looking at the display on the radar gun meter. "It shows 104.5 miles per hour," yelled Skip.

"Throw another fastball, Gary. I wanna make sure the reading is accurate," said Coach Watson, now surrounded by several curious ball players.

Gary again did his windup and putting every inch of his body into the motion, threw the baseball into the catcher's mitt with such power, it made Skip nervous, even though standing behind the protection of the catcher.

"104.4 miles per hour," yelled Skip, excitedly.

Coach Watson looked at Gary. "How old are you, Gary?"

"I'll be 18 in September, sir," replied Gary.

"Did your high school coach ever see you pitch?" asked Coach Watson, wondering why Gary had not been discovered by baseball scouts.

"I was only 16 and the coach said that at my age, I should restrain my pitch until I got a couple of years older," said Gary.

"Your high school coach was a very wise man. But you must always warm up your arm before you pitch, especially your fastball. I want you to throw another fastball for the record, then that will be all for today, and I want to talk to you, afterwards," said Coach Watson, who realized he'd found a real gem of a pitcher.

Gary threw another fastball, again cutting the center of home plate, this time with a speed of 104.5 miles per hour.

Coach Watson took Gary aside for a walk into the dugout.

"I don't know if you realize it, Gary, but you've got the makings of a professional baseball player, if you're managed right, and with your cooperation, I'll make it happen," said Coach Watson.

"Well, sir, I do love the game, that's why I play it, but I must tell you, that my future is in aviation. That's why I major in aeronautical engineering," said Gary.

"Really, aeronautical engineering, huh! Well, I don't see why you can't do both, at least while attending this university," said Coach Watson, knowing that the excitement in baseball could overcome his interest in aeronautics.

"Sir, I'd like to mention that my friend Alex Siegel who came with me, is a great first baseman and a strong hitter. I'd be very grateful if you would accept him to play on the team," said Gary.

"If he's anywhere as good as you, I'll put him on our first string. Did he play baseball with you in high school?" asked Coach Watson.

"Yes, sir, he did, and he goes where I go. We're a team, sir," said Gary.

"You're a very loyal friend. I like that in a man, consider it done," said Coach Watson, now doubly impressed by this young man's character.

It didn't take long for Alex to prove his athletic prowess and skill as a first baseman, and especially as a batter, sending the ball into the bleachers on a number of occasions. Coach Watson decided to put him on his first string, especially when Gary was on the pitching mound. These two ball players instilled a camaraderie that Coach Watson believed would inspire and energize the team.

At the next ball game, Alex was used on first base, but Gary just warmed the bench in the dugout, while Cid Koblen, their previous season's first line pitcher, took to the mound, and lost the game by two runs.

"Gary, you probably wondered why I kept you on the bench for this game," said Coach Watson. "I wanted you to observe this first game. Next weekend, we're playing against Castle University, and you will be the relief pitcher. I'm starting you slow for good reason, trust me."

"I do trust you, Coach. I'm ready whenever you are," replied Gary, with his easy-going smile.

That Saturday afternoon, Rachel and Jackie sat in one of the first rows of the wooden bleachers at the SUNYAB outdoor stadium, awaiting the start of the baseball game between the SUNYAB Bulls and the Castle Knights.

The Bulls came on the field, taking their positions, with Cid Koblen standing on the mound looking for his catcher, Jake Holden, to give him the signal to start throwing him a few warm-up pitches, while the rest of the players took their positions around the bases and in the field.

"There's Alex on first base," said Jackie, "but Gary is not the pitcher."

"That's because the coach told him he was using him as the relief pitcher, to get his feet wet," said Rachel. "We may see him later, if the Knights start hitting Cid Koblen, that's the name of the pitcher on the mound."

"I see Gary brought you up to date on the players. My brother seems to confide more in you than he does his own sister," said Jackie.

"Ha! C'mon, Jackie. In case you don't know it, Gary and I are going steady. I'm now wearing his class ring. That shouldn't be a surprise, considering that you have been seeing my brother Alex quite steadily, and he told me he was going to offer you his class ring, but don't tell him I told you, 'cause he wants it to be a surprise," said Rachel.

"Really, let me see," said Jackie looking at the ring finger of Rachel's right hand. "When do you think Alex is going to offer me his ring?"

"Probably today, after the game, when he's alone with you," replied Rachel. "You are going to accept it, right?"

"Of course I am. I love him," replied Jackie, surprising herself at the statement.

"Wow! I knew you liked my brother a lot, but I guess I should've known that was going to happen. We've been together the four of us since we were infants. I might as well tell you, Jackie, that I'm also in love with your brother Gary, and I know that someday we're going to be married, and have a boy and a girl, just like my parents did," said Rachel.

"God, wouldn't that be something. The four of us being married to each other. Holy cow. A carbon copy of the Great Generation to the Next Generation," said Jackie.

"I just hope nothing happens between now and then to change that wonderful future that seems to have been planned for us from the moment of our birth," said Rachel.

The sound of the bat hitting a baseball suddenly got the girls' attention as the batter was now running towards first base, while the short-stop retrieved the ball and threw it to the first baseman in time for the umpire to call him out.

"Luckily Alex is tall, at six three. He was able to catch that high ball," said Jackie with admiration.

"Yeah! Both our guys are tall," said Rachel. "They're almost the same height, with Gary only an inch and a half shorter. But my brother Alex is lanky with big hands like a basketball player, while your brother Gary has the body of a swimmer with the shoulders of a weightlifter. You'd think Gary would have blond hair like his mother, but he has only her blue eyes and dark brown hair like his father. But both my parents have black hair, so not surprisingly, me and my brother also have black hair.

"So you're wondering about the coloring of our children, already?" said Jackie. "I'll let nature surprise me."

"Hey! The Bulls are now at bat," said Rachel. "Hopefully, we'll get a chance to see Alex at bat."

After two batters for the Bulls struck out, Alex came at bat. Two balls and one strike were facing Alex. The pitcher threw a fast ball dead center and Alex struck it with a hard crack that sent the ball high into left field beyond the Knights' left fielder for a homerun.

As Alex ran around the bases, the crowd cheered, with Jackie and Rachel standing in ovation for their personal hero.

"Holy Molly!" yelled Jackie, "a homerun. That's my Alex," she said proudly.

"Yeah! And it's just like him to say it was nothing, just a game," said Rachel.

"And that's one of the reasons I love, him, 'cause he's modest and not a bragger," said Jackie.

The score remained the same until the fifth inning, when the Knights scored two runs, making it two to one in favor of the Knights.

At this time, Coach Watson, walked up to the mound and spoke with the pitcher, Cid Koblen.

"How do you feel, Cid?" asked Koblen.

"To tell you the truth, coach, my right elbow hurts," said Koblen.

"The one thing we don't want is to aggravate it. It needs some rest and maybe some treatment, so I'm relieving you and putting in Gary Longbow," said Coach Watson.

"That's alright with me, coach," replied Koblen, who started walking off the mound towards the Bulls' dugout.

As Coach Watson approached the dugout, he motioned for Gary to step up onto the field.

"OK! Gary, show 'em what you've got," said Coach Watson.

"Oh! My God!" exclaimed Rachel. "Gary is walking up to the pitcher's mound. He's going to be on for the next four innings."

"This was worth the wait, Rachel. This is so exciting, with Gary on the mound and Alex on first base. I think I'm going to pee in my pants," said Jackie.

"Huh! Huh! Stop it, Jackie. You're gonna have me do it," replied Rachel, laughing.

"Here they go with the first Knight at bat," said Jackie.

"You see that guy holding a movie camera, standing directly behind the catcher," said Rachel. "I didn't know they were going to film this game."

"That's not a camera, Rachel. That's a radar gun to measure the speed of the ball as it travels from the pitcher to the catcher, and he stands behind the backstop for protection, according to Gary," said Jackie

"Really, they can determine the speed of his pitch?" said Rachel.

"That's right, and the faster the better," replied Jackie.

The batter was a big man, known for his record of homeruns.

The catcher, Jake Holden, signaled with the fingers of his right hand between his knees, for a fast ball where he would place his mitt, which would be low and inside the home plate's border, close enough for the batter to believe the baseball crossed outside the home plate for the umpire to call it a ball rather than a strike.

Gary did his windup and threw his fast ball directly into Jake's mitt, which the batter mistook as a ball, but the umpire called it "strike one."

Skip looked into his radar gun, and with his walkie-talkie, told Coach Watson, the speed of that fast ball was 104.1 miles per hour.

Jake asked for another fast ball, this time high and inside the plate, which brought a swing from the batter that simply cut through the air, too late for a hit, for strike two.

Jake now called for a slider, and Gary aimed his pitch at the batter's shoulder. As the baseball travelled towards the batter's shoulder, it made him step back, only to see the ball slide almost two feet over the corner of home plate for strike three, and out.

The next two batters also struck out with no hits, resulting in the Knights taking to the field with the Bulls at bat.

As a catcher, Jake Holden was the most knowledgeable player regarding the types of pitches and their idiosyncrasies in the arsenal of a pitcher. He could recognize a curve ball from a knuckle ball and other pitches from the position of the ball's rotating stiches as it sped towards him. Hence, the catcher could be the most formidable batter facing a pitcher, and so the pitcher for the Knights was now facing Jake Holden, catcher for the Bulls.

The score so far was 2 to 1 in favor of the Knights. The Bulls needed to score two runs, and keep the Knights from scoring another run, to win the game.

The first pitch to Jake was a curve ball which he ignored, but the umpire called a strike, with which Jake strongly disagreed, but the umpire stayed fast on his call.

The second pitch was a fast ball which Jake partially hit, sending it into the backstop, for which the umpire called it a foul ball for strike two. One more strike and Jake would be called out. He couldn't afford to ignore another pitch, and the tension was mounting, not only for Jake but also his teammates and his fans.

This time, knowing he had an advantage over the batter with two strikes against him and no balls, the pitcher could afford to throw a ball outside the strike zone, hoping to sucker Jake into swinging at it for a third strike. However, Jake's experience told him to pass on this pitch and the umpire called it a ball.

The pitcher still had an advantage with only one ball called against him, but decided to end it all with a fast ball right down the middle of home plate, and Jake hammered it over the short-stop between center and left field, while he ran over first base, stopping at second base for a double base hit.

The right outfielder for the Bulls came to bat, and after one strike and two balls against him, he hit a fast ball and sent it deep into right field which was caught by the Knights' right fielder for the Bulls' first out.

The third baseman for the Bulls now came to bat, and after hitting a fly ball high over the infield, it was caught by the pitcher for the Bulls' second out.

This was the ninth and last inning, and the last chance for the Bulls to score. They needed two runs to beat the Knights and then prevent them from scoring another run when they came at bat for the last time. The full weight of this dramatic moment fell on the next batter for the Bulls, and everyone sensed the importance of this next confrontation between the batter and pitcher.

At this moment, the Knights decided to substitute their pitcher with a relief pitcher, fresh and ready for the challenge. He was a big fellow, and a left handed pitcher, which can present a problem for many batters.

A tall lanky ball player walked up to the plate and dusted his shoes with his bat, then took a look at the catcher, then the pitcher, sizing him up. He then swung his bat a few times to loosen up, and readied himself for the first pitch.

"It's Alex. Oh! My God," exclaimed Jackie, making the sign of the cross.

"I hope he doesn't strike out. This is his chance to bring Jake home with him and win the game," said Rachel.

The pitch came fast and low, for ball one. A sigh of relief could be heard from Jackie and Rachel.

The second pitch was delayed as the pitcher threw the ball to his second baseman, in an attempt to catch Jake off base and end the game, but Jake got there first.

The pitcher stretched both arms up in the air, then brought them down together for a brief moment against his chest. He leaned back and threw a curve ball that Alex hit outside left field for a foul ball and strike one.

The pitcher realized Alex had a bead on his curve ball, therefore decided to throw his best pitch, a fast ball intended to be high, but whose trajectory came in waist high, meeting the fat part of Alex' bat that sent the ball high into the air to the center-field bleachers for a homerun that brought Jake home from second base and Alex to home plate where he was greeted by some of his teammates as he tried to make his way to the dugout.

"He did it, he did it," shouted Jackie, now jumping with joy and embracing Rachel. "Oh! God. I love that man."

"The game is not over, Jackie. The Knights have their last chance at bat, and if they score just two runs, they win the game. So Gary has to keep them from scoring any runs during this last inning," said Rachel.

"Holy Moly! I think I'm going to need a drink after this game," said Jackie. "and I really don't drink, but this game has got me so wound up, I'll need a tranquilizer."

"I know you're exaggerating, Jackie, but I know what you mean, and I think if they win, we'll have to celebrate at a pizza place with a beer or two," said Rachel.

The Knights were now getting ready to put their best batters in their lineup, while the Bulls, now out in the field with Gary on the mound and Alex on first base, waited for the onslaught.

Everyone in the Bulls dugout, especially Coach Watson, was on edge, knowing that this last inning would determine the outcome of the game. Watson knew that even four innings can seem like an eternity, and he had no one else of equal stature to relieve Gary, if he should need replacement. The first batter for the Knights, their first baseman, took his position in the batter's box, swung his bat a few times to loosen up, then waited for the pitch from Gary.

Jake Holden signaled Gary to throw a fast ball on the inside to move the batter back and intimidate him.

Gary did his windup and sprung from the mound with a lightning fast ball that Skip recorded at 104.9 miles per hour. The batter pulled back and did not swing his bat, and the umpire called it a ball.

Jake signaled for Gary to throw a slider which would have the same trajectory as his previous fast ball, but would break a few feet from the batter and cross home place in the strike zone. The ruse worked. The batter failed to swing his bat and the umpire called it strike one.

Jake signaled Gary to throw another slider, but Gary shook his head in the negative. Jake signaled for a fast ball center high, after witnessing the batter swinging his bat waist high during his warmup.

Gary did his windup, leaped from the mound with his right arm releasing the ball, finding its mark in Jake's mitt within a second, missing the bat by at least two inches, at a speed of 104.7 miles per hour.

The batter, now facing two strikes and one ball against him, gave the pitcher the advantage, in that the pitcher could now waste at least two pitches before he was left with the choice of one strike or one ball that would walk him to first base. Gary also knew that.

Jake signaled Gary to throw a slider towards the center of home place, knowing it would break away from home plate and out of reach of the batter's bat. As predicted by Jake, the batter swung at the pitched ball and missed for strike three, putting him out of the game. A loud cheer could be heard from the fans of the Bulls in their home field.

"Holy Moly! This is so exciting. Only two more to go and we win," said Jackie.

"There's a lot of pressure on Gary, right now, but he seems to be handling it well," said Rachel. "He's just like his father, cool as a cucumber under fire, my Dad told me."

"He's a chip off the old block," replied Jackie. "That's my brother, God love him."

The next batter, was their centerfielder, a big bruiser with arms like tree trunks, who looked like he could drive the baseball into space.

Jake sized him up, watching the height of his warmup swing and his stance from home plate. He signaled Gary to dust him off on his first pitch with a fast ball towards his upper body, which effectively moved the batter back from his stance, wondering if the pitcher had poor control of his pitches, hence readied himself for other wild pitches, causing his stance to be unsteady. The batter now faced one ball and no strikes. The batter's timing was not accustomed to pitches exceeding 90 miles per hour, hence he faced an unknown adversary.

Gary received a signal from Jake for a fast ball just below shoulder height, cutting the inside edge of home plate.

Gary knew this batter had the potential of hitting a homerun if he connected with his fast ball. He had to be very precise in this pitch to cut the inside corner of home plate, just below shoulder height, with a fast ball that required total coordination, and release of the ball in exactly the correct trajectory that would cross the strike zone where Jake's mitt was ready to receive it.

Coach Watson was holding his breath, as Gary did his windup, and with his right hand holding the ball, nearly touching the ground behind him, jettisoned off the mound like a coiled spring with an exploding 105.1 mile-per-hour release of the ball, ending in the catcher's mitt, without a swing from the stunned batter, now facing a one strike and one ball count against him.

Jake heard Skip announcing the 105.1 mile per hour throw, and decided to call for another fast ball, this time low, just above the knees, a cut inside the strike zone. Jake deliberately held his mitt high and center for the batter to see, then at the last minute when the batter focused on the pitcher, he moved his mitt to the desired strike zone.

With no one on base, Gary had the luxury of being able to fully windup his pitch for maximum power, and released the ball with a recorded 105 mile per hour speed that elicited a late and wide swing from the batter for strike two.

Now facing a dire situation, the coach for the Knights called for time out to speak to his centerfielder.

"Listen, don't try for a homerun, just hit the ball that will get you on base. Scott is next, and we're counting on him to bring you home," said the Knights' coach.

In the meantime, Jake walked up towards the mound to meet with Gary.

"You haven't yet thrown a drop pitch, and I think this is the time to do it, but land it below the strike zone," said Jake.

"You mean, throw it at knee level to bait him to swing, but the ball will drop below the strike zone a few feet from it," said Gary.

"That's right Gary. If he swings and misses, he's out with strike three. If he doesn't swing, it's only ball two. So we have nothing to lose," said Jake.

"OK! Let's do it," replied Gary.

The big centerfielder stood in the batter's box, poised to get some wood on the ball, enough to get him to first base.

Gary went through his usual windup and threw a drop pitch as planned which did draw a swing from the batter who missed the ball as it dropped just a few inches above home plate, outside the strike zone. Having swung and missed the ball resulted in strike three, putting him out of the game.

All eyes were now on the next batter, who was the catcher for the Knights, and their best hitter. A stocky and robust man with an air of confidence, the batter stood in the batter's box, with his bat held high over his shoulder, ready for action. He didn't provide warmup swings for Jake to see and evaluate. Gary was facing his most formidable opponent, and Jake knew it. He also knew it was his job to evaluate the batter and advise Gary on his pitching strategy for each batter.

The coach for the Knights called time out as he walked over to speak to his catcher, up at bat.

"They all expect you to go for a homerun to even the score, and the effort to accomplish that has a high degree of failure. However, what I have in mind will surprise every-one and get you on base, which is what we need right now. Then the next batter can also make a strategic move to get on base, until we get a man on third base who can be brought home to even the score. Then we'll have a whole new ball game. So I want you to bunt. That's right, I want you to bunt the ball to the left infield, so that the third baseman and the pitcher are equal distant from the ball, and one of them has to decide to run after it, while you make it to first base," said the coach.

"But I think I can beat that pitcher, and hit the ball out of the park," said the catcher.

"That's what all the batters before you thought and they all struck out. So you do as I say and bunt. Got that?" said the coach, not as a question, but as an order.

"Yeah! I got it, coach," replied the catcher.

The catcher walked back into the batter's box and took his position, indicating he was ready for the first pitch. As a catcher, having faced hundreds of baseballs thrown at him, it made him especially qualified to judge which pitch was best suited for a bunt.

On the mound, Gary knew he faced his most challenging batter, and wondered which pitch Jake would ask him to throw, and the answer came quickly with his best fast ball, high and on the inside corner of the strike zone.

Gary agreed with Jakes' signal and threw a fast ball exactly where Jake wanted it, but the batter let the ball pass him without a swing. However, the umpire called it strike one, because it was within the strike zone.

Jake signaled for a slider aimed at the center of home plate, which would move at least a foot away from home plate and the batter, who might be tempted to swing at it.

The velocity of the slider, being slower than Gary's extreme fast ball, made a better target for a bunt, if the batter moved forward before its slide, which is what the batter did, bunting the ball halfway between home place and third base. Gary got into a crouch to give his third baseman a clear pitch to Alex on first base when he got hold of the baseball, but the infielder fumbled it, then retrieved it and threw it to Alex, but not in time for the batter to step on first base for a base hit.

Now Gary had to position himself with his back facing first base, while he stretched both arms above his head, then bringing them down to his chest with the ball in both hands to a complete stop, before throwing the ball past the batter to his catcher. From such a position he could quickly step off the pitcher's plate and throw the ball to any of the basemen, when a runner attempts to steal a base.

The Knights coach sent his short-stop infielder to the batter's box. He was a fast runner and place hitter, in that he could spot hit the ball within the infield, making it hard for infielders to reach the ball in time before the short-stop reached first base.

Jake and Gary knew they needed only one more strike out to end the game in their favor, hence this was a most important moment.

The short-stop batter was a left hander which demanded different tactics from the pitcher, who needed Jake's experienced advice.

Jake signaled for Gary to throw a slider aimed at the shoulder of an imaginary right-handed batter, giving the illusion of a wild pitch traveling outside the strike zone, but sliding over home plate and the strike zone at the last minute. The batter, being a left hander, would find the ball's trajectory almost out of reach and out of the strike zone, thus not swing at it. As predicted by Jake, that's exactly what happened for a call of strike one.

Gary noticed that the Knights' catcher on first base, was taking a very long lead away from first, towards second base, in an attempt to steal second base. In a quick move, Gary threw the ball to Alex on first base, but not in time to catch the batter before he returned to first base.

Nevertheless, he kept the batter from stealing second base and gave him fair warning he had him within his sight.

Jake now signaled Gary to throw a fast ball over the inside corner of home plate, waist high, which Gary executed with astonishing speed of 104.9 miles per hour, catching the batter off-guard without any action, resulting in a call of strike two.

Gary knew that the next pitch could end the game. He had two strikes with no ball against the batter, a most enviable position for any pitcher, who could afford to waste a ball, even two balls, before weakening his position. Jake read his mind and signaled for a fast ball outside the strike zone with little time to judge.

Gary threw his fast ball as planned, but the batter managed to hit the ball with the tip of his bat, sending the ball between the third baseman and second baseman. The short-stop caught the ball and threw it to his first baseman, but it was a split second too late. Now, the Knights had a man on first base and another on second base, as intended.

The pressure was mounting on the Bulls and their fans, including Rachel and Jackie who understood the precarious position Gary was facing. All the Knights needed was a hit that would allow one of its runners on base to make it home to even the score.

Jake walked up to the mound for a chat with Gary.

"How's your pitching arm, Gary?" asked Jake.

"It's fine. I'm OK!" replied Gary.

"Whoever they put in at bat, you've got to strike him out, Gary," said Jake.

"Yeah! I know. I think we'll have to dispense with the drop and slider and concentrate on placing the fast ball within the least likely areas of the strike zone for him to hit," said Gary.

"And put as much steam as you can behind your fast ball," said Jake.

"Jesus, according to Skip, I've hit 105 miles per hour. I don't think I can top that," said Gary.

"Maybe, just don't slow down, that's all," replied Jake with a grin.

On the mound, Gary looked at the batter facing him, swinging his bat loosely, waiting for Gary to go into his pitching position.

Jake signaled for a fast ball, low and inside the strike zone. With deep concentration, Gary set all of the muscles in his body into action, achieving a pitching speed of 105.5 miles per hour, by far the fastest throw of a baseball in the history of the Bulls University stadium. The pitch was too fast and too close for the batter to react, resulting in a strike one against him.

Gary stood on the mound with the ball in his right hand, occasionally placing it in his gloved hand, then retrieving it again, while thinking of his next move, although Jake had already signaled him to throw another fast ball, this time high inside the strike zone.

Gary, signaled Jake in the negative and for him to come up to the mound.

"What's the matter, you don't like my call?" asked Jake.

"I've changed my mind, Jake. What if I throw the fastest slider I can muster, aimed at his head. It's bound to rattle him. It'll be coming at him so fast, he won't have time to differentiate it from a fast ball, and it'll slide over the inside corner of the plate, if I can put enough spin on it," said Gary.

"How much confidence have you got that it'll work?" asked Jake.

"Well, ninety percent," replied Gary.

"You think that's enough to risk the outcome of this game?" asked Jake.

"Yes, I do, Jake, and the umpire is getting antsy," said Gary.

"OK! Buddy, let's do it," replied Jake, who then returned to his catcher's post behind the batter.

Gary watched the runners on first and second base, and in particular, the second base who may attempt to steal third base, placing him in a position to steal home. He then did his windup and as planned, threw a fast slider at the batter's head which, as expected, caused him to step back allowing the ball to slide just inside the top corner of the strike zone for a call of strike two.

With a big smile, Jake threw the ball back to Gary, who was already thinking of the next pitch which could end the game.

Jake and Gary both knew that they had the luxury of having two strikes and no balls, hence could afford to bait the batter with a pitch outside the strike zone.

Jake signaled Gary to throw a fast ball, again shoulder high but outside the strike zone. Gary declined with a negative shake of his head.

Not knowing what Gary really wanted, Jake requested time out and walked up to the mound.

"What's wrong with that pitch?" asked Jake.

"I think we can end this right now, with a shoulder high pitch, Jake, but just inside the strike zone," said Gary.

"You think you can slice it that thin," asked Jake.

"I've been doing it so far," replied Gary. "Besides, if it goes outside the strike zone, it'll be what you originally asked for in the first place."

"Yeah! OK! If it works, it'll be the end of the game with three outs," said Jake, returning to his catcher's position.

Looking down from the bleachers, Rachel and Jackie were silently praying for Gary to strike out the batter, knowing it would win the game for the Bulls.

"Oh! God. I didn't know baseball could be so exciting," said Rachel.

"It's exciting because we know the principal ball players," replied Jackie.

"I suppose you're right. Nevertheless, next time I'm taking a tranquilizer," said Rachel.

"You're joking, of course. Aren't you?" asked Jackie.

"Of course I'm joking. What do you think?" asked Rachel.

"Well with you, I never know when you're joking," replied Jackie.

"Let's watch the game. Jake just left Gary and is returning to home plate," said Rachel.

Gary looked down from the mound at the batter, then turned and looked at the runner on second base, then turned again to take his pitching position. He did his windup and with all of the energy and muscle at his disposal, threw a fast ball that ripped through the air at 105.9 miles per hour, landing in the catcher's mitt exactly where he had placed it as a target that would cut the inside of the strike zone for a call of strike three, ending the game with a roar from the fans in the bleachers, and a jamboree from the Bulls climbing out of the dugout onto the field in celebration of their win over the Knights.

Rachel and Jackie watched from the bleachers as the ball players from the Bulls had raised Gary onto their shoulders in honor of his masterful shutout.

"We're not going to be able to get near Gary and Alex while they're celebrating their victory inside the clubhouse. So we might as well take our time, and let them vent their enthusiasm, which they deserve, and we'll wait for them outside the clubhouse," said Jackie.

"I guess you're right, but what a game that was," said Rachel.

"Hey! Let's not forget that Alex hit that homerun which gave us the winning score. They should've carried him on their shoulders as well," said Jackie.

"Yeah! You're right, but the pitcher, especially when the game depends solely on his performance, always gets primary coverage, you know that," replied Rachel.

"Yes, I know, but I'm so proud of Alex, and I'm going to let him know that," said Jackie.

Rachel, sitting in Jackie's 1935 Mercedes-Benz 500K Roadster, with Jackie at the wheel, waited patiently for Gary and Alex to exit the university stadium's locker room for ball players. Finally, the ball players started to appear from the stadium's exit, and Gary along with Alex, immediately spotted Jackie's candy red roadster, which Jackie inherited from her mother, parked across the street.

"Hey! Guys, you both played a terrific game, and we saw the whole thing up close in the bleachers," said Jackie.

"We won the game, that's what counts," replied Gary.

"Yeah! but you guys carried the game," said Jackie.

"So where are you guys going from here?" asked Rachel.

"The team is gathering at Salvatore's pizza parlor on Main Street in Williamsville. You wanna join us?" asked Gary.

"Yes, of course. That's why we're here waiting for you," replied Jackie. "You're very quiet, Alex. Is everything OK?"

"Yeah! Sure. You guys are doing all the talking. I'm just listening," replied Alex.

"Alright, then, you know where Salvatore's pizza is located, so we'll see you there," said Gary.

The Bulls baseball team practically took over the pizzeria in numbers, which included several young female university students, with Jackie and Rachel among them. One particularly attractive brunette female student stood behind Gary, seated at a long table occupied by the team, attempting to engage in a conversation with him, placing her right hand on his shoulder.

"You see what I see," said Jackie, "Amy is trying to muscle in on your boyfriend."

"Yeah! I see her. I'm taking care of that, pronto," replied Rachel, who silently walked over to where Amy was standing, and removed her hand from Gary's shoulder.

"That's my guy, Amy, so scram," said Rachel, who now had been joined by Jackie.

"Then you should put an 'off limits' sign on him," replied Amy, leaving to avoid an altercation, which got Gary and Alex' attention.

Alex got up from his chair and offered it to Jackie, and Gary did the same for Rachel.

"We're going to get two other chairs and squeeze them next to yours," said Gary. "Hey, you guys, can you make room for two more chairs?"

Sal, the proprietor of the pizzeria, brought two chairs and fitted them next to those occupied by Jackie and Rachel, making everyone happy. The party was very festive, and ended with no one inebriated, but full of animated camaraderie, brought about by an atmosphere of shared team effort and accomplishment.

The following morning, a Sunday, saw Gary and Jackie sitting at the breakfast table with their parents, James and Louise Longbow, discussing the previous day's baseball game.

"So how did the game go?" asked James.

"We won 3 to 2 and Gary pitched the last four innings for a shut-out," said Jackie.

"But we wouldn't have won the game if it hadn't been for Alex hitting a home run that raised our score from 1 to 2 to 3 to 2 in our favor," said Gary.

"Sounds like an exciting ball game. Wish I could have attended it," said James.

"Looks like you and Alex together brought the trophy home," said Louise.

"Actually, Mom, Jake, who's our catcher, had a lot to do with it. He's got the toughest job on the team," said Gary.

"Gary's got a point. I played baseball and pitched in my younger days, and I can attest to the important role the catcher plays, which can make or break a pitcher," said James.

"I agree with you, Dad, and I don't know what I'd do without Jake as my catcher," said Gary.

"It's a good thing that you recognize the ability of others and don't take all the credit for yourself, Gary. I'm proud of you, son," said James with a warm smile that spelled love.

"Next time you play ball, Jim, let us know, and we'll try to make it to see you play," said Louise.

"We play against the Tigers from Queens College, next Saturday, and it's a home game here in Buffalo," said Gary.

"Well, it's a Saturday, so we should be able to attend, can't we, Jim?" asked Louise.

"Yes, I don't see why not. Where can we get tickets for the game?" asked James.

"I'll get those for you, Dad," said Jackie. "Maybe Rachel's parents can come too. I'll mention it to her. That would be just great."

"You mentioned, Jackie that Gary pitched the last four innings. Were you the relief pitcher?" asked James.

"Yes, I was, Dad. I don't know if he'll have me as the starting pitcher next week, but I'm satisfied being the relief pitcher," said Gary.

"After pitching a shut-out, Gary, I think your coach is going to think twice about keeping you on the bench for five innings. I wouldn't be surprised if he has you starting the next game," said James.

"Nine innings is a long time, and I really don't care if he does use me as his relief pitcher, as long as I get into the game," said Gary.

"How are you doing in school, Gary?" asked Louise.

"I'm doing fine, Mom. They've got some great programs at UB, and next semester, I start the aeronautical engineering studies with Alex. We're also enrolled at Falcon Aviation for flight lessons starting in two weeks," said Gary.

"Are you going to have enough time between your studies, baseball games and flight lessons?" asked Louise.

"Sure, Mom, don't worry, I won't let anything interfere with my studies on aeronautical engineering," said Gary.

"That's good to hear, Gary. Don't neglect your studies. That's your future, son," said James.

The following Saturday arrived, and the Longbow and Siegel family sat in the bleachers of the Bulls stadium, waiting for the game between the Bulls and the Tigers to start.

In the Bulls dugout, Coach Watson called Gary over to speak to him privately.

"I'm starting Cid Koblen today, Gary, because I don't think your pitching arm is ready for nine innings, and you're too valuable a player to take any risks. You're only 18 and still growing, so you're the relief pitcher today, and I'll give you the last five innings again, unless Cid falters requiring earlier relief. You OK with that, Gary?" asked Watson.

"Yeah! Sure coach. It makes a lot of sense," replied Gary.

"Good, I know you'd understand. By the way, the speed of your fast ball got around, and I spotted the talent scout for the New York Yankees, moseying around. Be careful, Gary, and don't sign anything without first talking to me and especially your father, before you decide anything," said Watson.

"Thanks for the warning, coach," replied Gary, who understood that now being eighteen years of age, he was considered an adult and anything he signed became a legal document.

The talent scout managed to seat himself behind the backstop next to Skip who was holding the radar gun.

"My name is Pete Monroe. I'm a talent scout for the New York Yankees," he said, holding out his hand for a handshake.

"Really! "I'm Skip Webb. Glad to meet you."

"I hear that you clocked the relief pitcher for the Bulls last Saturday at 105 miles per hour. Is that right?" asked Monroe.

"That's right, and he did it more than once," replied Skip.

"Well, I'd like to see it with my own eyes. So I hope you don't mind if I glance at your radar screen for confirmation," said Monroe.

"No, I don't mind," replied Skip.

The baseball game started with the Bulls taking to the field, allowing the Tigers to be the first at bat.

"Looks like they're using Cid Koblen as the starting pitcher, Dad," said Jackie.

"Looks that way. I think they'll be using Gary as the relief pitcher in the later innings, which is OK. I think I know what the coach is doing. He's saving Gary's arm until he matures, and can endure a full nine innings, which is smart," said James.

"I might as well go get myself a hot dog and a coke, then," said Jackie. "Anyone else want a hot dog?"

"Wait, I'll go with you," said Rachel. "Mom, Dad, you want a hot dog and coke?"

"No dear, maybe later, we'll get it ourselves," said Marie.

"The same with us, Jackie. Don't worry about us. You just take care of your own taste buds," said Louise.

At that moment, Eric Longbow, James' father and Gary's grandfather arrived.

"Sorry folks if I'm late, but I got held up in traffic. So what's the score?" asked Eric.

"The game just started, Dad, and Gary is not the starting pitcher, so you haven't missed anything," said James.

Five grueling innings transpired with a score of 4 to 2 for the Bulls, which did not require Cid to be replaced by a relief pitcher, being two points ahead. However, the sixth innings changed all that.

The Tigers were now at bat, and Cid threw a curve ball that met wood and landed in left field, allowing the batter to make it to second base. The next batter, a left hander, hit the ball in right field for a base hit, advancing the first batter from second base to third base. Now came the Tigers' catcher, who allowed two pitches to go by him without a swing. Then the third pitch met his bat sending the ball into the left bleachers for a foul ball. Cid knew this batter could change the game with two men on bases. He decided to throw a knuckle ball as a change of pace. The batter pounced on that ball with such force that it climbed to heights difficult to follow until it landed in the center bleaches for a homerun, bringing the score 5 to 4 for the Tigers.

Coach Watson waived Gary over to him. "It time for you to go to work, my boy, and bring home the bacon."

"Gotcha, Coach. No problem," replied Gary with confidence.

"Well, it's about time Gary got on the mound," said Jackie.

"Now we're going to see some real pitching," said Rachel.

"And hitting with Alex in the mix," added Jackie.

"He's got only three innings to make things right for the Bulls," said James.

"I'm sure Gary will do his part, but he'll need support from the hitters if they're to win the game," said Eric.

"This is turning out to be the most exciting part of the game," said Susan, who'd been quiet until now.

"Yeah! Mom, especially since Gary is now in the game and Alex is his batting support," said Rachel.

Gary threw mostly fast balls ranging in speed from 103 to 105 miles per hour, that astonished talent scout Monroe, looking over the shoulders of Skip, who was operating the radar unit. Gary struck out all three batters facing him.

At bat for the Bulls came the short-stop, who hit the ball into the left outfield for a base hit. He was followed by the catcher Jake Holden, who also got a base hit, a double, pushing the short-stop to third base.

"Oh! My God. Alex is now at bat, and there are two men on base. This is his chance," said Jackie, with the family members sharing her personal excitement.

Alex knew this opportunity with two men on bases might not reoccur, so he had to strike the iron while it was hot. He let the first pitch pass by him for a ball. However, he swung at the second pitch, a fast ball, and got some wood on it, but it went over the left field foul line for strike one.

The next pitch, also a fast ball, came down the center, begging for Alex's bat which did not disappoint him, sending the ball high into center field, bouncing off the bleacher wall. Both runners on base scored, and Alex made it to third base, but had to stop when he saw the catcher receiving the ball from the second baseman. Now the score was 6 to 5 for the Bulls, with a man on third base.

Jackie and Rachel were jumping with joy, while their parents watched them with big smiles on their faces.

"I knew Alex would do it. He's my hero," said Jackie, unashamed of her zeal for Alex in front of the family.

"There are two more innings. Let's not count our chickens before they're hatched," said David.

The right fielder for the Bulls came to bat, and hit a high fly ball into right field that was caught by the right fielder for the first out.

The center fielder came to bat and hit the ball almost straight up, leaving it up for grabs for the pitcher or the catcher to get it. The catcher caught the ball for the second out.

The second baseman for the Bulls now came up at bat, realizing it was up to him to bring Alex home, and he only needed a base hit to accomplish that.

"The pitcher threw a curve ball that invited the batter to strike it, which he did, sending the ball directly into the glove of the pitcher who immediately threw it to the catcher, preventing Alex from scoring, which ended the inning with a score of 6 to 5 in favor of the Bulls.

Gary realized that he had two innings left in which he had to prevent the Tigers from scoring, hence he needed at least a shut out or even better, a no-hitter.

Jake walked up to the mound to have a chat with Gary, and share his observations so far of the Tigers' batters.

"Cid does not throw sliders and his fast ball is nowhere as fast as yours, so the Tigers are in for some surprises, and since we have only two innings left, by the time they get acquainted with both those pitches, the game will be over," said Jake.

"So you're suggesting that I throw sliders mixed in with well-placed fast balls for the remaining two innings, and I'll have a no-hitter," said Gary.

"I think you can do it, Jim. They're ripe for it," said Jake.

"OK! Let's play ball," said Gary, and Jake returned to his position behind home plate.

The first batter for the Tigers came to the plate, and as Jake predicted, he just watched the slider coming in inches from his hands holding the bat. He waited for the umpire to call it a ball, when it slid over the home plate for a strike. The next pitch, a fast ball cut the inside corner of the plate for another strike that the batter failed to swing at. Another slider which the batter failed to swing at resulted in strike three and out.

The next two batters suffered the same fate, both striking out. However, the Bulls, now at bat, while not striking out, failed to score any runs due to the excellent fielding of the Tigers who caught two flies in the outfield and a ground ball to first base, ending that inning.

The Tigers were now again at bat, ready to score at least one run to even the game or two runs that would win it for them.

Gary decided to use only his fast balls with precision cutting the inside corners of home plate to end the game with a no-hitter

Jake used his mitt as a precise target for cutting corners which Gary effectively pounded with 105 mile per hour fast balls that eluded the batters, whose timing had never experienced such volatile rocketballs. Few batters took swings at the fast balls, and all struck out, ending the game with a score of 6 to 5 in favor of the Bulls. Gary had pitched a no-hitter, but only as a relief pitcher, not the whole nine innings required to earn that title.

There was jubilation not only in the bleachers where the Longbow and Siegel families were gathered, but also in the dugout, where coach Watson was congratulating his players for their outstanding performance. As Gary and Alex were leaving the locker room, they were accosted by Pete Monroe, the talent scout.

"I would like to congratulate you, Mister Longbow, for your exceptional talent as a pitcher," said Monroe, directing his congratulatory remark at Gary. "I'm Pete Monroe, talent scout for the New York Yankees, and I would appreciate just a few minutes of your time for a brief conversation about the possibility of you playing for the New York Yankees.”

Not wanting to be rude, Gary agreed, but invited Alex to join them, which Monroe accepted, inasmuch as Alex had also impressed him with his hitting and fielding, with possibilities for recruitment.

“How old are you, Gary…may I call you by your first name?” asked Monroe.

“Yeah! Sure. I’m eighteen,” replied Gary.

“How would you like to play professional baseball for the Yankees?” asked Monroe.

“Well, I don’t know. That’s something I would have to think about,” replied Gary.

“What is there to think about Gary. You’re being given an opportunity to play for the New York Yankees, the greatest major league baseball team. Most young men would give their eye teeth for such an opportunity,” said Monroe with pride.

“I do have other interests, Mister Monroe, such as aeronautical engineering, which I plan on making my lifetime career,” replied Gary, as Alex listened with great interest to the exchange.

“Well, that’s a very noble profession, but it wouldn’t pay anywhere near as much money as playing for the Yankees,” said Monroe.

“That may be true, Mister Monroe, but being only eighteen, I’m going to have to talk to my parents about your offer, sir, and get back to you,” said Gary.

"That's most reasonable, Gary. Here's my business card. Please call me when you're ready to talk business," said Monroe, who then gave his business card to Alex. "Young man. I understand your name is Alex Siegel. I'm also extending an invitation for you to attend a tryout at the Yankee stadium, for possible recruitment to our Triple A farm team."

"Triple A...isn't that minor league baseball?" asked Alex.

"Yes, but we have to see how you perform before you can step up to the major league Yankees," said Monroe.

"Thank you, for your offer, sir. Like Gary, I'm going to consult with my parents before making such an important decision," said Alex, who had already made up his mind that he wasn't going to give up a career in aeronautical engineering for minor league baseball, where he could remain without ever playing for the Yankees.

"As the boys headed toward the bleachers, Alex asked Gary, "Aren't you going to Salvatore's pizzeria to join the gang?"

"Naw! Not this time, Alex. Let's catch up with Rachel and Jackie and join the folks for a bite somewhere," said Gary.

"OK! The girls are parked over there waiting for us," said Alex.

The girls agreed to join their parents who decided to eat dinner at Marty's restaurant in North Buffalo.

Upon arrival, they found their parents, including James' father Eric, already seated in Marty's Italian restaurant.

Management pulled a couple of tables against the tables occupied by the parents, giving it a family atmosphere.

"What held you guys up?" asked Louise.

"A talent scout for the New York Yankees offered Gary a chance to play for the Yankees, and me for their Triple A farm team," said Alex.

"Is that right?" said James Longbow, as a statement rather than a question.

"What was the scout's name?" asked David Siegel.

"Pete Monroe," answered Gary.

"Did he quote an amount?" asked David.

"No, because I told him I would have to consult with my parents, so he gave me his business card, and asked for me to call him when I had made a decision," said Gary.

"What about you, Alex. What did you tell him?" asked David.

"The same thing as Gary. But I had already made up my mind that I'm not interested in playing in a minor baseball league," said Alex.

"You know, Gary, that as a pitcher, your arm is expected to last about five years, maybe a bit longer. But after that, what do you do? Hopefully you've saved enough money to retire, but what do you do with your life. Whereas, an aeronautical engineer, has a profession that will last a lifetime, full of accomplishments and pride, that overall will provide you with just as much income and a sustainable retirement for you and your family," said James.

"Your father is right, Gary. You should enjoy the ride as an outstanding athlete and baseball pitcher while at the University, and upon graduation, look at it as a period in your life for you to remember as a wonderful dream and a game that had to end, in order for you to develop and nurture your major talents as an aeronautical engineer, a profession that will benefit all mankind," said his grandfather, Eric Longbow, whose wisdom everyone respected.

"You know, Grandpa, that thought occurred to me, and I agree with you. I will turn down Mister Monroe's offer," said Gary.

"I was hoping you'd say that, Gary. I'd hate to take those flying lessons without you," said Alex.

"I think you made a wise decision, Gary. I'm so proud of you," said Louise.

"Well, now that's settled, what shall we order?" asked David with gusto.

At Falcon Aviation, Gary and Alex reported for their first flight lesson, and were surprised to learn they had a choice of training on a Cessna 172 Skyhawk, single-engine, high wing, 4-seat aircraft, or a Brantly B-2, 2-seat helicopter and Brantly 305, 5-seat helicopter. They decided to postpone their decision until they had an opportunity to talk with their fathers.

Gary and Alex gathered with their fathers, on the patio in back of the Longbow house, to discuss the issue of fixed wing versus helicopter aircraft training.

"While we've had for some time at Curtiss-Wright, fixed wing aircrafts, such as the Air Travel 6000-B, and recently the Cessna 172, a most popular single-engine 4-seat aircraft, we've also acquired a Fairchild-Hiller FA-1100, 5-seat helicopter, which we found to be more suitable for business trips and landing choices," said James Longbow.

"Have you been trained to fly helicopters, Dad?" asked Gary.

"No, I haven't, and neither has Dave, so the company had to hire a helicopter pilot," replied James.

"You might consider the fact that when you two graduate from UB, you'll be eligible for the draft, and their need for helicopter pilots. You might also consider the fact that you have a guaranteed job as aircraft designers at Curtiss-Wright Corporation, where Jim and I are in charge of that division. If you are FAA certified as helicopter pilots, you could fly the company's helicopter, discontinuing the need for employment of a helicopter pilot, which would add to your salary, and usefulness to the company," said David Siegel.

"I might add that you would be able to use the company's helicopter, which seats the pilot and four passengers, on special occasions, with the president's permission," said James Longbow.

"Sounds like you both are recommending we train as helicopter pilots. Is that what I'm hearing?" asked Gary.

"That's about it, Gary. I just think that under the circumstances, it makes perfect sense for you guys to get certified as helicopter pilots. Just remember that your expected tour of duty in Vietnam is 12 months, and as helicopter pilots, you can opt to fly Med-Evac helicopters rather than attack helicopters. If you should later decide to also get certified as fixed-wing aircraft pilots, you can always do that at Falcon Aviation as time permits," said James.

"I have to agree with Jim. Your best bet is to train as helicopter pilots, and as you explained to us, Falcon Aviation will train you in both the Brantly two-seater and the four-seater helicopters, giving you a real leg-up on other Air Force cadets in training," said David.

"That's what we did, when we joined the Air Force. We were already FAA Certified as pilots, so we were able to skip training 101, and move directly to the next level of training, and graduating at the top of the class gave us a better choice of assignment," said James.   Gary looked at Alex, then addressed their fathers with a decision he felt was shared by Alex.

"I'm glad we decided to consult with you first. What you have said about the advantages of training as helicopter pilots makes a lot of sense, and unless Alex disagrees with me, which I don't think he does, we're going to train as helicopter pilots and get FAA certified," said Gary.

"I agree with Gary. I think it'll be fun flying those helicopters," said Alex.

"Well, I'm glad we all agree on this. It's an important decision, and you've addressed it in a most sensible and mature way. Thank you for consulting us," said David.

The two ambitious aviators, nevertheless, did not neglect their studies which formed the nucleus of their goals for the future, and they still had time to play baseball for the Bulls, although their attendance at practice sessions was less than Coach Watson expected of his star ball players. Talent scout Pete Monroe attempted one more time to recruit Gary Longbow, who convinced him that no amount of money or other incentive could change his decision, hence not to bother him again, and Alex gave Monroe the same answer, ending Monroe's recruitment hopes.

The University of New York at Buffalo's Graduation Ball was only three weeks away, and neither Jackie nor Rachel had been asked by Gary and Alex to be their date for that celebrated ball, which culminated their four-year attendance and graduation with bachelor's degrees in aeronautical engineering.

"What's keeping these guys from asking us to join them at the graduation ball?" asked Rachel.

"I guess they're just taking us for granted. We've been doing things together, including sailing, for so long, that they just expect us to know there can be no one else for them to bring to the ball," replied Jackie.

"Well, I think they need some prodding, and I'm going to mention it to Gary when I see him later," said Rachel.

"While you're at it, prod your brother Alex, will you?" said Jackie.

"OK! I will, with pleasure," replied Rachel.

"You know, Jackie, they're now going to be eligible for the draft into the Army, and possibly be assigned overseas to Vietnam. Has Alex brought up the subject of marriage yet?" asked Rachel.

"No, he hasn't, and I don't think it's because he doesn't want to. He just doesn't think he's quite ready, and Gary takes from his father, who didn't want to marry my mother until he had a steady job to support her. So I think he won't propose to you until he's discharged from the Army, and has a job at Curtiss-Wright Corporation, and Alex will follow those guidelines too," said Jackie.

"Well, that's fine, but I think we should still bring up the subject, and get an agreed commitment from them, that after they're discharged and have a job, we'll get married," said Rachel.

"That sounds too direct and almost an ultimatum, Rachel. You have to maneuver them gently into the conversation about love and the suffering anguish we'll be going through worrying about their safety in Vietnam. Their assurance of marriage upon their return would lighten the burden we'll be carrying during their time of peril in the Far East," said Jackie.

"Good God, Jackie, you should write romance novels. They'd be on the New York Times Best Seller List," said Rachel.

"Now wait a minute, Rachel. I meant every word of it. I would die if anything happened to Alex. Nevertheless, sometimes you have to use some finesse to bring your thoughts into action, that's all, " replied Jackie.

"Yes, I know you love my brother, and I love your brother too. It's just that I don't take anything for granted. Maybe I'm insecure. I like to be sure about things that are important to me," said Rachel.

"Hey! I don't blame you, Rachel. But in this case, Gary is a sure thing," said Jackie.

Two days later, Gary and Alex formally invited Rachel and Jackie to the Graduation Ball, and during a romantic moment at the ball, the girls managed to extract a commitment of marriage upon their discharge from the Army. What may have precipitated their agreement, was the fact that coitus was being withheld until their wedding night, a lesson learned from their mothers, who only violated that promise because of extreme circumstances brought about by their fiancés' dangerous bombing missions over Germany during World War Two.

CHAPTER VII

Service as US Army Helicopter Pilots in Vietnam War

The war in Vietnam in the summer of 1968 was at its height in activity with more than half a million United States Army servicemen serving in that country. They were there to assist the South Vietnamese in their fight against North Vietnam's invasion to unite Vietnam as a communist country. The major city and capital of South Vietnam was Saigon, considered the Paris of Asia, and most US servicemen on leave, made it to Saigon for its entertainment and female companionship. Drugs such as marihuana, heroin and cocaine were readily available, and some US servicemen availed themselves of these addictive drugs to relieve the severe anxiety of combat in a thick and impenetrable jungle, where the temperature and humidity reached 100 degrees Fahrenheit. Its nightmarish environment was infested with over 100 different species of snakes, including cobras and vipers, most of them poisonous. It also included two snakes that could crush a person to death, namely the Burmese python and the Boa constrictor. As if that wasn't enough, especially when camped out at night, soldiers had to contend with wild boars, tarantulas the size of a frying pan, rats, lizards, scorpions, bats, orangutans, spiders, monkeys, centipedes, and long-beaked malaria carrying mosquitoes that could bite through clothes. And then, they had to watch for booby traps and ambushes by the Vietcong. But draftees with assignment to Vietnam were not made aware of those conditions until they were in the country, facing the reality of war in Vietnam.

Gary Longbow and Alex Siegel reported to the Army Induction Center in Buffalo, New York as required, now that their educational deferment from the draft had expired. After providing documentation of their graduation from the University of New York at Buffalo and their FAA Certification as helicopter pilots, they were sworn in as Second Lieutenants in the US Army, and ordered to report to Fort Sam Huston, Texas for officer basic training, then on to Fort Wolters, Mineral Hills, Texas, for primary training in a 2-seat TH-55 helicopter for a period of nine months. This involved pre-flight training, pre-solo learning to hover, then cross-country flying, even though they both held FAA Certification as helicopter pilots. They were told they had to learn to fly the Army way. They were then transferred to Fort Rucker, Alabama for advanced flight training on instruments, and the Huey B & D model helicopters, which lasted four months. Finally they graduated as basic aviators, and were given ten days leave of absence, before reporting to McGuire Air Force Base, New Jersey for shipment to Vietnam via Travis Air Force Base, California. Having already served thirteen months in training, they became eligible and were promoted from Second Lieutenant to First Lieutenant.

Gary and Alex quickly booked a flight from Dothan Regional Airport, about 22 miles from Fort Rucker, to Buffalo International Airport, anxious to be with their family before shipment to Vietnam.

While in the air, the two aviators discussed their experience with Army flight training, and their expectations once in Vietnam.

"We've both been assigned to the US Army Vietnam Med-Evac Detachment," said Alex. "So, at least we'll be saving lives, not taking them."

"Well, that's true, but we'll also be very vulnerable to attack in the air and on the ground," replied Gary.

"Yeah! But won't we be escorted by Cobra gun-ships, which have two machine guns on each side, and seven rockets on the port and starboard side of the helicopter. That's a lot of fire power," said Alex.

"That's the plan of action, but the reality may be different. We'll see. But let's not divulge to the girls the dangers we'll be facing. Let's just emphasize that we'll be evacuating the wounded to various hospitals, which is the truth," said Gary.

"Yeah! And we can show them our Special Orders assigning us to a Med-Evac Detachment," replied Alex.

When they arrived at the Buffalo airport, Jackie and Rachel were there to meet them with a loving embrace, and salutations from their parents who would see them later. These two tall, handsome aviators wore their uniform bearing helicopter wings over their breast pocket with the pride of the Yankees, had they accepted that career.

"You guys wear that uniform as if it had been tailor made," said Jackie. "I'm so proud of you."

"Yes, and we're going to show you off, when we go dancing at the Lakebeach Yacht Club this coming Saturday," said Rachel.

"You still have your sailboats in the water?" asked Gary.

"Yes, the season is not over yet, Gary. Mom and Dad still use it on occasion, and so do Dave and Susan," replied Jackie.

"Well that's good, but I don't think we'll have time to make use of it while we're here, with only eight days left before we leave," said Gary.

"Only eight days?" asked Rachel.

"Yes, we have orders to report to McGuire Air Force Base, where we'll be boarding a plane for Travis Air Force Base in California. That's the point of embarkation for our flight to Vietnam," said Alex.

"My God! It's happening already. Now I know how Mom and Louise felt when their fiancés left for England," said Rachel.

"Like watching an old deja-vu movie, huh!" said Alex.

"Personal episodes, like history, have a way of repeating themselves," said Gary.

"Yeah! Well, I hope their incarceration as prisoners of war is not one of those repeatable episodes," said Jackie.

"Amen!" said Rachel.

"I hope you guys are not tired from your travel," said Jackie. "The whole family wants to greet you this evening for dinner at the Lackawanna mansion. We'll stop at the house first, so you can freshen up, then we want you to wear your uniform this evening. You know how that will impress grandfather."

"Let's not forget our own parents who proudly wore the Army Air Corps uniform, and now you guys are carrying the baton for our generation," said Rachel.

"I never thought of it that way, Rachel, but you're right. We're carrying on the tradition for this generation, and we'll have to get to work on the next generation to continue this honorable tradition," said Gary with a mischievous grin.

"I think you're getting ahead of yourself, Gary. There are a couple of hurdles you have to jump over before you cross the finish line, my friend," said Jackie.

The large dining room at the Sontag mansion easily catered to the entire Sontag, Longbow and Siegel family, including Gary's grandfather Eric Longbow, a widower, whose son James, now a Brigadier General, was his sole heir and devotee.

Marie Sontag, the matriarch, governed the kitchen and cooks she hired for the occasion, enabling her to occasionally mingle with her guests, and sit down to dinner next to her husband Michael.

James sauntered into the kitchen, captivated by the wonderful aroma of freshly cooked meat, and observed his mother-in-law at work overseeing the cooks.

"On this special occasion, Jim, now that you're a Brigadier General, I think you should have worn your uniform with the silver stars on your shoulders. Gary and Alex are proudly wearing their uniform, although I noticed that Dave did not wear his, probably following your lead," said Marie Sontag

"I just didn't want to steal the boys' thunder. This is their celebration on the occasion of their newly appointed commission, and graduation as helicopter pilots," replied James in deference to his mother-in-law.

"I suppose you're right, Jim. I never thought of that," replied Marie. "You're a very thoughtful man. I can see why you got promoted to General."

"Well, I hope it wasn't due to my good manners, Marie," said James in good humor.

James left the kitchen to join the rest of the family, and found his wife Louise conversing with her best friend and next door neighbor Susan Siegel.

"I see you've been in the kitchen," said Louise. "Found anything good to eat?"

"Marie's got everything under control, and I wouldn't dare touch any of the food before it's ready to be served," replied James.

"Marie runs a tight ship and the kitchen is her domain. Even Michael doesn't go in there, unless it's to smell the cooking and compliment her," said Louise.

"So, what topic of conversation have I interrupted?" asked James.

"Well, it's about our sons going to Vietnam. We've been reading in the newspapers about the conditions there, and the savagery of the Vietcong towards our soldiers, and it worries us," said Louise, with Susan agreeing.

"Actually, Gary and Alex will be flying helicopters rescuing our wounded soldiers from the field of combat. They're not ground soldiers, fighting the Vietcong in the jungles of Vietnam," said James.

"Yes, but what if they're shot down, then they could be captured and become prisoners of war like what happened to you and Dave in Germany," said Susan.

"I'm sure they'll be escorted by helicopter gun-ships to protect them during their rescue operations," said James, attempting to minimize Susan's fears, and those of Louise as well.

"Is there ever going to be a time when we'll have enduring peace, so our children will never see another war?" asked Susan rhetorically.

"The only way to have enduring peace is to be so militarily strong that no one in their right mind will dare start a war with us," replied James.

"Yeah! But the operative word is *right mind*," replied Louise.

With the dinner nearly over, Michael Sontag stood up and raised his glass of wine to toast his two guests of honor.

"To Gary and Alex, our generation's warriors, we wish you success in your mission, honor in your duty to your country, and safe return to your family and friends," said Michael.

"Aye! Aye! Cheered everyone, now standing around the dining table with raised glasses of wine, which they imbibed merrily.

That Saturday evening, the Lakebeach Yacht Club was crowded with members and guests, every dining table occupied. Gary and Alex, accompanied by Rachel and Jackie, sat at a table for eight, inasmuch as they were joined this evening by James, Louise, David and Susan, who knew they might not see their sons again for a very long time.

During the evening, several members of the yacht club came over to greet Gary and Alex, wearing their Army uniform, to wish them well. However, those younger members of draft age with whom they had sailed in various races and regattas, were not present, and the Vietnam war was to blame for that interruption in their lives.

"The atmosphere in the club is not the same, now that its youth has gone to war," said James.

"Reminds me of what we went through twenty-four years ago," said Louise.

"Well, at least you know you'll be in Vietnam for twelve months only, then you'll be home," said David.

"Yes, that's a relief in itself," said Susan. "In the last war, our men remained in Europe for four years before returning home."

"That must have been tough on you, Mom, and you too, aunt Louise," said Alex.

"Well, that's over now, and I'd just as soon forget about it. But you boys have now been given the responsibility of rescuing our wounded soldiers so they can return to their families. Just make sure you come back to us safe and sound," said Susan.

"Don't worry Mom, we don't intend to remain in Vietnam any longer than we have to," said Alex.

"I'll say Amen to that. I'm not a tropical creature, and I hear that the temperature in Vietnam reaches 100 degrees and the humidity is oppressive," said Gary.

"Look fellows, go there with a positive attitude, and make the best of everything. Believe me, things will go a lot smoother if you learn to deal with each situation, regardless of its difficulty, with audacity and determination to succeed," said James.

Gary and Alex listened to James, now a Brigadier General, with pride at having him as their role model. They secretly promised themselves they would earn his respect, and that of David, now a Colonel.

The day of their departure, Gary and Alex were driven to Niagara Falls Air Force Base by Rachel and Jackie, after having said their farewell to their parents in Williamsville, New York.

Standing at the doorway to the airport terminal, the two couples embraced with tears in the eyes of Rachel and Jackie, as they finally said goodbye, releasing them from their yearning hands.

"I'll write to you, Rachel, as often as I can," said Gary.

"Me too, Jackie, and don't worry, we'll be alright," said Alex.

The two aviators walked towards the C-47 military transport aircraft, and reaching the top of the metal staircase, turned and waved goodbye, then disappeared inside the aircraft, for the short flight to McGuire Air Force Base, New Jersey. Their connecting flight to Travis Air Force Base, Fairfield, California was not due for departure until the following morning. The flight from McGuire Air Force Base to Travis Air Force Base was long and uneventful, however upon disembarking the aircraft, Gary and Alex witnessed the sobering unloading from a C-141 long-range transport aircraft, of several plain, unpainted aluminum coffins containing the bodies of soldiers from Vietnam.

"Jesus, what a welcoming reminder of where we're going and what we're getting into," said Alex.

"Well, in a war you can expect some people will die. Hopefully there won't be many, and it won't be us," replied Gary. "Let's get a room in the Bachelor Officers Quarters."

The following morning, Gary and Alex boarded a military chartered Boeing 707 jet aircraft from Continental Airlines, contracted by Military Assistance Command Vietnam (MACV), with destination Tan Son Nhut Air Base, also serving as the Saigon International Airport.

The flight made a refueling stop at Wake Island, which Gary was told by one of the stewardesses, was located in the middle of the Pacific Ocean, and some 2000 miles west of Honolulu, Hawaii. A second refueling stop was made at

Clark Air Force Base in the Philippines. Finally, after some 22 hours, they landed at Tan Son Nhut Air Base, Vietnam.

The first thing they noticed were the flags representing the various countries engaged in the Vietnam war, flying on top of the airport terminal building, and then the humid heat.

Upon entry into the terminal, the military passengers were met by an Army Lieutenant and two sergeants, requesting to see their special orders for their unit of assignment in Vietnam.

Gary and Alex were directed to a bus waiting outside the terminal with a sign above the windshield reflecting the name Camp Alpha, located a couple of miles adjacent to Tan Son Nhut Air Base. Upon arrival, they were billeted in barracks reserved for officers, and told they would be there for a day or two for processing and assignment to their respective units.

Upon receipt of their special orders, Gary and Alex compared notes.

"I've been assigned to the 247 Medical Detachment at Nah Trang. How about you?" asked Gary.

"Same Detachment, thank God," replied Alex. "Let's take a look at the map you've got of Vietnam."

"Looks like it's about 20 miles north of Cam Ranh Bay, and about half-way along the coast to the DMZ and North Vietnam," said Gary.

"Yeah! But I'm wondering if we're each going to be assigned a separate helicopter or fly together as pilot and co-pilot, which I would certainly prefer," said Alex.

"We'll find out soon enough when we get to the 247 Med-Evac Detachment," replied Gary.

The next day, Gary and Alex boarded a C-130 aircraft and upon arrival at Nah Trang, they were met by a US Army officer who introduced himself as Captain George Sealy. He invited them to join him in his jeep for transport to Detachment Headquarters consisting of a refurbished French Colonial house from the days of French occupation that ended with the Dien Bien Phu offensive. Inside his office, Captain Sealy briefed them on their assignment at the 247 Medical Evacuation Detachment, with the desired news they would be assigned together as pilot and co-pilot with Gary as the flight commander. They would be flying the Huey UH-1D helicopter.

"You'll be flying a Bell UH-1D Huey helicopter, and your crew chief will be Staff Sergeant John Esposito, and your patient protector will be Staff Sergeant Tom Savorski. You'll also have a medic on board to take care of the wounded, and determine which medical facility is best equipped to treat your patients, using your radio," said Captain Sealy.

"By patient protector, you mean door gunner?" asked Gary.

"That's correct. He'll be armed with either an M-16 or an M-60. In case you're not familiar with the M-60, it similar to the Browning Automatic Rifle familiarly known as the BAR. We use the term *patient protector* to comply with the Geneva Convention," replied Sealy.

"Will we be accompanied by a gun-ship, sir?" asked Alex.

"Occasionally, depending on the intensity of the fighting. We don't have any gun-ships here at Nah Trang. The nearest are some 20 miles away," replied Sealy.

"Where do we go to get our gear and flight suit?" asked Gary.

"I'm having Sergeant Marcos drive you to our supply warehouse, where you'll be issued your flight suits, fatigues, boots, and other equipment,. You'll get your Smith & Wesson .38 caliber pistol with shoulder holster from Unit Supply, with a pocket strip of additional ammo," said Sealy. "Any questions before I have Sergeant Marcos drive you to the warehouse and unit supply, and afterwards to your billets, where you'll meet other pilots who'll be glad to bring you up to speed and share their experiences with you?"

"No sir. Thank you for the briefing," replied Gary for the two of them.

"Well then, welcome aboard, and I'm sure you'll be well received by our other pilots and crew," said Sealy.

At the warehouse, Gary and Alex were issued their clothing and equipment, including a US RT-159 survival radio, and a .38 caliber pistol with holster from Unit Supply. In addition, they were given a B-4B canvas suitcase with large side pocket in which to carry their stuff. They were then driven to a World War Two barracks, partitioned into single rooms. Upon entering the one-story building, they were immediately met by four Chief Warrant Officers dressed in flight suits.

The nearest one, a stocky, dirty-blond haired man in his mid-twenties, greeted Gary and Alex with a reserved smile.

"I'm Rufus White and this is my co-pilot Max Schmitt."

"Glad to meet you," replied Gary, extending his hand for a handshake. "I'm Gary and this is my co-pilot Alex."

"And I'm Bill Paxton and this is Tom Grover, my partner in crime," shaking hands with Gary and Alex.

"Are you the only Med-Evac crew besides us? asked Gary.

"No, two crews are still out in the field, and one crew is probably in the snack bar," said Rufus White. "You guys complete the Med-Evac Detachment, which has only six Huey helicopters. Welcome aboard. Those two bunks over there at the end are reserved for you guys,"

After settling down with all of their gear stored away in their wall and foot lockers, Gary and Alex got into conversation with their fellow aviators.

"This must be your first time in Vietnam," said White.

"Yes, it is for the both of us," replied Gary.

"Well, has anyone told you about the snakes in this country?" asked Schmitt.

"I read there were several poisonous ones to be aware of," replied Alex.

"Just be careful when you land your helicopter in the jungle, that snakes won't crawl into your chopper. They're real fast and deadly, but we found a sure-fire way to keep them out," said Schmitt.

"Oh! Yeah, how?" asked Alex with Gary looking on with great curiosity.

"By urinating on the floor to both door entrances, which animals do to demarcate their territory, and it works," said Schmitt, with White agreeing with him.

"Well, I guess Army Headquarters must have heard of your urinating solution, because we were issued a snake repellent canister and told to spray the two entrances to our helicopter, and it would prevent any snakes from entering it," said Gary.

"Really! Where did you get those canisters?" asked White with great surprise and curiosity.

"The same place you got your pissing solution, wise guy," replied Gary with a smile that brought loud laughter from Tom Grover, but not from White and Schmitt.

"Oh! So you're a smart ass. What did you say your last name was?" asked White.

"I didn't, but my last name is Longbow and Alex' last name is Siegel. Is that a problem?"

"Well, now, that depends...judging from your family names, aren't you an Indian and your co-pilot a Jew?" asked White.

"Yes, what of it?" replied Gary.

"In that case, you two deserve to get the only black medic in the Detachment. Leroy Washington," said White.

"I'll bet you're from either Alabama or Georgia, and belong to the Klu Klux Klan," said Gary.

"That's pretty clever of you, Tonto. I'm from Montgomery, Alabama, and yes, I'm a member of the Ku Klux Klan and proud of it," said White.

"And what about you, Max? Are you also a member of the Ku Klux Klan?" asked Gary.

"As a matter of fact, I'm also from Montgomery, and in the same KKK Unit," replied Max Schmitt. "We don't agree with the Army's desegregation policy, and strongly resent having an Indian and a Jew in the same barracks with us. Thankfully, Leroy Washington, as a non-commissioned officer, can't be billeted with us officers."

Alex watched Gary's quiet, stealth approach towards White, knowing only too well Gary's quick, aggressive action when offended, he readied himself in support.

"I'm from New York and so is Alex, and we have no tolerance for racists, and the Ku Klux Klan is nothing more than an American terrorist organization that needs to be destroyed. I'm glad Leroy Washington was assigned to my flight crew. He's probably the best Medic in the Detachment," said Gary, now only a couple of feet facing Rufus White.

"I don't mind you calling me a racist, but when you insult the Ku Klux Klan, those are fighting words, Mister," said White.

"Whitey, you asked for it," barked Gary, hitting Whitey on the jaw with a powerful punch that knocked him flat on his back, unconscious. Alex immediately stepped in to block Max Schmitt from joining the fight.

"You want to join him, Max?" asked Alex, now in a fighting configuration.

Max remained silent, realizing the futility of any further aggression.

"Hey! C'mon, guys," said Tom Glover, stepping in between them, while Bill Paxton was kneeling down to revive White. "We're here to fight the Gooks, not each other, for Christ-sake. Let's call a truce."

"You tell Whitey that Leroy Washington is part of my crew, and if I hear of any abuse of Leroy, I will take that as a personal affront, and deal with him accordingly. You got that Max?" said Gary.

"In case you didn't, Max, Let me tell you that we Jews won't tolerate discrimination and racism. I thought the Second World War had taught you Krauts a lesson. In case it didn't, I WILL," said Alex whose big frame was ready to back him up.

Rufus White regained consciousness, and was helped into a standing position, feeling his jaw with his hand while looking at Gary with his back turned, walking back to his cubicle with Alex in tow.

"Man, this guys' got a quick temper, and a fighting disposition," said Max to White.

"If I were you, Rufus, I wouldn't advertise your membership in the Ku Klux Klan, not around here anyway," said Tom Grover, from the Pine Tree State of Maine, with no affiliation with the Ku Klux Klan or other subversive organizations. "Someday, you may just need those guys."

Gary decided not to wait until the following day to visit Leroy Washington, residing in the next barracks, and he was accompanied by Alex Siegel in his visit.

Upon entering the barracks of non-commissioned officers in the various ranks of Sergeant, Gary and Alex were greeted by the full complement of crew members for the six helicopter flights.

Noticing the only black crew member, half-way through the barracks, Gary and Alex walked up to him and introduced themselves.

"Hi Leroy. I'm Gary Longbow your flight commander, and this is my co-pilot Alex Siegel. We thought we should make your acquaintance right away, and welcome you to our crew."

"That's very thoughtful of you, sir. I'm glad to be part of your crew," said Washington.

"Where're you from?" asked Gary.

"From Philadelphia, the city of brotherly love, sir," replied Washington.

"We're both from Buffalo, New York, not far from you," replied Gary.

"I know the area, well, sir. You're located between two Great Lakes, Erie and Ontario, a nice place to visit and live, I'm sure," said Washington.

"Just so you know, Leroy, the Army has not yet completed its integration, so if anyone gives you any flak because of your race, I want you to tell me right away, so I can put a stop to it. OK?" said Gary.

"Yes sir, I appreciate that, but I can take care of myself, sir. Don't you worry about that, sir," replied Leroy Washington, whose physique could have earned him a place as a full-back on a football team.

"If you need anything, just let us know. I presume our Crew Chief, Sergeant John Esposito and our Door Gunner, Sergeant Tom Savorski are billeted in another barracks," said Gary.

"Yes, that's correct, sir. But they'll be at the briefing tomorrow morning for you to meet them," said Washington..

"Alright then, Leroy. See you tomorrow at the briefing," said Gary, shaking Leroy's hand.

Gary and Alex decided to visit the snack bar for a hamburger and a milkshake, and as they sat down to a table, they were joined by Tom Grover.

"Do you mind if I join you?" asked Grover.

"No, pull up a chair," said Alex.

"I'm sorry about what happened. I wasn't aware of those guys' affiliation with the KKK," said Grover.

"What about Bill Paxton, your flight commander. He just watched and never said a word," said Alex.

"Yeah! Well, Bill is the quiet type. He's from Manassas, Virginia, and frankly, I don't know anything about him. He never talks about his family, and is a very private person. But the mere fact that he avoided any participation in tonight's action, tells me he just wants to serve his time and go home," said Grover.

"I can't say I blame him," said Gary. "We all want to serve our time and go home, hopefully alive and in one piece."

"So, two crews are out in the field right now, huh! said Alex.

"Yeah! They went out together, because of the number of casualties they had to evacuate," said Grover.

"Captain Sealy won't send you guys out right away. Not until you've gotten the hang of using the Personnel Rescue Hoist," said Grover.

"We didn't get to use the rescue hoist in our training," said Gary.

"Well, the hoist is a winch mounted on a support anchored to the roof and floor of the helicopter cabin with a moveable metal arm inside the right side door behind the pilot's seat. So when the door is open, the hoist located at the end of its metal arm, can be rotated to position the cable and pulleys outside the helicopter, and clear of the skids, so the cable carrying a litter or harness can be lowered as far as 250 feet below the chopper, and raised from the ground carrying as much as 600 pounds," said Grover.

"Whose job is it to operate the hoist?" asked Alex.

"That job goes to the crew chief or the medical corpsman, and sometimes the crew chief lowers the medic to bring the wounded back up into the chopper," said Grover.

"That's really exposing the medic to enemy fire," said Gary.

"I'll tell you one thing. You don't want to hover and hoist casualties for more than a few minutes, if you don't want to get shot down by RPG's, that's rocket propelled grenade launchers, and potato masher styled hand grenades, which we refer to as CHICOM's," said Grover.

"I think we should've stayed home. What do you think, Gary?" said Alex, in good humor.

"Naw! These guys need our help. Besides, the Army made us an offer we couldn't refuse," replied Gary.

"What's that?" asked Grover.

"Why, that great hazardous duty pay, of course," said Gary with a contagious laugh.

"You know, you guys are a laugh a minute," said Grover, smiling.

"By the way, when you get back to the barracks, check your bedding to make sure you weren't short-sheeted. It's Rufus White's way of initiating newcomers to what he considers his barracks," said Grover.

"Thanks for the warning, but we've been schooled by our veteran fathers about that, and other pranks on recruits. You fold the bottom sheet in two, bring the end up to look like the top sheet, so when I climb into bed, my legs can't go more than a couple of feet," said Gary.

"Looks like you guys have everything under control. I'm glad I spoke with you. See you at tomorrow's briefing," said Grover, getting up from the table and exiting the snack bar.

"That Tom Grover is really a nice guy," said Alex.

"Yeah! The only two bad apples are Whitey and Max, but I think we've got them in check," said Gary.

"Huh! Huh! The more I know you, the more you remind me of what my Dad told me about your father's quick temper and readiness for action," said Alex.

"You must know more about my father than I do, 'cause he seldom talks about his experiences in the military. But your Dad knows my father better than anyone, having served with him as his co-pilot on those B-17 Bombers over Germany, and then being prisoners of war together in a Nazi concentration camp," said Gary.

"Yeah! My Dad told me a lot, but not everything, I'm sure," replied Alex.

The following morning, while eating breakfast in the Mess Hall in the officers section, Gary and Alex were joined by Captain Sealy.

"When you're through with your chow, c'mon over to base operations where you'll meet your crew, including the medic assigned to your flight. You've got some flight training to do before you're sent on any med-evac missions," said Sealy.

"We're looking forward to the training and the missions, sir," replied Gary, not mentioning his meeting with Leroy Washington the previous evening.

"I'm glad you're on board, because our sixth Huey was unused for some time, until you got here. Now we're at full strength," said Sealy.

At Base Operations, the Detachment Commander, Captain George Sealy, was joined by the Executive Officer, First Lieutenant Steve Crawford for an in-briefing about policy and procedures to the new crew consisting of First Lieutenants Gary Longbow, Alex Siegel, and Sergeants John Esposito, Sergeant Tom Saverski, and Leroy Washington.

"Welcome to the 247th Med-Evac Detachment. Chief Warrant Officer Mark Kowalski will be your flight instructor on the Huey UH-1. He will conduct your in-country standardization ride, local area orientation as well as Landing Zone training and hoist operation. This training will take two days. Afterwards, you'll be assigned operational missions. Based on your performance, one of you Lieutenants will be assigned as the aircraft commander," said Captain Sealy.

At the conclusion of the in-country checkout, Lieutenant Gary Longbow was assigned the position of aircraft commander, with Alex Siegel as his co-pilot.

A week transpired before a call came through from Base Operations for two med-evac aircraft to fly to Phu Bai, and assist in the evacuation of the wounded during Operation Safe Harbor. Crews headed by Gary Longbow and Rufus White departed Nha Trang to Tuy Hoa for refueling, then onto Phu Bai where combat operations were taking place with two Cobra gunships firing at North Vietnamese regulars, assaulting a US fire base, with several casualties evident and ready for evacuation. Rufus took the lead in landing at the firebase and his aircraft was immediately taking fire, receiving heavy damage to the aircraft, and wounding some of its occupants, including Rufus White who had left his position to help in the rescue of patients near the downed helicopter. Longbow landed nearby, and the gunner Tom Savorski and Medic Leroy Washington, left their aircraft to rescue the Rufus crew.

Rufus had sustained wounds in both legs incapacitating him, while his co-pilot Max Schmitt lay in a pool of blood inside the aircraft with fatal injuries to the head. Leroy Washington ran over to Rufus, and quickly realizing the gravity of his wounds, threw him over his shoulder and brought him safely back to the Longbow aircraft where the remaining Rufus crew was already on board. They immediately departed the area, flying to the nearest hospital located at Da Nang.

Rufus White was quickly admitted for surgery which saved both his legs. Lying in a hospital bed, the doctor told him that his quick rescue and rapid transportation to the hospital saved not only his legs, but also his life, due to the loss of blood. White grasped the irony of his rescue with the realization he owed his life to Leroy Washington, a black man.

Back at the 247th Med-Evac Detachment, Captain Sealy was informed about the death of Chief Warrant Officer Max Schmitt, and the hospitalization of CWO Rufus White, who would not be returning to the 247th Med-Evac Detachment. He was being transferred to the United States for medical rehabilitation and reassignment. This meant that the 247th Med-Evac Detachment now had only five medical-evacuation crews available with no replacement in sight.

The next several weeks saw a significant increase in the demand for medical evacuation rescue flights from the 247th Med-Evac Detachment, that so far, had not cost the detachment any loss of crew personnel. Then a call for assistance came from a small combat unit located four miles south of Thanh Hoa, that had suffered a single but serious casualty. Longbow's flight crew was assigned that rescue mission.

Gary Longbow and his co-pilot Alex Siegel, with their usual crew consisting of his crew chief, Staff Sergeant John Esposito, his door-gunner, Staff Sergeant Tom Savorski, armed with an M-60 automatic rifle, and his Medic, Leroy Washington, took flight on their Huey UH-1, for the jungle a few miles south of Thanh Hoa. Upon arrival at the coordinates provided to Longbow and Siegel, they used their air-to-ground radio to contact the platoon leader who indicated he would use a yellow grenade due to the thick green foliage surrounding them. Owing to the dense terrain preventing a landing, Esposito was instructed to lower the hoist attached to a litter to bring up the wounded soldier. The small opening in the thick foliage in which Esposito had to lower the litter presented a problem with the force of the wind. The litter finally disappeared through the foliage and when the line slacked indicating it has reached the ground, a rocket propelled grenade hit the propeller housing causing the helicopter to crash through the dense jungle that actually softened the impact, with its crew suffering bruises but no disabling injuries. They quickly exited the damaged aircraft, and found themselves under fire, along with the platoon that now numbered only 27 of the 39 infantrymen they had started out with. It appeared they were facing a much larger enemy force then previously reported.

The Lieutenant, Martin Lovejoy, in charge of the platoon, now called for air support, as did Longbow, but their defensive position became untenable when the large Vietnamese force, seemingly indifferent to the loss of life, overran the platoon, killing several US soldiers and capturing the remainder, including the Longbow crew, minus Sergeant Tom Savorki, who became a target when he used the M-60 rifle against the oncoming enemy, and lost his life.

"We're outmanned and outgunned, fellows," said Longbow to Alex, Esposito and Washington. "Drop your gun belts and keep your hands raised, 'cause they'll shoot you if you look at them sideways."

"There must be a whole battalion of them. I guess the Lieutenant didn't see them," said Alex, as they were being assembled by the North Vietnamese soldiers with rifles pointed at them to discourage any resistance.

A North Vietnamese officer in the rank of Major, suddenly walked up to the assembled prisoners, and singled out Lieutenant Lovejoy from the bars on his lapels as the apparent officer in charge. In surprisingly good English, he addressed the Lieutenant in a condescending tone that left no doubt about his contempt for him and his men.

"I am Major Chien Duong. You are all prisoners of the Democratic Republic of North Vietnam, and will be imprisoned for the duration of the war. You will now march to your new home as uninvited guests. Any attempts to escape will be punishable by death. Is that understood Lieutenant?"

"Yes. May I ask how far we'll have to walk to reach your prison? Some of my men are injured," said Lieutenant Lovejoy.

"At least five miles, then you'll be taken by trucks to prison. Those who cannot sustain the march will be shot," said Major Duong in a firm, non-emotional voice.

"I must object to this forced march of several injured soldiers, which is against the Geneva Convention," said Lovejoy.

"Who is your second in command, Lieutenant?" asked Duong.

"Master Sergeant Philby," replied Lovejoy, motioning Philby to step forward.

Major Duong pulled out his revolver and summarily shot Lovejoy in the head killing him instantly. "Sergeant Philby, you are now in command of the prisoners. Any questions?"

"No, sir," replied Philby, stunned by the cold brutality of the Major.

A junior North Vietnamese officer walked up to the Major and told him that the helicopter crew had two officers, pointing to Longbow and Siegel.

"When we get to the Son Tay prison camp, let's separate these two officers from the enlisted men, for intense interrogation. Make sure they survive the march," said Major Duong.

During the march through the jungle, one US soldier got bitten by a viper and collapsed. When his buddy tried to help him, he was stabbed with the point of a North Vietnamese's rifle, and told to get back in the line of prisoners, which he did, leaving his friend to die. By the time they reached a dirt road where two trucks were parked with several Vietnamese soldiers standing by, the prisoner count went from thirty-one, including the Longbow crew of four, to twenty-four. The platoon lost seven men to the jungle of North Vietnam, but only one by reptiles. The other six soldiers, wounded during the skirmish with the North Vietnamese, and unable to endure the forced march, were summarily shot and left in the jungle.

CHAPTER VIII

Dangerous Escape from Camp Hope, North Vietnam

Upon arrival at Son Tay prison camp, the prisoners were made to stand at attention in military formation, two-men deep, in front of Major Chien Duong. Several North Vietnamese soldiers holding rifles and AK-47 assault weapons surrounded the prisoners.

Major Duong walked up to Longbow and Siegel and told them to step forward, which they did. He then instructed one of the guards to escort them to their new home, which turned out to be a large cage made entirely of bamboo sticks tied together with twine, allowing a one to two inch space between the vertical bamboo poles sunk into the ground covered by nearly five feet of tepid water. At gun point, Longbow and Siegel were ordered inside the watery cage through the only entrance door, also made of bamboo, secured with a chain and padlock.

During all of their time in transient to their bamboo cell, Longbow and Siegel remained silent in order to avoid undue attention to themseves. Now alone and confined in their watery bamboo cell, they finally had a chance to compare notes on their precarious situation.

"Well, at least the water is not cold, so we won't suffer from hypothermia," said Longbow.

"Yeah! But snakes can get in through the space between these bamboo poles," said Siegel.

"You know, Alex. When we were brought into this camp, I noticed very few buildings to hold prisoners. This prison camp may be just a holding place until we're transferred to a bigger prison, or else they're going to expand it to accommodate more prisoners," said James Longbow, now looking through the bamboo poles to his right.

"I thought of that too, Gary. What are you looking at?" asked David Siegel, as he waddled through the water towards Longbow.

"We're located next to a river and I see some small boats, and a few canoes tied to a wooden dock," said Longbow.

"Yeah! I see that. I wonder which river this is?" asked Siegel.

"Well, if we consider the location where our aircraft was disabled, the direction of our march which I constantly monitored, and its duration, and the time it took for the trucks to bring us here, figuring they were travelling at about 35 miles per hour, I figure we must be near the Son Cong river, which is a tributary of the Red River. If I remember my North Vietnamese geography, we must be at least 25 miles west of Hanoi, their capital," said Longbow.

"Yeah! That does make sense, Gary. But doesn't that river flow past Hanoi into the Gulf of Tonkin?" asked Siegel.

"Yes, but so what. If we can escape from this cage and steal one of those canoes, we can paddle south west in the hope that one of our patrol helicopters will spot us, and lift us with their hoist for a successful escape. Furthermore, we can then inform our Intelligence unit about the location of this camp, and number of American prisoners, so they can mount an assault on the camp and free those poor guys," said Longbow.

"That sounds good, Gary. but just how do you propose we get out of this hellhole?" asked Siegel.

"Let me think about it, Alex," replied Longbow, examining the structure of their bamboo prison.

Inside the one-story wooden building with corrugated metal roof serving as Major Chien Nguoyen's prison headquarters and office, sat the Major with his deputy Lieutenant Cong Dang and Battalion Commander Lieutenant Sang Pham.

"When do you want me to interrogate the two pilots, sir?" asked Dang.

"Let them appreciate their desperate situation and conditions for three days, then bring one in at a time. First, the co-pilot, and then the pilot. With their bowl of rice, bring them drinking water. We don't want them to suffer dysentery when we interrogate them, " said the Major with a confident smile.

Two days passed with only two visits a day when a bowl of rice with bits of pork and an empty bottle of wine filled with water were brought to them.

"I have a plan which will take both of us to make it work," said Longbow.

"I'm all ears, what is it?" asked Siegel.

"In the far corner which is a sufficient distance from the entrance door not to be noticeable of any change, we'll remove two of those vertical bamboo poles, which are probably planted into the ground below us by about a foot or two, which means that when we pull them up from the ground, they'll be about eight to nine feet long. So we'll have to break them to a length of about five or six feet. But that's OK, because when you break a bamboo pole, it's not an even break, but a splintered break which makes for a sharp point of a spear. Get the idea, Alex?" said Longbow.

"Yeah! I get it, but how do we remove them?" asked Siegel.

"We use our teeth to first break the knot of twine that holds the poles together. Then once the twine is removed, we can first twist the bamboo poles, then pull them up. We can then use them as spears to take out the two guards that come to us daily for our meals," said Longbow.

"That's fine, except that only one of them comes inside our cage to give us the bowls and water bottle, while the other one stands guard outside the cage with his AK-47," said Siegel.

"I thought of that, and this is what we must do. I still have my gold wedding band, right. So when the first guard comes into our cage, you stand back so he has to come towards you. I'll be standing in the front of the cage, but not near the entrance, so the first guard won't come to me. However, once he makes a bee towards you, I'll move close to the entrance and stick my hand out holding my gold ring for the armed guard to see. He'll come close to me to get the ring and that's when I'll shove my submerged bamboo spear right into his stomach while you do the same to the guard in front of you. But you must keep your spear well below the surface so he can't see it," said Longbow.

"Jesus, Gary. I've never killed anyone. I don't know if I can do it, when it's that close and personal," said Siegel.

"Listen Alex. Right now they're feeding us rice with pork and water to keep us in a cooperative mood, while we contemplate the futility of our situation and the possible consequences of our resistance. They haven't interrogated us yet, but they will, and soon.

When we refuse to provide them with the information they want, they'll torture us and even kill us, and that last option is most likely the final outcome of our confinement here. So I ask you, Alex, under these circumstances, when this guard is preventing you from ever seeing your wife and family again, doesn't that make you angry enough to kill him, so you can be free to be with your family again?" asked Longbow.

"Yeah! I guess you're right. If you can do it, so can I. I'm with you buddy," said Siegel.

"OK! Let's get to work on those two bamboo poles," said Longbow. They both worked at cutting the twine with their teeth and wearing their fingernails raw, untying the twine that held the bamboo poles together. Knowing their lives depended on it, they worked diligently until they had both poles out of the muddy flooring and ready for use when time permitted.

The following afternoon, about an hour after their bowl of rice and water was delivered; they heard someone coming towards them.

Two guards appeared at the doorway, and one of them unlocked the door and motioned for Siegel to come forward. He hesitated, so one of them moved inside the cage, and pointing his pistol at Siegel, ordered him to exit the cage, which he did, while Longbow looked at him, wondering if he would ever see his friend again.

Siegel was brought to a one-story building adjacent to the prison's headquarters. Once inside, his hands were tied behind his back with rope and he was seated in an armless wooden chair facing Lieutenant Cong Dang standing before him with a swagger stick.

"I'm Lieutenant Cong Dang, and if you are wondering where I learned to speak such good English, it is because I lived in Los Angeles and attended the University of California and graduated with a Bachelor's degree. So you see Mister Alex Siegel, yes we know the identity of your entire crew, from the papers we found on the wreck of your helicopter and your own wallets. We also know you wear dog tags with your identification. So let's not waste time with the obvious.

Now I'm going to ask you some questions, the answer to which I know some, which will tell me whether you're being wholly truthful or lying, in which case you will be punished," said Cong Dan.

"According to the Geneva Convention, I'm only required to reveal my name, rank and serial number, that's all," replied Siegel.

"The Geneva Convention is a joke. This is war, Mister Siegel. Either you answer my questions, or you will be severely punished," said Cong Dan.

"I am Lieutenant Alex Siegel, serial number 12389076," replied Siegel.

Cong Dan struck Siegel on the side of his head with his leather swagger stick immediately causing swelling and a red mark on the side of his face. He felt excruciating pain but tightened his jaws to keep from yelling. Regaining his composure, he looked at Cong Dan with defiance.

"You can beat me to death if you wish, but I won't tell you anything other than my name, rank and serial number," said Siegel.

Cong Dan had the two guards, also inside the room, remove Siegel's shirt. They then fastened a rope around his tied wrists and threw the rope over an overhead horizontal beam, raising his hands up slightly above his head, causing the muscles in his shoulders to stretch to their limit. Siegel's head was forced downward by the rise of his arms, fully exposing his backside.

Cong Dan, now holding a leather whip, struck Siegel on his back, buttocks and legs until Siegel lost consciousness.

"Cut him down, he won't talk, I know his type," said Cong Dan in Vietnamese. "When he regains consciousness, take him back to his cage."

Inside Major Chien Duong's office, Cong Dan reported the results of his interrogation.

"He won't talk right now. But when his strength diminishes with his prolonged imprisonment in these conditions, he'll tell us everything we want to know. I want to concentrate on him, because I think he's the weaker of the two. When one falls, the other is not far behind him. The domino effect," said Cong Dan.

"We've both got our degree in psychology from the University in California, and are well aware of the type of individuals we're dealing with. So let's see how really brave they are tomorrow night at our private sports arena. We'll start with Commander Longbow, who I think is a good bet for this game," said the Major.

Longbow watched with grave concern, as two guards were helping Siegel walk from their jeep to the entrance to their cage. Once the door was opened, they shoved Siegel inside, into the arms of Longbow, who carried his friend to the other end of the cage for some privacy.

"Good God, Alex. They really worked you over, my friend, but you're still alive, and that's what counts. Let me see you back," said Longbow.

"You have a lot of welts but the skin isn't broken, so that will prevent infection, especially in this water. Listen, Alex, you did good, now you must recover quickly, because we must break out of here within the next day or two. You think in a couple of days you'll have the strength to go through with your end of it?" asked Longbow.

Looking up at Longbow with a slight grin. "Yeah! I'm ready to kill all those bastards," replied Siegel, now filled with hatred and a good reason for revenge.

That evening, around 1900 hours, the same two guards appeared at the entrance to the cage, and the one, with his pistol pointed at Longbow, motioned for him to come to the entrance, and when the door opened, he was ordered to exit. As he stepped out of the entrance, a lassoed rope was placed around his neck and tightened, with the guard holding the other end of the rope, preventing him from running away. Apparently, they didn't want to have any reason to shoot him, because he was to be the entertainment that evening along with heavy gambling.

As they approached the one-story bamboo building, loud voices in a party mood could be heard from Vietnamese military personnel inside. Upon entering the building, Longbow was pulled by the neck with the rope towards the edge of a four-foot corrugated metal siding to a circular pit, 10 feet in diameter, with stone flooring. The noose around Longbow's neck was removed and he was told to step into the empty pit, which he did. He noticed that there must have been twenty or more men standing around the pit. One man, a Vietnamese Army officer, was taking bets and accepting paper money. Major Chien Duong stepped to the edge of the pit and called Longbow over.

"You'll be given a hunting knife to defend yourself against one of our favorite jungle reptiles. I'm betting on you to win, so don't disappoint me, Mister Longbow," said the Major.

"I'll try not to, but not for your sake, Major," replied Longbow, who at that moment was thrown a hunting knife with a five inch shining steel blade at his feet.

Longbow picked up the knife and lightly ran one of his fingers against the blade to determine its sharpness and was not disappointed. From the Major's statement, he surmised they were going to challenge him with a snake, and he was sure it would be a poisonous one. When the bets were all taken, a man brought a wooden box to the edge of the pit, lifted the trap door allowing the snake to exit into the pit.

It was a cobra, about six feet in length. It immediately raised its head several inches above the ground to examine its surroundings, and upon seeing Longbow, now in a crouched position with knife in his right hand pointing directly at the cobra, the snake coiled itself, and in its usual defensive posture, raised its head a couple of feet, spreading the width of its neck several inches. Its piercing eyes usually struck fear in its victim's heart, but Longbow's survival instinct would not allow him that luxury. He remembered that in India, cobras were hypnotized with a flute by snake entertainers in the streets of Calcutta. He figured he could use his knife as a distraction by having the lights illuminating the large room reflect on the shining steel blade of his hunting knife.

Pointing his knife at a slight angle allowing the brightness of the blade to elicit the cobra's attention, he slowly moved the blade pointed at the cobra's head, from left to right in a hypnotic motion, until he observed the Cobra's head follow the tip of the knife, partially mesmerized. Soon, Longbow felt it was time to slowly move closer to the Cobra while maintaining movement of the knife, hoping that when he got close enough to attack the cobra, the closeness of the knife to its head would cause the cobra to open its mouth threateningly.

The blade of Longbow's knife was now within six inches of the cobra's head, which Longbow expected, threatened the cobra into an attack mode, mouth wide open, deadly fangs exposed. Longbow thrusted the blade of his knife deep inside the cobra's mouth, and with a sudden jerk, lifted the sharp edge of his blade upward, cutting the cobra's head in two, with the rest of the snake falling inert on the ground. Longbow threw the knife, blade first, into the ground where it stood exposing only the handle. He turned and walked towards the edge of the pit where he had first entered, and was met by Major Chien Duong, holding his monetary winnings in his hand.

"Congratulations, Mister Longbow. For that demonstration you have earned a bowl of rice and pork."

"Since I earned you a good sum of money, perhaps you can give me a second bowl of rice and pork for my friend," said Longbow.

The Major looked at Longbow for a while, and then decided to be generous.

"You are right, Mister Longbow. You shall have a second bowl of rice for your friend to take with you." The Major then ordered one of the low ranking soldiers to bring two bowls or rice and pork which he then gave to Longbow, who was then escorted, without a rope around his neck, to his watery bamboo cage, where he was received by Siegel with much delight at seeing him alive and with food.

"Jesus, how did you manage to get two bowls of rice?" asked Siegel.

"I told Major Chien Duong that if he gave me two bowls or rice with pork, I would after the war introduce him to Marilyn Monroe whose a good friend of mine," said Longbow.

"Yeah! C'mon, Gary, what really happened?" asked Siegel, laughing.

Longbow described the whole incident and taught Siegel to use the same tactic in the event he was subjected to that challenge.

"Listen, Gary, I think I'm strong enough to help us escape from this place. What about tomorrow, at dinner time?" asked Siegel.

"Eat your rice and pork, while we talk. You need that food to build up your strength, Alex," said Longbow.

"Well, what about tomorrow evening, Gary?" asked Siegel.

"Yeah! that would be a good time. It would get dark soon after, and we could then escape without being seen," said Longbow.

"That's it then. Goodbye cesspool, hello canoe. At least, I'll have dry feet again," said Siegel.

"I'm surprised we haven't been bitten by snakes or even rats," said Longbow.

"I didn't know rats could swim," said Siegel.

"Well, rats don't like to go into a water basin of any kind, like cats, but when they're hungry, they'll go anywhere. They can even swim underwater," said Longbow.

"Underwater? Are you kidding?" asked Siegel.

"No, I'm not kidding, Alex. They've been known to invade a building by swimming up the sewer pipes of toilets. But thank God, so far, we haven't seen any come into our cage," said Longbow.

"That's true. I suppose though, they can squeeze between the spaces of the bamboo poles, and snakes too," said Siegel. "Jesus, just thinking about it gives me the shivers. They're such disgusting creatures. I'm wondering why God created them in the first place."

"For the answer to that, you'll have to read Charles Darwin's theory of evolution in his book 'On the Origin of Species' published in the mid-nineteenth century," said Longbow, with a grin.

"Well, right now I'm not in any mood to read about Darwin's theory of evolution. I'm concerned about tomorrow. I just hope I don't let you down," said Siegel.

"You won't let me down, Alex. You never have so far, and when that guard comes at you, just remember the beating you got, and shove that bamboo pole right through him, knowing it'll get you away from here," said Longbow, motivating his friend into the right state of mind for the required action that will take a man's life.

Siegel remained quiet, thinking about Longbow's words of justification and encouragement. He rested in a seating position against the bamboo wall with the water level at his chest, enabling him to sleep. Had he and Longbow been shorter men, they would have had to learn to sleep standing up or else drown. That should have been enough motivation for anyone to escape from that watery cage. But the closeness of his human target, as he plunged his homemade spear into his body, is what troubled Seigel, and Longbow knew that his best friend's sensitive and kind nature found it difficult to reconcile with the deadly task ahead of him.

"Is the tip of your pole sharp enough?" asked Longbow.

Siegel lifted that end of the bamboo pole and showed the jagged tip to Longbow.

"Yeah! You did a nice job when you splintered it. It'll pierce him like a sharp knife in butter," said Longbow, who was simply trying to assure his friend of the ease in which it would go down, but then thought he was being too graphic. Now he needed to discuss the aftermath following the elimination of the guards.

"Listen, Alex. We'll have to hide the two bodies so they won't be discovered until we're far gone down river. So leave the spear inside the guard. We'll submerge both of them in the far corner of the cage, using the spear, which we'll drive through the side of the bamboo cage. That'll hold them below the surface," said Longbow.

"Yeah! That makes sense. Then the other guards will think they took off with us in tow somewhere else, and by the time they find out what happened, we'll be miles away," said Siegel. "You know, Gary. I hate to say this, but I'm glad you're here with me, because otherwise, I would have perished in this hell hole. Gee, I'm sorry, I know how it sounds."

"I know what you mean, Alex. No need to apologize. Frankly, if I weren't here, but was given a chance to join you, in order to help your escape, I wouldn't hesitate one bit, 'cause you're my best friend and brother-in- arms, remember," said Longbow.

They awakened the following day, knowing that this was the day of their deliverance, and they both said a brief prayer to God for his help and forgiveness for what they were about to do. It was 1830 hours with the sun resting on the horizon when one of the two guards carrying two bowls of rice waited, while the other guard unlocked the padlock from the chain that secured the door to the cage. The rice carrying guard entered the cage and saw only Siegel standing near the far end of the cage, because Longbow was submerged up to his chin in the corner of the cage nearest the entrance, therefore out of sight.

While the first guard slowly walked towards Siegel, who was holding his bamboo spear pointed in the guard's direction, hidden submerged two feet below the surface by the water's brown-reddish color, Longbow quickly moved next to the entrance door, and stuck his hand holding his gold wedding band through the opening between the bamboo poles for the guard holding an AK-47 assault rifle to see.

"Hey! Do you understand English? How would you like to have this gold ring?" asked Longbow.

The guard obviously did not understand English, but did know the value of a gold ring, and approached Longbow close enough to take the ring, at which time, Longbow drove his bamboo spear through the guard's stomach eliciting a gurgling sound. The guard then collapsed in front of Longbow, with the spear sticking out of his back. Longbow was so preoccupied with the guard in front of him, that he didn't hear, nor was he aware of Siegel's elimination of the rice-carrying guard until he turned to see if Siegel needed his assistance. Siegel just stood still holding his end of the bamboo spear stuck through the guard's mid-section, with his head just above the water.

"Alex, move him back to the rear of the cage. I've got to bring the other guard inside before anyone sees him," said Longbow, who walked out of the cage and dragged the guard's body with the spear still inside him, through the entrance and to the rear of the cage.

As planned, they submerged both bodies and drove the bamboo spears through the vertical bamboo poles of the cage, effectively holding the guards submerged.

"Did you take his pistol," asked Longbow.

"No I didn't. Do we need it. You've got your guard's AK-47 rifle," said Siegel.

"Nevertheless, two weapons are better than one," replied Longbow, who then reached into the water and finding the pistol inside the waist holster, removed it and gave it to Siegel.

"OK! Let's get out of here, and keep a low profile," said Longbow, as they exited the cage and replaced the padlock on the chain to make it look normal. Longbow picked up the AK-47 assault rifle by the strap and slung it over his shoulder.

Walking quickly in a crouched position, Longbow and Siegel made their way to the edge of the river. They spotted a wooden canoe that had two paddles which they selected as their get-away boat.

They submerged themselves into the river with only their heads above water, and being excellent swimmers from their years of sailing, easily and quietly breast-stroked their way to the canoe. They made sure they positioned themselves on the side of the canoe facing the river so as not to be seen by anyone on land. After loosening the rope from the canoe rather than the dock, they placed the AK-47 and pistol inside the canoe and slowly guided it away from the dock and along the shore line, until the slow river's current, which conveniently ran southeast, took them and their canoe a half a mile away from the Son Tay Prison Camp. They decided it was not safe to get inside the canoe and start paddling until they were as far away from Son Tay Prison as their arms would allow them.

CHAPTER IX

Rescue Operation on Son Cong River

Unknown to Longbow and Siegel, the news of their captivity by the North Vietnamese a week earlier, had swiftly made its way to Major General Claude Barclay, Wing Commander of the 174th Attack Wing at Hancock Field in Syracuse, New York. He decided to make a personal visit to the Longbow and Siegel families, with his Deputy, Colonel Tom Levin, who drove them, using his personal automobile, rather than the General's staff car bearing the flag of a two-star General. Barclay had visited the two families, residing next to each other in Williamsville, New York, overlooking Ellicott Creek, a year earlier, and considered Jim Longbow and Dave Siegel personal friends, as well as officers in his unit.

The drive took about four hours, and upon arrival on Creekside Road, Tom Levin pulled into the drive-way of the three-car garage of the Longbow residence, rather than Siegel's, since Longbow was the flight commander of the downed helicopter.

It was mid-afternoon and when Barclay rang the door-bell, no one answered, because Louise and her daughter Jackie were sitting around the picnic table in their back yard with their neighbor Susan and her daughter Rachel, discussing their dual wedding plans upon Gary and Alex's return from Vietnam.

"I think I hear the doorbell ringing," said Jackie. "I'll go see who it is."

The front door was open, but the storm door with screen was closed and locked. Looking through the screen, Jackie recognized General Barclay and wondered why he was calling on them in person, and immediately realized something grave may have happened to warrant their visit.

"Hello, General Barclay, would you come in please," said Jackie, inviting both officers inside the house. "My mother and the Siegels are sitting in the back yard. I presume you want to see my mother!"

"Yes, if you please, Jackie," replied Barclay, remembering her name.

The two officers followed Jackie through the living and dining rooms, and out into the back yard, where they were greeted by Louise, Susan and Rachel.

"Nice to see you again," said Barclay. "This is my Deputy, Colonel Tom Levin. I was hoping your husband would be home, but I guess he's still at work with your husband Dave."

"Yes, they won't be home until five-thirty, and we usually dine at about six-thirty. So why don't you gentlemen stay for dinner, and then you can visit with our husbands. Is there anything we should know?" asked Louise, looking straight into General Barclay's eyes which avoided hers, thus raising her suspicion that he may be the bearer of bad news about their sons.

"Well, I suppose you'll have to know sooner or later and it's better if it comes from an authoritative source," said General Barclay.

"It's about Gary and Alex, isn't it?" asked Susan.

"Yes, it is, Ma'am," "replied Barclay.

"Oh! My God!. What happened...are they dead?" asked Susan.

"No, not that we know of, Ma'am. Gary and Alex were on a medical evacuation operation when their helicopter, while on the ground rescuing a wounded soldier, was hit by a rocket propelled grenade that immobilized the helicopter, and from what was observed by a second helicopter on the scene, Gary, Alex and others from the platoon they were rescuing were captured by the North Vietnamese Army, and are imprisoned somewhere in North Vietnam. At this time, we have no further information, except that our reconnaissance flights have narrowed to three the number of possible prison camps they were taken. You can be assured that all measures available to us will be taken to rescue them," said General Barclay.

"Well, at least they're still alive," said Louise.

"I'd better call Dave and tell him about this, right away," said Susan.

"I wouldn't do that, Susan. "Let them come home, and General Barclay can then tell them in military detail what happened, and what can be done to rescue them," said Louise.

"You're not going to call Jim, then!" said Susan.

"No, I'm going to wait until he comes home," replied Louise.

"Alright then, I'll wait too," replied Susan, not wanting to have only her husband know of the incident with Jim held in the dark until he got home.

"What are their chances of survival in a North Vietnamese prison?" asked Jackie.

"Reasonably good if their health holds out," said Barclay.

"Gary and Alex are in great shape. They're super athletes, and should be able to withstand imprisonment until they're rescued," said Rachel with confidence.

"Hopefully they won't have to endure imprisonment too long," said General Barclay.

James Longbow with David Siegel as his passenger, arrived at his house, and saw the black sedan parked in his driveway.

"Hey! Jim. Looks like you've got a visitor," said Siegel.

"Yeah! I wonder who it is?" replied Longbow.

"Only one way to find out," said Siegel.

After exiting Longbow's automobile, Siegel started walking towards his house, when Longbow called out to him.

"Hey! Dave. There's an officer sticker from Hancock Field on the front bumper. I think you'd better come in with me," said Longbow.

"Jesus. I hope it's not bad news," said Siegel, as they entered the Longbow residence, and finding it empty, went into the back yard, where they were greeted by their family and General Barclay with his deputy.

"Hi Claude, Tom," said Longbow, dispensing with titles, especially since he himself was now a Brigadier General. "What brings you so far from home?"

"Well, as I already explained to your family, we got word from Army Headquarters in Long Bien, Vietnam that the med-evac helicopter flown by Gary Longbow and Alex Siegel, was hit with a rocket-propelled grenade while on the ground picking up the wounded, and as a result they were captured by the North Vietnamese military, and transported to one of their prison camps in North Vietnam," said General Barclay.

"How do they know they were captured and not killed?" asked Longbow.

"Because the Cobra gunship that had accompanied them, was unable to fire at the enemy, because they were intermingled with the platoon of soldiers with their wounded, and what remained of the crew of the first helicopter that went down, and the second helicopter, flown by Gary and Alex, was now also surrounded by North Vietnamese soldiers. So all the Cobra crew could do was take pictures and try to follow them from the air to see where they were being taken, but their trail soon evaporated when they went back into the dense jungle," said General Barclay.

"At least we know they're alive, but now the question is where were they were taken, and can we rescue them with any degree of success?" asked Dave Siegel.

"The Army had their reconnaissance aircraft make several sorties over North Vietnam taking pictures of known and suspected prison sites, and their intelligence service believes that the helicopter crews, and the platoon soldiers captured at Thanh Hoa, were most likely imprisoned in a relatively new prison camp along the Son Cong River in the northeast province of Thai Nguyen, Vietnam," said General Barclay.

"How reliable is that information?" asked James Longbow.

"I asked the same question, and I was told 75 percent," replied Barclay.

"So, armed with that information, is the Army going to initiate a rescue operation?" asked Siegel.

"That area is not more than 25 some miles from Hanoi, and heavily defended. Furthermore, I was told that right now, the rescue of some 20 prisoners is low on the priority list of combat operations at the US Army Republic of Vietnam," said Barclay.

"You mean Gary and Alex are just going to rot in that Vietnamese prison, without any effort from the Army to rescue them?" said Jackie.

General Barclay remained silent, trying to think of an appropriate response, when Jim Longbow, realizing the delicate situation Jackie had created for General Barclay, interrupted.

"Jackie....the General didn't say the Army wasn't going to rescue them. He just said that right now, the Army is currently in the middle of some very important operations and can't jump on this rescue mission right away. But as soon as it's possible, they will take appropriate action to bring our guys back," said Longbow.

"Jim's right, Jackie, you've got to give the Army a chance to prepare for such an action. You just can't go in like gang busters and pull our guys out. It's not that easy. You've got to have a plan of action and a back-up plan in case the first one fails, and the list of things that must be done can be exhausting. So be patient and let the Army do its job," said Siegel.

"Listen, what are we having for dinner, Louise?" asked James Longbow.

"Since there're so many of us, we're going to throw some hamburgers and hot dogs on the grill," said Louise. "You girls can go in the kitchen and make us a salad, while Susan and I get the grill going. I'm sure Jim and Dave want to discuss this matter further with General Barclay."

"Let's take a walk by the creek," said Jim Longbow to Barclay and his deputy Tom Levin, with Dave Siegel tagging along.

"This is a beautiful place you have here. A million dollar view," said Barclay.

"Do you have any high ranking contacts in Vietnam, Claude?" asked Longbow.

"Yes, why?" replied Claude Barclay.

"Because I feel an urgency to go Vietnam and get a rescue operation going. Now, I never felt special because I got promoted to Brigadier General, but darn it, Claude, if being a General will help me rescue my son Gary and Dave's son Alex, then by God, I'll use my rank to influence those who can mount a rescue operation. But an Air Force Brigadier General will have little currency with Army personnel, unless an Air Force General in Vietnam is in good stead with an Army General in Vietnam who can give me a letter of cooperation with Army units in Vietnam. With such support I can visit the 247 Med-Evac Detachment at Nah Trang, and get a first-hand view of the situation there, and possibly organize a limited but effective rescue effort. So who do you know in the Air Force over in Vietnam, who can introduce me to a General willing to provide me with a Carte d'Assistance," said James Longbow, with David Siegel listening attentively.

"Wait a minute, Jim. Why can't I go with you?" asked Siegel.

"Because one of us has to stay here with the family. Besides, our boss at Curtiss-Wright won't be too happy with both of us gone," said Longbow.

"I also think, Dave, that since only one of you can go to Vietnam, a Brigadier General will have far more influence than a Colonel, no offense meant, Dave." said General Barclay.

"None taken, General Barclay, and I agree. It makes perfect sense that Jim should be the one to go to Vietnam," said Siegel.

"So who do you have in mind, Claude?" asked James Longbow.

"Well, as a matter of fact, my classmate at West Point is now Major General John Granville, assigned to the Military Assistance Command Vietnam at Tan Son Nhut Air base. I'll send him an urgent message, and ask him to introduce you to one of his Army buddies who can provide you with a Carte d'Assistance," said Barclay. "I'll also have to place you on active duty for a period of six months with orders assigning you to Vietnam for the purpose of investigating the possibility of mounting a rescue operation of our two officers currently imprisoned in North Vietnam. I'll have those orders for you within 48 hours. So when will you be ready to leave?"

"I'll be at Hancock Air Field within 72 hours, Claude, and I want you to know that Dave and I, and our entire family, owe you a huge debt of gratitude. Now our families will be able to deal with our sons' captivity with hope, knowing I'll be in Vietnam, working on getting them home," said James Longbow.

"You're most welcome. You and Dave have served our country in an exemplary manner, and I'm proud to be your friend. Therefore, I'm more than happy to be able to provide you with the help you need, and God willing, you'll be successful in bringing those boys home," said General Barclay.

"I do have one other favor to ask you, Claude. Please don't mention my going to Vietnam to our wives and daughters. Dave and I will tell them after you've left. My wife and daughter might initially find my departure to Vietnam worrisome, but with patience and a reasonable explanation, they will accept my going to Vietnam as a necessary and hopeful assignment," said Longbow.

"No problem, Jim. I understand," replied Barclay.

That evening, after the General and his Deputy, as well as the Siegels had left the Longbow residence, Jim Longbow asked his wife and daughter to join him in the living room, and told them of his conversation with General Barclay, and his decision to go to Vietnam to arrange for the rescue of Gary and Alex.

"What if something happens to you while you're in Vietnam. Then I'll be without a husband as well as a son. What can you do that the Army can't do?" said Louise in tears.

"Time is of the essence, Louise. I know Gary better than anyone. He's very much like me. He knows that his best chance to escape is soon after his capture when his strength is still at its optimum, so he'll want to escape as soon as possible, and he'll find a way to do it, because he has a 'can do' attitude. Claude told me their reconnaissance photos indicate our boys may be imprisoned at a new camp along the Son Cong River in the northeast province of Thai Nguyen. Gary and Alex are excellent swimmers and sailors. If they manage to escape from that prison, they'll surely take to the river and possibly steal a small boat, and try to make it back to friendly waters, and perhaps they'll even be spotted by one of our aircraft and rescued from the river. The thing is, I'll be there to expedite things and give it direction, because I'm more motivated than anyone in the Army. Now, do you understand why I must go to Vietnam?" asked James Longbow, who had gained their riveted attention.

"Well, General Longbow, you made a most convincing argument, which I accept with my sincere wishes for success," said Louise, reaching over and kissing him. "I'm glad I married you, James. I'm so proud of you."

"And I can see why they made you a General, Dad. You give 'em hell when you're over there," said Jackie.

James Longbow, wearing his Air Force uniform bearing his silver star on his epaulettes, was greeted by Major General Claude Barclay upon arrival at the Hancock Air Field aboard a C-47 Transport aircraft from Niagara Falls, New York. Longbow had decided to fly rather than drive his automobile, because he didn't want to leave his vehicle at Hancock Field for what could turn out to be several months. Hence he had his wife Louise drive him to Niagara Falls Air Field, a distance of about ten miles from Williamsville.

After Longbow's landing, General Barclay invited him to enter his staff car bearing a flag with two stars off the front fender, which gathered the attention of everyone whose path it crossed. At Wing Headquarters, General Longbow was introduced to Barclay's staff, and again to his deputy, Colonel Tom Levin.

"I've had Tom arrange for you to be given a flight suit and boots, also a Smith & Wesson revolver with shoulder holster, because where you're going, you just might need it, and this will save you a lot of red tape and unnecessary delays," said Barclay.

"Thanks, Claude, I appreciate that. Has General John Granville made any contact with anyone in the Army, yet?" asked Longbow.

"As a matter of fact, he has. When you arrive at Tan Son Nhut Air Force Base, you'll first meet with General Granville. He'll give you the 'Carte d'Assistance' which will ask anyone in the US Army and Air Force as well as the South Vietnamese Army, to render any assistance you need in the performance of your mission. Then he'll provide you with transportation by air to Nah Trang Air Field where you will be met by Captain George Sealy, Commander of the 247th Med-Evac Detachment, who has agreed to provide you with all assistance necessary in the accomplishment of your rescue mission. John said Captain Sealy was actually enthusiastic about your arrival, and more than willing to help you rescue his downed pilots and crew," said Barclay.

"That's great. I'll be working directly with the unit to which Gary and Alex were assigned. That's going to expedite things tremendously. When do I leave?" asked Longbow.

"Tomorrow morning. Your flight leaves at 0800 for McGuire Air Force Base to Travis Air Force Base, then onto Tan Son Nhut Air Force Base. Tom, will now take you to Base Supply for your gear, then your BOQ where you'll be billeted for the night. I hope you'll agree to join me and my wife Betsy for dinner at the Officers Club this evening," said Barclay.

"With pleasure. What time?" asked Longbow.

"1800 hours," replied Barclay.

The following morning, James Longbow, carrying a B-4B canvas suitcase with side pocket and an AWOL bag, after shaking hands and saying goodbye to General Barclay, walked towards the metal staircase abutted to the door of the transport aircraft, and boarded it, not knowing if he would ever return with his son.

It was raining cats and dogs when James Longbow landed at Nah Trang Air Field, suggesting he may have arrived during the Monsoon season. Luckily he had been advised about the tropical weather and the wearing of the summer uniform. To his delightful surprise, Captain Sealy was there to greet him when he descended the staircase from the transport aircraft, with a salute which the General returned.

"How was your overseas flight, sir?" asked Sealy.

"Uneventful, but it gave me time to think about the challenges before us," replied Longbow.

"I have you billeted at our modest BOQ, sir. We're not accustomed to visits by General officers," said Sealy.

"Well, George. I hope you don't mind if I call you by your first name. We're apparently going to be working together on a very special project which will have no place for formalities. I'd like to get to my billet and change into my flight suit, then immediately have a conference at your office with your staff to discuss a possible plan of action. I do have one in mind for your approval, George. I also recognize that I'm just your guest, and need your kind and expert assistance in rescuing my son and Lieutenant Siegel, which I appreciate with immense gratitude," said Longbow.

"Sir, when General Granville told me you needed my assistance, I was overjoyed by your arrival, which meant that I was now going to be getting help from a General officer with the muscle to get things done, and fast. So my staff and I are most grateful for your entry into this war to rescue our crew," said Captain Sealy.

"Well, George, I'm glad you feel that way. Now to the BOQ, so I can change, and get this conference going. There's no time to lose," said Longbow with a tone of urgency and determination.

Captain Sealy waited while Longbow quickly changed into his flight suit and boots, but left his revolver in his B-4B suitcase for later placement with his clothes in his dresser drawers.

Sealy drove James Longbow to their Base Operations, where they were met by Lieutenant Steve Crawford, the Executive Officer, and Chief Warrant Officer Mark Kowalski, Flight Instructor and Base Operations Med-Evac coordinator.

Upon seeing the silver stars on Longbow's shoulders, everyone present stood at attention.

"At ease, men," said Captain Sealy. "General Longbow is here as our guest to assist in the rescue of his son Gary Longbow and Alex Siegel, whom you knew as part of the crew, whose helicopter was disabled while attempting to rescue casualties of an embattled platoon of US soldiers, resulting in their capture by the North Vietnamese Army. We've been asked by Major General John Granville at Military Assistance Command Vietnam to provide General Longbow with whatever assistance he needs to execute a successful rescue operation of Lieutenants Longbow and Siegel, and other crewmen captured during that failed rescue. Just so you know something about General Longbow, he flew B-17 bombers with Alex Siegel's father from England over Germany, and was shot down on one of those bombing raids, resulting in their imprisonment in a Nazi Concentration Camp for the duration of the Second World War. So he's no stranger to danger. I'm now going to have him tell you about his thoughts concerning this rescue operation that might help us formulate a rescue plan with some measure of success."

"I'm very grateful and encouraged by your willingness to accept and include me in your rescue operation of my son and Alex Siegel which may well lead to the rescue of the remaining crew members in captivity there. I've been doing some research on the known North Vietnamese prison camps and their proximity to Thanh Hoa , where they were captured. I checked with Army and Air Force Intelligence, as well as the National Security Agency, for any information they may have gathered from photo reconnaissance flights over North Vietnam, and I've come to the conclusion that our crew was taken and confined at Son Tay Prison, a relatively new prison camp also known as Camp Hope. It's located off the Son Cong River in the northeast province of Thai Nguyen, Vietnam. The Cong River flows from Nui Coc Lake and passes through the town of Son Cong into the Red River, flowing past Hanoi onto the Gulf of Tonkin. Camp Hope's geographic coordinates are 21 08 36N 105 30 01E, and it's located near Dac Tru Village, about 23 miles west of Hanoi. That is the latest information I have acquired from what I consider reliable sources, " said Longbow. "Is anyone familiar with that area?"

"I'm Lieutenant Steve Crawford, sir. Our helicopter crews have flown several sorties over the Son Cong River, which is a tributary of the Red River with a span of about 60 miles. Our own experience and research has reached the same conclusion you have, sir. Camp Hope appears to be our best bet, sir."

"I'm glad we've come to the same conclusion," said Longbow, "because that gives us assurance that we won't be wasting valuable time searching that area, and I do mean search, because the Army cannot, at this time, allocate the necessary resources required for an all-out assault on Camp Hope. However, I have a different plan of action. Now please hear me out. Gary and Alex are sailors since early childhood and great swimmers. Camp Hope is situated alongside the Son Cong River. My son knows that the best time to escape is soon after capture because your strength is at its best, and diminishes rapidly when in captivity. So they've been imprisoned for about one week now. I feel strongly that they will soon make their escape on the Son Cong river, stealing a small boat, possibly a canoe or row boat, and float down in a southeast direction, according to geographic records, in the hope that one of our patrol helicopters will discover them and lift them up to safety."

"General Longbow, sir, I think you've been reading our minds, because that's basically what we thought should be done, although we didn't have that personal information about your son and Lieutenant Siegel," said Lieutenant Crawford.

"Your research, General Longbow, is right on target, sir," said Captain Sealy. "I think we should allocate one Huey UH-1 with hoist and two Cobra gun-ship to patrol over the Son Cong River from Camp Hope going Southeast, and as time progresses, increase the length of the patrol past Hanoi until we find them. I think that we will need three passes a day, one in mid-morning, one in mid-afternoon and one just before sundown, for at least one week, and if no results, reevaluate our plan of action."

"I do have one request which I hope you will honor," said James Longbow. "I would like to ride on the rescue helicopter, because I can recognize my son from afar and readily distinguish him from others, and as Captain Sealy said, I'm not a stranger to danger and combat."

"I'm sure I'm speaking for our entire crew, that it will be an honor, sir, to have you onboard our helicopter," said Captain Sealy.

The following morning, General James Longbow, dressed in a flight suit, wearing a double shoulder harness and holster with cartridge loops, containing a .38 caliber with 5 inch barrel revolver, arrived at the Base Operations where he was greeted by Captain Sealy.

"Sir, I would like to introduce you to our two Cobra gun-ship crews from the 119th Assault Helicopter Company at Cam Ranh Air Base. This is Chief Warrant Officer Chris Stepson and his observer Chief Warrant Officer Adam Prescott, flying the lead Cobra, and Chief Warrant Officer Charlie Copanski and his observer Chief Warrant Officer Conrad Watson who will fly the second helicopter. They're going to give our Huey protective cover during this rescue effort we've named Operation Bamboo," said Captain Sealy.

"We've been told of your reason for being here, sir, and we're glad to be of help in this rescue operation," said Chris Stepson, speaking on behalf of the two gun-ship crews.

"Chief Warrant Officer Mark Kowalski, our flight instructor, will be piloting the Huey, and Chief Warrant Officer Frank Minelli will be his co-pilot. Tech Sergeant Matthew Conway is our Crew Chief, and Staff Sergeant Dean Remington will be the door-gunner and hoist operator. Our Medic is Tech Sergeant Harry Metcalf. I think

I've got everybody that's involved in this rescue operation," said Captain Sealy.

"I am most thankful to all of you who are risking your lives in this rescue operation. Your assistance will be remembered with deep gratitude long after its conclusion," said Longbow.

Onboard the Huey, now flying high with a Cobra gunship on each side, sat Longbow, next to Sergeant Conway and Sergeant Dean Remington, while Medic Harry Metcalf was in conversation with Frank Minelli, the co-pilot, sitting next to Flight Commander Mark Kowalski, piloting the helicopter.

"I see you've got a coil of rope with knots in it, that must be more than one hundred feet long," said Longbow to Dean Remington.

"Actually, it's two hundred and fifty feet long, and the knots in it, spaced a foot apart, are to provide a grip to whoever is climbing it," said Remington.

"But why would you need that rope when you've got the mechanized hoist?" asked Longbow.

"Because the hoist is known to jam up and freeze when it reaches more than 200 feet, even though it's 250 feet long. We've sometimes had to cut the wire and let it drop when that happens, so the rope is the sure alternative," said Remington.

"Well, that makes sense. I just hope we don't have to use it when we find our guys," said Longbow. "Did you come up with the idea of using a knotted rope or is this something the Army came up with?"

"Actually, I did sir," said Remington, "after I saw one casualty we had to cut loose because of a hoist malfunction, I had nightmares over it. So I decided that next time we had a hoist malfunction, we could still bring up the casualty with the rope, unless it's a litter case," said Remington.

"This is an excellent idea, and you should be commended for it. I think that all med-evac helicopters should have the rope alternative, and I'll make sure you're credited for it," said General Longbow.

"Thank you, sir, but I can't take all the credit. I swung the idea by Matthew and my other crewmembers, and they agreed with the idea, but we haven't had occasion to use it yet.

"Let's hope not. But if we do, I'm giving you credit for it," said Longbow.

"We're now in North Vietnam, over the Son Cong River, following its path northwest. We've got six pair of eyes focused on the river, so we're not likely to miss our guys. If they're on that river, we'll spot them," said Mark Kowalski to the Huey crew and General Longbow.

After an hour's flight over the river, Frank Minelli spotted what he believed to be an overturned canoe floating in the middle of the river.

"Let's get down closer, Mark, to check out that overturned canoe. There may be someone hiding under it, using the pocket of air that accumulates between the water and the bottom of the overturned canoe," said Minelli.

"Well if our guys are hiding under it, they'll surely come out when they hear our helicopter," said Mark Kowalski.

As they hovered some fifty feet over what had appeared to be an overturned canoe, they discovered it was only a large log.

"Just a false alarm, only a log," said Kowalski to the Huey crew.

"We've covered this stretch of the river twice, Mark. Let's come back just before dinner," said Frank Minelli.

"OK! Frank, let's do that," replied Kowalski.

Minelli radioed the pilot of the lead Cobra they were heading back to Nah Trang Air Base, and returning at 1600 hours. He then advised the crew of the Flight Commander's decision, and no one disagreed with it.

At that precise moment, Gary Longbow and Alex Siegel were recovering from a long sleep in their stolen canoe, hidden under overhanging heavily leafed branches of trees bordering the river. They had rowed through half the night, and exhausted from a week's deprived sleep in their watery bamboo cage, they finally were able to sleep lying down in a dry canoe. It must have been near noontime when they awakened to the noise of tropical birds. The temperature was nearly 100 degrees Fahrenheit with equal humidity.

"Man, I could drink a gallon of fresh water and eat a whole chicken," said Alex.

"Keep dreaming, buddy, because that's all you're gonna get until we're rescued," replied Gary. "I think we'd better get going soon, if we're to be seen by helicopter patrols,"

"We could make spears out of some of those branches, and spear us some fish. I don't mind eating them raw," said Alex.

"It's not worth the time and effort. I have a feeling we're gonna be found by our patrol this afternoon. We've been gone over a week, so they must have figured out where we were confined, and expect us to try to escape. Being confined next to a river makes this the logical place for them to look for us, don't you think?" said Gary.

"Yeah! I suppose you're right. But I'm concerned that the Viet Cong or the North Vietnamese Army will discover us before the helicopter patrol. Why don't we wait here under cover until we hear the engine noise of the helicopter patrols, then paddle into the open river where they can see us," said Alex.

"That does have merit, Alex, but what if they don't patrol this far north. We should be paddling southeast where our chances are better at being spotted by a patrol," said Gary.

"Yeah! But if they know where we were confined, they would patrol as far north as the prison camp," replied Alex. "Let's compromise. Let's sit here 'till mid-afternoon, then paddle down river."

"Alright, I'll go along with that, Alex. I'm sure tempted to drink some of this water, but its reddish-brown tint is a surefire turnoff."

"Yeah! There's no telling what kind of parasites are in that muddy water," said Alex. "Besides, if you're right, we'll be picked up by late afternoon."

"Say a prayer, just in case," replied Gary.

Late that afternoon, it started raining, as the Huey Med-Evac helicopter piloted by Mark Kowalski with his crew including General Longbow, took off from Nah Trang Air Base, escorted by the two Cobra gunships. The rain limited their visibility, but nevertheless, the crew was determined to find their missing comrades. Undaunted, they started their run at low altitude along the Son Cong River in a northeast direction and were about fifteen miles south of Camp Hope when the pilot from the lead Cobra, Chief Chris Stepson, radioed Mark Kowalski.

"I see two guys paddling a canoe at twelve o'clock, and they look American," said Stepson.

"Yeah! I see them too, and they're waiving at us. We're going down to meet them," said Kowalski.

"General Longbow, I think we've found our guys. I'm going to hover directly over them. See if you can identify them," said Kowalski.

While the Huey hovered over the canoe, slowly descending to an altitude that permitted the lifting of the two Americans, the two Cobra gunships positioned themselves between the Huey and the shore line, ready to fire their machine guns and rockets at anyone on shore that appeared threatening. However the heavy rain offered some protection with its limited visibility.

Leaning over the edge of the large door opening of the Huey, Longbow, recognizing his son Gary and Alex Siegel, both sporting short beards, yelled out to them.

"We're lowering a harness to you. Put it on and we'll hoist you aboard," said James Longbow, who didn't want to get into small talk, when every second they were exposed could cost them their lives.

"You go first, Alex. I'll be right behind you," said Gary.

Alex slipped the harness around his upper torso and Dean Remington engaged the electric hoist, which slowly brought Alex up into the door opening where Harry Metcalf and Remington grabbed him and pulled him inside the helicopter, and into the arms of James Longbow, who sat him down in the corner of the helicopter, and gave him a bottle of water.

"Welcome back, Alex," said James Longbow.

Remington lowered the harness and Gary put on the harness, abandoning his AK-47 and the canoe, as the hoist started to lift him, until he had reached about 20 feet above the water, when the hoist suddenly stopped.

"Jesus, not now!" said Remington.

"What happened?" asked James Longbow.

"The Goddamn hoist froze up and won't continue the lift. Son-of-a-bitch. I don't believe it," said Remington.

"Well, we can't leave my son dangling down there," said James Longbow. "Let's use the rope."

"Is Gary in any shape and strong enough to climb up that rope or do we have to pull him up, Alex," asked James Longbow.

"I think he can pull himself up," replied Alex.

"Good, then let's get that rope down to him," said James Longbow, not realizing that Remington had already thrown the looped end of the rope down to Gary Longbow.

"Listen, Gary," yelled Remington. "If you can't pull yourself up, put your foot in the loop and grab the rope above one of the knots, and we'll pull you up."

"I can pull myself up, thanks," replied Gary, who grabbed the rope, when all of a sudden, all hell broke loose as the two Cobras unleashed their armament at the east shoreline, devastating that whole area into a smoke filled carnage of death and destruction, that motivated Gary to climb that rope with the speed of a squirrel. As he placed one of his hands on the edge of the floor of the Huey, General Longbow grabbed his wrist and pulled him up with the help of Conway standing on the other side, into the helicopter. James Longbow gave his son a manly hug and welcomed him with a bottle of water, then had him sit next to Alex.

Remington cut the hoist wire with a bolt cutter, while Conway raised the rope into the aircraft, then yelled the OK to the pilot to take off.

"The hoist is free and everyone's aboard. Ready to take off," said Crew Chief Conway to the pilot, who then radioed the lead Cobra of his departure and return to Nah Trang Air Base.

The two Cobras waited about a minute behind to make sure no other threats to the Huey existed, then quickly left the area to join the Huey, now flying at a high altitude for safety.

"How are you guys feeling?" asked James Longbow of his son and Alex.

"We're OK. Just tired and hungry for something other than rice and pork," said Gary, eliciting a laugh from Alex.

"I won't bother you with questions regarding your experience while in captivity, because when we arrive at Nah Trang Air Base, Army Intelligence will want to debrief you right away, while your memory of events is still clear in your mind. Then, after you shower and shave, and get new clothing, we're going to have a sumptuous dinner at the Officer's Club," said James Longbow.

"My mouth is watering at the very thought of a steak dinner," said Alex with a grin.

"Before you leave this aircraft, you should thank the crew for their outstanding service in this difficult rescue operation. I personally intend to recommend individual citations for every member of this crew," said James Longbow, within earshot of the crew.

At Nah Trang Air Base, Gary and Alex were taken immediately to Base Operations where two Army Intelligence Officers were waiting for them. Upon seeing a Brigadier General accompanying Gary and Alex, they immediately saluted him, and identified themselves as Major Norman Ansley and Captain Jason Butler.

"I'm General James Longbow, and this is my son Gary Longbow, and Lieutenant Alex Siegel. I hope you don't mind if I sit in on your debriefing."

"No, sir, we don't mind, General Longbow. I'm sure you have the necessary clearance for it," said Major Ansley.

Gary and Alex related all of the events that took place, from the time their helicopter was incapacitated and they were captured, to their escape, a story which left the listeners in absolute awe.

"Do you know what happened to the other crew members?" asked Captain Butler.

"No, not really. We only got a glimpse of them upon arrival at the prison camp. After that, we were separated, and as we said, we were put into a bamboo cage filled with water up to our waist," said Gary.

"How many prisoners do you estimate were there in captivity," asked Captain Butler.

"I would estimate about twenty-five, but more could have arrived while we were in captivity," said Alex.

"Well, I think your escape is almost miraculous, and shows exceptional ingenuity and courage beyond any expectations. I'm sure Headquarters will agree and merit you both accordingly," said Major Ansley.

That evening, dressed in new flight suits and boots, Gary and Alex joined General Longbow for a delightful dinner at the Officers Club.

"I spoke to Major General John Granville at Military Assistance Command, and he agreed for you two Lieutenants to be immediately transferred to Fort Rucker, Alabama to serve out your remaining months before discharge from the Army, with a 30-day leave of absence on route to Fort Rucker," said James Longbow.

"You mean, we're not going back to the 247th Med-Evac Detachment," said Gary with Alex looking on in disbelief.

"That's correct. You both earned this 30-day leave, and those few remaining months can be served in the US," said James Longbow.

Gary looked at Alex, before replying. "Well, Dad, I feel like I'm deserting those guys at the Detachment who risked their lives to save us," said Gary.

"What do you think, Alex?" asked General Longbow.

"In a way, I do feel like Gary, but then, I'm certain, that if any of those guys were in our shoes, they'd jump at the chance to return to the States early. So I'm for taking that 30-days leave, so I can see Jackie, Rachel, and my Mom and Dad, who, I'm sure, were worried sick over my capture and imprisonment," said Alex.

"You know, Gary, your family comes first, and when you consider the agony that your mother went through when she learned of your imprisonment in North Vietnam, she cried herself to sleep almost every night. Your beloved Rachel did not fare much better, not knowing if you were ever going to survive your imprisonment. So I think you owe them your love in person and without delay," said General Longbow.

"I hope that someday, Dad, I'll attain your wisdom. You're right, I should be grateful for all you've done to make our rescue possible, so we can be united with our family again," said Gary.

"That's it, then. We leave tomorrow morning for Tan Son Nhut Air Base, where we'll board a MATS aircraft that will take us to Travis Air Force Base, and from there to Fort Dix, New Jersey. So get your stuff ready for departure and say goodbye to Vietnam," said General Longbow.

"I can't believe we're leaving Vietnam. Just a little more than a week ago, we were caged like an animal in a North Vietnam prison," said Alex.

"Don't remind me. I'd like to forget the whole thing," said Gary.

"Can't say I blame you. But believe me, Gary, the memories will always be there, ready to surface when you least expect it, and you learn to deal with it," said General Longbow.

"You know, Dad, that took a lot of guts for you to come all the way over here to have us rescued. I'll never forget that," said Gary.

"And that goes for me too, General Siegel," said Alex.

"Once we get to Travis, you guys can make a long distance call to Louise and Susan, while I call Dave at work, and tell him the good news," said General Longbow.

"Man, will they be surprised," said Alex.

"That's an understatement. Mom will probably pitch a tent at Niagara Falls Air Force Base, waiting for our arrival from McGuire," said Gary in good humor.

"Your Mom adores you, Gary, and your rescue is the greatest gift she could ever have received, bar none," said General Longbow.

There was silence, then General Longbow spoke again.

"Well, fellows, let's call it a night because you have to be packed and ready to leave on the 0900 flight to Tan Son Nhut Air Base. So we'll leave the BOQ at 0700 for the Mess Hall, and have breakfast, then go to the Base Ops and the terminal to board our 0900 flight," said General Longbow.

"We'll be ready, Dad," said Gary.

"When we're in the company of other members of the military, please don't refer to me as Dad, Gary. Let's observe military courtesy, OK!" said General Longbow.

"Yes, sir, Dad," replied Gary, eliciting laughter from Alex and the General.

At Tan Son Nhut Air Base, General Longbow, accompanied by his son Gary and Alex, boarded a chartered Boeing 707 jet airliner for the long flight across the Pacific Ocean to Travis Air Force Base, Fairfield California.

Inside the terminal at Travis Air Force Base, Gary and Alex each got into a telephone kiosk with a bunch of loose change to make their call to their mothers, and possibly their sisters, while the General called his buddy David Siegel at work to tell him the good news.

"Curtiss-Wright Corporation, Siegel speaking."

"Dave, this is Jim. I'm calling you from Travis Air Force Base. I just landed from Vietnam with your son Alex and Gary. They're in the next telephone booth calling their mothers," said James Longbow.

"That's fantastic news. Holly cow, how'd you do it, Jim," said Dave Siegel excitedly.

"I'll tell you all about it, Dave as soon as we get home. We're scheduled to board a flight this evening at 2300 hours, arriving at McGuire AFB at about 0500, Then we'll try to get a flight out of there to Niagara Falls Air Base. I'll call you the moment I learn the time of departure to Niagara Falls, so you and the girls can meet us there upon arrival," said James.

"Roger that. Man, I'm in the mood for a celebration, my friend," said David.

"Hold that thought until we get there. I'm going to sign off now, and see you soon, Dave," said James.

As he stepped out of the phone booth, he saw Gary exiting his phone booth, then Alex, both in a pensive mood.

"How did your Mom take the news?" asked James.

"She couldn't stop crying, Dad. I think she was simply overwhelmed with the sound of my voice, and the realization I was alive and back in the States. I think she was in shock. Maybe you should call her, Dad, and reassure her it was me that called her," said Gary.

"I think I'll do that, then she can go over to Susan's and reassure her as well," said James.

"How about you, Alex. How did Susan take the news?" asked James.

"About the same as Louise, She cried a lot and kept asking me where I was calling from, although I kept telling her I was at Travis Air Force Base," said Alex.

"Let me call Louise, right now," said General Longbow.

"Louise, this is James, your husband. Gary just called you, and he's with me and Alex."

"Oh! God, Jim, when I heard Gary's voice, I just couldn't stop crying, and hardly comprehended what he was saying. My prayers were answered, it was a miracle," said Louise.

"The miracle is they escaped from their prison and were rescued by our helicopter patrol from North Vietnam, and are now coming home to you and Susan. We're getting on a plane tonight and arriving at McGuire Air Force Base tomorrow morning, early. We'll try to get a flight out of there to Niagara Falls Air Base. I talked to Dave at work and he'll let you know when we'll be arriving at Niagara Falls Air Base, so you can all meet us, OK!" said James.

"Oh! James, I've been crying with joy. Hurry home, darling," said Louise.

"I love you, Louise. Goodbye for now," said James, ending the telephone conversation.

CHAPTER X

A Wedding for the Next Generation

During the flight aboard the MATS chartered Boeing 707 Airliner destined for McGuire Air Force Base, New Jersey, Alex sat in a window seat, while Gary sat next to him, with General Longbow in the aisle seat, rubbing elbows with each other, which facilitated personal conversation.

"You know, Gary…this Vietnam experience has made me realize that we're not immortal, and our lives can be cut short at any time. So as soon as I get home, I'm going to ask Jackie to marry me," said Alex.

"Really! I mean, you're still in the Army for several months before discharge. Why not wait 'till then, and have a job before you take on that responsibility," said Gary.

"Because I love and miss her, and I just don't want to wait anymore," replied Alex. "What about you, Gary? I thought you were in love with my sister Rachel."

"I am, but I thought there was plenty of time for me to pop that question after I got discharged from the Army," replied Gary, within earshot of the General who found the conversation fascinating.

"If you ask me, fellows, I think the girls will have something to say about the timing of that fateful event," said General Longbow.

"Well, we do have thirty days' leave, which might give us time to get married, or at least engaged," said Alex.

"Since you lovesick guys are both planning on getting married to each other's sister, why not have a double wedding in the same church. All four of you can get married in a Catholic church where a Rabbi is invited to participate in the ceremony. In fact, I attended a Jewish friend of mine's wedding in a Catholic Church to a Catholic woman, with a Rabbi participating in the ceremony at the invitation of the priest. In the conduct of the Jewish rituals, the Rabbi had the groom crush a glass wrapped in a napkin, symbolizing the destruction of the Jewish temple in Jerusalem, and the finality of the marital pledge, in that the broken glass cannot be put back together into its previous state," said General Longbow.

"You mean we don't have to convert to the other's religion to be married in the church of their faith," asked Alex.

"Times have changed, Alex. No, Jackie doesn't have to convert to Judaism in order to marry you, nor does Rachel have to convert to Catholicism in order to marry Gary," said General Longbow.

"Frankly, that was a big concern for me," said Gary, "because I heard it can take from one-to-two years for the conversion to take place. But this solves that problem. However, what about the children that will follow? How does one decide which religion that child will be indoctrinated, and who decides?"

"That's something the parents discuss in a rational and empathic manner. But there's no reason the children can't be indoctrinated in both religions, and as they mature, decide for themselves which one meets their spiritual needs and beliefs," said General Longbow. "However, I believe that the Jewish faith requires that the religion of the mother determine the religion of the child, in that case, Judaism. Nevertheless, that doesn't prevent the child from being eventually exposed to Catholicism, providing the child with an ultimate choice."

"I'm still having trouble with the belief that the Catholic Church condones the marriage of Catholics to Jews without a formal conversion to Catholicism, and vice versa for the Jewish faith," said Alex.

"If you look at the Nostra Aetate, which is the declaration on non-Christian religions of the Second Vatican Council, promulgated by Pope Paul VI in the Fall of 1965, you'll find that the Catholic Church imparts that God had never revoked his covenant with the Jewish People. Therefore, Jews are not considered targets for conversion, but assimilation within the Christian community. In fact, the Pope has urged a reasonable and more moderate approach that will contribute to the ecumenical movement, with a dialogue between the ministers of Catholics and Jews," said General Longbow.

"I read somewhere that 35 percent of Jewish Americans who married within the past seven years have a non-Jewish spouse. But it didn't say what marital path they took," said Gary.

"I'm sure that Jackie and Rachel, with Louise and Susan's assistance, will resolve those issues to everyone's satisfaction," said Alex.

"We're all mature and intelligent adults, so we should be able to address those issues when they come up. In the meantime, I think you provided us with the answers we needed, Dad," said Gary.

"Then, if you're with me, Gary, I think a double wedding would make for a very special wedding ceremony, the likes of which have never been seen in Erie County. The reception that would follow could be equally superlative and something to remember the rest of our lives," said Alex, excited at the thought of it.

"I think a double wedding in a Catholic church officiated by a Priest and a Rabbi is the ultimate solution. Which Catholic church would you recommend, Dad?" asked Gary.

"First of all, not every Catholic priest is yet receptive to the Pope's urging for the cordial cooperation between Catholics and non-Catholic ministers. I would highly recommend Father O'Malley at Saints Peter & Paul Roman Catholic Church in Williamsville, to officiate your wedding ceremony. He's conducted weddings with a Rabbi in attendance for Catholic/Jewish couples, therefore is no stranger to this type of ceremony. Of course you still have to get blood tests and apply for a marriage license at City Hall, and do a myriad of other things, which I'm sure, Jackie and Rachel will be able to iron out, with the help of

Louise and Susan," said General Longbow. "I think that after you've conferred with your fiancées and your mothers, you'll realize that your thirty days leave will not give you enough time to accomplish all of the requirements of a double marriage in church, and a lavish reception. Therefore you may have to be satisfied with an engagement with ring, and the promise of marriage after your discharge from the Army."

"Yeah! I think you're right, Dad. Makes a lot of sense. What do you think, Alex?" asked Gary,

"I agree. We don't want to rush such a memorable event that we'll all treasure the rest of our lives," said Alex.

"Good. Then it's all set. When do you want to propose to Jackie?" asked Gary.

"Well, I think that's something very personal, which should be done in private. However, we could both propose the same night, so the next morning, the four of us would be engaged, and able to plan together for the forthcoming wedding," said Alex.

The sun was rising as the Boeing 707 Airliner, carrying General Longbow, his son and Alex Siegel, landed at McGuire Air Force Base.

Being a General officer, James Longbow, accompanied by his son Gary and Alex, was given priority in flight reservations aboard a military aircraft bound for Niagara Falls, New York. Since it was a short flight, anything that flew was acceptable to them, and a C-47 transport aircraft designed to transport cargo, was scheduled for departure to Niagara

Falls Air Force Base, at 1120 hours, giving them enough time to eat breakfast at the terminal before departure. General Longbow found a telephone and called Louise to inform her they'd be arriving Niagara Falls Air Base at approximately 1330 hours that afternoon.

The only seating inside the C-47 were the long seats hanging against the walls of the aircraft, and the inside temperature was near freezing once above ten thousand feet. But this was merely an inconvenience, considering what Gary and Alex had experienced in Vietnam, and the General flying B-17's over Germany.

The C-47 landed at Niagara Falls Air Force Base at 1340 hours, and taxied to a designated parking area within walking distance of the terminal where a wheeled staircase was abutted to the doorway of the aircraft. The General and his two companions were the only passengers on the aircraft, and as a fatherly gesture, Longbow allowed Gary and Alex to disembark first, knowing they'd be greeted with overwhelming embraces from Jackie, Rachel and their mothers and David, leaving him to witness with joy, the family reunion.

While Jackie and Rachel had their arms wrapped around Alex and Gary, Louise, Susan and David made their way to General James Longbow. and greeted him with a warm reception that needed no explanation.

"James....you did the impossible, bringing our boys back home, and I have no words powerful enough to express my gratitude and love," said Louise.

"Thank you, sweetheart, but I only arranged for their transportation back home. They themselves carried off their own escape from prison, and with luck, they were found and rescued by the helicopter patrol," said James Longbow.

"I think you're minimizing your role, James, and as far as I'm concerned, you're my hero," said Louise with finality.

"James, thank you for bringing our son home," said Susan, with David standing next to her.

"You are welcome. He came as a package deal," replied James with a grin.

"Jim could never take a compliment well," said David, also grinning. "Let's have a drink when we get home, and you can tell us everything that happened over there."

"Sure, but I think our boys have a lot more to tell then me," replied James.

"No doubt, but let's give the boys time to settle in, before we start to interrogate them," said Louise.

"Actually, I have more to tell you than you would ever expect, but for the time being, it will be for your ears only, OK?" said James Longbow.

"Really! What have you been up to, James, and when are you going to confide in us?" asked Susan, with David looking amused at James' verbal fencing with the girls, reminiscent of earlier days gone by.

"As soon as we get home and have a drink to loosen my tongue," replied James in good humor.

They all converged at the Longbow residence, so that the immediate family could hear and participate in the story to be told by Gary and Alex about their capture and escape. The General decided to wait untill later, when Jackie and Rachel were not present, to give Louise, Susan and David the impending news that Gary and Alex were going to propose marriage to Jackie and Rachel, but postpone the wedding until they were discharged from the Army. Furthermore, he would give them the double wedding plans to be officiated by a Priest and Rabbi.

All went well, and that very evening, Gary and Alex swiftly took Rachel and Jackie to dinner at a local restaurant, and together, they proposed marriage, with the promise of a ring of their choice when they could accompany them to a jewelry store.

"You mean I don't have to convert to Judaism in order to marry Alex?" said Jackie. "Are you sure about that?"

"Yes, I'm sure. Dad told us of a friend who did it, and he knows Father O'Malley at Saints Peter & Paul Roman Catholic Church here in Williamsville, who has performed such mixed marriages," said Gary.

"Yeah! And I heard him tell us on the plane, that a rabbi will be invited to participate in the ceremony, and Gary and I will break a glass in the Hebrew tradition," said Alex.

"Wow! That's great news," said Rachel.

"Yes, it took a great load off my mind too," said Gary.

"So when are you going to be discharged from the Army?" asked Jackie.

"We're due for discharge from the Army on the 21st of November 1970, which is only three months from now," said Gary.

"So where are you going to receive your discharge papers?" asked Rachel.

"At Fort Rucker, Alabama," said Alex.

"Sounds like it's in the boondocks," said Jackie.

"It's in Dale County, and you're right, it's in the boondocks," said Gary.

"Well, it's only three months, then you'll be civilians again," said Rachel.

"When you think about it, that's not much time before the wedding preparations," said Jackie. "Did you tell Mom about the date of your discharge?"

"Yes I have, and I'm sure she told Susan about it too," said Gary.

"Good, then I'll be able to wear my wedding band soon," said Jackie.

"Jackie, like her Mom, didn't want an engagement ring, because the protruding stone would be an impediment when sailing. She wanted a broad, small diamond studded, multi-color gold-silver wedding band with Indian characteristics," said Alex, "and when you see it, you'll all agree, it's a magnificent wedding ring."

"Where did you get it from?" asked Rachel.

"Erik Jewelers. They made the ring to order, an original," said Alex.

"I won't ask what you got, Rachel, because I think I know you got an engagement-wedding ring combination with large stones," said Jackie.

"Yeah! You're right, but only the engagement ring has a large stone, a diamond. The wedding band has several different precious stones on it. I figure when I go sailing, I'll remove the engagement ringing, but never the wedding band," said Rachel.

"Chacun as son gout," said Jackie.

"That's right, each to his own taste," said Gary.

"Have you guys decided on where we'll spend our honeymoon?' asked Rachel.

"Well, I, for one, want to spend it where Jackie will be happiest," said Alex. But I thought we'd all go together on our honeymoon. After all, we've always spent our holidays together since we were kids."

"I'm for all of us spending our honeymoon together, and Paris would be my first choice," said Jackie. "That's where my mother spent her honeymoon, and at the Ritz, no less."

"What about you, Gary. What's your first choice?" asked Rachel.

"Paris, without a doubt. But there's only one problem. Paris is best visited in warm weather, between June and September, which means that we'd have to postpone the wedding until June at the earliest," said Gary.

"Holy cow, that's a long time for me to wait for my wedding band," said Jackie.

"Let's look at this logically. We won't get discharged until the 21st of November, and I don't think the family would want the wedding to take place during the Christmas holidays, which puts us into January at the earliest," said Gary.

"And January is too close to the Christmas and New Year celebrations, which leaves us with February onward," said Alex.

"Therefore, we would only have to wait until June for the wedding to take place, followed immediately by our honeymoon in Paris," said Gary.

"And June is a wonderful month to be married," added Rachel.

"Then do we all agree for the wedding to take place in, say, mid-June of next year?" asked Gary.

They all looked at each other, nodding their heads in the affirmative.

"Looks like we have a unanimous decision of mid-June for our forthcoming wedding, and Paris here we come," said Alex.

"How about staying at the Ritz Hotel, the swankiest hotel in Paris?" asked Jackie.

"Hey! We might as well go first class, all the way," said Gary, with everyone agreeing.

A fortnight later, James Longbow received a telephone call while at work at Curtiss-Wright Corporation, from Major General Claude Barclay.

"Jim, this is Claude at Hancock Field, how are you?"

"I'm doing fine, getting things ready for a double wedding of my son Gary and Alex Siegel," said Longbow. "You'll be getting a formal invitation to the wedding, but it won't occur until they're discharged in about six weeks."

"I appreciate the invitation, and unless my wife has other plans, we'll be glad to attend," said Barclay.

"The reason I called you, is because it will shortly be in the news, and I wanted you, your son and Lieutenant Siegel to hear it first and accurately. The information your son and Lieutenant Siegel provided in their debriefing by our Intel agents, caused a major reassessment of our intelligence information on Camp Hope, resulting in the final decision to mount a major rescue attempt on Camp Hope to rescue our American prisoners of war. The assault and rescue operation involved the Air Force, Navy and Army Special Forces. Fifty-eight Green Berets and 30 aircraft manned by 95 airmen landed on Camp Hope, and while the assault and rescue operation was successful, none of the American prisoners were there in the camp. In fact, the camp had been abandoned. My guess is that when the North Vietnamese learned of your son and Lieutenant Siegel's escape, they realized the infrastructure, management and horrific conditions of the camp would be revealed to the US Military Command. They felt that this information would encourage the US Military to invade the prison camp to rescue the American prisoners, and they were right. So they moved them to another prison camp," said Barclay.

"That does make sense, but no help to those American prisoners," replied Longbow.

"Well, now it's back to the drawing board to find out where they were moved to," said Barclay.

"Yeah! In the meantime, more will die from malnutrition, disease, torture and murder," said Longbow.

"The best thing we can do is bring this war to an end," said Barclay.

"Hopefully, it will be sooner than later," replied Longbow, ending the conversation with a reminder of the wedding invitation.

The double wedding of Gary with Rachel, and Alex with Jackie, took place as planned at Saints Peter and Paul Roman Catholic Church in Williamsville, New York. Presiding were Father O'Malley and Rabbi Meir Starr. The church was filled with the entire Sontag, Longbow and Siegel family and friends, who witnessed the only double interfaith wedding ever to take place in that church, and perhaps in any church in Erie County. The wedding ceremony ended with the two brides and grooms walking through a shower of confetti to the limousine awaiting them for their short trip to the Sontag Mansion in Lackawanna, where the wedding reception took place.

All arrangements for the newlyweds' honeymoon to Paris, France were made, with their bags packed and stored in the baggage compartment of Michael Sontag's limousine, ready to take them to the Buffalo International Airport, anytime they elected to leave the reception.

As the newlyweds rode in the limousine on its way to the Sontag residence, Rachel looked at Jackie's wedding band.

"Let me see your wedding ring up close," said Rachel. "Oh! It's so beautiful, and it sparkles no matter which way you turn your hand. That was a good choice, Jackie."

"You didn't do so bad yourself, Rachel. That's some rock you've got on your engagement ring. You'll never be poor as long as you have that ring," said Jackie, getting a laugh from everyone.

"Listen, guys. When we get to the house, Rachel and I are going upstairs into the guest bedroom, and change into our traveling dresses, so we can leave the reception whenever we decide our presence is no longer required," said Jackie.

"Yeah! I expected that. Luckily we don't have to change. Tuxedos are fashionable anywhere," said Gary.

The Sontag mansion was quickly inundated with people in a celebrating mood. A bar was set up with a bartender, and two large tables with an assortment of hors d'oeuvres, some of them on a bed of ice, and others in hot metal trays, were surrounded by appreciative, hungry guests. No expense was spared, and the reception included a who's who in industry and politics. A professional pianist played lively music, creating an atmosphere of gaiety and active conversation.

Gary and Alex, dressed in their tuxedo, walked across the large living room where James stood with his wife

Louise, and David with Susan, overlooking the crowd of people, many of whom they did not know.

"There must be a couple of hundred people here," said Gary.

"Yeah! I didn't know we had that many friends," said James Longbow.

"Where's Jackie and Rachel?" asked Louise.

"They're upstairs changing into their travel attire," said Gary.

"So you're ready to take off for Paris, huh!" said David Siegel.

"We sure are, and we don't want to miss our flight to JFK International," said Alex.

"What time does your flight leave Buffalo?" asked Susan.

"11:45 and we're staying at the Marriott overnight just outside JFK. Then at 10:30AM we'll be taking our flight aboard Air France to Paris," said Gary.

"Just make sure you're at Buffalo Airport at least ninety minutes before flight time," said James Longbow.

"Don't worry, Dad, we'll be there on time," said Gary, smiling at his father for his unwarranted concern.

"I see that my father has joined Michael Sontag and his wife Marie over there in conversation with Senator Mike Blanchard. He's a democrat isn't he, Dave?" asked James Longbow.

"Yeah! I don't think he's gonna change their party affiliation," said David Siegel.

"Oh! There they are," said Louise, observing Jackie and Rachel coming down the stairs on the other side of the living room, Jackie wearing a beige dress cut at the knee, with a gold necklace, gold loop earrings, and tan shoes, while Rachel wore a red dress, also cut at the knee, with a white gold necklace with diamond pendant, diamond stud earrings, and black shoes.

"Excuse us, please," said Gary. "We're off to join our wives before they're overwhelmed by the attention of all those single men."

Gary and Alex, dressed in their tuxedos, standing tall, and in animated conversation with Jackie and Rachel, looked like a picture from a high society magazine.

"Look at them, full of life and aspirations. Reminds me of when we were young," said James.

"Yes, and now we've passed the baton to the next generation," said David.

"Yes we have, and with grace and everlasting love," said Louise

"Amen!" said Susan softly.

THE END

* 9 7 8 1 7 3 2 2 1 1 4 1 4 *